Black by Rose

When killing is the only way forward

Andrew Barrett

The Ink Foundry

Praise for Black by Rose

~ An outright masterpiece.
~ The writing is urgent, exciting, at times upsetting, even terrifying. It is utterly convincing and extremely brutal where it needs to be.
~ Fast paced, thrilling, thought provoking. I couldn't fault this book.
~ You really get to care about Eddie and your heart is in your mouth when you read about what happens to him.
~ If you like CSI type books that are fast paced, gritty and with great believable characters, this is the book for you.
~ This book has love, tears, humour and drama. A well written story with tension and some edge of the seat moments.
~ When I was reading it, I struggled to put it down; when I wasn't reading it, I was itching for an opportunity to pick it up again.

Preface

Proud to swear in British English

Contents

1. Ten Years Ago   1

2. Today   3

3. Do Not Panic   5

4. Bad Memories and Bad Men   11

5. A Game Called Dying   15

6. Slade and the Whore   19

7. Killing Speed Limits   29

8. The Robbery and the Red Marker Pen   35

9. A Neck for Old Rope   41

10. Keep Your Friends Close   47

11. Paperwork and Politics   57

12. The Death of Anticipation   63

13. Writer's Cramp and Winston's Murder   67

14. The Birth of Operation Domino   73

15. A Fistful of Horror   77

16. Finding Life in a Graveyard   81

17. Charlie and The Spinney Nook   87

18. First Day, First Confrontation   91

19.	The Brook in a Shallow Valley	99
20.	The Second Taste of Ben & Jerry's	103
21.	The Theory	111
22.	The McDonald's Confession	121
23.	The Briefing	131
24.	One Man's Joy...	139
25.	I Love You, Rosaline	149
26.	The Job	157
27.	The Daily Grind	173
28.	No Such Thing as Judgement Day	179
29.	Scaffolding Poles	185
30.	The Moonlight and a Window Seat	193
31.	The Flowers, The Tablets, and The Briefing	197
32.	Back at the Murder House	207
33.	Flowers and Blood	213
34.	Hide, Charlie, Hide	223
35.	Dented Shining Armour	235
36.	Can't do Right for Doing Wrong	249
37.	And Then the Police Came	255
38.	Trembling All Over	265
39.	A Cold Bath and a Hot Whisky	271
40.	The Fat Lady Takes a Deep Breath	285
41.	Sophie Grew a Spine	293
42.	Missing	301
43.	Speculation and Bluster	315

44. Respect at the Graveside   325

45. Heartbreak   327

46. Behind The Magic Carousel   339

47. Nearly There   347

48. A Present for Jagger   361

49. The Long Soak   367

50. Epilogue   379

Acknowledgments   383

Dedication   385

About the Author   387

Also By Andrew Barrett   389

Chapter One

Ten Years Ago

THE BASS WAS AMAZING. It thundered through the lower ground floor of the Tangerine Oasis nightclub as though the walls were going to fall down. Freak Like Me, the new one by the Sugababes, pounded loud enough to create mime from speech. Sophie felt the bass resonate inside her chest. She held Lisa tightly, nuzzling into her neck, and felt her sweat against her own skin, and revelled in her odour. Lisa suddenly broke the embrace and pulled her towards the toilets.

It was still loud in here, pumped through small wall-mounted speakers so that even after the door swung closed, it reverberated through their throbbing bodies as though nothing else in the world existed. Nothing mattered anymore and Sophie kissed her with a passion reserved for their more intimate moments back in the flat. Their hands searched each other and the kissing grew rampant, urgent, energy-filled like a need, tongues delving, fingers probing, sweat mingling, breath hot and sweet and fast.

And then the door opened.

The added bass pulsed into the room, echoed on the tiles and the girls looked around. Chloe stood there in shock, her mouth open for an instant before it closed and her lips pulled back into a silent teeth-filled sneer of rage. And then she screamed, "Fucking bitch!" and was on them in a second.

All three slid on the shiny tiles, and under Chloe's momentum, they hit the floor heavily in a mess of arms and legs. Bags scattered, shoes came off, make-up rolled across the floor. Nails scratched and gouged. Then Chloe punched Sophie in the mouth and grabbed her by the hair, leapt on top of her. Blood spattered in tiny droplets across the white-tiles, and Lisa was pushed to one side. She looked in horror as Chloe smashed Sophie's head into the floor, clumps of hair in her fists.

Sophie screamed, arms flailing, and Lisa sat there stunned as if it was all happening in slow motion. Painfully slow. She grabbed something, it was a shoe, and she swung it at Chloe, an arc that had no aim or purpose other than to disrupt.

And then everything stopped.

There was no music. The silence was crushing. The passion was dead.

Lisa held her breath, hand covering her mouth, eyes wide as Chloe lurched and then fell to the floor, scattering lipstick tubes, eyes open staring through the ceiling into an abyss. Unblinking. Blood dripped onto the floor, a rivulet chased the lipstick.

Lisa screamed.

Sophie got to her knees, rubbing the back of her head. Her other hand smudged the blood that had splashed across her chest; more had misted on her face.

Lisa scurried into a cubicle, ready to vomit. She retched, coughed, and panted, seeing the silhouette of her reflection in the water. Sweat fell from tangles of hair. Ripples erased her.

And then the sound came back, and with it her other senses. She could feel the goosepimples on her arms, could feel the tiles with her toes, could feel her body shaking and the bile in her throat. The door opened and the bass came louder, and Lisa held her breath.

Someone behind her screamed and ran back out of the toilets yelling something almost incoherent. The one word she heard very clearly was 'police'. Over and over again.

"Lisa!"

Lisa turned in the cubicle and saw the tears in Sophie's eyes.

"Go. Get out!" Sophie was shouting at her. "Run, dammit. Fucking run."

Chapter Two

Today

SOPHIE MORAN SAW UNRESTRICTED sunlight for the first time in almost nine years. She stood on the stone steps and admired its quality, which seemed strangely altered to her now. Perhaps free people saw with different eyes, rich with full HD colour.

Banging against her leg as she walked down the steps was an HMP carrier bag. In it was just about everything she owned. The rest of her stuff, the passport and driving licence, things like that, were in her solicitor's storage somewhere in Leeds.

She breathed deeply, listened to the hum of traffic on the distant road, and saw cars in the nearby car park that she didn't recognise, all sleek and modern now compared to how boxy they were almost a decade previously.

Sophie crossed the car park and found a wooden bench next to a dustbin on a stretch of grass. The bin was overflowing with McDonald's fast-food wrappers that attracted a dozen or so wasps. She sat at the far side, away from the bin, and marvelled at a view that didn't include bars, gates, screws, or inmates, of sounds not obliterated by keys, shouts, screaming, crying, echoing...

Sophie Moran looked at her watch; marvelling that it was the first time in years that the time actually mattered to her. And it mattered because her sister was due any time now. Sophie burst into tears.

Two days after stepping out of prison, Sophie stepped into Leeds. She had business there; mainly consisting of things to get her feeble life back on track, to pick up the threads of existence that had been severed so cruelly, and begin making something of herself.

For a good portion of her remaining time inside, and constantly over the last two days, she'd wondered how Lisa would be living. She wondered how she was doing, if she missed her at all, if she even thought of her. Every day, the torment grew a little until it blocked the view of everything else. It was huge inside her head, and it grew prickles like the spiky husk of a horse chestnut seed.

There was nothing else left to do; there was just a craving for a normality she hadn't felt for nearly a decade, and since her life had ended while being in the throes of a blazing romance with Lisa, it seemed that the obvious thing to do in order to get normality breathing again, was to find her.

Like haemorrhoids surrounding an arsehole, a ring of solicitors' and barristers' properties surrounded the courthouses in Leeds city centre. It was from one of the barristers' offices that Sophie Moran exited, carrying a new plastic bag. In it were her personal papers, driving licence, passport (now expired), bank details, file of correspondence from the solicitors and barristers, discipline criteria and notice of summary employment termination from West Yorkshire Police, letters of support from The Police Federation, letters of condolence from her landlord, 'Sorry – you're evicted', and details of the storage company where all her remaining stuff was – probably ruined by mice now anyway.

She had £628.42 to her name, no job, no prospects of a job, and the title of 'murderer'.

But she had Lisa.

Finding Lisa was priority number one.

Chapter Three

Do Not Panic

OUTSIDE THE SUPERMARKET WERE two CCTV cameras, both aiming inwards, roughly to where the main entry door was. They weren't working right now because Pikey and Ste had been up on the roof three hours ago and disabled them. It would take the service technician, based across in Manchester, until at least eleven to get here. He was a busy man, because crews across West Yorkshire had been out overnight doing similar things to other CCTV cameras operated by his company. And when the service tech came in to work this morning, he and his colleagues would be overwhelmed with requests for their expertise.

At exactly nine o'clock, the red security truck, with Seven Security Services sign-written in large white letters down the side and across the front, pulled into the car park right outside the automatic entrance doors to the store. The driver had parked in a blind-spot, unprotected by surveillance equipment, and because this was the first of their scheduled seven drops this morning, the truck was literally sagging with cash.

Pikey looked on. All they had to do was get inside the bloody thing. Without destroying the cash.

It would be good too if they could manage the whole job without hurting anyone, and especially without killing anyone, but needs must, and if the guards were uncooperative, they could look forward to a decent insurance pay-out and a desk job with wheelchair access. Or a really snazzy burial paid for by a grateful company. Pikey gave the nod as the passenger guard climbed out and slammed the door shut. He walked around the front of the truck and along the driver's side to the revolving hatch. As the hatch opened and he took out the cash box, a drunken male fell against the passenger door and then clumsily walked into the rear-view mirror, knocking it upwards and away from the side of the van. Now the driver was blind to the passenger side of his truck; all he could see in the mirror was lightly clouded sky. The drunken man stood upright, wobbled, and waved an apology and a kiss to the driver, who gesticulated towards him as he wandered off clutching his bottle of cider.

The guard walked inside the building with the cash box.

Another male, this time not drunk at all, ran along the passenger side of the truck carrying a creeper board. The creeper board was the kind of thing a mechanic would lie on and wheel himself under your car to fix a blowing exhaust. As he ran, he leapt onto the creeper like a luge rider might do. He quickly guided himself beneath the truck and from a belt pouch removed two small metal boxes each fitted with an adhesive magnet. He stuck one of the boxes, about the size of a cigarette packet, to a section of floor just aft of the driver's seat where the comms equipment and auxiliary battery were located, and the other just under the passenger seat where the main vehicle battery was. He flicked a tiny toggle switch on each box, and red LEDs lit up.

Then he got the hell out of there.

People walked past the car park, mostly oblivious to what was happening sixty feet away. And those who saw the drunken man or the tobogganer carried on with their journey. Either they didn't believe what they were seeing, or they did and just didn't want to get involved. Other people entered the supermarket while speaking on their phones, or while thinking about what to buy, or while watching some drunken man having an argument with himself a few yards away; either way, people were too distracted to notice or care.

Then the police arrived.

Outside the car park, on the wide footpaths, they parked two plain white Vauxhall Astra cars with flashing roof-mounted light bars. Megaphones attached somewhere in the cars began pushing out repeatedly the following message read by a female with a soothing, smiling voice: Do not panic, this is a training exercise. Do not panic, this is a training exercise...

A plain-clothed officer alighted from each car.

The guard with a now empty cash box, walked back out of the supermarket as the two charges detonated. The sound was a sharp crack that had an almost piercing quality about it, yet it dissipated quickly as the truck lifted an inch or two on its springs. A cloud of dust and metal fragments boomed out on a mini shock wave just prior to the exhaust pipe falling off. The truck's hazard lights stopped working, the engine cut out and suddenly by comparison everything was very quiet except the megaphones and the debris tinkling to a stop thirty yards away. From beneath the van, battery acid dribbled onto the lightly cratered tarmac.

Do not panic, this is a training exercise.

In the same moment, a masked man used a metal bar to take the guard's feet from under him. The guard hit the floor on his knees and collapsed quickly onto his side. The clear Perspex shield over his face fogged from a muffled scream. As the guard writhed on the chewing-gum encrusted floor, the masked man knelt on his chest, pointed a gun at his abdomen and said, "If you press your panic button, I will shoot you in the kidney. Do you understand?"

The guard, face a crumpled mess of pain, nodded vigorously, the back of his helmet scraping on the ground.

"If you do not do as I say immediately, I will also shoot you in the kidney. Understand?" Another scraping nod. "Get to your feet." The masked man stood back and continued to point the gun at the guard's abdomen as he stood, hopping on damaged legs. Shoppers walked by the scene as though nothing was quite so important as their morning milk and eggs. A few of the more alert customers peered out from inside, standing alongside a couple of impressed security guards. They stared in silence, watching the training scenario with fascination. A woman stopped the pushchair and crouched at the side of her child, pointing and laughing. The child giggled.

"Tell your colleagues you have a weapon pointed at you and they are to get out of the truck without activating their panic buttons. I will shoot if I detect a panic button. Understand?"

The guard nodded and limped to the driver's window where he banged on the reinforced glass. The driver looked stunned by the blast directly behind him and stared blank-faced at his colleague through a thin haze of smoke. He listened for a moment, eyes wide and shocked, his face loose, mouth gaping, and eventually nodded his understanding.

A single person stopped alongside one of the police cars, rested his elbows on the car park wall and watched the proceedings with nothing short of delight on his face. Less than thirty seconds later, there were twelve people watching, seemingly enjoying the show. Do not panic, this is a training exercise, spoiled their experience a little, but they endured it with a mixture of smiles and astonishment, some commenting upon how realistic it all seemed, and others wondering if it was part of a film they were making.

The truck driver spoke into the mic, seemed to realise it wasn't working anymore, and so banged on the bulkhead behind him, and shouted some instructions. The driver's door opened. The reinforced doors at the back of the truck opened too as a white van reversed up to them. The dazed cash man joined his sobbing buddy and the slack-jawed driver at the side of the truck where the revolving hatch was, and all three knelt on the floor as though attending a private prayer meeting. The gunman stood over them offering communion.

The drunken man suddenly sobered up; he and the bobsleighing mechanic climbed into the back of the cash truck. The white van's rear doors opened and the two plain-clothed police officers climbed aboard; one received cash boxes from the stricken cash truck, the other took them and squeezed them into a specially constructed wooden frame bolted to the van floor, while another drilled two 8 mm holes in the ends of each polyethylene case.

It was like a production line. Smooth and well-rehearsed.

Do not panic, this is a training exercise.

A sixth man, dressed in a leather floor-length apron, clear face shield, and wearing long, heavy duty leather gauntlets, pushed an adapter into one of the holes in each case and from a distribution manifold behind him, fed a small tube onto each adapter.

When the cash truck was empty, the drunk and the bobsleighing mechanic jumped off, collected the cider bottle and metal bar, strolled to the white van's cab and casually joined the driver inside.

With all the cases secured, all drilled, adapters and tubes fitted, the leather apron man turned on the liquid nitrogen canister mounted in a sturdy wire cage beyond the manifold. Then the plain-clothed police officers left the van and closed the rear doors, leaving the drill-man and Mr Nitrogen in the dark until the overhead lights blinked and came on. Mr Nitrogen diligently checked for leaks, then read the cylinder's gauges and made adjustments as the van began moving away. He and the drill-man watched as creeping frost grew on the pipes.

The van travelled for less than a minute before it stopped.

The two plain-clothed officers and the masked gunman walked across the car park and climbed aboard their police cars. They turned off the flashing lights and megaphones and slowly drove away to an appreciative applause from the gathered crowd. They even waved.

Both cars joined the van half a mile away on a deserted lane. The plain-clothed police officers set the incendiaries and locked their cars. They deposited the roof lights in the already open hatch of a plain blue Ford Mondeo parked in front of the van, while the masked gunman threw his balaclava and his gun into the boot as well, and turned his black jacket inside out, put it back on and climbed into the driver's seat.

The plain-clothed officers walked to the van, pulled off and rolled up the white magnetic sheets that covered bright blue and orange signage across the side, front, and rear panels; unhooked the false number plates and placed everything in the Mondeo's boot and climbed aboard before it drove sedately away followed by the van.

The newly exposed signs on the van said Rapid Removals. And it had been too; the whole operation from start to finish took nine minutes and twenty-four seconds. Both plain-clothed police officers allowed themselves a laugh and a congratulatory high-five. The driver smiled at them, and the relief on his face was evident; he was delighted it had gone well because he was due in court in a few hours, on trial for rape. His name was Blake Crosby, and he was looking forward to the trial judge throwing the case out within the first few minutes of the hearing, and looking forward to a piss-up tonight to celebrate his continued freedom, and to toast wonderful British justice.

Chapter Four

Bad Memories and Bad Men

— One —

EDDIE WAS STUCK IN traffic. It was turning into a hot day and the temperature was rising in roughly the same proportion as his anger.

He wound down the window and could hear X99 hovering somewhere close by.

In front of him was a large Mercedes van with a bad case of rampant rust and an even worse case of oily smoke burping out of the blowing exhaust. It smelled awful, and Eddie closed the window back up.

Eventually the Mercedes took off and left Eddie to drive through its haze of smog. He nudged up to second gear and then he saw the reason for the helicopter and the temporary road block; there was police activity thirty or forty yards to his right as he drove by a small supermarket with a red truck parked outside. Looked like a cash-in-transit job maybe; scene tape all over the place, and CID standing around wondering what the hell to do. And there was a CSI walking around with a camera dangling from her neck.

Eddie's eyes sprang wide, and he was sure that for a second or two his heart stopped. What the hell... that was no ordinary CSI; that was Ros. Well, it looked like Ros. Same face, same swagger, same everything. No, the hair was different. He pulled over to the kerb and put the handbrake on.

"Daft bastard," he said.

No way could that have been Ros. He'd obsessed about her for the last two years. Okay, 'obsessed' might be a strong word to use, fixated might be a better choice. She's walked out of the office and out of Eddie's life and not a single day had passed where he didn't find himself thinking about her, what became of her, where did she go, and who was she with.

Eventually he calmed down, though he had a queasy feeling in his gut. He wondered if it was time to go and seek advice about this. He seemed to see her everywhere; at first it was only in his dreams, and then he began seeing her out and about too. But it was ever more regular, and now, dammit, it was getting quite frightening. "She was so real..."

With some regret, he selected first gear and drove on.

— Two —

Benson nudged Cooper.

Cooper looked up, cleared his throat and that made Lisa Westmoreland look up too. She got out of the car and marched across to the courthouse steps, blonde hair raging like fire in the slanting afternoon sunlight.

"What's she doing? Christ's sake," Benson looked at his DCI, and watched his emotionless face as he stared at the gang swaggering down the steps, giving high-fives and lighting spliffs as though they were untouchable. "We should take the fucking lot out."

"Don't tempt me," Cooper stepped out of the car, leaned against the door and lit a cigarette.

Benson joined him and they watched DCI Lisa Westmoreland drag aside two of the cheerful group. She was talking closely to them, pointing a threatening finger up at them. She was five-foot-seven, towered over by two of Chapeltown's meanest bastards and she made their triumphant smiles die on their faces.

"She's got some balls."

"I wasn't joking, boss," said Benson again.

Cooper sighed, "There are thirty-eight gangs around Leeds—"

"I didn't mean all of them."

"Okay; there are three main gangs. Chapeltown, Harehills, and Middleton. What's that, twenty-five top people plus another ninety wannabes?" Cooper turned to Benson, "What you going to do, bomb them?"

"It's a fine idea, but I'm sure I could think of something slower, more painful."

Cooper smiled. He knew Benson was serious. Old coppers like him would love to stop playing tiddlywinks with these arseholes and start playing hard ball like they used to in the eighties. In the eighties, a copper could get away with all sorts – murder included.

"I'm sure you could. But until then, I want to know how they got off."

"Expensive lawyers."

"Nah, it's more than that. As a force, we spent eighty-five grand on exhibit tracking software, and suddenly an important piece of evidence can't be found. Poof," he said, "it just disappeared as if by magic. Explain that to me."

Benson stood silently for a moment, dropped his cigarette in the gutter and said, "Someone cocked up: that's how we lost the evidence."

"Or someone's bent and they destroyed the evidence."

"Ha, and you accuse me of still living in the eighties."

Lisa Westmoreland walked back towards the car; anger stretched her lips into a thin dark line. She glared at Benson and Cooper as she approached. Over her shoulder, Cooper could see the two gang members giving her the finger, laughing with their mates.

Chapter Five

A Game Called Dying

THEY PRESSED HIS FACE into the carpet and knelt in the small of his back until he complied, until he calmed down and stopped thrashing about. He snatched gulps of air and felt them bind his wrists, heard the zip of a cable tie and hissed as it bit into his skin.

"Last time I ask; give me names."

The pressure left his head. Tony Lambert stared at the digital photograph frame on the marble hearth. The one of him holding a salmon proudly in both arms flashed onto the screen. Last summer up in Perthshire; he and Shelly had a ball. They went out for a meal that evening, and he'd proposed to her. Down on one knee, the full mashings. A great time.

He closed his eyes, not really wanting to see the photographs anymore.

The knee came off his back, and they hauled him upright.

"Any more fucking about, we'll stop being so pleasant. Alright?"

Tony panted.

"I said, alright?"

Tony nodded.

"Good. Give me names."

Tony said nothing. He'd survived worse than this. In fact, he was a little stunned they'd been so lenient with him. If he'd wanted names, he would have begun hitting by now. Hard. But these two, Blake and Tyler Crosby, sons of the infamous Slade Crosby of Chapeltown, were hesitant; as if they didn't really want to be here, mixing it up with a copper. Tony relaxed slightly, knowing it would soon be over and these two would be on their way, none the wiser.

It was strange, though. Them being here at all. Wait till Cooper hears about this, he thought. And he wondered, briefly, whether mentioning that to the Crosbys might not scare them away right now.

Blake stood before Tony with a coil of old blue nylon rope hanging off one shoulder, and he nodded as if in response to some silent request from Tyler, who stood behind him. Blake disappeared through the lounge door, and Tony heard him quietly ascending the stairs. Towards Shelly. She was well out of it though; always had problems sleeping these days – understandably, and the doc had given her something to help her rest.

"Hey, wait—"

"You had your chance, now shut it."

"Don't make this any worse—"

Tyler twisted the cable ties and they dug into his flesh.

"I'll tell you their names, just—"

"Too late. I told you, I don't fuck about. When I say something, I mean it. You already had your last chance—"

"Don't you fucking dare touch her." Then it hit him. Why they were mixing it up with a copper. Why they hadn't done a runner already. They had no intention of running; they weren't here just to scare him, were they?

"Ssshhh. Don't want to wake her just yet. Shelly, isn't it?"

"Please! Look, I'll tell you their names. Phil Gibson, he's one, and Dom Thompson, and Jimmy Akhtar; just leave her alone."

"Upstairs, Tony."

"Tyler, there's no need—"

"Enough."

He moved forward, the hand in his back pushing him on. And now it had gone past the point of no return. It had gone past the questions and the denials, it had gone past the gentle slapping about and the low-level threats, and now it was into the lands of big pain. He knew it, and no one, not even the two men, could stop it now. Once Shelly woke up things could never go back to how they were.

And the tears came. Tony Lambert was a hard bastard himself; he knew the drill, had practised it a thousand times until he'd become very good at it. And each time he beat the shit out of a small-time villain, he became harder, more proficient and less inclined to stop until the job was done.

He mounted the stairs with heavy feet, and his nose filled up. "Look," he whispered, "I told you all I know, there's no need to involve her."

"What's the password?" Tyler whispered.

Tony looked up and at the summit of the stairs, peering into the front bedroom where Shelly would be sleeping, was Blake. His face was expressionless, but his eyes said he was ready to finish the job off too. Is that how I looked, he wondered; all steely-faced, determined, mechanical? Tony had no doubt at all that they would finish it off if need be. "It's 'Violet'," he said. "Now come on, I've told you it all, you can leave—"

The man at the top of the stairs slid the coil of rope from his shoulder and dropped it on the landing floor. He pushed the bedroom door fully open, turned on the light and hurried inside.

Tony's eyes widened. "No!" he screamed, "Shelly, wake up!"

Panic.

All she could see was the ceiling light; bright and edged with stars as her eyes watered. There was a buzzing sound too, a little like the sound you hear when listening to a seashell; but it was growing louder, and then she couldn't see the ceiling light at all. He was big and he cast his shadow across her face. She caught the briefest glimpse of Tony, another man holding him across the other side of the room. She saw the pleading in his eyes. The fear on his face broke her heart. His mouth moved but she couldn't hear anything.

And all she could feel was pressure, immense pressure inside as his grip tightened. A fire burned in her chest. She was very afraid, but she couldn't scream. And her world was shrinking. At first she could feel her legs and her arms and hands. But they had receded somehow, become automatic appendages she had no control over. They kicked and they flailed, and her hands grabbed feebly at his jacket, but it was nothing to do with her; she had no control over them. Only her eyes, wider, wider, seeing less and less. Darkness claimed the edges of her vision, spreading inwards towards the centre. Buzzing and booming in her ears.

Something inside her throat snapped. Her tongue filled her mouth.

He grinned down at her and she could feel the leather of his gloves cold against her throat. And even though she couldn't breathe, she could smell blood.

Somewhere in the background, a man screamed, Tony; muffled as though it came through a pillow. But it was shrinking, becoming quieter. The fear subsided.

And then the light turned dark. And the silence came too.

Chapter Six

Slade and the Whore

— One —

SLADE LIT A CIGARETTE and reclined on the expansive leather sofa. He watched the young woman put her bra and pants back on. She would've been perfect, he thought, if she had bigger tits. Not much bigger, mind; just enough to get them swaying properly. Still, can't have everything. She was new here, part of a consignment of twelve girls last month. And she was the pick of the litter, this one. Very handsome.

"That was good," he said.

She looked at him, a blank expression on her pale face.

In fact, her whole body was pale. These Poles had no fucking colour at all.

"I said," he shouted, "that was good," he gave her the thumbs up, and she cracked a smile at last. "Da," he shouted.

She nodded. "Tak."

"Talking to my fucking self again." He threw fifty quid at her. "Tea?"

He nodded, watched her hips as she walked into the kitchen. This was one of those swanky apartments – not flats, mind – apartments that had sprouted up in Leeds city centre over the last decade. It was open-plan; all wood floors, prints of New York skylines on the magnolia walls and some other abstract stuff that made his eyes go queer. Not bad, the apartment, modern, sleek. Totally unappealing if you preferred carpets and proper curtains. Why did everyone want fucking blinds these days? No character at all.

It had a view too, this apartment. Right over the canal. Rumour had it there was a troll living under one of those canal bridges. Bollocks, of course, but it didn't stop some enterprising restaurant owner putting up a banner, creating a treasure hunt and making a bundle from the residents and tourists. Tourists? In Leeds?

How things changed.

Still, Slade admired the man for his entrepreneurial streak.

He had given the girl fifty quid not because he had to – she was free, she was his – but because he believed in keeping things harmonious between employer and employee, just as he'd done when he took his cut during the building of these very apartments. And six others in Leeds. Two-hundred and twenty-thousand quid he'd made that year from back-handers and supplying the "security" for the building sites.

It was his best year yet. Better than the drugs by almost fifty grand. But not as good as property management. That was where to be these days; it was a posh title for being a landlord, mainly in the Holbeck, Beeston and Chapeltown slum areas where the DWP put the dossers and the kids and he charged them ninety quid a week for one room in a crumbling rodent-infested shithole.

"Cukier?"

"What?"

She turned, showed him the sugar bowl, and he shook his head.

"Sweet enough, dear."

She nodded.

"Not a fucking clue."

She walked to the side of the sofa and placed a steaming mug of black tea on the table. The mug had Pooh Bear on it; was a heavy old thing, a bit like a Toby jug.

"You haff wife?"

His head snapped around at her. "What? What did you say?"

The girl's friendly smile shrivelled up, and she backed a couple of steps away. "Just I wonder."

Slade's gaze eventually left her, and he poked his head forward like a pigeon, like a man whose collar was too tight. "She died. Years ago. Maureen." He took big breaths, but the mood was spoiled now, ruined by some stupid foreign bitch.

"Galfriend. You haff?"

And now she was taking the piss out of him. Never mind the sorry-looking wide blue eyes; she was laughing at him. Wouldn't be surprised if she was in cahoots with Rachel! Slade swung his deformed legs off the bed and took hold of the hot cup.

She tried to turn away and put her hands up to her pretty face, but she was way too slow. He threw the tea in her face. She managed to scream pretty well though; a sort of startled scream when she worked out what was happening, and then a real agonised scream as the pain bit.

The door to the apartment burst open and Monty strode in, "Chief?"

"Out."

The door closed behind Monty.

Her knees sagged, and she hit the floor, hands smothering her face, a child's shriek escaping the clenched fingers, shoulders heaving.

"Never," he whispered, "talk to me again."

And then he brought the Pooh Bear mug down on her head and she stopped screaming quite suddenly.

— Two —

"Take me home, Monty."

Monty selected 'drive' and pulled out into the city traffic. "You shouldn't let them wind you up, chief." Monty looked in the rear-view mirror, his brow heavy with concern. "You do too much for them; and how do they pay you back?"

"I know, I know. I'm a soft touch."

"You gotta watch your blood pressure," he said. "You need any work doing on 'em, you come and get me; it's why I'm here, chief. They're taking the piss out of you. You been like a father to them." Monty smacked the steering wheel.

"I am, I know."

The Grange used to be a farmhouse, back when the surrounding countryside was countryside, and not rows of houses. These days The Grange was twice the size it once was; extended by the Crosbys over the last forty years, but even now, with eight bedrooms, three lounges, reception rooms, utility rooms, a massive kitchen, a games room, and a sauna, it was dwarfed by some of the houses they'd thrown up in recent years. They were like hotels, ghastly monstrosities some of them. Still, sighed Slade, even some people with stacks of cash had shit taste. Money was no guarantee of style. But, big as the house was, Slade lived either in the kitchen, or in the front lounge. Months, sometimes years, would pass between visits to the other rooms. It had been Maureen's place... and he saw fit to keep it and to keep it as she would have liked.

The gates rolled back on their tracks and the driveway lit up as though guiding its owner through the last few yards until he was home from a hard day at the office.

In fact, Slade's day had consisted of golf in the morning, followed by two "meetings" in the afternoon, followed by a shag in the evening. The shag had resulted, probably, in someone's death, one of the meetings definitely had resulted in someone's death – possibly two someones – and the golf had lost him thirty-seven thousand pounds but gained him a new acquaintance on Leeds City Council. Money very well spent. Slade had more pies than he had fingers. But that was fine, because inside the house, he had another twenty fingers to go at.

They belonged to Tyler and Blake Crosby. Tyler would be king when Slade turned his toes up; not just because he was the elder by two years, but because he had the brains and the ruthlessness needed to run things. He had the respect of those who worked for the family and crucially, of its enemies too. Whereas Blake, although not exactly stupid, was just too immature to wear his dad's crown. And he was soft. He got involved because he was told to get involved, and he did ruthless things because he was told to be ruthless. Left to his own devices, he would probably pay off someone when he should have killed them, and kill someone when he should have paid them off. He struggled with the intricacies of the role, struggled with politics and diplomacy, something Slade had in abundance, or so he liked to think.

Rachel was the oddity. She had nothing to do with the business. She knew what went on, and she distanced herself from their seedy activities as though getting too close might infect her holier-than-thou pride with something incurable: wealth.

The BMW silently glided to a halt before the pillared doorway. Monty shut the motor down and Slade looked across the turning circle and saw a silver Mercedes and a black Range Rover. "Ah," he smiled, "they're back."

Across the turning circle, and largely out of sight from The Grange, was another house. It was a lot smaller; some of the staff lived there when they needed to stay close. And because it was well hidden, it was a good place to hide in too; had its own self-contained cellar fitted out just in case. So far it had never been used; that "just in case" had never materialised. But Slade was a planner, always had been and always would be.

The staff house was the gathering place. It was where Slade mingled with his trusted people. It was where he had a laugh with the lads and it was where the deals were sorted, the payments made and the plans planned. And it was where Slade hobbled to when he got out of the car, his walking stick kicking up gravel. Monty locked the BMW and walked at Slade's side.

"Have you heard anything?"

"Nah," Monty said.

Slade opened the door and walked into the kitchen. The new man, Jagger, was filling the kettle. "Know how I take my tea?"

Jagger turned off the tap. He looked at Slade Crosby and just nodded. "Boss." And then to Monty, "You want one?"

"Coffee. No sugar."

Slade headed into the lounge where Blake sat on the bare floorboards, legs outstretched, feet crossed, whisky nestled in his lap, and smiled up at the old man. "Well?" asked Slade.

"I felt her neck snap."

Ste and Pikey giggled, and Tyler shook his head, and took the tissue away from his nose. "I keep telling him, her fucking neck didn't snap; it was her hyoid cartilage."

"It was her neck!" The smile had gone.

Tyler held out a hand "Okay, okay it was her neck."

"Never mind all that," said Slade, "did you do it right?" He looked at Tyler, saw the bloodied tissue. "What happened to you?"

Monty kicked Ste off the scratched leather chair, consigning him to one of the uncomfortable dining chairs scattered around the periphery of the small, smoky room. Pikey chose not to be kicked out of his seat, but instead stood up and nodded at Slade, then joined Blake on the floor with a fresh bottle of beer and lit a cigarette.

"It went according to plan, Dad," said Tyler. "Apart from a bust nose."

"Why, what happened?"

"I was holding him while The Boston Strangler there did his stuff..."

Blake gave him the finger.

"...And he nutted me. Thrashing about like a fucking fish on a dock. It bled like a bastard on the way back here. But apart from that, it went fine."

"Hope so, boy." Slade eased himself into the chair, hooked the walking stick over the back of a dining chair, and took a cigarette from the packet on the low table next to him. "Hope so," he said again.

Jagger walked in and handed out the drinks to Monty and Slade, then went back for Ste's and Blake's. He tried to blend in by sliding down the wall and stretching out on the floor, cigarette in hand.

"Names. Did he give any names?"

Tyler nodded and then slid a glance at Jagger.

"Fuck off, Tyler," Blake shouted. "I said he was okay, didn't I?"

Slade palmed Blake's protests.

"Dad; he's either in or he's out. Make your mind up."

Slade sipped tea, looked at Jagger.

Jagger shrugged and stood up. "Suit yourself. I'll get my coat. You can mail my money."

"Monty, give him the keys to her apartment."

Jagger looked at Monty. "Whose apartment?"

"Tanya," Slade said. "Or whatever her name is."

Monty threw a set of keys at Jagger. "Waterfront View. Entry number is 1066. Flat is number 89."

"Apartment!"

"Apartment 89. Go make sure she's okay."

Jagger stood. "And what if she isn't okay?"

"Ring me," Slade snapped.

Jagger was almost at the door, when Slade called him back.

"Don't worry 'bout this." He half nodded to the room. "You'll be in when the time is right. Okay?"

"Fine."

"And then get off home. Be back here tomorrow at noon; you've got some shopping to do for a job."

— Three —

Jagger stood still as the lift doors opened. There was no activity downstairs or even outside the flats. But he took his time anyway; listening, watching. He exited the lift and turned right, checking for those black-eyed security cameras that seemed to be in every building these days. He walked swiftly up the carpeted corridor with purpose, as though he'd been here a thousand times before, glancing at the door numbers rolling by. At number 89 he faced the door and listened again. Nothing.

He knocked lightly and was rewarded with nothing again.

So far, so good.

And then he turned the key, stood aside and opened the door, expecting a bullet to hit the wall opposite. Slade and the gang had given no indication that he was disliked; no indication even that he wasn't trusted – except for the names thing, whatever that was all about, but he still needed to be careful. Being fresh in a crew was a dangerous place to be until you earned their trust. Checking on the girl, he hoped, would be part of that ritualistic entry to the Trusted Club. An initiation of sorts.

No bullet.

Jagger cautiously entered the flat, and as soon as he was near the kitchen, he could see a pair of naked legs. Already, he didn't like this.

She was lying face down, her blonde hair turned red by her own blood. Nearby, a smashed pottery mug, one of those thick ones that would cause a shit-load of damage if it hit you on the head. "Bastard," he whispered. And then he went to turn her over. Her face made him grimace. "Why the fuck..." her left eyelid was blistered, and all the left side of her face was red like she'd been half in the oven at 200 degrees for an hour. "Poor kid."

So far as he could tell, all the blood was from a scalp injury and they always bled like hell. She appeared okay apart from that, and the face of course. She had a pulse, regular and fairly strong, and as he watched her, her lips moved slightly, and a string of saliva fell from the corner of her mouth.

Okay, time to ring Slade, who would want her fixed up by some doctor he had on his books. Or... Wait a minute. He's scarred her face; he knows she's damaged goods now, he knows she will bring in pence now where she should have brought in pounds.

There would be no doctor.

Okay, decision time.

Jagger made sure the door was locked and then sat on the settee with his phone to his ear, looking at the sorry piece of shit on the floor.

— Four —

"So who are they?"

Ste shrugged and Monty looked at Blake and Tyler. Blank faces.

"Never heard of them," said Pikey.

Slade ignored the rest of the tea, and knocked back a Pernod, "They must work under operational names."

"Well, Tony Pearson did." This from Tyler. "He used a false name with us. I checked his house out; he has mail addressed to Tony Lambert.

"Okay," Slade said, "when Wasp gets here tomorrow, you have him nip across to his mate in Harehills, see if those names mean anything to Shylock's crew."

"Okay," Tyler said.

And then Slade's phone rang. He nodded at Monty, who reached across the table and answered for him. "Yes."

"It's me, Jagger."

"Go on."

"She's dead. Want me to ditch her and clean this place up?"

Monty looked at Slade. "The girl's dead."

Slade tutted and finished his Pernod.

"Yeah, do that. Where you taking her?"

"There's a place I know up in Otley; she'll never be found."

"Right, good. Here, how you gonna get her out of the flat?"

"Apartment!" Slade shouted.

Monty nodded an apology.

"She's tiny. Easily fit in one of the cushion covers off the leather sofa."

Monty laughed. "Like it. See you at noon."

He pressed end and slid the phone back on the table. "He seems okay, does that Jagger."

"Think so?" Tyler stood and arched his back. He took a can of lager from a six-pack and swigged it in one.

"And you don't, I suppose?" Blake looked at Tyler, "Why don't you like him? Every time I introduce someone, you have to—"

"Shut up, you prick. Nothing to do with who introduced him."

"What then?"

"He's too reserved." Tyler looked around the room, and suddenly everyone laughed, even Slade, who threw the

Pernod glass at him. It was a poor shot, and Tyler didn't have to move. He smiled at his dad, but said, "Seriously. I mean we don't know who the three people are that Tony mentioned; how do we know he ain't a copper?"

Slade stopped laughing. "Because I fucking checked!" Slade was on his feet, heading for Tyler on shaky legs.

"Well Tony was one; didn't check him out too well, did you?"

Monty yelled, "Watch your lip, Ty!"

"How do you think I sussed him out?" Slade grabbed Tyler by the arm and drew him close. "Don't fucking cross me, boy," he growled. "You're too old to go over my knee, but there are other ways... D'ya get my meaning?"

Tyler swallowed.

"Eh?"

"Yes," he said.

Slade eventually smiled, "Good lad," and patted him on the arm, "Now get me some more Pernod." He returned to his seat. "Anyway, Jagger's done time in Parkhurst. Know what for?" Slade turned and saw a row of blank faces. "He's done time for cash-in-transit robberies. Six of 'em. And he knows his way around cash machines too."

Chapter Seven

Killing Speed Limits

EDDIE STARED AT HER for a long time.

She was beautiful, and for a fleeting moment she reminded him of Ros. But it seemed every woman reminded him of Ros these days. And actually, it wasn't for a fleeting moment at all; it was for a good minute or two. And that was a long time when you were standing in a woman's bedroom gazing down at her like a fool, wondering what might have been.

Outside in the street below there was turbulence, car doors slamming and people talking loudly. The noise brought Eddie round again. He unfolded his arms and walked from the room, leaving the woman with the trail of blood from her nostrils, frozen against her pallid skin, drying on the crisp white pillow, like a scream at prayer time.

He returned to the landing, took up his customary stance on a stepping plate and stared at the woman's husband. The husband stared back, a questioning look on his face, yet a resigned, almost pitiful look in his eyes. He had strong hands, Eddie noted, big hands with thick fingers; plenty strong enough to strangle his wife and then hang himself.

But of course, he hadn't.

Eddie's radio bleeped loudly and it made him jump. It made him angry. He tore a ragged hole in the side of the plastic scene suit and yanked the damned thing off its clip, pressed the button and said, "Go away."

"Eddie, it's McCain, can you talk?"

He took a breath. "Yes," he said, "I've done it before."

"I've got some news on the suicide."

Whoopee, he thought. "It's not a suicide."

"Listen, there's someone on their way over to see you. And I'll be—"

"Who? Who's coming over? I'm busy!"

"Will you listen for just—"

Eddie took the battery from the radio and tossed both parts down the stairs. After they thudded against the front door, silence came back to him. He closed his eyes and tried to get back to where he had been. He looked again at the marks on the laminate floor and wondered if they'd develop with aluminium powder, or white powder maybe. He was about to turn and head down the stairs for his kit when the front door opened and the radio and its battery grazed an arc across the floor.

Eddie looked at the man, and heard the noise from outside louder now, intrusive. "Who the hell are you?"

The man, dressed in a white scene suit the same as Eddie's, closed the door, dropped a kit box on the ground and smiled up at Eddie. "I'm here to relieve you."

Eddie blinked. "That's very kind of you but I'm a little busy right now."

He wore his hair like an American Marine, right down to the wood, and he wore a grin too with perfect teeth, one that said he was humouring Eddie, one that said he knew all about Eddie's ways, that he'd been prepared for them. "Funny." The grin stayed put, and the perfect teeth grew more perfect. "Come on down, Eddie."

"What is this, The Price is Right?"

The grin levelled out a bit, the eyes narrowed.

"This is my scene, and I say who comes in here—"

"Not anymore."

"Where're you from?" Eddie began a slow descent.

"Major Crime. Name's James Whitely."

"This is logged as a suicide. So what's MCU doing here?"

"Ah," Whitely shrugged. "Can't tell you."

"Then you'd best fuck off," Eddie made it to the bottom step, stood a foot taller than Whitely, and folded his arms.

"Your boss was supposed—"

"Well he didn't, so get your arse—"

"He probably tried," said Whitely. "But it looks like you dropped your radio." He bent and collected the radio, slid the battery back on and powered it up. "Here," he handed it over, "butter fingers."

"You're not here because it's a suicide; you're here because of who he is." Eddie snatched the radio. "So who is he, then?" He nodded up the stairs.

"Sorry, can't tell you."

"That means he's either a politician or a copper."

A slight glint in Whitely's eyes.

Eddie nodded. "Copper, then."

"Look, Eddie—"

"PSD on their way too?"

"Yes."

"You'd best pretend you know what you're doing here then."

"What's that supposed to mean?" The grin had vanished completely now, replaced instead by a slight look of trepidation.

"You'll find out, Mr MCU man." Eddie entered the lounge, grabbed his camera kit and forensic case and was stopped by Whitely in the hall.

"Eddie, what will I find out?"

"You think you're here for a twenty-minute suicide, right?"

Whitely nodded.

Eddie laughed. "Good luck."

"Eddie, what—"

Eddie saw the nuances of fear in Whitely's eyes, and wondered why he didn't just barge past him and get the hell out of here; he had been relieved, after all. Instead, he sighed, "Follow me." Eddie dropped his kit and marched back up the stairs, across the stepping plates and into the bedroom.

Whitely stood at his side. "Shit," he said. "Murder-suicide."

"Half right," Eddie turned to leave.

"Has he left a note?"

Eddie made it to the landing again, "Why would he?"

Whitely gently grabbed Eddie's arm. "Please," he said.

Eddie looked again at James Whitely; only this time he didn't see a brave American Marine, instead he saw a frightened kid who was well out of his depth, and didn't have a hope in hell of impressing those who'd sent him here. If it had been a straight suicide, he could cope, no doubt. But now with murder thrown into the equation, he would struggle. "It's not a murder-suicide, Whitely. It's a double murder dressed up to look like a murder-suicide."

Whitely didn't even make it to his next sentence, a question: how the hell do you know that? before the door opened and a giant scene suit with a tiny head stuck on top squeezed into the hall.

"Fuck," Eddie whispered. "McCain."

"Eddie?" McCain's head swivelled left and right.

"What?"

McCain looked up the stairs. "Why are you still here?"

Behind McCain another scene suit, this one considerably smaller, and clutching a clipboard, followed him in.

"What is this?" Eddie shouted. "You lot run out of offices? This is a—"

"Shut it! And grab your kit and handover to MCU."

Eddie ground his teeth, could feel the heat growing in his chest.

"Eddie was just updating me, Mr McCain," Whitely said.

"Yeah, well he's finished updating. Eddie?"

Eddie thumped down the stairs.

The clipboard looked nervous, and said, "I'll wait outside, Peter." She turned and left before McCain could say anything.

And then Eddie was there. "What's your problem, eh?"

"Same as always, Eddie: you. Now get your kit—"

"There are two bodies here—"

"I don't care if there are 200 bodies. It's major crime's problem, so get out."

"You don't understand."

McCain sighed through the mask, "I don't need to understand, you prick. I need you at an armed robbery in Gipton. This scene has nothing to do with you anymore. How many more times!"

"So what are you doing here?"

"Making sure you leave. I know how anal you can get about a job." He took hold of Eddie's arm, and Eddie stopped dead.

He looked at McCain's chubby hand, and then he looked at McCain's sunken eyes. "I'll count to three."

McCain's hand dropped away. "I want you breaking speed limits in five minutes." He turned and left the house, and for a moment Eddie closed his eyes and tried to breathe deeply, tried to contact his inner self and calm down.

"I'll break your fucking legs in five minutes," he whispered, watching McCain rolling the scene suit off his rotund body, hoping he'd fall flat on his arse. The svelte lady, probably from the Professional Standards Department, put down her clipboard, approached McCain and they began talking, McCain nodding Eddie's way every now and then.

Whitely came down the stairs, and the place was quiet again now, quiet enough to hear the kid's scene suit rustling. "I'm going to have to call my gaffer," he said. "No way can I do this on my own."

"Yeah, well you wouldn't be on your own if he'd piss off."

"Thanks, but I don't want to get you in any more bother."

"You'd think we worked for competing companies, Christ's sake."

"So, just quickly, what makes you think it's a double murder?"

Eddie turned his attention away from McCain, looked back at the kid, and eventually said, "Four things, initially. There are drag marks leading to his feet—"

"Eddie!" McCain shouted.

Eddie grabbed the door, yanked it wide and screamed, "Will you just fuck off!" And then he was out of the house, scuttling down the driveway, almost running in his haste to get to McCain. McCain saw this and tried to get out of his suit even quicker, but snagged a shoe and went down heavily on his backside. Several neighbours laughed. The PCSOs laughed.

Eddie did not laugh. He stood before McCain and said, "This job is about to go tits-up because of you, you prick."

"I have my orders!" McCain almost screamed.

Eddie straightened. "Well shove your orders right up your arse." Eddie began walking towards his van.

Whitely called from the house, "Eddie, you forgot your kit."

"Put it on eBay," he opened his van door.

McCain got to his feet, "Eddie, you get—"

"And shove your job up your arse too. Plenty of fucking room for it."

McCain got his wish after all; within five minutes Eddie wasn't just breaking speed limits. He was obliterating them.

Chapter Eight

The Robbery and the Red Marker Pen

—One —

EDDIE SAT IN THE van, listening to the radio operator getting more and more wound up by the steady influx of jobs and the distinct lack of CSIs she had available to deal with them.

"Bravo-Seven-Two?"

That was Eddie's call sign. He ignored her.

"XW to Bravo-Seven-Two, receiving?"

He sighed, pressed the button, "Seven-Two."

"Seven-Two, are you free for details of a robbery in Gipton?"

"No."

"Can you give an ETA, please?"

"No."

"Seven-Two, CID are asking for CSI urgently please. Can you take details?"

Eddie ignored her.

"Eddie, take details now!" That was McCain.

Eddie pressed the button. "You take details. I'm going home to curl one out and file my corns."

He turned the radio off, stared at the steering wheel and listened to the exhaust ticking as it cooled down. There through the windscreen, a bunch of officers climbed into a van and sped out through the iron gates of a main police station that was slowly crumbling into decay.

He'd calmed down considerably on the journey back from Alwoodley and the copper's apparent suicide. But not enough to change his mind about what he was going to do. What was the point of the Major Crime Unit sending in a kid who couldn't handle a major crime? It didn't make sense. And what made even less sense was the First Attending Officer had neglected to find the second body. Christ, it wasn't as though it was buried under the floorboards or anything quite so cryptic – it was lying in bed!

But the icing on the cake, the pinnacle of all the foolishness that was running rampant throughout his own part of the police community, was the startling ineptitude of his supervisor to listen to sound advice and prevent a dire situation getting any worse. "Prick," he said again.

But there was more to it than he could nail down right now. What was the point of being tremendously unhappy in your work if all it did was enable you to exist, to enable you to come to work? Surely he'd be better off not coming to work and actually be happy for a change? And that prompted another question: even if he didn't have all this to contend with, would he really be a happy man then?

Eddie was not a happy-go-lucky kind of man; he never whistled while walking along, he never hummed a tune in the shower, he never rattled the change in his pockets. He was a deep thinker, and the more he thought about things, the worse they appeared, until they became almost insurmountable. Life was just too much of a struggle without adding this kind of burden to it.

And that was why he climbed out of the van and headed into the station for one last time.

— Two —

As he walked the corridor towards the CSI office, Eddie constructed a wall inside his mind. It was tall and it was robust and it was there to deflect any pleas that might come his way from Chris, the area forensic manager, the man who was in charge of the Eastern CSI hub, the man who was in charge of McCain.

On the other hand, he thought, there may be no pleas at all; instead there might be deafening cheers. Either way was fine.

Eddie punched through the door and made straight for his desk, reaching into his jacket pocket for the van keys.

"Back early, Eddie," Chris said. A phone behind him began to ring.

"I'm leaving."

Chris leaned against the doorframe of his office. "Again?" he smiled but it was lost.

"Here's the van keys, my radio, my locker key, my ID card," he pulled his wallet out, tossed the card on the desk. "You can keep whatever's in the locker, sell it, burn it, whatever you want."

"What?"

"My kit is still at the scene. Give it to my replacement."

"Whoa, hold on, mate—"

"I don't want a conversation about it. I'm leaving. Nice knowing you."

"Is this about McCain?"

"He's just one small turd in a giant shit factory."

"He phoned me, told me what happened at the suicide."

Eddie stared at the ceiling. "Apparently he didn't tell you what happened then."

Chris walked across the office. "What do you mean?"

Eddie took off his police jacket, threw it on the desk. "Because it wasn't a suicide." He pulled on his coat. "For the last time, for the record, for posterity, it wasn't a fucking suicide!"

A second phone began to ring. Chris picked it up, put it back down again. "If you know something that might help—"

"Bollocks. That scene was pulled right out from under me, handed to a kid who was quaking in his boots, and I tried to tell McCain what was happening, but all he did was bawl me out. So don't come that shit with me."

Chris held out his hands, palms towards Eddie. "Calm down, Eddie."

"Piss off with your calm down. I'm not talking about it anymore, I'm off."

"You can't just go like this."

"Host a leaving party if you want, but I'll be busy washing my hair. Don't bother with a whip-round or a card, eh."

"You have to give notice."

"I hereby give notice—"

"Eddie! You have to give a month's notice."

Eddie smiled at Chris as he slammed his desk drawer. "So sack me." He headed for the door.

"Think about what you're doing. Think about what you're giving up—"

"Okay, I'll indulge you, shall I? What am I giving up? I'm giving up working seventy-hour weeks; I'm giving up being ordered around by that egotistical arsehole who's forgotten what it's like at the pointy end these days; I'm giving up rushing from one fucking job to another because we suddenly lost a shit-load of staff when the government 'restructured' us." He smiled then. "But anyway, look on the bright side, I'm giving someone a job. There, everyone's happy."

Chris closed his eyes, said dejectedly, "I need it in writing, mate."

The phone began ringing again. Eddie stopped; he bit his tongue, trying to prevent the impetus he had nurtured during his walk up the corridor, the brick wall he'd built, from slowly crumbling like the station around him. He swiped the ringing phone off the desk and headed for the white board at the head of the office. He picked up a red pen and scrawled, "I quit." And signed it, "E. Collins."

"Look, why don't you take the rest of the day off and just give it some thought."

Eddie headed for the door just as McCain walked in through it. Suddenly his impetus returned. "No need."

Chris said, "Eddie—"

"I'll mail you a letter."

McCain stopped and stared. "What's going on?"

"The writing is on the wall, tosser," Eddie pointed back over his shoulder. "Haven't you got a robbery in Gipton to go to?"

Chapter Nine

A Neck for Old Rope

EDDIE PULLED UP WELL back from the cordon and climbed out. The traditional throb of police activity was all around him, except since he was here last time – only an hour ago – it had doubled in intensity.

He could see CID cars littered around, parked half on the residents' driveways and half on the road; marked vans canted at strange angles on the grassed verges. And right in front of his car was a BBC outside broadcast crew. Amazing how these things got out so quickly.

As he walked towards the scene tape, he took out a cigarette and watched the clusters of coppers and CID embroiled in whatever it was they did at scenes like this. Certainly house-to-house will have been carried out by now, or maybe they're still under way with it, he thought, and they'll be securing the property round the back, working out shifts and personnel, and of course, since they now obviously thought the scene more than just a murder-suicide, they might even be considering armed officers to float invisibly among them.

Either way, with the number of officers standing idly around, it looked like the old police adage was still very much alive: hurry up and wait.

But as he neared the cordon, some of them looked at him. And for the first time in years, Eddie Collins felt like an outsider. Working for the police was a strange experience. There were seven or eight thousand of them in West Yorkshire, and he knew maybe a couple of hundred or so by sight and only a handful by name, but no matter where in the county he went, he could rely on a nod, and a smile and conversation if he felt that way inclined. He was part of the club, one of the in-crowd, nothing too secret to share.

But now that he was lighter by a warrant card, the doors to that club were closed. He could expect nothing more than common courtesy from his thousands of ex-buddies now, and that was an eerie feeling. He wondered if he'd be able to get close enough.

Eddie flicked his cigarette into the gutter and nodded at the approaching PCSO.

"Eddie, what's up?"

"Nip and get James Whitely for me, would you?"

"The CSI?"

"Yeah," Eddie said, almost bitterly, "the CSI."

"I can book you in if you want to come inside?"

Eddie smiled. Wouldn't be saying that if you knew my employment status. "I'm on my way home, just wanted a quick word."

The PCSO disappeared and Eddie looked around at the interested neighbours who gathered in clumps for a gawp and a natter as though all this was a day out at the seaside for them. He wondered how many knew of the secrets inside that rather pleasant detached house. How would this upmarket neighbourhood react to having a murder house in their very private little street?

Whitely walked briskly – as briskly as a scene suit would allow – over towards Eddie, ripping his mask off and sweeping the hood back over cropped hair that glistened with sweat, a "phew" hovering on his dry lips. "Thought you had a robbery to go to."

"Did you work it out?" He nodded to the house.

Whitely looked around as though about to impart some earth-shattering news, "Frankly, no I didn't. I've been concentrating on photography."

"What? Haven't you even studied the scene? Aren't you curious?"

"Of course I am, but I have to get the photos done for a—"

"Briefing, yeah I know."

"Why do you think it's a," he lowered his voice, "a double murder?"

"Lots of things. The front door was unlocked."

"So?"

"You going to kill your wife and then top yourself, you don't want granny from next door walking in to borrow a cup of sugar as you're tying the noose do you?"

"Suppose."

"So he let the murderers in. The murderers let themselves back out."

Whitely clicked his fingers, "No note!"

"They don't always leave one anyway, especially if their mind's all over the place." And I should know about having your mind all over the place, he thought, remembering the time his wife and kid left him, and the Ros at the same time. "So don't let that sway you."

"You said murderers. Plural."

"And the rope is foreign to the scene. Everything in that house is less than six months old. Nothing is dirty or well used; no way would he have a shitty old rope just lying around."

"He might have brought it with him."

"Where from, work?"

"Look," Whitely said, "he didn't work regular hours at the local nick, if you know what I mean."

Eddie looked away. It began to make some kind of sense to him now; having been ejected from the scene so that Major Crime Unit could take over. "I see," he said. "If that means what I think it means, you'd better make sure you're fucking thorough in there."

"I will. What else?"

"Don't forget the marks on the landing floor; drag marks. The landing will powder up pretty good, but get some oblique light on there, first job."

"Okay."

"And look at his wrists; his hands were bound, there are marks on them – low copy swab them. And then look on the handrail below the attic hatch, there's a footwear mark there."

"Might have been his."

"Nope. Not his, I checked."

"But you hadn't even powdered it up, how could you tell—"

"So powder it up. It's an Adidas."

Whitely stared in wonder at Eddie; even his perfect teeth saluted. "How the..."

"Right, I'm off."

"What?"

"I have a life to plan." Eddie turned and began walking away.

"What's that supposed to mean?" Whitely called.

"I've resigned." Eddie lit a cigarette and walked away.

"No way! And you came back here?"

Eddie waved as he walked, but had made it no more than thirty yards when a besuited woman coughed in front of him. He looked up, saw the figure, saw the chest, and then saw the eyes. They were great eyes, but the chest was better.

"He was a policeman, wasn't he?"

She had a voice to match her looks too, he thought, heavenly like a slow drink of Grand Marnier that trickles down your throat. "Who are you?"

"Sarah Moran," she said, "BBC."

For a second he'd expected her to say Kelly... Don't know why, it just seemed natural. And Kelly? Now there was a name to add a cloud to the brightest of days. Eddie looked down and walked on, "Sorry, can't help," he said, her soft voice and wonderful figure already forgotten, already replaced by a slightly harsher voice and a face full of mischief, full of beauty and wonderment. Eddie walked across the road, feeling more than a little dejected, and was almost hit by some arsehole in a Corsa; probably more CID. You could never have too many CID when some shit like this kicked off. It added to the pandemonium; was quite entertaining actually. He got in the car and slammed the door.

All it took was something innocent like that to set him off again, to set him back months again; just a name, maybe even a smell of her perfume or the way a woman might smile – anything could instantly propel him back to his life before, as a husband to Kelly, and a father to Sammy. It was an old life, long gone now.

There was a knock on his window and he looked up to see the BBC woman again. He started the engine and then wound down the window. Stared at her.

She saw his dampened eyes and appeared genuinely upset for him. "Oh I'm sorry," she said, "was he a friend of yours?"

"I'm no one's friend," he muttered as he drove away.

Chapter Ten

Keep Your Friends Close

— One —

IN THE RECEPTION HALL was a semi-circular desk with the force crest in a subtle 3D design discreetly lit from above. Below the crest it said, "Major Crime Unit & Crime Division". DCI Lisa Westmoreland signed in, went through a set of double doors and took the stairs to the first floor, and into the main office. She nodded a "good morning" to the admin people, walked by her own office, and headed straight for Cooper's. Cooper was waiting for her, closed the door after her.

"Coffee?"

Westmoreland shook her head, and sat down in one of two small arm chairs separated by a circular table. "Definitely suicide, is it?"

Cooper shrugged. "He was found by a neighbour." He closed his old man's eyes and dropped into his own seat behind an empty teak-effect desk. "This could fuck up two years' work."

"Local CSI are already on it so I've sent my CSI out there to take over. We'll soon know if it really is a suicide. I can't spare more than one right now—"

"Better hope it is. A suicide, I mean."

"I presume he had family?"

Cooper nodded, "A wife. No kids. She miscarried a week ago." He looked at Westmoreland and said, "Even if it's not suicide, we tell everyone it is until I can contact the others."

"Where's the wife?"

"Not heard anything about her yet. I just hope... Well, right now I don't know what to hope."

"How many others are out there?"

Cooper shook his head, almost imperceptibly.

"I have to know, Francis. If you want me to help you then you're going to have to start sharing."

"I can't—"

"Bollocks. Share or I pull my people off it right now and you can go cap in hand to Serious Organised Crime, see if they can spare a scene examiner. Or let the locals back in there. And I guarantee it'll be in the media within—"

"Eight. Three of them deep."

"How come he was at home? On leave, what?"

"Look, there are some things I'd rather keep—"

"You pulled him in, didn't you?"

Cooper sighed. "He was stressed out. Because of the miscarriage. He took his eye off the ball, got slack."

Westmoreland raised her eyebrows.

"And I swear, Lisa, if any of this gets out—"

"What do you take me for—"

"If any of it gets out, I go to the ACC with details of this meeting."

"Fair enough." She could see Cooper was stressed out too. Operations like this could turn you sour; and if things started to go wrong – unplanned things, like miscarriages – then it could put lives at risk. Then the whole game of cops and robbers turned really nasty. "Things like that have a habit of screwing with people's brains, so maybe chance is on your side; it most likely is suicide."

"I hope it is. He was well inside a Leeds crew and they're not renowned for being pleasant with people who've crossed them."

"Have you got suppression orders in place?"

"First thing this morning. Even if it is a suicide, if the press shows a picture of him on the news, it'll spook the crew – they'll know we had someone on the inside."

Lisa shuffled in her chair; she felt uncomfortable with this. All this cloak and dagger stuff wasn't in her job description. Of course she had secrets, anyone in her rank had, but playing about with publicity versus playing inside gangs that weren't averse to heavy violence was a tough act to balance, especially when there were policies and procedures and laws on disclosure to bear in mind. Especially when there were real people, people with families, to bear in mind too. "I can see you're twitchy; but you have thought about getting the others out until you know for sure this is a suicide?"

"Of course I've thought about it. Can't do it though. There's more work still to be done—"

"But you might—"

"The pisser, the real pisser about all of this is that I had a missed call from him last night. I always keep my phone switched on and near me. Always. But I put it on silent last night."

"Why?"

He sighed. "Can you believe I went to the flicks." He looked almost ashamed. "Of all the nights to have a fucking social life..."

"Your call, but you should make them aware at least."

"My boys stay out there until I say so." Cooper looked at the clock ticking on the wall above Westmoreland's head. It was the only feature; nothing else broke up the monotony of magnolia walls. "I have to know one way or the other as quickly as possible, Lisa. And whoever examines that scene has to be 100 per cent sure."

— Two —

Westmoreland made the call to DI Taylor from her own office. "Alan, it's me. Keep everything close to your chest, but I want you to get down to the Alwoodley scene now and make an assessment for Cooper."

Taylor sat up in his chair. "What kind of assessment?"

"I need to know the cause of death."

"I thought it was a suicide."

"It needs confirming. Urgently please."

"I'll ring the CSI."

"No, don't ring him; go see him. I want accuracy, no Chinese whispers. And take Jeffery with you to interpret the findings. Now." Westmoreland hung up.

— Three —

They turned into the estate, drove around a BBC outside broadcast van and almost collided with a man crossing the street with his head down, shoulders slumped. Following him was a well-dressed woman. Jeffery slowed, peered in the mirror and saw the man. It was Eddie Collins, he was sure of it. Looked like he was talking to the press. Jeffery mumbled something under his breath.

He found a spot to park in and cut the engine. "I don't see what's so important about this job." Jeffery unbuckled and looked across at DI Taylor.

"Is that a question?"

"It's a suicide. And yes," he said, "it's a police officer. Regrettable, I admit. But I don't see the significance of a trip down here when James is perfectly—"

"I can't say too much. I need to know for Cooper." He climbed out of the car and left Jeffery staring blank-faced at the steering wheel as though expecting it to perform a trick.

Together they walked to the cordon, spoke to the PCSO and awaited James Whitely.

"Our Cooper? Crime Division Cooper?"

Taylor nodded.

"This one of his lads then?"

Taylor turned to Jeffery. "It is." He frowned, "Please, no more questions."

Whitely came down the driveway to meet them, walking from the shade into the sunlight, squinting like a pit pony freshly released. "Jeffery," he nodded. "Mr Taylor."

"How far have you got, James?"

"I'm still on with the photography. Is there a problem?" He looked from one to the other.

Jeffery came in closer, stretching the scene tape, and whispered, "Is it a suicide? That's what we need to know."

James bit his bottom lip. "I thought it was."

"But?"

"I took over from a CSI called Collins. He's convinced it's a murder."

Taylor and Jeffery looked at each other. "Why?"

"I was going to ring you, but Eddie Collins just came back to offer some help."

"Go on."

"It's not a suicide. It's a murder. In fact it's a double murder; his wife is in the bedroom, asphyxiated."

"Fuck," Taylor said.

"Why is he so convinced?"

"You want to come in? I could show you."

"No," Jeffery said, impatience gathering, "just tell us, will you."

— Four —

Jeffery thanked Chris, pressed end, and dropped the phone into his jacket pocket. He shook his head, and then wondered why he was surprised by anything Eddie Collins did these days. Once through the doors of the Major Crime Unit, Jeffery and Taylor headed straight for Westmoreland's office, knocked and entered, then closed the door.

Westmoreland asked, "How well do you know this Collins?"

Jeffery took a deep breath and exhaled a long sigh, "Well enough."

"And? Jesus, why is everything like pulling teeth today?"

"He's an alcoholic. Or at least he was the last time I worked with him. A leopard never changes its spots, they say."

"That it? He's an alky?"

"As we pulled up to the scene, I thought I saw him. A reporter was following him across the road."

Westmoreland stared.

Jeffery shrugged. "I don't know if he was talking to her or not."

"I'll have him in court if he's said anything." She stared at the carpet, bit her lower lip, and then asked, "Apart from that?"

"You want to know if what he told James Whitely makes any sense, don't you?"

"Well of course I bloody do."

"Yes, it makes sense. And Eddie Collins is just about the best crime scene examiner in West Yorkshire. He has a knack, an eye for detail that no one else does."

"You still sound doubtful of him?"

"I'm just wary of him, that's all. He's got a temper, and he's not good at taking instructions."

Westmoreland smiled. "All artists are extreme, Jeffery. But it shows some kind of dedication if he's prepared to come back to a scene he's been unceremoniously released from to make sure it's done correctly after he's resigned." She thought about her words. "Passion."

And Jeffery thought about them too. He wondered why Collins had given in his notice and then just picked up his coat and left. Chris at the CSI office was unable to shed any real light on it, citing Collins's dismay at statistics and examination times as the main reason. But Jeffery suspected Peter McCain was high on Eddie's list of reasons too. "I wouldn't place too much weight on his abilities in this case though; James would have worked it out soon enough."

"I don't share your optimism, Jeffery. Sounds to me as though Collins convinced him it was a double murder. And people tend not to have open eyes about things, let alone open minds."

Jeffery looked away, knowing the open minds remark was aimed at him directly.

"Okay, I need to see Cooper with the bad news. And while I do that, I want you to contact the CSI office again. Find out Eddie Collins's address."

Jeffery raised his eyebrows. "Why?"

"I want him."

"I beg your pardon!"

"Is there a problem?"

"There are a lot of people in the main office out there, and in Crime Division who used to work with him, and—"

"Benson, you mean? Ruffled his feathers a bit did he?"

"There was a big falling out a couple of years ago, and it was more than feather-ruffling. There'll be hell to pay if you bring him here." Jeffery bit his bottom lip.

"No there won't. If I want him, he comes; Benson – and whoever else you're referring to – had better put the past behind them. I know what happened back then, but if people had done their jobs correctly, a lot of nastiness could have been avoided. And yes, before you ask, I'm talking about Benson and his demotion."

"But there's—"

"Now if you'll excuse me, I must go and see Cooper."

Jeffery cleared his throat. "It's my decision who is employed as an CSI, Lisa, not yours."

"Then make the decision to hire him. Right, Jeffery?"

"What about following procedure? What about advertising the post?"

Westmoreland moved closer. "We have a vacancy, don't we?"

"Yes, but—"

"Advertising and interviewing... two months, minimum. You happy with that? Will your overworked staff be happy with that?"

"I know all that—"

"And when we follow procedure, human resources give you someone like James Whitely. Don't they?"

"He has potential."

"Potential is good. For the future. Right now we need experience."

Jeffery sighed. Game over.

"Just do it. Please."

— Five —

When Westmoreland left, Cooper sat back in his chair, one leg perched on the top of his desk, a certain resignation creeping through his body.

He wondered if this was the beginning of the end of the operation. Tony Lambert had been a massive source of information concerning Slade Crosby and his Chapeltown gang. Everything from dates and times of jobs to snippets of intelligence he'd gathered about the other Leeds crews. He had been in among them for nine months, and was well trusted.

Cooper had pulled Tony out of the crew last week, on the pretence of a family tragedy in Ireland, just so he could be at home with his wife, who naturally was feeling depressed about the miscarriage. Depending on how quickly Tony resurfaced, he had every intention of sliding him back into the crew to resume his duties.

It seemed as though the crew had other ideas though.

Somehow they'd found out he was a police officer. Somehow they'd found out where he lived. And then they'd killed him and his wife. It sent a message: it said they had become brave these days, it said they didn't tolerate this underhand way of prosecuting them for illegal activities.

The most startling thing was they had disguised it as suicide. They hadn't gone in there and shot Tony and his wife, or just bludgeoned them to death. They'd thought it through, kept scene disturbance to a minimum, trying to deflect suspicion away from murder. "Why?" he whispered to the empty office.

The obvious answer was that the police would begin looking for the murderer in the Crosby gang. And gangs these days knew the police granted them a certain amount of latitude. Not a stalemate as such, more of an unofficial status quo: we'll leave you to do your stuff so long as it isn't child sex offences or terrorism, but step over this invisible line and we'll have to call on you. Sorry. That's how it was these days: a battle for psychological territory.

But a gang who capped an officer and his wife and didn't sufficiently cover their tracks were going to collect a heap of shit from the law. One thing the police were famous for was looking after their own when tragedy struck. They would pursue the responsible gang relentlessly; there would be zero tolerance (a term Cooper detested, but it had its place) and their activities would be shut down.

So why didn't the police do that anyway? Because another gang, one foreign to the neighbourhood, one that didn't know the very personal culture of the district, might step in and take control. And then the police would be right back to square one – no intelligence on anyone. There would also be a period of elevated violence that would negatively affect residents and businesses – very bad for stats and satisfaction survey results.

And to hound a gang as endemic as the Crosbys, who'd leached into the community, would prove fantastically resource-heavy, and time consuming. But Slade Crosby had overstepped that mark, that invisible line.

Cooper slid his leg off the desk and sat forward in his chair, elbows on the desk, head in hands. This was turning into a very difficult situation for him. He had a hand to play, and he had good cards too; but he couldn't afford for the gang to think they'd won.

The slaying of a copper and his wife was wonderful underground PR for the gang, a real status boost. If Tony's picture went public, and the press reported the event as a double murder, the gang would see it. They'd know their attempt at disguising it as murder-suicide had failed and they'd try to cover their tracks. And that's when things would become dangerous for all other police officers, covert and overt. Play those cards close to your chest, he thought, and the gang remains unaware of our progress, and they leave themselves open to arrest.

But arrests would be later, much later. For now, Cooper wanted to concentrate on the big event, and pursuing those responsible for Tony's death had become an integral part of that effort. Slade Crosby's days were numbered.

Cooper was beginning to think that Benson might be right, that any way to take Crosby down was acceptable. Any way at all.

Chapter Eleven

Paperwork and Politics

EVEN BEFORE HE'D UNLOCKED the front door to the cottage, he could hear the damned phone ringing. He closed the door after him, and locked it as the first drops of rain landed, and thudded through into the house just as the phone rang off and the machine picked up.

He stood still and listened, watching the red digital display tell him he had three missed calls already. No one ever rang Eddie. He wasn't Mr Popular, and that suited him just fine.

But today, apparently, he was Mr Popular.

"Eddie," said the phone, "it's Chris from work," Eddie closed his eyes and sighed. "Mate, can you give me a ring. Pretty urgent. Erm, yeah. Cheers."

Eddie stood the bottle of Metaxa on the sideboard and took hold of the phone and its base in one hand and he walked to the kitchen. Even when the line between the phone and the wall socket tightened, he kept on walking until the plug twanged out of the wall and hit him in the back. Then he opened the bin and threw the whole lot inside.

"Hello, Chris," Eddie mocked as he walked back into the lounge. "No I can't ring you. Piss off."

This was something new for Eddie. He had never been out of work. And this didn't feel like a week of leave either, it felt different, very strange as though he was his own man, could do anything he wanted, and wasn't beholden to anyone, cut free. Because even if you have a week off, or two weeks, or even a month, you know you're going back to it; and you know they've still got you by the balls.

Freedom – every man's dream. That was a feeling, he guessed, you only ever got once you'd retired and your body was too knackered to take advantage of the fact. Or, he supposed, raising eyebrows as he peeled off his uniform in the bedroom, if you were a lazy idle tosser and had never worked a day in your life. Then it might feel like this.

In his boxer shorts, Eddie went to the kitchen and took out a roll of bin bags from beneath the sink, and filled the kettle while he was there. He returned to the bedroom, stripped the belt out of his trousers, and threw loose change into the shoe box by the bed.

But no, even that would feel different because you wouldn't have had all the years of hard graft to give you the comparison. "See," Eddie said, "that's what I like about you; deep thinking already, mate." He collected together all the bits of uniform the police had seen fit to give him over the years, including the steel toe-capped boots that wouldn't look out of place on a storm-trooper, and stuffed them all into the bin bag.

"Gonna have me a fire tomorrow." He walked through to the kitchen, found a mug that wasn't too grubby, rinsed it and shook a little coffee out into it. "I could make it into a ceremony." He poured the water, dribbled some milk. "I could light some candles." He opened the drawer, searching for a teaspoon, and wasn't surprised to find none. He took out a knife and stirred the coffee with the blade. It went everywhere, splashing across the worktop, but it didn't dampen his spirits. He just mopped up the spilt coffee with the nearest tea-towel. "I could invite a few close friends around." He grinned as he walked into the bathroom and set the taps running, added bubbles, and then added more bubbles. "So, that'll be me and... me then," he laughed.

Or perhaps you'd feel like this if you were stinking rich, say a lottery winner, and had just walked from your mundane job stacking shelves at Sainsbury's. How great would you feel then, he wondered? As good as this feels now? Probably a whole lot better, actually. Eddie sank into the bath letting its heat cure his body and letting the bubbles run up the crack of his arse. He giggled.

It would feel like that, he supposed, like getting the biggest and best "Get Out of Jail Free" card in the world, if he wasn't almost broke.

"Maybe not the best time to walk away," he conceded. From now on though, there never would be a best time. He reckoned he had about 800 quid in the bank. Possibly. It had been a while since he'd checked; he made a mental note to check tomorrow, because, as he looked around at the bathroom, he knew he was leaving. There was nothing to stay here for anyway.

After Kelly, he'd sold their house and bought this cottage, aiming to be in the countryside but within an easy commute to work. And he'd more or less succeeded there – he was kind of in the countryside, but there was a busy road only 300 yards away, and when the wind was in the right direction, it was like living next to the M1. The commute had been quite good though.

Only now, he didn't have a commute to do. Ah, that thought again, it made him smile, and he wondered how long it would take him to get used to the idea. Freedom.

And that untangled him, made him take a big carefree breath. He could really aim for the countryside now, had a second chance to get it right. A second chance to get out of the clutches of this bastard city and live somewhere isolated; somewhere remote where you'd struggle to hear any man-made sound at all. The thought filled him with a tingling need. And he could do it; put this place on the market tomorrow and start looking for somewhere to grow old and senile in.

No more early morning starts. No more late finishes, no more half nights or full nights to contend with. No more pissed-up complainants holding him responsible for the trouble they'd brought on themselves. And the thing that made him smile widest right now, as the water cooled, was the thought of no police bullshit: paperwork and politics. Bliss.

There was a knock at his front door.

Eddie blinked in astonishment. He closed his eyes and held his breath, teeth clenched tightly.

The knock came again, and Eddie submersed himself. But he could still hear it, dulled but incessant. He surfaced, spat water and shouted, "Go away!"

"Eddie," the muffled voice came back, "it's me."

It's me, he thought. Who the hell is "me"? It didn't really matter who it was, Eddie was not in the mood for entertaining today; he was in a "this is the first day of the rest of my life, and I want to wallow in it by myself" kind of mood. "I don't care who you are. Go away!"

There was another knock at the door again, only this time it was more of a bang. And that didn't improve Eddie's temper at all. Growling, he climbed from the bath, threw a towel around his waist and headed for the door, water dripping from his chin, and anger brewing inside.

He opened the door. "What?"

McCain stood there. "Can I come in?"

"No."

"But it's raining."

"Better talk quick then."

"Eddie. I'm getting wet."

"Frightened you'll shrink?"

"Please?"

After a pause, Eddie threw the door open wide and stepped back. "Why can't you leave me alone? I resigned."

"Thanks," McCain said as he brushed past Eddie into the lounge.

Eddie closed the door, folded his goosepimpled arms, and said, "Well?"

"I won't stay long—"

"Correct. Now what do you want?"

"About earlier..."

Eddie stared.

"I er, I wanted to apologise about my behaviour at the scene. I was out of order."

Eddie stared.

McCain looked away.

"That it?"

He shifted uncomfortably, and then cleared his throat. "I wondered if you'd reconsider your resignation."

"Who wondered if I'd reconsider?"

"I did."

Eddie stared again.

McCain sighed, "Alright, Chris did. As well, I mean."

"Look, I resigned because you're a prick, let's get that out in the open before we go any further; no point pussyfooting around. And your personnel skills are non-existent," he paused there, wondering if McCain had the balls to throw that back at him. Evidently, he didn't. "But it's not just you. I resigned because no one gives a shit about the job anymore. Everyone is too busy ticking boxes to realise it's more than collecting footwear evidence and searching for blood... all they want is their quota of jobs doing; they don't care what we find at scenes any more—"

"That's not us, mate, that's the government—"

"Exactly! And that's why I quit."

"But—"

"Examining crime scenes isn't about production-line shit; each one is different and needs individual attention. It isn't about pushing us from one job to the next till the fucking list is clear, it's about helping people."

Now it was McCain's turn to stare; he had a dumbfounded look in his eyes. Eddie also detected a part of them that clearly said, "Yeah right, if you say so".

Eddie almost laughed, but managed to haul it back just in time; it was no good having McCain think he'd suddenly gained a new friend, or rather just a friend. "I realise I'm no cuddly bunny, but the job is there to be done correctly for the victim, not done quickly for the government – otherwise what's the point? And it never will be done properly and for the victim, so that's why I quit, and that's why I'm telling you to piss off. I'm not coming back."

"You sure about this?"

Eddie nodded.

"What shall I tell Chris?"

Eddie gently eased McCain out of the front door and into the rain again, "Tell him whatever you want, mate. Goodbye."

He closed the door and then a moment later, opened it again. "McCain?"

With something approaching majesty McCain spun around, clearly hoping that Eddie had changed his mind. He wore an optimistic smile. "Yes, Eddie?"

"Wait there!" Eddie disappeared back inside, and McCain looked confused until the bin bag caught him on the side of the face.

"Ow!"

"Sorry," Eddie smiled, "must've been the boots." He closed the door. And only a few seconds passed again, just enough time for McCain to shove the bag into the boot of his car, before Eddie opened the door again. "McCain?"

"Yes, Eddie?"

"Don't come back." He slammed the door.

After a minute, he heard McCain drive away, and Eddie stood in the lounge, slowly drying but still cold now. The first thing he saw was the bottle of Metaxa brandy.

He could barely remember buying it. But he was glad he had; he was very glad, because he had some serious remembering to do, and maybe a little planning too.

Eddie clutched the bottle and waltzed into the bathroom. He licked his lips and cracked the seal, throwing the lid on the floor and then he poured the entire bottle down the toilet and flushed it.

With pride, and yet with dampened eyes, Eddie put the empty bottle down and climbed back into the bath.

Chapter Twelve

The Death of Anticipation

SHE PARKED AT THE end of the street.

The Bitch lived in a cul-de-sac of sorts, a modern estate in a south Leeds village called Oulton. The estate had one entrance road only, so she knew he'd have to drive past her to get out. It was raining again; always seemed to these days, there was no respite from it, it was incessant, and it was frustrating. It always rained. And she was always in a bad mood these days too. But that had little to do with the weather, if truth be told. This had to do with him. And The Bitch of course.

The lights of approaching traffic were too bright and they appeared to starburst on the smeared windscreen and that made it even more difficult to see. Of course, she could just turn around and drive to The Bitch's house, see if his pickup truck was parked there. She knew it would be. But if that were the case, she thought, then why put yourself through this, why not just go back to work and forget all about it?

Naff off!

She knew where his pickup was, but it still needed confirming. She had to know because…

Her heart beat faster and she rolled the window down a couple of inches, trying to get some cool air into the van, trying to stay focused without having a damned heart attack at the thought of what she was doing. What she was doing? Okay, without having a heart attack knowing what he was doing. With The Bitch.

The rain spattered her face through the open window. She squinted, but didn't wind it back up again.

I don't know if it's even happening yet.

Of course you do; you can live in denial if you want—

Okay, okay! I don't know—

There it is! His pickup drove straight past her; the sound of its massive tyres ploughing through the standing water deafened her, the spray following like a cloud of red mist – the devil's afterburner. She flicked the wipers on full to make sure it was actually his pickup and not one just like it. It's a Dodge Ram, stupid; there's about five in the whole sodding country.

So that's it then.

She turned off the wipers and the screen blurred, just a rectangle with streaks of white and red floating around inside it. She was stunned, quite literally. It was like being told you were about to die. Sorry, nothing we can do. You've got a week left to live.

Stunned was a mild word. She was cloven in two.

"You've got a week left to live," had a liberating quality to it, though; it was the flag of freedom waved aloft in bright summer sun; it was an end to the wondering, the speculation. It was the death of anticipation. It was the last sigh of a lifetime of sighs given by the last breath. Now it was real. She could feel her throat closing up and her nasal passages blocking too, could feel the prickle behind her eyes.

"Don't you dare bastard cry!"

You've got a week left to live also made her angry as hell. She'd known about it for months and had chosen to ignore it; had chosen the easy option, the Let's see if it dies a natural death option, when she knew deep down it never would. Deep down she knew it was springtime in their world; it was a world still full of anticipation, still brimming with raw desire and with lust. And she hated them for it.

She started the van, turned on the wipers and cleared her throat. Then she grazed a sleeve across her eyes and turned around, heading for The Bitch.

Within a minute she was outside 28 Priory Road, and didn't even remember driving there. Her world was silent, as though it was holding its breath. She killed the lights and the wipers, and stepped out of the van. She walked along the pavement and down the drive, and stood at the front door with rainwater running off her hair and not even noticing. She stood there with her hands curled into fists and her cheeks throbbing, her chest pounding and hatred leaking from her.

And then sound of the rain came back, calming. Traffic noises re-emerged into her world as though someone had turned the volume back up; water trickled down her neck, her hands ached and were cold. She blinked, and a single sob burst out of her mouth.

As she climbed slowly back into the van and turned around, the woman at the upstairs window of 28 Priory Road let the curtains fall back into place and picked up the phone.

Chapter Thirteen

Writer's Cramp and Winston's Murder

EDDIE WATCHED THE SPIDER walk across the carpet. It would pause every now and then as though inspecting something. He watched with interest as it turned and headed towards him. "Hello," he whispered. "What's your name?" The spider stopped walking and Eddie wondered if it was watching him, wondering what he was. "You look like a Winston to me." Winston was the first guest in Eddie's cottage that he didn't mind sharing air with.

Eddie shook out the newspaper and slurped tea. He resumed his search for properties up in North Yorkshire, somewhere in the Dales he thought; it would be idyllic, and best of all it would be out of Leeds, away from all the scrotes and all the coppers and all the CSIs.

Hmmm, he thought, that's the best bit!

It was after eight o'clock; the light in the lounge was growing dim, and despite sitting by the window, Eddie was struggling to read. He put down his cup, ready to go and turn on the light. And then he heard it, quite plainly among the background of silence he so adored. The crunching of stones beneath tyres. And the very faint purr of an engine. This did not please Eddie. He folded the paper, sat still and waited.

And there it was, the closing of a car door; ah, and another. Who the hell is this? His forehead creased and his fists clenched. Can't be travellers, he thought; they have diesel vans that make an awful clattering noise. Can't be friends either, because I got rid of them all one way or another. Who wants to hang around a miserable bastard for long? No one.

So who is it then?

Someone knocked on the door.

Eddie closed his eyes. He knew who it was.

Well they can go fuck themselves, he thought. I'm not in.

He and Winston sat in encroaching darkness for a full five minutes as they banged on the door, as they sidled through the nettles around the back and tried that door, peering through the kitchen window, no doubt. Eddie tapped his fingers; this move couldn't come soon enough.

And then he heard voices, soft, muffled. And a car door slammed. Eddie smiled at his victory and stood. He knocked the half full mug of tea and it fell to the floor where it shattered. "Bollocks."

Someone knocked at the door again.

"Eddie?"

"Shit," he whispered.

"Eddie, stop sodding about and open the door."

"Stay there, Winston." Eddie turned on the lounge light and headed reluctantly for the door. "Who is it?"

"It's me, Eddie."

Eddie sighed. "Why is everyone called 'me' these days?" He turned the key and opened the door.

Jeffery smiled at him. "Can we come in?"

"Is it bob-a-job week already?"

"What?"

"Never mind," Eddie said. "What the hell do you want?"

Jeffery half-turned and revealed a woman in a suit standing to his left, "Eddie, this is Lisa Westmoreland."

Eddie looked across, nodded. "Great. That's really good to hear," he began closing the door, "so pleased for you."

"Eddie," Lisa Westmoreland stuck her hand into the decreasing gap, forcing Eddie to shake. "Good to meet you at last." Westmoreland smiled widely.

With a resigned sigh, Eddie opened the door. "What the hell are you doing here?" he asked Jeffery. "I thought you'd crawled so far up your own arse, you'd finally asphyxiated yourself."

Westmoreland laughed and Jeffery shot glances at them both.

Eddie closed the front door and when he turned around, both had made themselves comfortable on his sofa. "Please," he said, "sit down."

"Don't suppose there's a coffee on offer is there, Eddie?"

"This isn't a Little Chef, you know." Eddie stepped past the sofa towards the window seat and as he did, he saw a black smudge on the rug. "Bastards," he said, looking at Jeffery and Westmoreland, an accusing look on his face. "You killed Winston!"

"What?"

Eddie pointed. "My pet spider."

Jeffery and Westmoreland exchanged glances. "Sorry," they said.

"We'd been through such a lot together."

Eddie tutted and retook his seat. "Now what the hell do you want? I'm busy."

"We heard from Chris Ashley at CSI that you walked a couple of days ago."

"You came here so I could confirm it for you?" He stared between Jeffery and Westmoreland and then nudged aside the broken mug. "I'm not coming back. I thought I'd made it plain." He studied Jeffery. "Anyway, what did happen to you? You just vanished from CSI."

"I took him on permanently," Westmoreland said. "Major Crime Unit."

"And who are you?"

"I'm the head of MCU Leeds. Detective Chief Superintendent Lisa Westmoreland."

"Do you ever get writer's cramp?"

"So why don't you want to go back?" Jeffery asked.

"Can't you just go and ask McCain? I went through all this a couple of days ago."

"Who's McCain?"

Jeffery looked at Westmoreland, "He's the supervisor at CSI."

"He's a prick," Eddie said.

Jeffery nodded, "Can't argue with that."

"Is that the only reason you left?"

Eddie sighed, apparently unable to stay off the subject of work for very long – despite not actually working there anymore. He lit a cigarette, reclined in his chair. "I'm sick of the hours. I'm sick of the shifts. I'm sick of the shit way we're forced to do our job, and then being criticised for it."

"That's the modern police culture for you," Jeffery said. "It was coming in before I left."

"It's not how I like my staff to work." Westmoreland looked defensively at Eddie.

"I'm happy for them." He flicked ash. "But if there's nothing else—"

"Why did you go back to the suicide?" Westmoreland leaned forward, elbows on knees.

"I'm going to have a card printed up. It's going to say, 'It wasn't a fucking suicide!'"

"Okay, fair point. But why did you go back?"

"Read the card! I just told you. You lot had it flagged as a suicide. You," he pointed at Jeffery, "sent a young lad in to a scene that was obviously a double murder."

They watched Eddie as he stood, threw his cigarette into the ashtray and marched around the lounge as though his head was on fire.

"And McCain was going to just leave it with him; I mean, he was content – no, he didn't give a shit whether it was suicide or, to use his words, 'whether there were two hundred murdered bodies in there', we were off the job and that was that. He shouted at me to get my arse out of that scene. And that young kid, Whitely or Wheatley or whoever, was bricking it! No one would listen!"

They watched him.

Eddie calmed down eventually, scrubbed a hand across his face and then lit another cigarette, saw the one he'd left burning in the ashtray, closed his eyes and sighed. "Either the kid would have found out it was a murder, in which case good for him; or he would have processed it as a murder-suicide and no one would ever have known that it was a double murder, in which case—"

"The killers would have got away with it."

"At fucking last," Eddie said, sinking into his chair, holding a cigarette in each hand.

"And they'd be free to kill again." Westmoreland cleared her throat. "I want you to come and work for me, Eddie."

Eddie coughed smoke into the room and finally stubbed out one of the cigarettes. "What? No way."

"Why?"

"Because I'm happy being a bum."

Jeffery looked at Westmoreland, a "told you so" look on his face.

"It's not like working as a CSI," Westmoreland said.

"There's no tedious volume crime, Eddie. It's all major stuff, or it's proactive. It's a small unit—"

"It's all bullshit," Eddie smiled. "Look, I appreciate you popping round, really, I do, despite you killing my pet. But I left because not only is the job shit, but it's full of arseholes." He stared at Jeffery.

Jeffery stood. "See," he said, "told you he was a knob," and walked to the front door.

Westmoreland laughed. "I like you," she said to Eddie.

"You still drinking, Eddie?" Jeffery asked.

"You still a prick?"

"Okay," Westmoreland stood, held out her hand, "it was good of you to see us anyway, Eddie."

Reluctantly, Eddie shook, nodded his head and walked to the door.

"We'll get off then." Jeffery opened the door and then paused, "Oh, your phone," he said, "it just rings out. Is it broken?"

"It's in the bin."

"Right," Jeffery said, not at all surprised.

Both left, and Eddie closed the door, locked it and headed for the kitchen, "Strange," he said.

Chapter Fourteen

The Birth of Operation Domino

COOPER WASTED NO TIME as he entered Westmoreland's office. "What did you get from Tony's scene?"

"Sit down, Francis." Westmoreland looked him over as he brushed his tie straight and took a chair. He looked older than ever right now; she'd never seen him so drawn, and it concerned her. "You know what we got." She stared at him, at his drooping eyes, his wispy white hair, and then she sighed, "You want a coffee?"

"No, I don't want a coffee. I want to know, forensically, who killed Tony and his wife."

"I'm sorry," she shrugged, "We were lucky to find out he was murdered at all, but—"

"Come on, Lisa, you work at the cutting edge, don't give me bullshit."

"I beg your pardon?"

Cooper rubbed his face, sat back. "I'm sorry." He sighed, "I just need everything from that scene. Has it been gone over thoroughly?"

"We're still waiting for some lab results, you know. The answer might be there."

Cooper was silent.

"If I think of anything we could do, I'll get it done, okay?"

Cooper nodded. "I want to set up a joint operation. Major Crime Unit and Crime Division."

Lisa leaned forward, peered into his pale old eyes, searching for duplicity of any kind. They might both work for West Yorkshire Police, but some people were always out to make a fast buck or impress someone enough to get them another stripe or another pip. Joint operations were a good way to get those things, and if you managed to get an advantage by blaming any deficiency on your partner, absolving yourself from blame, you could be in the good books come the promotion board.

Lisa knew this from first-hand experience.

"Objective?"

"To secure the demise of the three main Leeds gangs."

That was a bold objective. And in accordance with her surprise, she raised her eyebrows and gave Cooper the smallest of smirks. A teaser.

"We can do it, Lisa. I have some intelligence on a few jobs of theirs, some drugs factories, cannabis farms, amphet caches and the like. We take that lot out, they'll be in tatters; nothing to stop us totally dismantling what's left."

"Hardly in tatters. On the back foot maybe, but not in tatters, Francis."

He stared at her, "We have to begin somewhere."

"But what fills the void?"

"Police work fills the void. Police work can keep this shit off the streets."

"Utopian crap."

"What?"

"You dredge the sludge out of a sewer, new sludge will accumulate in no time."

"Maybe so," he said, "but you give the sewer a break, you let things flow more easily for a while. Any new sludge that begins to gather can easily be washed away."

She thought about this for some time. There were two conflicting emotions within her right now: the fierce cry of independence, and a reluctance to be left out in the cold. She needed information right now, lots of it; and what he proposed, especially on the big event, was compelling enough for her to nod, and say, "What's the structure?"

"Joint decisions where it matters. Crime Division provides the undercover surveillance, CHIS remains private; we investigate covertly. We'll arrange for property confiscation, we'll gather and share intel. Major Crime Unit investigates overtly, provides forensic expertise. Whatever we get, we share."

"What about CID?"

"No go, Lisa. I'll meet with the divisional commanders. Any gang-related activity of note gets logged and passed through to both our departments at source. We keep them out of it."

"Okay," she said, "but if there's a big investigation, we're going to need their manpower; we're overburdened as it is."

"Fair point. I'll sort out some abstractions."

Lisa took a breath and weighed up the proposal. On the surface she was in a win-win situation. She and the Major Crime Unit could only benefit, and privately she kicked herself for not suggesting the plan to him first. She did, after all, need all the intelligence he could give her. "You're on."

"Good. Operation Domino," he said.

"Why Domino?"

He smiled, and then he actually laughed. "When one falls, kiddo, they all fall."

Chapter Fifteen

A Fistful of Horror

RACHEL KISSED DECLAN ON the arm, and then she rubbed it until he stopped crying. "There," she smiled, looking right into his eyes as though no one or nothing else existed; making him feel special, "is it better now?"

The last of the tears rolled from Declan's round face and he stared at her with innocent eyes. Eventually he smiled and he threw his arms around her, sinking his face into her pink hair. "Thank you, Miss."

Over Declan's shoulder she saw a Range Rover glide into the car park. Her smile withered. "Okay," she whispered, "go play now, you've only got five minutes before it's home time." She relaxed her grip on the boy and he was off into the playground.

Rachel stood and folded her arms, suddenly cold.

***

She dug her hands into her jacket pocket and approached the Range Rover as the window opened. Around them, cars were filling up with kids, footballs rolled past, parents jabbered and kids squealed. "What do you want?"

Blake looked at her. Missing from his expression was the usual Jack-the-lad, the usual hateful smirk. "Get in, sis," he said.

"I have work to do."

"Please."

That was shock enough for her. She climbed into the passenger seat and sealed the outside world away. "What?"

Blake licked his lips and tapped the steering wheel. "I want some advice."

"About what?"

He cleared his throat. "Women."

Rachel opened the door and had almost climbed out before he grabbed her. He looked at her, pretty much the same way she'd looked at Declan, eyes focused and burning. "Please."

She closed the door again but left her hand on the latch. "Giving you advice about women would be setting up some poor cow for a very unhappy future."

"I've changed—"

She didn't interrupt him, but he stopped short at the look of incredulity on her face.

"I have!"

"Going to throw a tantrum now?"

"Give me a chance, man."

She folded her arms. "Go on, then, I'm listening."

Quietly, he said, "I haven't got no one else to ask, but I've met someone, and I want to know how to treat her right."

"You could try not raping her. That'd be a really good start to any relationship. And then you could try—"

"Shut up, Rachel!"

She did, stared front.

He tried to smile at her, and then took a deep breath. "I'm not like that anymore, I already told you that. I don't want one of Dad's whores, and I don't want some junky tart either; I'm looking for a decent relationship."

"Where's all this come from?"

He shrugged, "What do you mean?"

"Why the change? Dad's whores have been good to you; they never call the police afterwards."

He ignored the snipe, "Like I say, I'm ready for a change. She's a lady; she's a bookkeeper. Respectable. I'm ready for commitment."

She raised her eyebrows at this.

"It's true, man. I just need to know how to treat a lady." He stopped looking at her; her facial expressions – mocking one minute, chastising the next – were putting him off. He looked at the dashboard. "I haven't got no one to ask, do I? I can't ask Dad—"

"No, because he's a rapist too!"

"Okay!" He sighed. "So, I can't ask him; I can't ask the guys because they'll just take the piss. It was Monty suggested I come and speak to you. You're the only normal member of the family left." Now he did look at her. "I get nervous, tongue-tied, and stupid." He grinned at her. "I just need to know where to take her, Hilton or a pub, or a club even? Do they like flowers, chocolates, that kind of crap, or is that just wasting time, would she think I was stupid because men don't do that stuff anymore?"

"So what's she like then, this amazing woman. And what does she call her Labrador?"

He ignored the remark, and said, "Well, I haven't actually met her yet."

She smiled, "I'm listening."

He swallowed nervously, yet it was obvious he was longing to share his news. "I'm taking her out this Friday. I thought maybe the Hilton at Garforth?"

"How did you two get to know each other?"

"Internet dating site."

"Oh my God!"

"What?"

"You haven't told her you're a business man with a Range Rover and his own house, have you? Have you told her about your prison—"

"Stop it!" His face was contorted like that of a child who'd just been told off for whipping a puppy. "I'm trying!"

"You can't control yourself, Blake!"

"I can, dammit!"

"Internet dating sites are an excellent way to trap vulnerable women." She pointed a finger at him, "And now you'll pretend to me that you didn't know that, you were just trying to find a decent woman outside your crumby circle of friends."

"That's right, Rachel. That's exactly what I'm doing, man. I want someone not connected to any of this shit. I want someone who doesn't know my past so I can start all over afresh; someone who won't judge me by past deeds."

"Did you read that on the side of a bottle of Rohypnol?"

Blake grabbed her arm in his left hand, thumb digging in to her slim bicep, and with his right he aimed a row of bony knuckles directly at her nose. She was prepared. She closed her mouth, screwed up her eyes and pursed her lips, ready for the crunching blow. But it didn't come.

She opened her eyes and the fist was there, right before her face. But her brother's eyes were staring past her out of the passenger window. Rachel turned to look. Outside, was the face of a small boy. He was probably clinging on to the door handle and standing on the chrome running boards. He had tears in his eyes, and a look of abject horror on his face as he saw what was happening inside the car.

"Declan," she whispered and opened the door.

Blake's fist dropped and his clamping left hand released her. She closed the door and walked away, holding the kid's hand.

Chapter Sixteen

Finding Life in a Graveyard

— One —

EDDIE HAD NEVER REALLY believed in God.

He believed that God, any god, was nothing more than a placebo for the faithful. And that was fine by him. If that belief held people's anger in check, if it guided them morally or even spiritually, and if it made them help others, then religion was alright in his book.

But Eddie still didn't believe in God.

Eddie believed in facts. Evidence. And he believed in searching out that evidence, those facts, and he believed in one thing above all others. Himself.

Strange then, that this creature of fact should find himself in a church because of a sudden fancy that struck him. It was a Norman church, built around 1100AD, and it was the building itself, the architecture, the romance if you like, that caused him to stop his car, walk past the familiar graveyard, head down, watching his feet, and arrive inside as though guided by some spiritual sat nav. There was no one around.

He was entirely alone; just him, his thoughts, and the pews, the stone floor. And the feeling of being watched.

It ran like a shiver up his back yet when he turned, emptiness was all he saw.

There was something else, however. It was a strange intangible feeling he supposed that a church-goer, a believer, might call the Presence of God. But Eddie didn't believe it. He preferred to think of it as a thinning of two worlds; a place where one might connect with things forgotten or with things wished for.

Stephanie Collins, Eddie's mum, had been dead twenty years. And of course, Eddie had been to her grave in the churchyard outside often, thinking at first that her soul was where her body was, that it was where he might touch her again, and relive the happy times. It was a fallacy. He felt her presence more in abstract dreams than he ever did looking at a granite block in a field. He missed her. But he didn't go to her grave much any more. He didn't feel bad about it either, realising that the grave was nothing more than a marker – something a person can leave so the rest of the world knows they existed. To Eddie, she had never really left.

It was hard to forgive her, and he probably never would. But he knew she was a good woman at heart, and that's why he still came here, to pay his respects – and he still had a lot of respect for her.

He never left flowers, and never read the cards tucked inside the flowers he sometimes saw here. It felt wrong to – a violation.

Yet here, in the church he felt strangely peaceful, as though it might, after all, be possible to touch your dreams at the thinning of the worlds.

"Bollocks," he whispered, denying the mysterious feeling creeping over him like a spider edging closer to its prey. Eddie shivered, sniffled and brought himself back round by gazing, almost mesmerised, at the sunbeams spinning a rainbow of patterns across the transept, dust motes dancing in the warmth.

Irrespective of the unfamiliar feelings spreading within him, Eddie felt quite close to tears; that preamble, the slight stinging behind the eyes, the stinging in the nostrils, and, "Sod this!" Eddie turned to leave and almost screamed.

Leaning against the doorframe, the light spilling in from the open door behind her, framing her, turning her hair into a glowing mass, and silhouetting her, was a woman. When he turned around, she stood straight, took her hands out of her pockets and began walking towards him. Her shoes echoed in the stillness and Eddie caught his breath.

She was smiling.

"Mother?" His chin was already quivering, his eyes made the vision of her ripple. But she was smiling at him. This is what abstract emotions could do a man, dammit.

"Don't be a dick."

He couldn't see through her, so she was solid, she was real. The furrows in his brow cleared, and he grinned wide. "Ros."

Her eyes shone. "Hello, Eddie."

She was back, and despite thanking Him over and over again, Eddie still did not believe in God.

— Two —

There was fresh coffee diluting the smell of cigarette smoke. The cottage was a tip, and he felt almost embarrassed. But neither spoke a single word until they were seated across from each other. Despite the anticipation mounting, he figured after waiting two years, he could afford another moment to soak her up. Eddie stared at her, he traced her face and her eyes, and she was content to allow it, and she just smiled.

"Why?" he said at last.

"I asked them to."

"Was I that bad?"

"No. Not really. It wasn't you, it was me." She fidgeted in the chair, held his gaze. "I'm sorry, Eddie. I'd just had enough of being your doormat; and I knew you'd never leave Kelly and Becca, and I'd be left on my own again, ready to catch you when you fell."

"Probably. She left me, though."

"Really?"

Eddie nodded, embarrassed. "I was horrible to you, wasn't I? They say you never know what you've got till it's gone."

She nodded, "They do say that." She picked at a cushion.

"You're different, Ros."

"Dyed my hair."

"No, not that." He fidgeted with his fingers, shy now that she was finally here. The things he'd planned to say to her if ever he should meet her again, faded like a dream in the morning. All except, "I loved you."

She looked up quickly. "How the hell would you know that? You wouldn't know love – you wouldn't know any emotion if it bit you in the arse. You were self-obsessed ninety per cent of the time. The other ten per cent you were moping round Kelly – I saw you!" Her hands clawed the cushion. "So don't you dare throw that crap at me now, Eddie Collins. Don't you fucking dare!"

With trembling hands, he shook out a cigarette and lit it. "I'm sorry," he said, "you're right."

"I should go."

"No! Please, please. Not yet, Ros." He leaned forward, whispered, "You saw me? Moping with Kelly?"

Her face straightened, she cleared her throat, "Why did you leave CSI?"

Eddie took a drag on the cigarette, stared at her, and a sudden realisation struck him. "How did you know I left CSI?"

"Jeffery told me."

"Jeffery told you?"

"I work at MCU, Eddie."

Eddie threw himself back in the chair. "I don't fucking believe this. You've let me go on thinking you bailed out this whole time, and you... you couldn't even bring yourself to get in touch. You worked a few miles away and every day you went to work knowing I craved you?"

She laughed, "You craved me? How the hell was I supposed to know that?"

"Considering you just upped and left, you wouldn't know, would you?"

She stared at him for a moment. "Never mind," she whispered. "It doesn't matter now."

"Everything matters now."

"Nothing matters now."

He looked at her, wondering what she meant, but knowing it would do no good to keep on pushing. It would keep. "They sent you here to recruit me, didn't they?"

She shook her head, "No. Jeffery said it was my decision. He'd promised to keep my appointment a secret from you; and he was relieved you declined their offer because it meant he wouldn't have to break a promise."

"I applied to work at MCU, and they knocked me back."

She looked at him and just shrugged.

"So how come you're here now?"

"Because we could use your help. You're a good—"

"Wait, wait, hold on. You went all corporate there for a moment, Ros." He squinted at her, "This is not personal, is it? This is just a recruitment exercise for MCU, isn't it?"

"It is personal, Eddie. I could've told Jeffery I didn't want you in our office, and it would have gone no further. And you'd never have known. So it is personal."

"If it's personal, why leave it two years to get in touch?" He stabbed out the cigarette with a little more force than was needed. "You must have known at some point that Kelly had gone. Or are we both good at keeping our secrets?"

"I knew."

"So why wait?"

She grabbed the cushion. "It doesn't matter."

"I'm confused. Tell me what makes you think it's suddenly got personal."

"No," she said. "I won't. It doesn't matter. Either you want the job or you don't." She stood up. "Thanks for the coffee."

"No," he rushed to her, took hold of her arm, "don't leave. Not yet."

"I have to, Eddie."

"Not like this, Ros. I found you again and I don't want to lose you."

She smiled up at him. And it was a sweet smile, a Ros smile, and her eyes shone again. But there was regret in there too, sadness. "Take the job." She kissed him on the cheek and was unlocking the front door before Eddie could gather his wits.

Chapter Seventeen

Charlie and The Spinney Nook

EVERYTHING WAS IN THE detail.

Charlie stared at herself in the mirror. And then she smiled. And then she grinned. She peered closer, "Got lippy on my teeth," she said, rubbing it away and trying again. "Better."

Panda nuzzled her.

"Ooh, you want some food? Panda hungry?" Panda meowed and leapt from the chair, tail in the air, glancing back as she ambled to the kitchen.

Charlie put the mirror aside, dropped her make-up bag on the carpet and followed the cat. These jeans are wrong, she thought. "They'll give the wrong impression." You want to look sophisticated, feminine.

She giggled to herself, and scooped food into Panda's bowl, running painted fingernails down the fur on Panda's back and watching her spine arch in response.

"Good gal," she said. "Do you think I've overdone the eye-liner?"

Panda ate and purred.

"Yes, I agree," Charlie whispered. "Jeans'll have to go, though."

She looked out of the kitchen window. A few hundred yards away a heat-haze rose from the playground's tarmac surface;

all the children were rippling. Charlie loved seeing the kids and she smiled, delighting as they laughed and shrieked.

You could try that cotton skirt. It is very warm out.

"What do you think, Panda? Cotton skirt? The white one?"

I thought you'd say that.

Charlie crossed the lounge and skipped up the stairs. In her bedroom, she sat in the wicker chair in the corner by her night stand. And she didn't move for nearly thirty minutes.

Am I doing the right thing? What if he's awful? He looked great on the site, but they all look great on the site. Some of them even look like Tom Cruise. I bet he Photoshopped his picture.

Blake, he was called.

"Rape alarm. Don't forget the rape alarm."

Am I doing the right thing?

You wanted a male friend. That's what you said.

She cringed. I know, but... Well, I've got by alright on my own—

You're very brave, you know.

You think?

Oh yes; it's good that you finally plucked up the courage to go out and mingle. It really is. Mum would be so proud of you.

She would be, wouldn't she?

If you're wearing that skirt, don't forget your handbag. And I would quickly run an iron over it first; it's been in the wardrobe for months.

Should I wear a jacket? Or will I be okay in this?

She stood and went into the bathroom where she could see herself in the large mirror over the sink.

I must get that tap fixed. I wonder if Blake is any good with plumbing. I wonder if he's any good at kissing, I wonder if he's any good— "Stop it, naughty," she giggled again.

She turned sideways on, pushed her boobs up slightly. "They're sagging a bit."

You're thirty-four, dear, not eighteen. But you could still turn a man's eye.

I didn't need a bra at eighteen. I might have to buy an uplifting one next time. And anyway, I'm not after turning his eyes. I want company, that's all. I want someone to take an interest in me, and I want to laugh.

"Ooh, Mum's brooch!"

Charlie considered the brooch to be good luck. And so it was precious to her. Everything Charlie held precious was locked away in a secret place.

She went back into the bedroom, pulled aside the quilt on her double bed and lifted the mattress. It rose easily, powered by two gas rams, like the ones that held up the hatch on her car. And it stayed open all by itself. In the void beneath the mattress, she kept a small wooden box inlaid with brass at the corners and a small brass latch on the front. It was her jewellery box. She took it out and opened it up and selected the brooch. It nestled among her mother's engagement and wedding rings, among a few precious photos and a lace doily made by her sister. The brooch was a cameo, and its silver edges gleamed.

For too long she had been alone. She wondered often what it would be like having someone to share things with. Nothing grand like trips to Italy or anything; just sharing a hot cuppa on a cold day, or sharing an episode of Friends, buying each other keepsakes at Christmas, and a treat out at the Jorvik centre on her birthday.

She sat in the car and looked at the front door as though she could see right through it and into the lounge, as though she could see Panda sitting on the arm of her favourite chair licking her paws.

Charlie swallowed and started the car.

As she drove to The Spinney Nook, she became ever more afraid.

It had been a challenge to begin with. No, not a challenge; it had been an adventure to begin with. Michelle at work had said it would do her good. And Michelle had said all those things about treats on your birthday, and eventually Charlie had come around to her way of thinking. She wasn't saying being single was abnormal or anything; but what she kept on saying was that there really was so much more to life when there were two of you to share it.

But all that wisdom didn't stop the nerves as she approached the car park.

And before she pushed open the doors to The Spinney Nook, a sudden chill brought goosepimples to her arms and she thought about turning around right then and getting the hell home.

"Should have worn that jacket after all," she said as she pushed the door open.

Chapter Eighteen

First Day, First Confrontation

— One —

HOW COME IN THIS day and age, when they can send machines to Mars, they can't make a wiper blade that swishes silently across a windscreen? Why must it always grate and leave a series of cartwheel spokes on the glass? Eddie gritted his teeth and turned the wipers off, preferring the danger of having just a rough idea of where he was going over enduring that bloody racket.

He was doing quite well; he could see the non-descript building up ahead and pulled into the driveway where a huge green spiked metal gate loomed. And then he drove straight into the bollard in the centre of the entrance road, the bollard with the intercom mounted on it.

He closed his eyes and forced himself to think of a beach at sunset, of gulls circling in the twilight skies and the waves gently breaking on the warm sand in which he stood. Then some arsehole blew their horn at him. Eddie opened his eyes and flicked the wiper switch. The wipers grated across the glass and Eddie growled as he selected reverse, ignoring the scraping noise from the front and ignoring the impatient driver behind him. Once clear of the intercom post, he climbed out into the rain, didn't even look at the car behind and marched up to the intercom, but his march drooped, became an amble. And suddenly Eddie felt a little sheepish, a little self-conscious. He swallowed, leaned low, since the intercom was now at quite an angle, and pressed the button.

A squeaking electronic voice said, "Can I help you?"

"Quarter pounder and large fries, please."

There was a pause, and Eddie almost smiled up at the camera perched on top of the gatepost.

"Mr Collins?" the voice asked.

Eddie blinked, he was impressed. "Yes. I'm here to see Mrs Westmoreland."

"Ms Westmoreland isn't in at the moment."

Eddie stood upright for a moment, and thought about her response. Then he bent, pressed the button, "I can wait here if you like. But there's a queue forming."

The car behind Eddie's beeped its horn again. Eddie stood and stared at the blue Vectra, shaking his head. He couldn't see through the screen because of the grey sky reflected in it, but he guessed it was some twenty-two-year-old prick with a testosterone surplus.

The gate clicked and began rolling back.

Eddie marvelled at the new dent in his Discovery and then climbed back inside and drove the hundred yards towards what looked like the main entrance. There were no markings anywhere, no helpful arrows, no signs, no insignias; the glass was mirrored. He parked up and rushed through the rain to the double doors. They buzzed as he approached, and he entered.

Eddie stopped and looked around. This place was like something from Lloyd's of London: all glass, marble floors and oak furniture with chrome adornments, high skylit ceilings, subtle spotlighting, and a receptionist with the world's most perfect smile. Ever. She had been moulded, had been lightly machined and then airbrushed. Turn her upside down and you'd find the words, Made in China stamped on her feet.

"Did you just drive into the post?" Her voice was just as squeaky in real life, but without the added hiss of electronics.

Eddie dripped rainwater and walked to the desk aware of the monitors to her right, all with incredibly clear pictures. Three were of the entrance. "Your hair looks... natural. And your eyes too."

She raised her eyebrows. "I beg your pardon?"

"Well, put it in the middle of a road, it's going to get hit. Silly design."

"Did you have your wipers turned off?"

"Look, where can I wait for Ms Westmoreland?"

"You'll need to sign in."

Eddie smiled and reached for the pad. "Pen?"

Miss China slid a Bic over, then folded her arms. "And use your real name."

Eddie looked suitably chastened. "Spoilsport."

In the far corner a door bleeped and then squeaked open. "Eddie, this way."

He looked up from the doodle and saw Jeffery holding the door open. Eddie turned to the receptionist, "Thank you, Miss Moneypenny."

"Very droll."

— Two —

Eddie had followed Jeffery up carpeted stairs, along corridors, through security doors and into a large open-plan office. He tried to look around and see who was there, but they were all just nondescript faces, people busy doing things on their computers. Here I am again, he thought. Bloody déjà vu.

"You could have made an effort, Eddie."

"I did. I'm here aren't I?"

Jeffery ushered him into a smaller glass-fronted office with a neat oak-effect desk, typical brown carpet tiles and walls totally bare except for a fire emergency evacuation plan and a long service certificate. How very flash, Eddie thought. Jeffery closed the door, waved Eddie to a seat, and then perched on the corner of his desk with his arms folded, looking very much like a school teacher whose patience with a disruptive pupil had finally run out.

Eddie looked up at him. He smiled. "Does this place have a coffee machine?"

"I'd forgotten what it was like working with you. These last two years have been pure bliss."

"It's nice that I've been missed, thank you."

"Do you still have a drinking problem?"

Eddie pushed his chair back, adding a more comfortable distance between them. "Took your time. I'd have asked that in the reception area."

"I'm diplomatic."

Eddie took a breath. "I don't have a drinking problem, and I never had a drinking problem."

"Really?"

"What? You're asking me a deeply personal question, so have the courtesy to listen to my answer."

Jeffery nodded, "Go on."

"I bought a bottle of brandy only last week. Metaxa, Five Star. Lovely stuff."

Jeffery sighed, went and sat in his chair, deflated it seemed, but maybe a little relieved that they'd hit the wall now rather than in a few months' time.

"And I poured it down the toilet. I bought a fine bottle of Glenfiddich the week before. It went down the kitchen sink. Yesterday, I bought a six-pack of Tetley's. I drank two tins, and I put the rest in the fridge. I can take it or leave it."

"Then why buy it in the first place?"

"To show me who's still in control. I am in control."

"Eddie—"

"I got legless twice, maybe three times in all the years I worked there. Whoopeedoo. Some people do that every week!"

"So you're not an alcoholic?"

"No. Never have been."

"Then why do you have a reputation as being one?"

Eddie shrugged. "Might have something to do with where I get drunk, or in whose company."

"Really?"

"I am in control. I don't have a drinking problem, Jeffery. I didn't have to tell you the control freak part, did I?" He held out his hand. "Steady as Mount Rushmore."

"And how's the mind?"

"Fuck's sake! Go have a word with Chris at divisional CSI, have a look through my personnel file. Check it for mental stress, sickness absence, hidden bottles of tequila... whatever you want. You'll find I'm firing on all cylinders, and despite my lack of enthusiasm for the human race as a whole, I think you'll find I too am a diplomat."

"I already checked."

"Knew you would've. You checked it before you even came around to my house to offer me this job. So you knew back then I didn't have a drinking problem."

"True."

"So why ask me in front of Westmoreland?"

Jeffery stared at him.

"You asked me in the hope it would scare her off; hoped she'd take back the offer." He paused, returned the stare. "I don't have a lot of fans, I know that. But I'm honest, good at my job...And you've seen my file, you know I'm clean; so what have you got against me now?"

Jeffery raised a finger and was about to respond when the office door opened, and Westmoreland bounded in with a smile on her face and rain in her hair. "Morning, Jeffery." She turned to Eddie. "Eddie! Great to see you," she held out a slender hand, "so glad you finally decided to join us. I was behind you at the gate, I beeped my horn."

"Oh, the Vectra, yeah, sorry," Eddie shook hands, "I was busy with the receptionist."

"Ah yes," she laughed, "Miss Moneypenny, wasn't it?"

Jeffery shook his head, and Eddie smiled shyly.

"Don't worry, I think she liked it." She turned back to Jeffery, "What were you discussing?"

"Eddie's pension rights; they'll carry on as if employment was continuous."

"Yes, super, super. Come on, let's get you out there. We've got a desk for you." She looked at Jeffery, "We did clear Kirsty's desk?"

"We did, yes."

"What happened to Kirsty?" Eddie asked.

"Come on, let's get you settled in."

— Three —

Westmoreland walked with Eddie out into the office, cast an arm wide and declared she loved working here. "There are some super people here," she enthused.

Jeffery, trailing behind, mumbled something.

"It's one big family in MCU. Over there are the detectives, headed up by DI Taylor who sits in the end office next to mine. This area is where the DSs and DCs work; they're all exhibits-trained. You've been in Jeffery's office – he coordinates jobs coming in through the DIs or though divisional CID, and Crime Division, and sometimes the National Crime Agency." She turned and pointed to a triangular desk with a bank of six monitors in their centre. "That's where our clerical support sits. Craig and Melanie are on today. They'll sort out any queries you have; they update some of your computer work. And beyond my office is crime division. First is DCI Cooper..." She turned to Jeffery, "Have you explained the stores and stock floor?"

"Not yet."

"Okay, well, I'm sure Jeffery can fill you in on the rest." Westmoreland extended her hand to Eddie again, "But if I can help you, just pop in and see me, okay?"

Eddie nodded, held his breath as he shook hands.

"Super," Westmoreland headed towards her office.

Eddie looked to Jeffery, who simply nodded and began walking.

Eddie's new desk was beside the window and the photocopier. The copier was larger than a small car and probably just as expensive. The view out of the mirrored window was nothing to get the watercolours out for; it showed the car park and it showed the green spiked gate and a small yellow post canted at a strange angle.

"Information pack I printed for you." Jeffery waved a wad of paper at Eddie then dropped it on the desk.

"Gee, thanks. If I ever get bored—"

"You won't."

"Who am I working with?"

"In it you'll find your shift rota—"

"I thought you didn't work shifts here? You told me you—"

"Calm down; you work days, and you work nights when operationally required. Also weekends on a rota system – it's in there," he pointed to the pack.

"You made this place sound so appealing. But I've walked from the frying pan—"

"Shut up." Jeffery stepped closer. "You've been here half an hour and already you're pissing me off."

Eddie shrugged. "So I'm a little rusty."

"You're lucky to have a job at all—"

"Okay, stop there. If you want a deep and meaningful – and I'd say you're itching for it – let's go back to your office where I can shout at you without disturbing people."

It was by then a little too late to worry about disturbing people. They'd already stopped work and were looking at Jeffery and Eddie, some with consternation at having their work interrupted, others got comfortable in their chairs and waited for the show to begin.

Eddie stared at Jeffery.

Jeffery looked at the onlookers, and he swallowed. "You'll be working with Ros initially; she can get you acquainted with the place, how it works here, where things are; she'll sort you out with a van and some kit," he said, rather more quietly than before. "And when you're up to speed, I want you out with James Whitely. He needs someone with experience; he hasn't been here long." He stepped closer to Eddie, "But please, show him the ropes, don't show him your bad habits."

Eddie smiled. "Jeffery. I don't have any bad habits."

"Quite," Jeffery turned to leave.

"Oh, one last thing before you abandon me to find the coffee machine all by myself. What happened to Kirsty?"

Chapter Nineteen

The Brook in a Shallow Valley

"WAIT," SHE SAID, "WHERE are you taking me? My car's that way." She looked across at him, wearing a half smile in case this was all just an innocent misunderstanding; no point over-reacting. The Spinney Nook, remember?"

"I want to show you something. No need to worry."

The car bounced off the main road and onto a rutted track between two fields. The indicator self-cancelled and the underside of the car hit the edge of a pothole. Long grass and nettles brushed paintwork; the wheels kicked up small stones, and a lazy cloud of dust formed in their wake. The sun was in her eyes, almost kissing the horizon, and nervously she swallowed.

She looked across at him still, studying his face, waiting for the smile she'd so admired to surface. It didn't.

"Blake," she said, "this can wait, I have to get back home; I told—"

"It'll only take a minute." And now he did glance across at her, and there was a smile but it wasn't in his eyes. His eyes were cold.

The car rounded a bend, and the long grass gave way to tall, thick shrubs, and the noises of the main road behind them vanished almost instantly. She could hear birdsong. And still he didn't stop as shade crept over the car and a sudden chill brought goosepimples to her bare arms.

This was spontaneous. She didn't do spontaneous.

"Blake—"

"Nearly there."

She clutched her bag tighter, almost unconsciously. He was going to show her a wonderful view or something, that's all. Those feelings you have inside are just rumours thrown up from a worrisome mind. They gave you some good advice at work; take it! They said get out more, live a little, enjoy other people's company; you've got a week away from here, they said – go and do something with it. And she had – wait, no, that's not right, she thought. She was trying to. She was beginning to. It was a trust thing–

And then the car stopped. "See," he said, already opening his door, "didn't I tell you this was worth seeing?"

"Well, I—"

"We should have brought a picnic!"

She climbed out and stood there against her open door, watching him stride away up a slight incline towards the beginnings of some woodland about 200 yards away. From her right, the dying sun speared between boughs and glinted off the roof; somewhere far off crows cawed, and closer by, starlings screamed with aerobatic delight. She saw a squirrel dashing up the trunk of an oak. It was beautiful. It was alive, and she felt good. Maybe spontaneity wasn't so bad after all. Maybe he wasn't so bad after all. Did he qualify for a second date?

Perhaps home could wait, she thought. And maybe they were right; maybe she should enjoy other people's company and stop being so scared. She closed the door, grinning at her own personal piece of nature; and she trotted after him, looking forward to sharing a little time with him, towards the sound of what turned out to be a brook in a shallow valley crowned by weeping willows and oak. "Blake," she laughed, "wait for me!"

"Down here."

She ducked beneath the gently swaying low branches of an oak, and almost danced towards the trunk. She could see the brook hopping over stones in its path, lapping at delicate shores; and subdued light played on the water's surface. When she reached the trunk he appeared and punched her hard in the face.

Chapter Twenty

The Second Taste of Ben & Jerry's

— One —

"DOES IT ALWAYS WORK like this?"

"Like what?"

Eddie sighed, stared at her. "You get a job and you're given a briefing."

"Yup. You need an overview of what you're dealing with."

"Sounds great."

"It is. No volume crime to deal with, only major stuff. So you have to know the background."

Eddie laughed. "Background? A kid found a body near a stream?"

Ros didn't laugh. "The car nearby belongs to Blake Crosby, he's one of the main men in Leeds. He's one of the Crosby gang that MCU are investigating."

"And?"

Ros shook her head and drove.

"Nice weather we're having—"

"Eddie, shut up!"

Eddie was never one to think too deeply when people told him to shut up; he was used to it. But when Ros told him to shut up, and on their first working day together, it rattled him. Things that unnerved him speared through his mind. Things like, why is she talking to me like this? Does she hate me? Why did she invite me to come and work with her, then?

But the worst thing his mind conjured up was: here we fucking go again! What possessed me, not only to come back to forensic work, but to think that things could ever be the same between us?

Of course "the same" was a very loose theme. There never had been a "the same" before. They had been friends, and she had supported him when no one else would. She had been wonderful. And then, if he remembered correctly, she had been in love with him, or at least slightly besotted with him. And he could do nothing about it; he was still married at the time. Though he admitted he had certain feelings towards her.

But now?

Ros turned off the main road and immediately ran into the outer cordon. She wound down her window at the approaching officer and began to give their details.

Eddie was in a world away from this one. "You ever eaten Ben and Jerry's rum and raisin ice cream?"

Ros wound up the window and waited for the officer to lift the barrier tape so she could drive beneath it.

"No."

"The first time I ate Ben and Jerry's rum and raisin ice cream I almost fainted, it was so good. I practically had a hard-on." He looked at her, she was unresponsive. "It was a few years till I had it again. I was really looking forward to it, you know because I'd remembered it was soooo good." Still nothing. "And when I took that first spoonful... it was just rum and raisin. Nothing special. Bit of a let-down, actually."

"Really."

"It's true."

Ros pulled up at the inner cordon and switched off the engine. She turned to him. "I want you to start with general photography of the vehicle while I arrange recovery. When you're done, get suited up and start peripheral photography of the body without going closer than ten metres. We'll use stepping plates if we need to when the time comes to get up close."

Eddie stared at her. If he hadn't seen her with his own eyes, he'd say she was a different Ros. He didn't much like this Ros, and he wanted his old friendly Ros back again. "Yes, boss." Eddie climbed out and slammed the van door.

He slid open the side door and began prepping the camera as Ros reached by him for a clipboard. "My point is," he said, "no matter how much you're looking forward to your next Ben and Jerry's rum and raisin ice cream," she looked at him and his face turned icy, "nothing's ever as good the second time round."

Eddie took the camera and left her staring into nothing.

— Two —

It only took half an hour for the rain they had left behind in the middle of Leeds to catch up with them, turning the infinite blue of a wonderful sky into a grey and turbulent bruise that stretched right across the horizon. It was very light rain, the kind that settles on your clothing like tiny silver balls rather than soaking in. Wood pigeons and chaffinches provided the tunes, an accompaniment to the stream and the slow rustle of a million leaves caressing each other.

Ros watched Eddie work. He was unusual in his approach to crime scenes and it was nothing that could be taught; his was definitely a home-brew method. And the impressive thing about it was that he was thorough in a seemingly haphazard way. She supposed those who taught scene examination techniques would frown at him because he didn't work to a protocol. Not their protocol, anyway. He stood still a lot of the time, and he looked; appeared to be daydreaming, and she'd asked him about it when they worked together before. All he said was that he was looking. Small answer for a big definition. He wasn't just looking, he was seeing, and he was gathering the feeling of the place. It wasn't witchcraft and it wasn't spiritualism. It was just Eddie, listening and absorbing.

Just Eddie.

Until last week when she'd found the courage to go and seek him in the church where his mother was buried, she hadn't seen him for two whole years. The last time she'd seen him, he'd called around for some advice the evening before she left that house and everything behind her. After she'd been offered the job with MCU, she'd asked Jeffery to make sure Eddie didn't know she was here, and she made sure Eddie's application to work at MCU was declined.

And that was the hardest thing she'd ever done. Even harder than finding him in the church had been. Things had happened to her since those days – good ol' days, she now called them – when Eddie worked scenes with her. The worst of it was she now blamed him for those things. Each time she thought of him, the voice inside her head would begin with, If only... Not fair really. On him. It wasn't his fault. And if she thought about it deeply enough, it should be him giving her a hard time, not the other way around. But she couldn't bring herself to shed the burden. Part of her wanted him to suffer, and it was the lead part right now.

"...from the body."

Ros snapped awake, looked at Eddie. "What?"

The body was on a slight incline between a big old tree and a stream. Another ten feet or so and it would have been on a very steep incline, where it could have rolled down the embankment and ended up in the water. It was maybe 200 yards from the car, and not visible from it. The foliage was thick, the ground a mixture of compact, dusty soil, moist black earth and woodland floor covered with flora.

Eddie trudged up the banking towards her, pulling the mask down to nestle in the stubble below his chin. His eyes didn't sparkle like they used to. And she felt sad; it was her fault. Everything was her fault.

"I said there's another scene about twenty yards from the body."

"Right, we'll—"

"You think this is a gangland murder?"

She shrugged. "Haven't had a chance to formulate a conclusion yet."

"I'm not asking for conclusions."

"I'm not ready—"

"Fine! I'll go look at the disturbance. When you're ready we can formulate together." He marched away to get more stepping plates. "Won't that be fun?"

"Eddie?"

Eddie stopped; he seemed to deflate before turning around.

She looked at him, and then the words she wanted to say ran away and hid. "Nothing."

Ros made her way towards the body, being careful to negotiate the banking without falling on her arse. Eddie had placed a stepping plate a foot further downhill, away from any disturbance but within easy reach of the corpse, and it gave them something safe to stand on.

Already the flies were gathering, their constant drone an annoyance she could do without. He wore a dark blue shirt and black slacks, shiny shoes and black socks. He was no oil rig worker; his hands were clean, nails short and clear. He lay face down and a slender ribbon of blood had run from his ear to pool into the soil below his cheek. He looked like a business man trying to engage with nature; and the shiny Range Rover up there being recovered right now, fitted the stereotype perfectly. And then she saw it. Upper right back, a tiny hole in the cloth of his shirt, its edges blackened and ragged. A gunshot wound.

———

Eddie was on his hands and knees looking at the disturbance. It was long smooth grass here, pitted intermittently by patches of bare earth. No chance of decent footwear marks, but there were drag marks running across the natural nap of the grass. And there, in the centre of a four- or five-foot area of tussled grass and raked earth, was something very interesting for Eddie. A red stain.

That's when everything fell into place, and he knew what had happened.

He placed a marker by it, took several distance shots and then closed in, adding a scale before taking close-up shots of it. The sky was darkening further, and Eddie reached into his new kit box for a swab.

Even in a scene suit that fitted where it touched, she was beautiful. Petite.

Eddie sighed, and made himself think of the job as he approached the crest of the embankment and looked downhill towards her. To his right was the remnant of a dry-stone wall that separated the grazing land beyond from the dangers of running water. The wall was part demolished; scattered stones being slowly swallowed by a thick tongue of moss – except for one which lay a few yards to the side of the tree he now stood near. Its mossy side was down when it should have been up; it had dented the earth, scattered a little soil, rolled and shed some moss.

Eddie looked up at the tree. It complicated his views of what happened here somewhat, but the theory still held together nicely.

And there was that feeling again. The same one he'd had in the church that day about a week ago; the one where he could almost feel someone watching him. Back then it had been Ros, but she was busy right now. He turned but couldn't see any of the coppers looking his way. He shuddered, and returned his attention to the tree, allowing himself one glance at Ros.

Ah, the feeling was correct again. She'd stopped being busy it seemed, and she was looking at him. Of course, when he turned to face her, she looked away.

"Live by the sword, die by the sword," she whispered. Blake Crosby was a hateful man by all accounts; and the accounts MCU had on him were plentiful. Ros had read them all, as well as soaking up the briefing before coming here. He was a rapist, though never convicted. Indeed the last person who was brave enough to come forward and accuse him of rape, said it happened right here too. This must have been a favourite spot for him. Some people have no imagination, she thought. And then she remembered how that case had gone tits-up – the semen sample he'd left behind had vanished and the judge threw the case out. Incredible. Utterly unbelievable too; the victim must have been distraught when he walked away free. The briefing also said he was a gun-runner and drug supplier; he was involved in prostitution, money laundering, identity theft, and protection rackets, as was the whole Crosby family, headed by the father, Slade. They were Leeds's answer to the Mafia. He was scum.

She was glad he was dead, but worried too because dear old Slade wouldn't let the death of his son pass without making waves. He'd make a damned tsunami.

* * *

"Talking to yourself again?" Eddie edged towards her down the banking and crouched beside her.

"Gangland killing," she said.

"That's your formulated conclusion? Why?"

"He's been shot in the back. Wallet's still in his back pocket so it isn't robbery, car's still there too."

Eddie reached across the body and patted the top of its head. His fingers sank into the skull and he could feel edges of bone beneath fingertips that came away red with blood. "Okay," he said, "this is what I've got. Contact-smeared blood over there by marker four; drag marks through the grass leading to it. He's got massive depressed fractures to the top of his skull and there's a rock up there that's out of place. Still gangland?"

"He's been shot in the back."

"Post mortem. No blood."

"So what do you think happened?"

He stared at her, less than a foot away. "I've been thinking about this a lot; I'll tell you what happened. I think you got me this job because of some residue of loyalty or friendship from two years ago. And I think you're pissed off with me because I somehow didn't work out where you were working and come running."

"I'm pissed off at you because you wind Jeffery up; I acted as guarantor for you, and you've gone out of your way to protect your reputation as an arsehole."

"Since when did you care about Jeffery being pissed off?"

"It's a good office; it has a good atmosphere. I don't want that destroying."

"You're lying."

"I beg your pardon!"

"You were annoyed with me or even angry with me when you tracked me down to the church. And you still were when you were in my lounge asking me to take the job. It has nothing to do with Jeffery. And it certainly has nothing to do with the sodding office – you know I'm not a people person."

"Let's bag him up, get the hell out of here," Ros stood and Eddie grabbed her wrist. She winced.

He let go. "Sorry," he stared at her, confused, "I don't know my own strength."

"I sprained it yesterday on the stupid van door."

"Well, I am sorry. I mean—"

"I said it's okay."

Eddie stood, pulled his mask down again. "You alright, Ros? I mean is something bothering you?"

"Tell me about your theory, if it's not a gangland killing."

Chapter Twenty-one

The Theory

— One —

EDDIE BREATHED IN DEEPLY, and then sighed it all the way out. He knew she was suffering; he knew something was bothering her and it had nothing to do with his spoiling the office atmosphere or upsetting dear old Jeffery. "Okay," he said, "follow me."

They scrambled up the banking again and Eddie came to a halt beside the large oak tree. "So far as I can tell, it all starts here." He bent down, pointed across the crown of the embankment towards marker four. "See the marks through the grass. There are two distinct marks as though one person has been dragged; and the grass was pulled that way, away from us, so that's how this person arrived at marker four. At marker four there is a site of disturbance the size of a person lying down." He looked at Ros; she was squinting towards the marker. "In the centre of the disturbance is a small patch of contact-smeared blood."

"It's started to rain, have you swabbed it?"

Eddie sighed again. "The next thing I noticed is this rock. It's been disturbed, it's rolled, which is pretty unusual for a square rock, I think. I wouldn't mind betting there is a hair or two caught in it."

"Okay."

"Look up. What do you see?"

Ros craned her neck and followed the trunk up to the first bough, then the second. "Ah," she said, "more blood."

Eddie nodded. "It explains the fractured skull and the dislodged rock. And I bet you a pound to a pinch of shit, the blood at marker four is the same as the blood up the tree."

"Okay, but it doesn't explain the hole in his back."

"One car. No discernible tyre tracks. Whoever was here came with him," Eddie nodded at the corpse. "They arrived in the same car. And he's dressed to impress."

"There may have been more than one passenger. He might have been killed by two people."

"It was only a theory, Ros. Best I can come up with."

"You saying the killer is a woman?"

"Not exactly, but most likely. I don't know his sexual orientation. But I am saying the killer was frightened."

Ros looked away.

"She shot him with his own damned gun after she remodelled his skull. Trajectory rods'll confirm that."

"He raped her, didn't he?"

Eddie nodded. "I think so. Unless she killed him because she was extremely disappointed by his performance."

"Not funny, Eddie."

"No, that was a bit callous. Sorry."

Ros turned to him, and she seemed to be studying his eyes. "What?" he asked.

"Nothing. Don't think I ever heard you say sorry and mean it before."

He had. He was utterly sure of it. In fact, he had apologised less than ten minutes ago when he grabbed her injured wrist. And no doubt he'd said it a thousand times before. Women seemed to have a peculiar knack of forgetting when it was to their advantage. He stared back, trying to see into her eyes also, trying to see what all this hostility was about. He couldn't get in, couldn't see clearly; it was as though the doors were open but the fly screens were firmly in place.

"Did I run over some kid's puppy on my way into work?"

"Okay, so what's next with him?"

"Are you changing the subject?"

"What's next?"

"Ah, right. Although it was very subtle, that was definitely a change of subject."

She stared at him.

"What's next. Right. Fibre tape the branch, swab the blood. Take the rock; see if we can find hair or skin on it matching our victim. Bag his hands and head, tape exposed flesh and then bag him up and bugger off in time for tea and biscuits."

"I'll start on the body. You can climb the tree."

Eddie saw some movement over Ros's shoulder. It was Jeffery, his bobbing bald head coming into view up by the summit. He saw them and waved.

"You go," said Eddie, "I'm not good friends with him right now."

"You shock me."

"It's true."

"Don't you want to explain your theory?"

Eddie turned away, "I'd rather work scenes. You tell him; say it was your idea if you want."

"Well? Is it him?" Jeffery looked tense, almost bordering on flustered. The walk from the outer cordon hadn't helped him, by the look of his red cheeks.

"Think so, yeah." Ros nodded.

"He got any ID on him?"

"Wallet in his back pocket, though we've not looked yet."

"Okay, Westmoreland is eager to have his identity confirmed. Pull the wallet, bag the driving licence etc into clear bags, then bag the wallet up, hand them all to DI Taylor. He's your exhibits man on this. Then I want you to tape his hands, swab them if you see fit, and then take his elims—"

"What?"

"I know. Westmoreland is very eager."

"We've never had to do elims—"

"Please," Jeffery said, "for me. Then Taylor will take them to the fingerprint bureau: they're expecting them."

"And the body?"

Jeffery shrugged, "Finish soon as you can and get the body removers in. I have James and Duffy on standby for the PM while you two finish up here." His eyes drifted past Ros to the tree. "How's he getting on?"

She nodded, "Okay."

"No problems with him?"

"He's fine, Jeffery, really."

Jeffery took a long breath in, nodded, "Okay, we'll see though; I just hope Westmoreland knows what she's doing."

"I have a theory. About Crosby."

"Go on."

"He was raping someone. That's why he was here. And when he finished, he went back to the car for his gun. While he was away, the victim took a rock, climbed a tree."

Jeffery smiled, "All seems very far-fetched, Ros."

"When Crosby returns, she throws the rock, it smashes his skull, and then she takes his gun and shoots him."

"Did you get that off Midsomer Murders?"

"It's how the evidence is pointing."

"Okay, well, I look forward to your report." He turned, ready to walk away, "Hurry up with the elims and the ID, will you?"

"Righto," Ros began walking away.

"Oh, Ros?"

She turned, walked back. "Yeah?"

"The theory sounds good, well done." Jeffery smiled at her.

She knew he'd been running the management stuff through his head again, making sure he motivated his staff and proffered praise aplenty. She almost laughed. "Thank you. But it's Eddie's theory."

Jeffery stopped smiling. "Really. Well ask him how he's so sure the rape victim knew Crosby would walk right up to the tree she was hiding in." He nodded at her, almost smiled and then walked away.

Ros re-joined Eddie. "Just a thought," she said, as she approached. "How could she be sure Crosby would walk right up to this tree?"

"How's Morse?"

"Huh? Oh, Jeffery's happy with your theory."

"I bet he was, till he found out it was mine and not yours." He looked up at her, "I'm guessing that's about the time he asked you that question."

"Okay, smart-arse, how could she be sure he'd approach this tree?"

"She was wearing a white cotton skirt or dress; one of those floaty summer things."

Ros shook her head, confused. "I'm lost."

"She wedged it against the tree using that stick. The wind blows from the top of the hill downwards, and it wafted the skirt out so he'd see it from over there by marker four, which is where he'd left her when he went to get the gun. You can just imagine the bastard creeping up here with a smile on his face and his gun at the ready."

Ros squinted at him. "Really thought this through, haven't you?"

"Not really. It's there, plain as day; white fibres caught in the bark, more on the end of the stick."

"I'll make a start on him."

— Two —

Ros put on fresh gloves and knelt by the cool body of Blake Crosby. Certainly from behind, he looked like Blake Crosby, same build, short black hair, and half sovereign rings on his left hand.

She reached into his trouser pocket and came out with a black leather wallet.

"It's still illegal to rob the dead," Eddie shouted from by the tree.

She ignored him, opened the wallet and took out the driving licence. "Blake Crosby." The name was repeated on three credit cards. There was over £200 cash inside, and most intriguingly, there was a folded slip of paper, well worn, the edges feathered, the sloping handwriting faded, almost worn away. It had three words written on it: Black by Rose.

Ros photographed it, slipped it carefully into an exhibit bag and sealed it. She dropped it into a large brown sack and repeated the process with the wallet and its other contents.

She found his mobile phone in his other pocket. It had seven missed calls from Dad and Ty. She bagged it too; it would no doubt provide good intelligence.

Crosby was face down in the dirt. And Ros needed him face up so that she could do the tapings from his hands easily, but turning him over would allow body fluids to seep out and ruin any evidence in the gunshot wound in his back. She wanted his shirt as an exhibit, but she couldn't begin to undress him for fear of losing trace evidence, so her only option was to cut out a six-inch square of cloth around the hole. She began by photographing the hole with a scale alongside, and then took a pair of sterile scissors and removed a piece of shirt roughly the size of a hand.

She looked up the bank and saw, unsurprisingly, Eddie sitting up in the tree, camera dangling from its strap around his neck. He was looking at her, legs swinging to and fro as though he'd just finished a picnic. His face was blank though, the mask pulled down to his neck again, and she could see he was miles away.

She smiled at him, but there was no response.

Ros went back to her own work.

Now she had the wound facing her. A neat hole no wider than the nail of her little finger, ringed with a thin smear of black, like a kid had traced it with a soft charcoal pencil. Gunshot residue. And it was quite intense, which meant the weapon was close when fired. After close-up photography of the wound, Ros put on fresh gloves, took out the swabs from a GSR kit and removed the black residue.

Once the GSR swabs were sealed inside a bag, Ros turned the body over and photographed it. She noted how the shirt wasn't tucked in at the front as it had been at the back; and the zip on his trousers was undone, as was the leather belt – it added strength to Eddie's theory. And his shoes were still neatly polished except for a little contact dirt in the stitching, so she knew if anyone had been dragged towards marker four, it hadn't been Blake.

The flies were growing in number and in curiosity; their bravery was also increasing, and with it, Ros's temper grew correspondingly shorter. Even the soft perpetual music of the stream nearby couldn't calm her down. The worst was the flies seemed attracted to her own sweat, and after being wafted away from the corpse, would try and alight on her forehead or neck.

In Ros's experience, the hands of a corpse were often frozen into fists, which made it the devil's own job to powder ridge detail, but Blake Crosby had hit the ground palms out and that's where he'd stayed through the developing process of rigor. He lay now face up, pale creases among the lividity in his face, dirt stuck to his cheek, insects scurrying away from the light. Hands face up, fingers straight out; he looked like a man in a glass coffin, trying to keep the lid from crushing him. Ros almost, but not quite, smiled at the thought.

She couldn't know for sure whether Blake Crosby was right- or left-handed. And since she thought it might be wise to know if he'd handled a firearm recently, it would be a good idea to swab for gunshot residues in the web of his thumbs and along the edge of the index fingers before swabbing the rest of each hand for contact DNA.

She remembered Jeffery asking for tapings of his hands too, but after all the swabbing, and after being crushed by his own body weight for several hours she thought it unlikely to produce much in the way of results. But still, she had to show willing.

Once all the swabbing was complete, Ros changed gloves again, got herself as comfortable as she could and prepared the tapings kit. And that's when her phone rang.

— Three —

Eddie had photographed the rock, taken the embedded hairs from it, and even seized it. He didn't yet know how thorough MCU were, and so he thought he'd better err on the side of caution. And then he set to gathering the white fibres from the trunk of the oak after recording their height from the ground, and photographing them, and gathered the white fibres too from the twig nearby. The twig was smooth, its young bark was shiny, and half way along its three-foot length were bits of ridge detail in blood, very very faint, but still, it was every scene examiner's dream to find them.

Eddie would have been whooping on any other day, but today he simply photographed them, swabbed the blood, swabbed again around the blood for contact DNA, and then just bagged the twig while barely thinking about it.

And now he found himself half way up the tree, having extensively photographed the trunk and boughs, scaled and swabbed the contact red stain, and dabbed tape over it in the hope of collecting more, if different, fibres. That's when he stopped.

Below him, by about twelve feet, and away from him by about twenty, Ros was kneeling over some dead guy, swabbing the palms of his hands.

Floating above her head was a glowing red question mark. He could see it like he could see the oak leaves flicking back and forth in the breeze like tiny flags. Eddie let his legs sway back and forth as he watched her, engrossed with her even though she was wrapped up in a white scene suit. They were traditionally unflattering, but Ros would look good wearing a landfill site.

The question mark flashed on and off in time with Eddie's heart. It was there, he knew, because that was how he felt about her right now. Why the hell would she go to the trouble of inviting him to work with her at MCU, why go to the trouble, and obvious heartache, of breaking her two-year vow of silence towards him – and then go out of her way to make him feel like shit? She couldn't be colder towards him if she had Frigidaire stamped on her forehead.

The worst part was not knowing what he'd done wrong; how had he upset her? The second worst part was her refusal to tell him. Christ, women were hard work, really hard work.

And that prompted another, more disconcerting thought to flutter in Eddie's mind. This one had brought an anchor that wouldn't have looked out of place on the QE2; it wasn't going anywhere for a very long time. The thought was this:

he would give MCU one week and if things hadn't improved, he would leave. Simple as that.

It had taken two things to get him to quit divisional CSI: a slow and gradual build-up of distaste encouraged by a shit system and propagated by really shit management, and a final injustice done to the very job they were here to do.

And although he was skint, Eddie had enjoyed his week or two away from such an intensely complicated and stressful world where people didn't always want you to succeed – where people would rather you let a murderer go if it proved them right about you being a wanker. And then they'd talked him back round and he'd let them. He shook his head, eyes still on Ros.

Why had they done that? More to the point, why had he accepted? Getting to the point of finally closing the office door for the last time, especially with no other income about to magically spring up, took some real balls. And now look... back here again. Only now it was worse, because in Ros he had found apathy where once there had been a good friend.

Yes, a week. And then, if things were still the same, he would walk again.

The gentle swaying of the branches, the soft music of the leaves and the gentle hum of the stream were pierced by a shrill sound. Eddie watched Ros as she fumbled the gloves off and retrieved her phone from her pocket. She looked at the caller display then bit her lower lip.

She looked up at Eddie, and he wasn't surprised to see her turn away from him.

Unashamedly listening intently in her direction, he heard a few words, despite the noises from the trees and her hushed voice. She began with a hearty 'Hi!' but trailed off into monotone mumbling shortly afterwards. Before long, she had slipped the phone back in her pocket and pulled the mask way up high over her face before turning around again.

Eddie sighed hard. Now it was beginning to make sense. Some of it.

A boyfriend, obviously. And that had generated a conflict within her; a current boyfriend versus memories of her old... her old what? Her old relationship with Eddie.

And how did that make him feel?

He could sum it up in a couple of words: jealous. And resigned.

"Eddie!"

Eddie turned on the bough and looked towards the police vehicles as some short, skinny man with a grin too wide for his face lumbered towards him, waving. "Who the fuck..."

"Come for the exhibits."

"Great," Eddie said. "Ros?"

"I'm here." Carrying a bulging brown bag packed full of exhibits, she walked straight past the tree, underneath Eddie's dangling feet and met the man at the inner cordon. Eddie watched her fill out some paperwork, listened as they engaged in brief banter, and within moments she was back, looking up at him this time. "Come on. Let's bag him, and then we can get the hell out of here."

"Aw," he said, "I was enjoying the peace and quiet. Still, I expect there'll be plenty more on the journey back."

Chapter Twenty-two

The McDonald's Confession

— One —

THERE WAS DUST ON the screen, only a fine layer, but the rain had turned it to mud, and the mud had left streaks down the glass, and for some reason not known to him, it looked very sad. How could a dirty windscreen look sad? he wondered. He didn't know; it just did. Maybe it reminded him of women crying, the way mascara runs down their faces.

"Can we go now, please?"

Eddie started the engine, cleared the screen and set off from their first forensic scene examination together in over two years. He had wonderful memories of those times, and he wished they could've been replicated or reincarnated somehow, because working with Ros the ice-maiden these days was painful, like combing your hair with barbed wire. Not at all pleasant.

He wasn't so sure now whether his decision to give it a week at MCU was the right one under the circumstances. The circumstances being Ros and how she was hurting him by being so distant that he had to use binoculars to see her.

He'd already tried talking to her, asking her why she was different. And he'd already worked out that she had a boyfriend. That was a hard blow, and even now, as they drove through Garforth with only the sound of tyres on wet tarmac for company, he lived in hope that her relationship wouldn't last long. You could do that with relationships like that, you were entitled. You couldn't do that with marriage though. With marriage you had to respect the couple and their vows, as Ros had done with Eddie and Kelly a thousand years ago. She had done it with grace, too, far more grace than he could summon.

But she hadn't yet told him why she was different towards him; he was still good ol' Eddie, nothing new there. In fact, he was better than the old Eddie – he was single again. What was the problem?

And that's why he revised his earlier decision.

"When we get back to the office, I'm leaving."

"You have to do your paperwork, then you can go home."

"When we get back to the office, I'm resigning, then I'm leaving."

"You've only just started!"

"And I wish I hadn't." He didn't look at her, he just kept driving.

"Why?"

"Because you dyed your hair."

"What?"

"Because Ben and Jerry's rum and raisin ice cream is like combing your hair with barbed wire."

She was looking at him, and he sneaked a quick glance. She was smiling. Ros was smiling! He liked that, and though it faltered to begin with, he smiled back until she said, "I have no idea what the hell you're talking about."

"I meant that Ben and Jerry's rum and raisin ice cream is shit the second time around." The sneaky look this time told him she wasn't smiling any more. This time, she understood what he meant. This time, she looked sad.

"You already said that, Eddie. Are you running out of metaphors?"

"I'm running out of patience."

They drove on in silence again until they reached Elland Road, and a McDonald's. "Pull in here," Ros said.

"Why?"

"Just do it. I want a coffee."

"And here's me thinking you wanted a fucking Happy Meal!"

Eddie pulled the van into the car park and killed the motor. She looked at him and climbed out. Eddie got out too, locked the door and lit a cigarette. He leaned against the van and watched her walking away into the restaurant. And that's when he felt like killing himself all over again.

He breathed deeply and flicked the cigarette away.

———

She had chosen a booth away from any windows, tucked away in the corner where passing foot traffic was infrequent, and he was glad because he sensed it was all about to come out and he didn't want kids and fat bastards gawping as they walked by. It was still noisy in here though; kids shouting when they should have been colouring or eating, the slow mouldering voices of a deep queue at the tills, and some unidentifiable tinny music falling like miniature party-poppers from the overhead speakers to air-burst into your private thoughts or derail your quiet conversation; as obtrusive as the crisp packet rustlers in a visual scene at the flicks.

He stared at her, waiting for her to begin.

"I don't want you to leave."

"I have to. I can't work alongside you anymore."

"I'm not that bad—"

"Ros, be honest just for once. I thought of you as an ice-maiden earlier; I never thought I'd label you like that, not my Ros."

"I'm not your Ros."

"There you go again!"

"I'm married, Eddie." Her teeth were bared.

Silence. He stared at her but he didn't see anything. He had quite suddenly developed acute tunnel vision but the vision part was wrong, there was nothing there; he saw right through her but there was nothing on the other side. He saw nothing, he heard nothing.

"...sorry, Eddie."

"What?"

"I said I'm sorry."

He smiled, an autopilot response. "You don't have to apologise for being married; I hope you'll be very happy." He checked his watch. "We should go."

"His name is Brian."

"Great."

"He's a landscape gardener."

"Have you got a card? Got some nettles need clearing."

"Please," she whispered, "I need to tell you this."

"You don't have to, it's fine, I understand."

"No you don't. I was thirty-six, and..."

"Really, you don't have to explain."

"Shut up, Eddie." She sipped her coffee. "I was thirty-six. No spring chicken," she tried to smile. "More an ugly duckling, really. And I was single. Alone. I was growing into an old spinster."

"I was—"

"And then Brian came along. We got along well. I liked him; he was solid and reliable."

Eddie swallowed, looked away. "I'm pleased for you, Ros." He smiled at her. "Really, I am. You've done well." There were tears pooling in her lower eyelids and Eddie looked away again to save her embarrassment as she dabbed them away.

"I was being very selfish," she continued, "when I came to offer you this job. I'm sorry about that."

"Selfish?"

"Well, you know we had a kind of special relationship back when... y'know, when you were with Kelly. Didn't we, we were—"

"Really good friends," he said, "yes, we were."

"We were really good friends then, and I'd hoped we could be really good friends again. You know, just like before."

"Only instead of you being able to look but not touch, now it's my turn?"

"It sounds crude when you say it like that."

"But true."

"Yes. I thought about it, Eddie. Jeffery told me where you were; he told me Westmoreland wanted you to come to MCU, but the final decision was mine, because I was the only one who could persuade you to come. So I thought about it and wondered if it was fair to you. I knew it would be hard on me, at least to begin with, but it would be unfair to you. I suppose I just wanted you to be near."

"Perhaps you could have levelled with me."

"Told you I was married?"

He nodded.

"Would it have made a difference?"

He thought about it. Would it have made a difference? Well of course it fucking would. Ros was number one on his hit parade, and now after this little revelation, she wasn't even in the charts, and so he would have remained a happy bum instead of being back breathing aluminium powder and staring at a woman he could never be close to. And that was the saddest news he'd had in two years. But it had affected her more. "It would have made a difference to you, Ros. If you'd come clean to begin with, you wouldn't have needed to treat me like a disease all day."

And then she sobbed.

Eddie reached out and was about to stroke her hair, but he pulled back quickly. She was married. He had to make himself remember that. And despite suspecting she was unhappy with Brian, he had to respect her status.

"Is this the personal bit you wouldn't tell me about?"

She nodded. "Some of it."

"There's more?"

Her voice broke as she said, "I invited you to work at MCU because I wanted to punish you."

Eddie sat back and folded his arms. His cheeks throbbed as he ground his teeth, and he took short shallow breaths. "Why punish me? What have I done?"

Eventually she looked up, napkin held over her nose, eyes beginning to redden. "Because all the years I've known and worked with you, you've been out of my reach. You've been with Kelly.

"And when I considered coming here, I was thinking of you, and I was thinking of her, and I was thinking that everything you touch turns to shit and I should stay away from you—"

"A lot happened since—"

"I know! And I thought we'd turned a corner, Eddie, once she began having an affair."

"We had!"

"You had! I was turning into a fucking spinster! In fact you hadn't changed at all – you came to see me and I couldn't believe how well you were coping still being her doormat."

Just then a McDonald's general, with four golden stars pinned to a name plate on his left breast hovered at their table. "Sir, madam, I'll have to ask you to leave if you continue—"

"Okay, okay," Eddie said, "I'm sorry."

"There are children—"

"I said okay! Thank you, okay."

The general wandered off and Eddie looked at Ros.

"They told me you didn't want to see me, Ros. Why would you make them say that? It's beyond cruel."

Tears ran unobstructed down her red cheeks as she looked up at him. "I didn't know then that Kelly was leaving for good; you two had always been fiery; off-on, on-off. And I thought we'd simply go on being friends, and I didn't want that any more, Eddie. I couldn't face watching you turn yourself inside out every day because you tried to be the man she wanted, but just couldn't convince yourself it was a good idea. I couldn't bear that. I would rather be alone, and so I decided to walk away without looking back. And when Taylor told me they were forming MCU... I joined up."

"That explains why they knocked me back for the same job." Eddie sighed. He wanted a cigarette. He also wanted to fuck off and leave her here. "Well, your punishment was thorough, I'll give you that."

"I'm sorry."

But most of all, he wanted to reach across the table and stroke her hair; he wanted to hold her, and he wanted to reassure her. He wanted Ros. "Don't be," he whispered, "it's okay."

"It was lousy timing. I couldn't have you, we couldn't be together, and then when I found out that we could be together, it was already too late." She blinked, as if surprised by how things turned out. "There was Brian."

That was the real punishment, he thought. "But you eventually must have found out that Kelly was no longer on the scene. And you knew where I worked. What, eight miles away from MCU? Why didn't you—"

"I was a mess. My world was upside down. I had a new job, I had lied to my best friend, I wasn't around for you when she left... and by then it was too late. And Brian was there."

"Good old Brian. Waterproof shoulders?"

She half-laughed, "Yes, he had waterproof shoulders."

"But you're unhappy with him."

"Why would you say that?"

Eddie drank his coffee, watched her over the rim. "Because most people say they love their man, you said you like him, present tense; good old solid and reliable Brian."

"That's not fair."

He shrugged, "You're right; I'm sorry. It's not fair. None of my business."

"Am I forgiven?"

He smiled, "Nothing to forgive, Ros. You've done nothing wrong."

"Are you still leaving?"

"I wish you'd told me. I mean I wish you'd got in touch. I was mortified when you left. I grieved, Ros. And I wanted to find you. I wanted to say goodbye to you, just once. It would have been gracious of you—"

"I know it would. I'm sorry about that too."

Eddie finished his coffee. "We should go."

"Are you staying?"

Her eyes were full of hope, an eagerness that he secretly enjoyed. It would take him some time to come to terms with why she invited him to join her; but he thought he would eventually. And considering what he'd inadvertently put her through, he supposed her "punishment" was warranted, and it was quite mild. "On one condition."

She smiled, "Go on."

"You show me where the fucking coffee machine is."

— Two —

Eddie took a right and walked straight into Benson. Benson dropped the Mars bar he'd just unwrapped, and both looked at it, saw little crumbs of chocolate scatter into the dirty carpet.

"Twat," Benson said.

Eddie squinted at him, then stood on the Mars bar and twisted his foot. "Now I'm a twat," he said, and walked away.

"Stop."

Eddie stopped, and he wondered if now would be the right time to run. "What?" He thought he'd done a reasonable job at masking the utter disbelief at bumping into him. He'd shown no surprise because he didn't want to see Benson grinning. In fact, he didn't want to see Benson at all.

"What are you doing here?"

"At the moment," he said, "I appear to be talking to an arsehole."

"I expected you to be dead by now."

Eddie turned and walked back, stood just in front of Benson – a little farther away than he normally would have on account of Benson's larger gut. Other people were on the corridor, and they avoided the two, giving them a wide berth as though sensing these two were polar opposites, as though they feared fists flying any time soon.

He continued, "Good to see they fixed the broken leg. Amazing how strong modern metals are." Eddie laughed. "Anyway, shouldn't you be out there arresting the wrong man?" It was a throwaway line; always good for annoying coppers with, but for Benson, who had chatted amiably with a man who later turned out o be a serial killer, it resonated like a church bell, and there was a slight twitch in his eye that made Eddie feel warm all over.

"Since MCU have lowered their standards to accommodate those who can't take orders," he smiled, "that means you, Collins, I think we should come to some arrangement."

"Oooh, that burned." Eddie said, "You ignore me and I'll pretend you never existed?"

"Something like that, yeah."

"Should be easy enough," Eddie turned and walked away, "apart from the fucking smell."

"Oi!"

Eddie stopped again. "Now what? I'm busy; I've got evidence to ignore! Oh no, wait, that was you too, wasn't it?"

"A quid."

"You having a sponsored silence? I'll give you a fiver, mate."

"For the Mars bar. A quid." He held out a hand.

"You're serious, aren't you?"

Benson stared, hand still held out.

"Eddie?"

Eddie turned and saw Ros at the office door. Despite their earlier chat, she didn't look very happy, but Eddie was getting used to it by now.

"Just give him a quid, and let's get on."

Eddie fumbled in his pocket and could see Benson almost pissing himself with glee. "Fifty pence do?"

"Eddie!"

"Alright, alright." He flicked a quid coin at Benson and walked after Ros.

Chapter Twenty-three

The Briefing

— One —

"EDDIE?"

It was Jeffery. Eddie sighed and walked across the office, shoulders slumped, feet dragging. "Yes, boss."

"Where've you been?"

"I've been to lots of places; want to narrow it down a bit?"

Jeffery took a breath and folded his arms. It was his customary stance whenever he felt prickled by annoyance. "From the scene."

"I took Ros to McDonald's."

"How chivalrous."

"I was desperate to show her their new McFlurry. They do a Toffee Crisp one now!"

"Well at least you're honest."

"You knew about the Toffee Crisp one?"

"I mean about going to McDonald's. We have trackers in each van, just in case you weren't aware."

"And you've been glued to some screen watching the fucking van all day? You should get a hobby. I heard Sudoku is good. Always been a Spider Solitaire kind o' guy myself."

"Eddie... I understand that things must have been difficult between you two. It's fine."

Eddie blinked. "Really?"

Jeffery nodded.

"Thanks, Jeffery. We had personal things to sort out."

To his credit, Jeffery smiled. "Okay, really, it's fine."

Eddie walked away, feeling cautious. He kept looking back to make sure this wasn't some wicked joke, that Jeffery wasn't running after him. This was like going to sleep in a children's playground and waking up with the adults. It was quite a shock, and it skewed Eddie's perception of Jeffery somewhat. And that was a good thing, except it made him a little nervous; he'd have to redraw the battle lines, maybe even cut him some slack.

Eddie sat next to Ros. "So where's all the fancy gear then?"

"Gear?"

"Yeah, the touch screens and the subdued neon lighting."

"What?"

"I thought working at MCU would be like stepping into CSI Miami."

"Think again."

Eddie looked despondent. "This is just another bog-standard divisional CSI office isn't it? Pre-war computers with a permanent egg timer. Second-hand desks, and chairs with dodgy castors."

Ros sighed, put down her pen.

"I mean, look; you're even using a pen. I thought it'd be—"

"Well it's not. Get used to it."

"It's like I never left," he whispered, and slid across to his own desk. "How do I log on?"

"Eddie; this is still part of West Yorkshire Police. Nothing is different when you get back to the office."

"We still have the same non-functioning computer programs?"

She nodded. "I have work to do, and I want to be home before midnight."

"Still have the same old guy in IT called Geoff, who smokes a pipe and wears tank tops, and thinks Space Invaders is at the cutting edge?"

"Eddie!"

"Sorry." He hit the computer's power button. "It's like déjà vu. What with you and Jeffery, and now that knob-head Benson?"

Ros put her head in her hands.

Eddie looked around and Jeffery was standing there with his hands on hips – another favourite pose, like Man at C&A was still in existence. He nodded to Ros. "You know Ros," he said, "she can sleep anywhere."

Ros looked up, "Jeffery."

"You okay?"

"Yeah, yeah, I was just—"

"Have you uploaded the photos yet? I'm keen to show them to Westmoreland and Benson."

"Why Benson?" Eddie asked.

"He's doing the death warning later this evening."

"I'd like to be a fly on that wall," Ros said. "Just on with them now."

"I can imagine it won't be pleasant."

"Have you told Jeffery about the note in his wallet?"

"There was a folded scrap of paper that said 'Black of Rose' or... No, 'Black by Rose'."

"What's it mean?"

Eddie and Ros both shrugged.

"Okay, Eddie get your photos done, too, Ros will show you our dedicated Dropbox feature, and then we have a briefing in half an hour, okay?"

Eddie's face screwed up. "A briefing? Do I have to?"

"And tomorrow I want you back at Tony Lambert's scene."

"What? That scene's a week old now. And anyway, I'm sure James—"

"He did a thorough job."

"Then why do you want me to go back? To clean the powder off?"

Jeffery pulled a chair across and sat between Ros and Eddie. "Keep this to yourself, but DCI Cooper is desperate for something else, something that James may have missed."

"Like what?"

"A name."

"Basil Fawlty," Eddie said. And then, "I told him to swab the dead guy's wrists for low copy. No joy?"

"No joy."

"What about the woman's throat? Was that swabbed?"

Jeffery stared at him for a moment, and then his eyes drifted away.

"I promise it wasn't a trick question."

"I'd have to check Kirsty's notes; she accompanied James."

"Meant to ask," Eddie said, "what happened to Kirsty?"

"If you sent her," Ros said, "then it probably didn't get done."

There was a tightness to her voice, so much so that Eddie turned and looked at her. She appeared fine, but something was awry.

"If she didn't, then it's too late now," Jeffery said.

"Why wouldn't she—"

"And no one is saying James did a bad job, quite the contrary, he's very capable, but we need someone of experience to have a thorough look. Cooper's desperate to find the murderer."

Eddie said, "If James is so capable, why not send him back?"

"Don't be a tool, Eddie," Ros said. "You know you'd never spot something second time around – especially if you're going to be looking as hard as James would do."

"And it'll do his confidence no good either," Jeffery whispered.

"Okay. But who's to say there's anything more to find?"

"Won't know unless we try."

"But if you're worried that James may have been too inexperienced to look close enough, why the hell didn't you replace him on the day, or least get him some help?"

"We did get him help." Jeffery stood and pushed the chair back. "Ros, you can go with him, keep an eye on him."

"She's a bad influence, Jeffery."

"Oi," Ros kicked his chair.

"Briefing. Thirty minutes." Jeffery was about to leave, when he paused, bent low towards Eddie and said, "Protect the lad's pride; don't mention your re-attendance to him."

— Two —

DCI Lisa Westmoreland headed the briefing which, Eddie noted, took place in a room similar to those used for briefings in the TV show 24; all glass and chrome, polished wooden table and a posh phone in the centre. "Blake Crosby's PM results show massive cranial damage consistent with being hit with a rock, or by one being dropped from a tree." She lowered her spectacles and peered at Eddie. "That right, Eddie?"

Eyes turned to face him, and he could feel himself going red, despite there being only ten people in the briefing. Eddie didn't like being the centre of attention. He nodded. "That's right." Keep it short, he told himself. And don't smile; she's less likely to ask you anything else.

"Did you find anything on that rock?"

Shit! "Hair, belonging, we think, to Blake. Bit of blood too, probably his."

"Super. What else did you find?"

"It's all in the report," he mumbled.

"For the benefit of the briefing."

"Erm, contact blood. On the tree. Some more in the grass."

Benson shook his head at Eddie. Eddie swallowed.

Jeffery cleared his throat. "May I, Lisa?"

Thank fuck for that. Jeffery, I'll never spit in your coffee again.

Jeffery went on to give the account that Eddie had come up with, and to Eddie's surprise, he did it very well; concise and with a little flair. His account went well, and there was a lot of nodding.

He sat near the back in the briefing. Benson was right next to Lisa Westmoreland, looking around the room as though he owned it, which, in Westmoreland's absence, he probably did. He was The Big Cheese now, and he knew it, having being promoted to DI because of the valiant way he broke a leg, and it had nothing to do with a serial killer he didn't arrest.

Eddie would keep that little nugget for future use.

Benson kept looking at Eddie, and Eddie returned the stare, not blinking, not looking away. Whatever power Benson had in this place, Eddie was prepared to match it, despite feeling intimidated by his bulk, and eyes as cold as a dead man's.

Jeffery was sitting to one side, his shirt sleeves rolled up over skinny arms, and he continued to speak well, covering the gunshot wound that Blake Crosby had acquired, before moving along to the white fibres Eddie had found.

And then there was Ros, sitting a few chairs forward of Eddie. When he wasn't in a staring match with Benson, that's where his eyes settled. There was still something bothering her. Yes, he knew a lot could happen to a person in two years, and he'd accounted for that; but there was something causing her to be on the defensive all the time. Maybe she was afraid of something. Eddie didn't like the thought of her being afraid.

"And then he was shot in the back. Standard 9 mm round recovered, so we have no idea, other than it was a handgun, what weapon she used. The firearm wasn't recovered, by the way, so be careful if you do come across our suspect." Lisa Westmoreland moved along to the rest of the PM results, including the internal and external penile swabs which indicated recent sexual intercourse. The swabs were winging their way to the lab, as she poetically put it. "Results due in a day or so."

She nodded to Benson beside her. "Tom will be giving the death warning to the family... have they rung in yet, Tom?"

"Not as far as I'm aware. The Crosbys tend not to keep their members on a tight rein though; and anyway, the last thing they want is plod floating around asking them awkward questions."

There was a light titter in the room and when Benson looked at Eddie, Eddie winked. Benson's smile hit the carpet, and Eddie almost laughed.

"And we'll be locking Blake's house down pending a POLSA search, but I want his computer soon as possible, Tom."

Benson only nodded.

"Okay," Westmoreland continued, "Team One, get onto all county hospitals and check for recent female admittances with vaginal or anal injuries, also liaise with Topaz and see if they have anything outstanding they can share with us." She turned to Jeffery, "Anything from the car?"

"Yes, we have fingerprints galore, tapings and we've taken GSR swabs from the glove box, beneath the seats, that sort of thing. Though most of the stuff we have are just controls for when you get our suspect."

Westmoreland nodded.

"And we've had the marks checked out; of course the Crosby clan and some of their men are all over it; but I'm assured there's a few unidentified ones located around the front passenger side."

"Right, so our suspect isn't known to us; she just got very hard to find."

Eddie breathed deeply. Nothing like stating the bleeding obvious, he thought. And this thought was closely followed by thoughts of coffee and a cigarette. He sighed, folded his arms.

Westmoreland paused – more for effect, thought Eddie, than anything else.

"Get to it." And then, "Oh, one last thing. We found a scrap of paper in his wallet. Handwritten on it were the words, 'Black by Rose'. Anyone have any idea what 'Black by Rose' refers to?"

Lots of mumbling and shaking of heads ended the briefing and Eddie lunged for the door.

Chapter Twenty-four

One Man's Joy...

"I WANT TO KNOW where the fuck he is!" Slade threw another glass at the wall and Tyler stood silently in the kitchen, just shaking his head.

Monty came in through the back door and saw how tense things were. He glanced at the smashed glass, then at Tyler, and Slade barked, "Well?"

"No sign at any of the casinos, or his usual haunts. He ain't been seen since yesterday afternoon."

"And who saw him yesterday afternoon?"

"Vernon at The Gaping Goose. Blake was doing his rounds. Paid him as usual, he says."

"Was he acting strange?"

"Vernon?"

"Blake, you idiot!"

Monty shrugged. "Nah, he was okay."

"Who's out looking?" Tyler asked.

"Ev'ryone." Monty grabbed a biscuit. And then another.

"Yeah, well better start calling them back in, Monty," Slade said. "Some of them have a job in a few hours."

"Will do, chief." Monty took the biscuits into the lounge, pulling out his phone on the way.

"What do you want me to do?"

Slade looked at Tyler. "Who's he normally kicking about with these days?"

"No one. Except us, I mean."

"He got a girl?"

Tyler shook his head. "Who the fuck would have him?"

Slade limped around the room, his hand nervously scraping through his hair, eyes always down. "Fix me a drink, Ty."

"We should ring Shylock."

Slade stopped walking, looked at him.

"And Tymo."

"They wouldn't fucking dare touch one of my boys."

"But we should ask the question. And, if they had any sense, they could put their own feelers out."

Slade thought about it. "Maybe tomorrow. I want this job to go down without a hitch tonight. I don't want them knowing we're on our back foot."

Tyler nodded. "Shall I ring Rachel?"

"No need. He won't have gone near her. Poison, she is."

"Chief?"

Slade looked to the lounge. "What now?" He headed out of the kitchen, using the doorframe to steady himself. Tyler followed him.

Through the lounge window, they could see the gates swing open and the row of sunken lamps illuminate down the driveway. A car slowly drove up to the house, and Monty whispered, "I let them in, chief. It's the law."

Benson dried his eyes and lowered the window, reached out and pushed the intercom button and tried to keep a straight face. On the way over here, he had howled with laughter, and the tears had squeezed out of eyes that had seen some of the awful things Blake Crosby had done over the years, things that could never be proved. His stomach ached from that laughter. Benson was delighted that one of Leeds's biggest baddest bastards was dead. "It was just a shame," he said to Khan, "that whoever killed him didn't rip his nuts off first and stick 'em down his throat. Maybe gouge an eye out too. That would've been great."

Khan nodded more sombrely at his side.

They both marvelled at the opulence that being so high up the wrong ladder brought: electric gates, lit driveway leading to an immaculately-gravelled turning circle. Enough top-notch cars to keep Top Gear busy for a series, and a house like an embassy, all illuminated by a dozen sunken floodlights.

"We're in the wrong job, Tom," Khan said, eyes taking in the surroundings.

"Maybe, but at least the chances of your kids being shot are fairly slim."

Benson pulled up behind a silver Mercedes just outside the front door, hoping he was blocking the path of any other vehicles. "Okay," he said, looking across at Khan, "No fucking laughing."

They walked up the steps and stood beneath the columned porch waiting for the door. A light in the hall came on and the door opened. Benson looked at the fat man, "Monty," he said.

"Come in, Mr Benson."

Benson and Khan followed Monty along the hall and into the lounge. Slade Crosby and his equally evil son, Tyler both stood by the fireplace, watching them come in.

"He's dead, isn't he?" Slade asked.

Benson cleared his throat, "I'm afraid he is, Mr Crosby."

"How?" Tyler asked.

"We're still doing some work on that."

"Where?"

"Near a stream, in Garforth."

Slade closed his eyes and took a long breath in through his nose. He was going to say "Garforth, again?" but of course he couldn't; because as far as the law was concerned "Garforth, the first time" never happened.

"We'll be appointing a family liaison officer, Mr Crosby, to keep you informed—"

"Fuck that." Slade sipped from a glass. "All I want to know from you lot is who did it, and how."

"But that's—"

"I said no!" Slade handed the glass to Tyler. "Fill it." He looked across to Benson, "Want one?"

Benson shook his head, "No ta." Then Slade approached, and Benson breathed in, tensed up. Khan took a step back.

"Stick your liaison officer up your arse. Get me names."

Benson blinked. "Mr Crosby—"

Then Khan butted in, "We know you're upset, Mr Crosby, and we're doing everything we can..."

Slade stared fixedly at Benson, his eyes widening with each of Khan words until he peered around Benson's shoulder and stared at him. Khan became quiet, and Slade returned his attention to Benson. "Occupational hazard, Mr Benson." He turned away, took the drink from Tyler. "I've been waiting for this day for a dozen years; it's no shock to me."

Benson looked at the surviving son, Tyler, and was dismayed there was no discernible reaction from him.

"Just names, Mr Benson. That's all I want from you."

"I'm going across to Blake's house now."

"What for?"

"To have a look round. And I want his computer."

"Why?"

"To have a look round." Benson stared at Slade. Not many people could intimidate him, but Slade Crosby was one of them. He forced himself to remain rigid, indignant. "If you need anything from in there, you come to me; we're locking it down."

"How long?"

"Long as required. I won't ask if you know why anyone would want him dead."

Monty growled, "Out of order, Mr Benson."

"We'll apprise you of our findings in due course."

"When can we have his remains back?" Monty asked.

"Yeah, we have a funeral to arrange," Slade said.

Benson slid his hands into his pockets, eyes flitting around the room as though looking for something. "This is why a family liaison—"

Slade was in Benson's face in an instant. Khan backed away to the door, but Benson stood his ground and this seemed to inflame Slade even more. "Don't you fucking listen?" He spat into Benson's face as he shouted, but neither even noticed. "I'll crush you, Benson. You start fucking about with my family, and I'll crush you."

The two men stared at each other.

"Mr Crosby. Sit the fuck down. Now."

Slade looked from eye to eye, searching the man, greedily looking for the fear that he knew was there.

"I said sit."

Monty moved to cover Khan, not that Khan had the slightest intention of doing anything other than leaving, and Tyler moved closer to Benson's back, hands flexing into fists.

And suddenly, Slade's face relaxed, his eyes left Benson's alone, and a fake smile dismissed the snarl. He even laughed, "Okay, Mr Benson; everything's fine. I just lost my boy; you can understand that, eh?"

"We'll be in touch."

"Looking forward to it," Slade retook his seat and Benson walked to the door.

"Who works Garforth?" Slade asked. He'd watched the coppers leave, and he knew full well they'd be laughing their bollocks off. That must have been one of the highlights of Benson's shitty career to date; giving him some bad news. Well, Slade Crosby had had worse news from better coppers than him. It didn't change the fact that Blake was dead.

"I said who works Garforth?"

Monty swallowed the last of the biscuits and shrugged, "We ain't got nobody working Garforth. So small you could fucking spit over it; nothing there, man."

"So what the fuck was he doing there?" Slade fell into a chair and realised, quite suddenly, that he was getting somewhere near being drunk. Good; he liked being drunk. It took away the shit from the day and left him with his own thoughts. Being drunk was almost an impenetrable barrier for bad news.

Except that was crap too. He looked at the glass of Pernod and knew that his outburst to Benson, about it being an occupational hazard was to a degree correct. But he'd lied when he said he'd expected it for the last dozen years. "Can't show them your weaknesses." Truth was, he hadn't expected it all. Maybe Tyler – he was sharp and hard, and he got people's backs up sometimes – but Blake was a puppy dog. An arsehole, granted, but soft like a puppy dog.

And then Monty said something. Slade looked up, shocked. "Rachel?"

"Dad. Tyler."

"I thought I should ring her, chief."

"Rachel, come in, come in. Monty, get Rachel—"

"I'm not stopping, Dad."

Slade looked her up and down; from the pink hair down to the Converse trainers. He blinked, the disappointment clear in his face, and he held out a hand. For a moment, he looked like he might cry. "Please, Rachel; just for tonight. I'll have your room made up." She was shaking her head. "I need my family around me tonight!"

"Robin is in the car; I said I wouldn't be long."

"Oh," he said. "Robin. Right." And then he smiled at her, "Bring him in. Monty, bring Robin in."

"No, Dad. I'll tell you what I know about Blake and then—"

"What you know?" Tyler stood forward. "You've seen him?"

Rachel nodded. "Ten minutes. He came to see me at work. Wanted my advice."

Slade sat down, looked at her intently. "Advice about what?"

Rachel swallowed, appeared afraid of her father. "Women. He wanted to know how to treat them right."

Tyler gave a laugh, and was about to state the obvious, about to say "How does a rapist treat a woman right? He leaves her alone". But he saw his father's face, and obviously decided now was not the time, and this was not the company.

"And why would he say that?"

"He was about to meet someone, he said." She swallowed again, interlaced her fingers so tightly that her nails turned white. "From an internet dating site."

Slade covered his eyes with a hand that shook ever so slightly. "Why didn't he come and see me." It was not a question; it was a statement, a statement from a father who now believed he had failed his youngest son. "I would have helped, I could have—"

"I'm not here to get into a debate, Dad, about why this or why that."

"No, cos you couldn't give a shit!" Tyler shouted.

She looked at him. Nodded slowly, and said, "I think I'd better leave."

"No, no you don't. I want to know what else he said. Rachel, you tell me now. Please."

"That was it, more or less. He said he was ready for commitment; he didn't want to... he didn't want to go with prostitutes any more. He said she was a bookkeeper, honest and respectable. And that's why he wanted advice on how to treat a woman."

"When was he meeting her, Rachel?" Monty asked from the doorway.

"He didn't say."

"Did he say where?"

She shook her head, licked her lips, "No, sorry."

"Sorry!" Tyler shouted.

"Tyler, give it a fucking rest." Slade looked at him. He looked then at Rachel through a sheen of tears, "I'm sorry I swore, love. Look, Rachel, stay the night, bring Robin in. Maybe in the morning you'll remember more."

Rachel turned and took a few steps towards the door. Monty stood there, almost as wide as the doorframe, and an inch or two taller. Slade nodded at him, and he stepped aside, "Let me get the front door for you," he said.

"Rachel."

She stopped, turned slowly towards her father.

"No need to trouble the police with this. Okay?"

She nodded.

"Good girl. We'll be making our own enquiries."

As Monty was closing the front door, the gates opened again and an old diesel pickup truck ambled in and squealed to a stop. Monty watched as Jagger, Pikey and Ste climbed out.

Monty came down the steps to them.

"Any news?" Jagger asked.

"Blake is dead."

"What?"

"Killed in Garforth. We don't know who did it, how or why. So," he took hold of Ste, "if you don't want your faces all across the floor, man, best stay in the staff house till it's time for the job."

"Must know something," Jagger said.

Monty looked at the lad. The other two, Ste and Pikey, took off across the turning circle to the staff house, engaged in fierce whispering. "Where's Wasp?"

"He's meeting us later; wanted to get home for some reason."

Monty nodded, considering a response to the "must know something". "All we know is he was using an internet dating site."

Jagger's face screwed up, "I don't get it," he said. "He's got his pick of the girls—"

"Never mind why; that's what happened, that's where we think he ran into trouble."

"You checked his computer? It might give you her name."

"It'll be password protected. Anyway, the coppers are round his gaff now seizing it."

"Shame. Wasp is good at stuff like that; he's always on about breaking codes to get inside stolen laptops."

"Is he, now?" Monty turned; ready to go back into the house. "I'll mention it to Slade; you go get your gear ready for the job. And then shift that heap o' shit off the drive."

"You reckon it could've been Shylock?"

Slade held out his empty glass and Tyler took it. "You know something I don't? Forget the Pernod, get me a cup of tea."

"We've never seen eye to eye with him, have we? He's always trying it on, dipping his hands in our till."

"Petty theft. That's all that is; everyone does it now and then, just to re-establish boundaries. But killing my boy... that's fucking war talk is that."

"You reckon we should pay him a visit, sound him out maybe?"

Monty closed the front door, Slade heard the big man walking down the hall and into the lounge. "Chief?"

"I might go see him. Give it a day or two though." He turned to Monty, "What?"

"I called her. Hope you didn't mind."

"Called who?"

"Rachel."

"Why?"

"Cos Blake said he was gonna see her—"

"Wait, wait, wait. Rewind. He told you he was going to see Rachel?"

Monty nodded.

"When?"

"Couple o' weeks ago. Maybe ten days."

"Did he tell you why?" Tyler asked.

"Yeah, said he wanted advice; just like she told you."

"And you didn't think to pass this on to me?" Slade's voice was quiet, but beneath it bubbled pure anger. His fingertips tapped on the leather seat, but now they were scratching, gouging.

"It didn't matter until Mr Benson showed up, chief."

"Didn't matter?"

"So I thought I should ring her, Rachel, I mean, tell her to come and see you with what she knew."

"How come I'm the last person to know any-fucking-thing around here!"

"Sorry, chief," Monty's head hung low. And then he said, "Jagger just came up with something good."

Slade stared.

"Does Blake only have one computer?"

"How the fuck should I know? No one tells me anything, remember?"

Tyler brought a mug of tea through from the kitchen. "You mean did Blake only have one computer."

"Quick to forget, aren't you, boy?"

He nodded at Slade, and then he squinted at Monty as though in thought. "You know what, you might've struck gold there."

"Me? Why?"

"He's got an old desktop at his house. I don't think he uses it much. But he's always got his head stuck in his—"

"iPad!" Monty clicked his fingers. "Bang on!"

"And I'm pretty sure it's in the staff house."

"Go get it, Monty. And make sure they're ready to go."

"Righto," Monty turned to leave.

"And tell them, there's a two grand bonus each if it goes without a hitch, okay?"

Monty left, and Tyler put his drink down, "I'd better get ready too."

"What for?"

"The job."

"You're staying here where I can keep an eye on you."

"I'm second lookout, Dad."

"You're staying put!"

"Why?"

"Till I find out for sure who killed Blake, you're staying put. Is that fucking clear?"

Chapter Twenty-five

I Love You, Rosaline

— One —

STILL THE RAIN FELL.

It was midnight, and Ros drove home in a daze after finishing late at the office. Paperwork: the bane of modern policing. She had done most of it in a trance, and the trance continued now as she pulled into her road and parked at the kerbside behind a huge Dodge Ram pickup truck. She shut down the engine, turned off the lights, and sat in the darkness just letting her mind continue its wandering as the rain grew louder on the roof.

She was thinking about Brian.

Men called Brian were solid and reliable, maybe even a little boring. They were staid and dependable. Or so she had thought. It was just something about their name – the mundaneness of it, its banality. Men called Brian would never be heroes, they would never pull their damsel off the rails before the steam loco sliced them in three; they would never take a bullet for the president. Those attributes belonged to men called Kurt. But Brians could be counted on to be loyal, steadfast, strong and diligent.

Except her Brian.

Her Brian was a bastard.

He'd started out being strong and diligent. In fact he was a proper gentleman; he believed in old-fashioned values: he opened doors for her, he offered his coat if she was cold, he bought her flowers every Friday, just in time to begin the weekend with a little romance, weekends they often spent away. Scarborough one weekend, Paris the next, even a long weekend in Rome. He was wonderful, was Brian.

Ros sighed, and climbed out of the car and into the rain. She locked the door and looked up at the dark bedroom window.

He was still wonderful even after they got married. He was made redundant from the council where he worked as a gardener. The redundancy was a huge blow, but it was a cloud lined with pure silver as far as he was concerned, because he'd only mentioned a couple of times about setting up his own landscape business, before Ros had agreed to use her savings and fund him.

He was her husband. He was loyal, steadfast Brian Craven, and they did everything together. They laughed and cried together, they got rich and poor together.

Almost.

She unlocked the front door and closed it quietly behind her. Rain dripped from her coat and suddenly she felt cold. She peered up the dark stairs and could picture him lying in bed, dreaming of her. She shivered.

So, how was she going to handle it then? This couldn't go on for much longer. At the very least she would be reprimanded at work for mistakes, at the worst she would drive into a damned tree without even going near the brake pedal. It had to come out; it needed resolution. At the very least, for now, it needed airing.

She swallowed, and hung up her coat.

But dare she?

The business had floundered to begin with. The bank wouldn't fund him. Ros handed over another cheque, and then another cheque. Then it began to flourish at last. The advertising she had paid for finally yielded results, and she even passed his name around at work, put his business card up on the cork notice board, and eventually his phone rang constantly and his diary bulged. Things were on the up; his mood was buoyant at last and he began to smile like he did in the old days. But things weren't the same.

Was it the cessation of weekend trips because of his business?

She shrugged. Maybe, she thought. But there was something else going on too, there was a subtle shift in power. Ros had the upper hand mentally; she was the stronger of the two, the wiser, the more logical. He was fanciful, extravagant, artistic. Her upper hand had diminished like her savings, and with it the power shifted to him. He grew less tolerant, seemed content to let doors slam in her face, and was too busy to be romantic. He was tired, grumpy. He began shouting.

Ros withdrew to safety inside her mind. Evenings spent watching the television weren't relaxing anymore. They had tension in them; she became slightly uncomfortable in his company, but could never pin it down to anything.

I should just wake him gently, ask him if everything's okay. We can sort this out; we can talk our way through it like adults. But do I want to sort it out? Do I want to live with a man I no longer trust?

This is Brian, remember? Come on, you've shared so much–

"My money is what we shared," she whispered to the empty hall. Don't you care about your pride, Ros? Don't you care he's been shagging The Bitch?

Just wake him gently and talk. You'll see, it'll work out fine.

— Two —

He heard the door close. Heard her take off her coat, and then she mumbled something.

He swallowed.

He could sense a confrontation coming a mile away. He was ready for it though. Ros was a good woman, and he wanted to keep her. She was his stability, and she kept his business on the straight and narrow while his moral compass had spun so fast the fucking needle had come off. But she had become boring, tedious to be around. And the worst thing was that she had... she had devalued herself somehow. And that meant he valued her less too, until he didn't value her at all. She meant less to him now than ever before, less than a broken tool, worthless. The only thing keeping them together now was his pity for her; the way she made him feel, like dirty somehow, because she was as worthless as shit. He was doing her a favour, being kind to a dumb animal. Yes, she was his stability, or at least she used to be.

He was almost looking forward to her breaking the news that she'd seen him leave... she was nervous. She was bricking it, big time. He could tell. Over the last few days she'd grown very cold towards him. And since the bust up at her office, she'd been remarkably strong in not mentioning it to him directly. But tonight it was coming to a head; no way on God's earth could she keep it in any more. She was fit to burst.

In the darkness, he squinted. He could hear her in the kitchen, shuffling about, filling the kettle, plucking up the courage to rouse him and begin their awkward conversation. Well, awkward for her. And then he heard her coming up the stairs. The bedroom door opened and Brian closed his eyes. He was looking forward to this.

— Three —

She opened the bedroom door and peered in. The room was filled with a gentle orange glow from the streetlamp outside. She could see him. He was fast asleep, lightly snoring. Rain patted against the window. What had she said, wake him gently and begin talking?

In one fluid movement she turned on the light and threw the bucket of cold water all over him. He screamed and was out of bed and on the floor like a dying fish on the dock, gasping for breath against the shock.

"You bastard!" she screamed.

Boring and staid Brian was on his feet in no time and with a fluidity to equal her own, punched her in the stomach hard enough to have her double up. The breath belched out of her and she collapsed on the carpet unable to breathe, one hand clawing at thin air, the other embedded in her stomach, knees pulled up tight and eyes wide. She sipped air through clenched teeth and as soon as she filled her lungs, she emptied her stomach on the floor next to her; convulsing, the pain in her body but a fraction of that in her mind.

She stared up him and was horrified to see him smiling at her.

"Look what you made me do, Rosaline."

She gasped.

"Woman shouldn't treat her man like that. No." Water dripped from his long hair right into her face. He didn't move aside. He obviously liked to see it fall on her. "I coulda killed you, girl. And then what woulda happened, eh?"

"You're screwing—"

"Ah ah. No need for that kinda language," he smiled. "I can see you're a little upset," he soothed, "but there isn't no need to be. You're mine now. When we met, you were everything to me. You still are—"

"Then why?"

His face darkened, the smile vanished. "You forced me into it! I had no choice, Rosaline. You grew snotty with me, like I wasn't worth shit and you were better 'n me."

"I never did." She coughed, and spat out more vomit.

"Why did you have to change? We were doing great and you changed and you made me—"

"Oh I made you fuck her, did I?"

Brian knelt by her side, brought his face within inches of hers. She held her breath and then whimpered, fingernails digging into the carpet. She screwed her eyes tightly closed but refused to cry. "You be careful now, Rosaline," he whispered. "You're making me cross again and then whatever happens'll be your fault."

She whimpered again, shoulders jerking despite the resolve she thought she had. That though, was running away from her now until she felt totally vulnerable.

"You don't care about us," he whispered. "You never really have, have you? You got your man, and you made him how you wanted; you paid me like a prostitute, bought me stuff so I'd stay around with you. And now I'm... I'm like a trophy for you, all bought an' paid for, for you to show off, to make yourself feel good. You're selfish, did you know that? Treat people like muck when you've had it easy all your life. You're a sad woman, Rosaline. Very sad."

She sobbed.

"You drove me into her bed. Did you know that? You brought this on yourself, and now you have the nerve to accuse me, to accuse me, of doing wrong? Unbelievable." He tucked a finger beneath her chin and turned her head so she was forced to look at him. "But that's okay, Rosaline." He smiled again, his eyes shifting between her own as he made sure she understood his point of view. "I forgive you."

But before she could even open her mouth to speak, he put extra pressure under her chin.

"I said it's fine; I understand. And I don't hold it against you, okay?"

She stared at him.

"I said okay?"

She nodded, and the pressure beneath her chin disappeared.

"All this," he said, "all this silliness with the water, and you making me hit you; we can forget all that, and we can carry on as before. I won't hold it against you, Rosaline, you know I'm not that kinda fella. Forgive an' forget, that's me, eh?" He looked at her still, and then he grinned. "Okay?"

Her lip trembled and she found herself nodding just so he'd go away and leave her alone. She had to hold her breath so she couldn't sob, she wouldn't give him that satisfaction, but when she closed her eyes, a tear squeezed out, and that made her angry all over again.

"Good lass," he said. And then he stood.

She took a quivering breath, held it for a moment, and then said, "I want you to leave, Brian." She opened her eyes slowly then. She could see him in the dull glow from the ceiling lamp, standing over her, naked except for a pair of wet boxers. He had his hands on his hips and he was looking down at her with incredulity on his face, confusion, as though he'd offered her a diamond tiara and she'd declined it in favour of a piece of chewing-gum he'd peeled off his work boots.

"I see," he said. He raised a finger, "I got something to show you. You stay right there, okay. I mean it, don't move, I'll be back in a second."

When he'd gone, the breath she'd been holding shivered out of her and she hitched in another one, tears rolling out of her eyes now so fiercely and with such heat that she didn't even see him come back in the room. It was only when he resumed his earlier kneeling position right by her head that she knew he was there and shrieked. She could feel his breath on her cheek.

He laughed softly at her, "Edgy, Rosaline? Sign of a guilty conscience is that, y'know."

"Please, Brian—"

"Ssshhh," he moved closer. "I don't want to see you like this. You've always been a loyal woman to me, and I thank you for it." That's when he grabbed her roughly by the hair and brought the kitchen knife up to her eye.

He's going to kill me. That was the only thought circling her mind now. He's going to kill me. Brian, the gardener. She tensed up, closed her eyes and swallowed, just waiting for it, the feel of a cold blade against her throat and then the hotness as it entered, and then what? Then she could feel the blood running hot, steaming across her neck, could hear it pattering on the carpet with each frenzied beat of a weakening heart.

He clutched her hair tighter, and still she dare not look, and then he dragged her head sideways and into the vomit. She felt it, cold against her cheek, felt its stench sting her nostrils, and she gasped, almost threw up again as he moved her face in and out of it, tilting her head towards it and pushing her until it was on her lips, in her eye, up her nose. And then he pulled her back away from it, straightened her face up. She shivered, retched.

"Rosaline," he whispered.

She opened her eyes. He smiled at her.

And then she felt the blade at her throat and could no longer hold back the tears. He had broken her finally, and she wailed.

"Ssshhh, it's gonna be okay. You'll see." He stroked her hair and then pressed the blade in harder, and she sipped tiny breaths at the top of her lungs, just waiting now. "I'm not going anywhere. Neither are you. Everything's going to stay just as it is."

She stared at him, not daring to move, hands digging into the carpet still, legs trembling. Any second that blade was going to pierce her skin, to puncture her throat.

"Is that clear?"

She stared.

"Nod if you agree."

She stared.

The blade pressed harder and she closed her eyes.

"You won't have to torment yourself any more. We understand each other now, don't we, dear?"

She nodded, reluctantly at first, and then as the blade left her throat, she nodded more vehemently, and the tears came again, and with them the sobbing too.

"I love you, Rosaline. Remember that. I love you so much. We'll always be together. And don't worry; I really do forgive you. I'm your man. And you are my woman." He stood and she dared to open her eyes again. "Now go take a shower, clean yourself up. And then clean your mess up."

Chapter Twenty-six

The Job

— One —

Monty closed the front door and walked along the hallway into the lounge.

"They get away okay?"

"Yep."

"No hitches?"

"Nope."

Monty handed the iPad to Slade and sat down opposite him. Slade looked at the thing. It was a piece of glass with an aluminium plate glued to its lower half. Not one button on it. "And I do what with it?"

Tyler sighed and stepped forward. "Dinosaur." He prodded the recess and the screen turned blue, asked for a password.

They all looked at each other.

"Try his birthday year," Monty said. "He was always shit at remembering passwords."

Slade looked at Monty.

"One-nine-seven-eight."

"Don't you know our birthdays, Dad?"

"Son, I don't even know my own fucking birthday, so put your lip away."

A touchscreen keypad cursor blinked, and Slade's big clumsy finger punched the numbers hard. The machine came to life displaying row after row of inch square icons. Slade shook his head in despair and handed it to Tyler.

"These are called apps, Dad. You can get games, BBC news, Google..."

"Whoopee. Put one on my shopping list, Monty."

Monty laughed as Tyler scrolled through five screens of apps until he hovered above one in particular. "e-Dater." He pressed the app and the screen filled with a multitude of colours; it showed a side panel with pictures of happy couples sharing glasses of champagne, of sexy silhouettes of couples kissing at sunset.

"Jesus," Slade said. "I'd rather go see Tanya," he smiled. Then he remembered the mess he'd made of Tanya, "Or maybe Shauna instead."

Along the other sidebar were adverts; thousands of them, that scrolled continuously and offered everything from garden sheds on eBay to structured retirement plans with a free Parker pen, from decadent holidays in Barbados to private clinics in London.

In the centre of the screen were two boxes, a cursor blinking in the uppermost one. "Username," whispered Tyler. He looked up, "that'll be his email address."

"Coulda told you that," said Slade.

Tyler went back to the front screen and picked Yahoo, then read off and remembered Blake's address before returning to the e-Dater site. He entered "Blake1978@ymail.com" and the cursor moved to the blank box labelled password.

"This is where we have to be careful. Some of these sites will lock you out for a day or two if you enter the wrong password more than a couple of times."

"Oh good," Monty said, "that helps."

"How many goes do we get?"

Tyler looked at his dad, shrugged. "You have to get the third one right."

"Start thinking, boys. Monty: pen and paper, let's do this thing right."

— Two —

They circled the block three times, looking for signs of recent activity, for recently parked vehicles or for out-of-place youths walking the streets. They looked for open windows, blowing curtains on the upper floors of the building that faced onto their target. There were none. It was after two in the morning, mid-week, and nothing moved, thought Jagger, except bad men and coppers. It was raining heavily, was almost deafening in the back of the van. Jagger was sitting on a wheel arch, gloved hand curled around the bodywork to keep from sliding off. Between his feet was a large canvas bag.

A wiry kid called Wasp sat opposite him, dressed entirely in black. He never moved a muscle until it was time to rock, and then he was like a whippet. He had jet black eyes that seemed to stare forever, unblinking, studying; making mental notes. Jagger didn't much like him. But he wasn't paid to like him, he was paid to do the job and get the hell out. It was Wasp's job to make sure they did it unimpeded.

Waves of rain blew up the street, and a gusty wind nudged the van towards the gutter. Ste stopped it, pulled up the handbrake. "I don't like this, man."

Pikey turned in the passenger seat and faced Ste. "Why?"

Ste shrugged. "It just don't feel right."

"That it? It don't feel right?"

Ste looked away, "If you're gonna take the piss—"

"Park up where I said. Do it now."

Without acknowledging Pikey, Ste put the van into reverse and juddered his way onto the triangle of tarmac off the main road, at the back of the target building. The van itself provided good cover from any passing traffic; a scrubby growth of weeds and a short row of dilapidated outbuildings shielded the triangle further. The van crept backwards, tyres crunching over broken glass. Ste stopped, turned off the headlights, looked at the others and nodded.

Pikey looked at Ste, "Stay awake, and no smoking." Then he opened the passenger door and climbed out, "Channel 12," and pressed the door closed after him. The sliding door opened and Jagger passed out the angle grinder and climbed out with the black holdall, a long jemmy bar sticking out past the zip.

The triangle was crudely lit by one streetlamp that showed amber spears of wind-driven rain scattering like starbursts. It was only just bright enough to show the rear of the terrace. Jutting out like afterthoughts, a series of extensions along the block created hidden pathways to the concealed back doors, each coated with a blackness the streetlamp could not reach.

Wasp slid from the van, clapped Jagger on the back and then took off into the darkness as quickly and quietly as a cat. Jagger slid the door closed, and walked briskly, squinting against the rain, through the puddles to the back door of the shop where Pikey was already waiting, his balaclava pulled down into place. The saw was on the ground nearby. "Leccy box is to the right, along the corridor."

Pikey got the five-foot jemmy to work on the grille over the back door and Jagger added his weight until the bolt sheared and the grille sprang open on squeaky hinges, banging into the brick wall. Pikey lodged the bar between the door and frame as Jagger lit up the expanding gap with an LED head torch, searching for the magnetic contact he knew would be there. He found it and, leaning across Pikey, jammed a strip of adhesive magnet, the type you'd find holding all manner of crap to the fridge door in most people's homes, into the gap and across the contact. Pikey heaved, and the door cracked and burst inwards. Jagger entered first, took the holdall down the short corridor to the end of the extension.

As he approached the cupboard, he flicked the switch on the head torch again and doubled the light coming from it. Water dripped from his rolled-up woollen balaclava as he stared at the electricity metre and its array of circuit breaker switches. He swallowed nervously, looked left along the corridor to see Pikey staring at him.

"Hurry up!"

Jagger turned off the main power to the premises, and then smashed the alarm keypad off the wall with a lump hammer from the holdall. For a brief moment there was the shrill cry of an alarm sounding and then silence as Jagger pulled the wires off the back-up battery's terminals. He looked at Pikey. "Here goes," he flicked the mains switch back on. They listened. Silence.

"Nice one," said Pikey. "Come on."

Jagger rushed along the corridor, took a swift peek at the door they'd broken in through and continued past the small kitchen and into the main shop. It was supposed to be some kind of coffee shop for the Turks in the area, a meeting place with sweet tea and hookah pipes. Jagger looked around at the padded benches across one wall, an out-of-place dining table and half a dozen well-worn chairs; shelves full of spices next to boxes of toilet roll and tubs of some brown liquid. Funny fuckers, them Turks, he thought. And then his eyes fell upon the object of this evening's enterprise. In the corner by the shop window, a white-painted wooden cube, six feet square with all manner of wires poking out the top.

— Three —

After twenty minutes, Slade looked at his watch; he knew the crew would be more or less in position by now. He took out his phone and checked it was sufficiently charged, checked to make sure he'd not missed any calls and then put it on the table next to him. If it rang, he wanted to be on it immediately.

And then he looked at the list that Monty had scribed. They had seven possible passwords for Blake's e-Dater site. And, if he was honest, he didn't really think any of them were right. Blake was thick as pig shit; he'd be the first to admit it, so Slade wasn't being unkind when he thought that. But the kid also had a sensitive side – and that was borne out by him going to see Rachel for dating advice.

So, he was a slightly complex character who was no good at remembering things. And not one of their collection of words, ranging from 'Blake' to 'Heart', from childhood favourites like 'Ninja' to 'Nintendo', seemed to fit with him as a person.

"So? Which one?"

"So he's shit at remembering passwords?"

Monty nodded.

Slade picked up his jacket and fished out a second mobile phone. This one was bulky and looked expensive. It also looked brand new, or at least, hardly used. He scrolled through a menu, and hit a button. The screen flashed, and he placed it to his ear, looking with some amusement at Monty's face. He knew what he was thinking: Not bad for a technophobe! The phone clicked in Slade's ear and a crackly voice spoke.

"It's me," he said. "I know. I'm sorry." He paused. "I said I'm sorry, I ain't gonna say it again!" Another pause, "Okay, I want some info from you. Did you find anything on Blake's body that looked like a password? Anything in his car or in his pockets—" Slade stopped, held his breath, and eventually he smiled at his eager audience. "Yes, thanks." And then, "It's in hand; I'm expecting it concluded within a week." He nodded once, and then again. "Bye." He pressed another button and then slid the phone away without a word.

"Who was that?" Tyler squinted at his father.

Slade nodded towards the iPad, "Try this."

Tyler picked up the machine and said, "Yeah, go on."

"Black by Rose."

Monty and Tyler looked at Slade. "Black by Rose?"

"Try it! Capital B, capital R"

Tyler typed and then Monty asked, "Is it a pub? Or a club, y'know one o' them fancy topless bars?"

Slade frowned. "I have no fucking idea."

"I'm in." Tyler sat on the arm of the chair so Slade could see what he was doing, and Monty peered at the screen from behind them.

Tyler had navigated through the password box of the e-Dating site and was in Blake's personal domain, with his chat box and his contact list, and another box of thumbnail images of potential suitors. There was only one person in the contact list. "Angel666," he said.

"Kind of name's that?"

"They don't use their real names, Dad. There's all kinds of nutters out there."

No one made any comment in response to that, but there was a raised eyebrow or two.

"So we're stuck, then?"

"Not yet, we're not," Tyler said. "I'll browse through his emails to this Angel666, see if she's opened up to him a bit."

— Four —

Scrotes had a strange sense of smell. They were always cautious – if they were serious. The average crack-head or the average dunce who'd steal something on spec tended not to think too far in advance; they tended to think only of the opportunity, and of nothing more. This crew, these robbers, were not of that particular ilk; they had plans, it was easy to see. They took their liberty seriously and had prepared for the worst, posting one man around the front of the building, and another in the old blue van around here, at the back; both no doubt in radio comms with the two inside. Would they be armed? Cooper asked himself. Of course they would be. I would be.

Coppers had the same sense of smell, perhaps more acutely tuned, certainly more calculating. They didn't have their continuing freedom to consider, or the need for an escape route to confuse the thought process. They had the villain, and they had the crime; and paramount in the thought process was catching one in the act of the other.

And that was exactly what they would be doing during tonight's little operation. Only not directly. It was fine locking up a gang for screwing over a cash machine, but he wanted the kingpin. He wanted the big players, and the only way to get to the big players was to capture the little ones and in good time, persuade them to talk to the nice policeman about the big naughty men who paid their wages.

In an empty bedsit above a nearby shop, a man from the imaging unit was videoing everything, all the comings and goings. Right now there wasn't a lot to entertain him, but soon, no doubt, there would be.

Cooper, until recently rubbing his face and stifling yawns, sat bolt upright, eyes scanning the triangle of tarmac and the poorly-illuminated surrounding area. He faced the scene through the wiper-smeared screen of an old Toyota which was parked directly beneath a broken streetlamp outside a corner shop. He was less than sixty yards from the old Transit that had one fidgeting scrote inside. Cooper bit his lower lip as the wipers cleared the screen again.

There were two favourable escape routes for the robbers. Both were covered by plain armed response vehicles. Their remit was to follow them, interchanging with their colleagues every third or fourth junction so as to remain invisible. They were told to follow and radio in with details of the ultimate location – that was the important thing – that's when Cooper would earn his money because that's when he had to get the obs teams in quickly, find out what became of the money, and where the robbers went after that, and even more importantly, to whom they spoke. Cooper had plenty of information on Slade and his gang but anything new would be very welcome right now. Very welcome indeed. Operation Domino wasn't a typical operation. Working within its confines were people who dared play the game by their own rules. All in the name of clearing the streets up a little – cleaning out the sewers.

The other routes available to the robbers were possibilities, but unlikely ones; ones that would take them into the estates, the narrow, poorly lit back roads around Harehills and into Chapeltown. Not recommended. But if they chose that way, then cars would pick them up soon enough.

"Can't get my head round it."

Cooper looked across to Benson. "What can't you get your head round?"

"They'd leave a cash machine in a fucking Turkish teashop."

"Maybe they're expensive to relocate."

"Not as expensive as having one emptied though."

Cooper nodded, contemplating it; it was a stupid thing to do. Apparently, the shop had once been a travel agency and it seemed a good idea having a cash machine embedded into the window pane outside, with all its workings inside, enclosed by a large wooden box with a door in it. He could imagine that most people didn't even see that box as they'd entered, never noticed it; it was just another place for posters of beaches or pistes.

But his mind was elsewhere right now – it was on Jagger, he was the important one.

— Five —

Tyler followed the trail of their relationship back over the last three weeks. It had gone from the usual cool approaches to something almost intimate. And since Blake had neglected to tell her of his past, it was obvious they would meet up at some point. He had posted some pictures of himself that were very flattering, and he'd gone out of his way to emphasise what a wonderful guy he was, dropping little hints about charity work and liking puppies. It brought a smile to Tyler's face; the only charity work Blake had ever done was stealing collection boxes, and the only time he thought of dogs was when he was at Doncaster greyhound track.

Still, hats off to him: it had worked.

Angel666 was a bookkeeper for a small-time accountant somewhere on the south side of Leeds, so that was a lead they could follow up if things didn't open out a bit further as he scrolled through and read their emails. And then he discovered her name was Angela, but most people called her "Charlie". She didn't elaborate further on the name, or why "Charlie".

And lastly, there were emails leading up to the meeting. How nervous she was, how much she was looking forward to it, but how shy she was, how inexperienced. "Don't worry about experience, love," Tyler said to himself, "he ain't worried about trivial stuff like that." And then details of the meeting itself.

He was to meet her in a pub called The Spinney Nook in Castleford at seven o'clock. They could eat there and get to know each other a bit, maybe pop into the Hilton in Garforth, and listen to the pianist. It seems they had got to know each other quite well, thought Tyler; well enough for Blake to take a fancy to her, and well enough for him to lose control just like he usually did. No matter how hard he tried to restrain himself.

When it boiled right down to it, Blake Crosby was always going to end up dead prematurely one way or another: either by a relative of a victim, or in prison from a nasty accident.

— Six —

Jagger felt pumped up. The place was dark, the torches he and Pikey carried only made the place even more eerie, elongating shadows and reflecting from chrome pots and glass jars, refracting water in jugs to spill rainbows across the ceilings.

The room smelled sickly sweet, cloying. The floor was sticky under foot, and it was hot, with an ingrained stench of sweat. He dropped the holdall and then placed the torch across its bowed centre so it shone directly upon the large oval dining table as he pulled it roughly aside. Pikey strode past and his black shadow was like a moving stripe in his vision. Across the outside of the glass door and across the remaining shop window were the grey ribs of a roller shutter door, good sound insulation.

Jagger pressed the button on the wire, "One, you there?"

"One. I'm here."

"Two?" Jagger said, forcing open the flimsy wooden door of the cube.

"Yep. I'm here."

He took off the head torch, rolled the wet balaclava down his face, making sure the small earpieces from the radio comms stayed in place. He replaced the head torch, pulled on a pair of goggles and then delved inside the bag for the ear protectors. This was going to be loud, very loud.

Though he kept his mind on the task in hand, he couldn't help feeling nervous. He had Pikey staring at him, he had the others outside waiting, listening, watching, and then he had Slade back at the ranch waiting for news.

"Jagger, move it!"

Jagger snapped back, looked up at Pikey. He had broad shoulders, a shelf of a forehead hiding sunken eyes that peered out through the balaclava. "Plug me in," he said, throwing the flex of the angle grinder towards him.

And then he took out the template, a cardboard shape that fitted over the metal door of the cash machine. He drew around it: two vertical lines precisely 87 mm in from the hinge side and 118 mm in from the lock side.

Jagger nodded at Pikey, clicked the mic button, "Ready?"

"Okay, go," whispered Ste.

"Clear to go," said Wasp.

Jagger pulled on heavy leather gloves, knelt in front of the cash machine's rear 10 mm thick door, and flicked the grinder's switch. Silence shattered in a howl.

Pikey checked his watch as Jagger brought the cutting disc up to the metal door. A constant spray of sparks jetted from the machine and hit the floor in front of Jagger's knees as he followed the black line down the hinge side of the door. The disc broke through, and Jagger swallowed as he pressed on. A three millimetre slit followed the machine as it cut its way from top to bottom. Four minutes.

Wasp concealed himself in the doorway of Mahmood's Burger and Pizza directly over the road from the shuttered teashop. He squatted down and waited. From here he had an uninterrupted view right up Harehills Lane for maybe 200 yards, another 100 yards in the other direction down towards the junction with Spencer Place and on towards the top end of Roseville Road. The streetlights were better around this side, but the rain was just as heavy, sending a shiver scuttling up Wasp's damp neck.

It was two-fifteen and Wasp held back a yawn. His eyes watered though and his hands were fidgeting with change in his pockets one moment, then spinning the wheel of a cigarette lighter the next. He stood, feet never still, eyes flicking from side to side. "Hurry up, hurry up," he whispered, quite suddenly wishing he was somewhere else.

From across the road he could hear a faint squeal; the saw working on metal. Wasp was famous for being cool, laid back in the face of danger. And so far as he could see, there was no danger. But he felt far from cool. Ste had been right: this just didn't feel good.

At seven minutes the hinge side was through completely and the lock side was almost there. Steam rose from Jagger's wet balaclava, and twice he'd had to stop to wipe condensation from the inside of his goggles. At his knees lay an ever increasing pile of gritty metal dust, the cooled grindings that had left the door as sparks and had melted into the linoleum. The smell of burnt steel was heavy in the air. The Stihl ground onwards towards the bottom, and Jagger's arms were burning, aching from the exertion, and beginning to shake. Sweat trickled down his back.

It was at times like these that he understood why people did this. It was thrilling. Even if he didn't need the money, it would be a high, an adrenaline rush; the chance of being caught now or later, the meeting later with Slade, the sharing of spoils, the camaraderie, the beer!

The blade sliced into the floor and the heavy door tilted forward. Pikey tapped Jagger on the shoulder, and he slid backwards out of the way, grateful to shut off the noise and put down the Stihl. When he did, his hands carried on vibrating, like an external version of pins and needles. And when the disc finally stopped turning, Jagger's ears were buzzing.

Pikey grabbed the handle and used it to pull the door directly outwards into the shop. Jagger peered inside as Pikey put the door down by the dining table. "We missed the door wiring by less than half an inch."

"So long as we missed it, I couldn't give a shit."

"Three cassettes," Jagger said. "Full."

"How much, then?"

"Twenty-five or thirty. Or thereabouts."

"Not bad for an hour's work."

"We haven't got it yet." Jagger looked in closer. "They're fitted with TN41 locks."

Pikey looked at him, "Is that supposed to mean something to me?"

"I can't get past them."

"What!"

"I can't pick them, I mean. We can cut through them—"

"So cut through them and let's fuck off."

"It's not as simple as that."

Pikey sighed, "How did I know you were going to say that?"

"They're fitted with anti-tamper switches, which we can't disable. They're on a thirty second timer; once I begin cutting, we have thirty seconds to get the cassettes out – all of them."

"And if we don't?"

"The alarm sounds in some monitoring station somewhere—"

"Cool, by the time they phone the coppers—"

"The coppers will take an age to get here, I know. But the shitty part of the deal is if we haven't got them all out of the way in that thirty seconds, the dye-packs go off."

Pikey thought about it. "Bollocks." He took a step back, hand rubbing his face through the wet balaclava. "What about the wiring? Can't we cut it, or freeze it or melt it?"

"I dunno, I've never played with this stuff before. Chances are the wiring is well routed behind the cassettes – the wiring we need anyhow. And if we fuck up, the job's over."

"What about the dye-pack wiring? Can't we cut that?"

"It's at the front of the cassettes. No chance."

"Bastard!"

"And even worse, I don't know when the thirty seconds begins."

"I ain't going back empty-handed. He'll kill us. I'd rather go back with dyed notes than nothing at all."

"I mean, I don't know if the tamper circuit operates after I've cut through the first, or as I begin cutting through the first."

"This gets better."

"Look, I could probably be through one lock in four or five seconds. I just wanted you to be aware of the risks."

"The risks? What risks, other than ten years in the clink?"

"It's why you do it, isn't it, the risk? I mean, you're not short of a bob or two."

"You reckon you can slice all three locks in less than fifteen seconds?"

"With a new blade, yep."

"Fit a new blade, let's crack on."

Ste was scared shitless.

He was on parole, was due at the parole office in eight hours, and if he didn't turn up, he'd be straight back to Parkhurst. If a copper took a peek inside this van right now, at two-thirty in the morning, did a name check on him and found him to be outside of his curfew, he'd be heading south in a matter of hours.

If he went back to prison, it would be the last time he'd see his kids, she'd already told him that. And he knew she wasn't bullshitting. He looked at the radio, wondered whether to call them back. He could say he'd seen the law. That would get them back out in no time, and they'd be forced to abandon the job and he could go home and keep his appointment. And he could keep his freedom and keep his kids. Sounded good.

But he'd be in the same boat again next week or next month.

Ste shook his head, played with the volume knob on the radio, and wondered why he'd ever agreed to this shit. There were other things–

"Fuck!" There, up ahead, on Harehills Lane. A cop car. He turned off the wipers and leaned across the seats, getting low. "Oh please no, go straight on, don't turn down here."

Through the rain, Wasp could make out a youth walking towards him, maybe 150 yards away. No threat right now. Well, he was just walking this way, actually, not specifically towards him; Wasp couldn't be seen from the pavement up there. No chance. But it was the way the youth ambled that spooked him. It was pissing it down, and this guy was just walking along like it was seventy degrees out there and he didn't have a rush in the world. Must be out of his fucking tree, Wasp thought.

He crouched, focused his attention entirely on the youth. He left the cigarette lighter in his pocket alone, and instead, he curled his hand around the gun. And then he saw it, further up Harehills Lane, a cop car cruising slowly this way. He scanned right, towards the parade of shops, towards the shuttered windows of the Turkish tearoom. If the cop car kept coming, straight towards him, he would relax, but if it turned off the main drag towards their little triangle of glass-strewn tarmac around the back of that block, he would have to call it in.

Wasp watched.

Wasp listened to the incessant rain beating the pavement.

Wasp watched intently up the road.

He should have spared a glance behind him too.

Chapter
Twenty-seven

The Daily Grind

— One —

JAGGER STOOD CLOSE TO the machine, angle grinder in hand, ready to go. "I want you to count out loud," he said. "Thirty seconds after I touch the first lock, drag my arse away from here."

Pikey nodded.

"Okay, here goes." He flicked the switch and the grinder roared. One last look at Pikey, who nodded again, and he went forward, the spinning wheel contacted the lock and inside his own head, he began counting. The blade bit and he was making good progress through the first lock. Sparks flew.

Wasp was wide-eyed and unblinking, as through the rain he saw the cop car turn off the main drag and head towards their triangle. The deep muffled scream from the teashop had resumed, and on top of that, the youth who was gently sauntering towards him, continued to do so, now less than fifty yards away.

"Fuck." Wasp grabbed the radio and almost got it to his mouth, when he noticed a disturbance in the rainfall to his right, some change he'd not been aware of before. It made him turn just in time to see the grimace on the face of his killer as the knife sank into his throat.

Ste could hear the muted sound of the angle grinder over the constant pandemonium of the rain on the van roof. He peered through the rain-smeared screen as his worst fear began to materialise before him. He shrank even lower, lying across the seats as the police car's headlamps lit up the front of the van. He brought the radio to his lips. "Stop, stop, stop. Coppers."

Pikey grabbed Jagger's shoulder. But Jagger had heard Ste's message too, had flicked the switch and driven the blade hard into the lock to stop it spinning.

Fourteen. Fifteen. Sixteen. Seventeen.

He was most of the way through the second lock, and it seemed their luck had run out.

Jagger swallowed. Waited.

Eighteen.

Benson looked across at Cooper and said, "I hope to Christ that's just a routine patrol."

"It is, he's not slowing."

"Why do they always show up—"

"Ssshh," Cooper pointed, "who the hell's that?"

Behind the police car by thirty yards was a black youth scurrying towards the blue van.

"What's he up to?" Benson said.

Cooper keyed his radio. "Imaging unit, are you getting this?"

"Yup."

— Two —

"So tomorrow, take the crew and tell 'em what you found. You do a search of all the accountants south of Leeds. And you find her," he warned, pointing a finger. "I want her, and I want her alive. When you do find her, you let me know, and you take her to the lock-up under the arches. Clear?"

Tyler nodded, "What about my collections?"

"Don't worry 'bout them. This takes priority."

— Three —

The cop car slowed a little as it drove by. Ste was shaking, and he craned his neck to watch in the passenger mirror as it left the triangle and drove away up towards Cherry Row. Ste closed his eyes and breathed a sigh, even allowed himself a smile before bringing the radio to his lips. "It's okay," he said, "they've gone now."

Ste held his hand out in front of him, and even in the pissy light of the streetlamp he could see it shaking. He laughed, and sat up, "Fuck me—"

There was a gentle tap on the driver's window and Ste, smile still on his face, turned to see a man holding a gun almost up to the glass. The man smiled wide to show nothing but gums as he pulled the trigger.

Twenty-three.

The voice crackled in Jagger's ear.

"It's okay, they've gone now."

Twenty-four. The Stihl growled into life again and was through the second lock in a whisper, then tore chunks out of the third. Pikey grabbed the handle of the lower cassette and as soon as the blade ripped into thin air, he yanked it free, followed by the second cassette. Jagger threw the angle grinder on the floor with the blade still spinning, tore the final cassette free and slammed the wooden door just as a loud crack spat red dye. The alarm sounded, a sharp, shrill noise that pierced Jagger's thoughts.

He looked around, breathing rapidly to see Pikey throwing both cassettes into the holdall, and keeping it wide open for Jagger to do the same with his.

As soon as it landed in the bag, Pikey zipped it and headed for the door, "Hurry up," he shouted back.

Jagger rested his hands on his knees, panting through his damp balaclava, and looked around to make sure he'd left nothing of himself behind, squinting through the noise. Leaving the saw and the jemmy bar and the spare cutting blades was fine – they'd torn off or obliterated all labels and serials anyway; he just wanted to make sure he'd left no masks or gloves or whatever. It was all too easy to get complacent at times like this.

The alarm shrieked behind him.

As soon as Pikey exited the broken door and was outside in the rain and the puddles, he knew something was wrong. The fact that he couldn't see Ste's ugly silhouette through the side window of the van because it was covered in some black fluid alerted him straight away. But then his gaze was captured by a youth who showed himself at the front of the van.

Pikey reached inside his jacket for the gun he carried, pulled it out and flicked off the safety catch all in one liquid movement. But he was so captivated by the youth that he didn't see the other one to his right until it was a fraction of a second too late to react properly.

There was a loud crack, and suddenly Pikey found himself lying in those puddles wondering what the hell had happened. He looked up as a man reached down and took the holdall from him. Pikey mouthed something, but only a small groan came out, and his dulling eyes were filled with confusion and misunderstanding as his mouth opened and closed.

The man walked away with Pikey's bag, and a second later, the youth from the front of the van joined him. Pikey had lost the gun somehow as he'd hit the ground and he could see it now, over there, only a few feet away, and well within reach. He lunged for it, and the pain ripped into his chest and suddenly he couldn't breathe any more.

He was dying, he knew that now. They'd finally got him. But he grabbed the gun anyway, even as his lungs filled up with his own blood and his vision began to blur. He pointed the gun towards the two men and let all eight rounds go, hoping to Christ to meet one of the bastards on the other side.

———

"What the fuck just happened?"

Cooper screamed at Benson, "Go! Go, for fuck's sake."

"What? I'm not driving into a fucking gun battle."

"Go!"

"Are you mad?"

Cooper looked at Benson, thin lips, "Get on the radio then, and get my ARVs here. Now!"

Jagger took a breath and had begun to walk across the gritty, sticky floor, feeling pleased with himself, when he heard the distinct report of a shot over the shrill alarm. He flinched, and quickly turned off his head torch, and headed for the doorway. He crouched and took a quick peek outside but could see nothing. The van was still there, that's all he knew.

"Fuck," he whispered. He edged out into the rain, made it another two feet before he saw the van window covered in a dark liquid that was streaking slowly down the glass, and then he saw Pikey face down only ten yards away, firing a gun.

Jagger ran to his side in time to see the weapon drop to the ground, still gripped by Pikey's lifeless hand. He felt a tug on his trousers, felt heat in his calf muscle and then heard the report. He turned to see two men climbing into a taxi; one was grunting, clutching his side, helped aboard by the other who had just shot him.

The taxi almost stalled in the driver's haste to be away, and Jagger chased it for close on fifty yards before it pulled away into the night, and his leg finally gave way. As it did, he got a good view of the injured passenger who turned and faced him, screaming in pain. He appeared to have no teeth, just black gums.

Jagger stumbled toward a lamppost trying to get his breath back and hissing at the pain in his leg, when he saw the Toyota nearby. He could have sworn there were people inside it, and squinted against the rain trying to get a better look.

Chapter Twenty-eight

No Such Thing as Judgement Day

— One —

"MONTY, IT'S JAGGER. COME and pick me up."

"Why, what's happened?"

"We got jumped. Everyone's dead."

"What do you mean, 'everyone'?"

"Everyone. There's only me left," Jagger bit down on his lower lip. "Hurry up mate; I've been shot in the fucking leg."

"Go get their mobile phones. I'll be at the top end of Spencer Place in half an hour..." There was a pause, a muffled sound as though Monty had his hand over the mouthpiece. "Where's the money?"

"They got it."

The line clicked off.

Jagger put the phone away, unsurprised by Monty's last question, and searched among the bins and skips for a decent bin bag. He found one that only had cardboard in it, rather than food scraps, and emptied the card out. He slid his wounded leg inside, tying it above his knee. And then he headed for Pikey, as quickly as he could, wincing with each stride.

— Two —

The bag rustled in the wind, flapping about like a black flag, rain whipping it, and plastering Jagger's hair to his screwed up face. Hands in pockets, arms tucked into his side against the wind. He leaned against a tree up at the top end of Spencer Place, feeling conspicuous, taking the weight off his injured leg, shivering from the shock or from the cold, he wasn't sure which. Maybe both. He listened to the sirens, saw the odd streak of blue light and cringed as a car pulled up alongside the tree, wipers scooting across the screen, Monty's face just visible by the dash lights.

With much effort, Jagger climbed aboard and slammed the door, and let out a gasp at the pain.

"Why the bag? Monty asked.

"No blood trail."

Monty engaged gear, "Good; I don't want blood in the car."

"How's Slade taking it?"

"He's dancing round the fuckin' lounge."

Jagger closed his eyes. Sometimes he hated this job.

Jagger sat in the kitchen chair. He could see himself reflected in the mirror by the archway into the lounge. His face had been washed clean by the rain, except in the creases, the depth of which appeared amplified by the rusting metal dust embedded in there. More tiny metal particles from the safe door that had sprayed his clothes had turned brown with rust, and streaked down his sweater. His hair was a ragged mess and his clothes were wet through, and still he shivered.

The bag was still tied around his leg, and it could stay there too; he was reluctant to even look at it, fearing the worst.

Slade sat across the table from him, cup of tea on the mat, small cigar smoking in a glass ashtray. Slade's arms were folded, and all he did was watch Jagger. Jagger swallowed. By the archway, Tyler stood silently too, also watching. Monty filled a plate with biscuits and then put the kettle on again.

"In this life," Slade said in a quiet voice, "you have to grab what you can." He stared. "You come into this life with nothing. Nothing at all, except maybe the love of your parents. If you're lucky. But you haven't got nothing. And really," he continued, "you go out pretty much the same way. The old people," he waved over his shoulder, "I mean the ancestors, they used to bury all their shit with them, see. They believed you could take it with you. But you can't." He stared.

Monty fixed himself a coffee. Then he joined Slade at the table, munching on his biscuits.

"And there ain't no such thing as judgement day, son. Never worry about that shit; it's lies, like Father Christmas and the Tooth Fairy."

Jagger looked at Monty, getting ever more confused. Monty ate biscuits.

"What I'm trying to say is you take what you want in this life. And you give as little back as you can get away with. If it means hurting folk to get stuff, then you hurt 'em. Simple as that. You go from life to death, from A to Z, in as much comfort and style as you can fucking muster." Slade took a drag on the cigar, sipped his tea. His eyes never left Jagger. "You don't fret about the afterlife or about no judgement day. You live for the now; fuck the past, and never look forward. Am I right?"

Jagger looked at him. "Yes," he said.

"Yes. I am. So them people that ripped me off tonight. I don't blame them. They're only trying to get from A to Z in style, see." The room was quiet.

Slade smashed his fist into the table.

Everyone jumped. Monty's biscuits hit the floor along with the ashtray and cigar.

"Except they don't take from me!"

Jagger swallowed and had to look away.

"I do the fuckin' taking!" he screamed.

The room paused.

And then he smiled at Jagger as Monty put the ashtray complete with cigar back in front of Slade. His eyes shone at Jagger, "Now I have to decide whether I believe you… or not."

Jagger looked confused. "Believe me? Why wouldn't you believe me?"

"Because it's very convenient that you stayed behind in the Turkish place to make sure you'd not forgotten nothing. As Pikey was being shot to death twenty yards away."

"I haven't taken your money!" He realised that he was being incredibly brave – he refused to think he was being foolish. He had to defend himself, and with conviction too; if Slade detected anything in him, it had to be a feeling of being insulted. "I worked fucking hard—"

Monty back-handed him around the face and stared at him. "Watch your lip."

"I got shot, Slade," he whispered, peering up at him across the table, head bowed, hand massaging his stiffening leg. "And I'm no grass either."

"So how did they find out?"

"I don't know. Honest."

"Told you we couldn't trust him. I fucking said—"

"Shut up."

"I haven't let you down, Slade," protested Jagger. "I've been here four months, and in all that time, have I ever let you down? We pulled off the cash-in-transit robbery, didn't we? It went fine. I've done collection work for you, Tyler, haven't I? I've never given anyone cause to think I'm not loyal." Everyone stared at him. "Oh come on! I even ditched that whore and cleaned up the flat."

Slade looked away in thought. "Tea, Monty, please."

"Can I have one?" Jagger asked.

Monty looked at Slade, and Slade nodded. "And it's an apartment!"

"Dad!"

"I said shut it, boy."

"Only one I can think of is Wasp." Jagger said. "He wasn't with us all day. We got everything ready, we did all the prep work, and he wasn't around."

"Where was he?"

"Not at home," Monty put two cups of tea on the table. "I checked earlier when you mentioned the computer thing."

"Wasp wouldn't pull a fast one—"

"Tyler. Wipe the SIM cards."

Tyler stared at Slade, the muscles in his cheeks throbbing. Then he removed all the cards from the phones, including Jagger's, put them on a saucer and put them in the microwave oven. He pressed start and watched the lightning show for ten seconds. The oven bleeped. Done.

"Did you see his body?" Slade asked.

Jagger nodded. "I got his phone and the comms equipment off him before the police showed up."

"You sure this black lad had no teeth?" Monty asked.

Jagger nodded. "Pikey got him in the side, he was screaming when he got in the taxi."

Monty and Slade both said, "Tymo."

"And if he's been hit," Tyler slid the cards into the bin, "he'll be with Gryz."

Slade nodded. "Tomorrow we begin putting things right with Blake. Tyler, that's your job, right?" Tyler nodded. "Monty, you get some of the lads round, give 'em names, addresses and amounts; I want all them collections to go smoothly, on time, like we can absorb this shit no problem, right?"

"Right, Chief."

"But for now, we go get my money back."

Monty and Tyler nodded.

"What about me?" Jagger asked.

"Get tooled up; you're coming with us." And then Slade added, "We'll get your leg fixed up while we're there."

"How many shall I call?"

"Half a dozen should do it."

Chapter Twenty-nine

Scaffolding Poles

QUEEN'S MEDICAL PRACTICE WAS a fairly swish building considering the area it was in. It was a new, single-storey building in its own grounds with ample parking. Thigh-high bushes surrounded it on all sides, and splinted saplings in wire protection baskets were dotted around the car park. The whole building was alone, situated in a playing field off a side road in Middleton. Middleton was predominantly council housing, and old housing at that; populated more by youth than wisdom, and considered a punishment rather than a gift by those who lived there.

At this time in the morning the medical centre ought to have been totally quiet; there should have been no lights on inside and no vehicles outside. Sometimes, dealers and pushers used the car park. But not tonight.

Monty did a drive-by with Jagger in the back and Slade up front. Tyler and the rest of the crew waited in the truck a few hundred yards away.

Jagger pointed and shouted, "That's the fucking taxi!"

"Better hope they came straight here, I want my cash back."

Two pole-mounted security lights fought a battle with the darkness, and their small victory illuminated the taxi. They shone on the blood-streaked hand prints that had run down from the top frame of the rear passenger door like a dying man's tears, and reflected off the driver's spectacles each time he moved his head. From the slightly open back window, smoke plumed into the sky, and then the unseen occupant tossed out a cigarette end and then wound the window up. More blue smoke curled lazily from its exhaust as the taxi's engine idled.

An empty BMW blocked the entrance to the medical centre car park.

At the side of the building, a lone man puffed on a cigarette; his head swivelled slowly as he watched their car go by.

A second, unseen man, stood around the back of the building having a piss. And apart from the small loss of blood from a head wound, that was the last time any bodily fluid would leave him until he hit the pathologist's table the next day. There was no security light around this side, the bulb had blown weeks ago and no one had bothered fixing it. But he'd stood out as a silhouette against the illuminated window of the doctor's surgery.

A drunken man staggered into the car park, arms outstretched as though he was afraid of walking into something. He stopped twenty yards short of the taxi; those inside, and the lone man beneath the security light, watched him. There was a click as solenoids locked the taxi's doors.

Two men readied themselves behind the bush just the other side of the taxi.

The drunken man swivelled slightly, then doubled over and threw up before collapsing onto the wet tarmac. He stirred for a moment, then regained his feet and saw at last, it seemed, the taxi. He smiled and tried to wave, then staggered across towards it with vomit stringing from his chin. The man beneath the security lamp walked a few paces, hand reaching inside his jacket. The taxi window came down a few inches.

"Hey mate," slurred the drunk, "giz a lift to Morley, wouldya."

"Go away," said the driver.

"Aw go on. I got cash, man. I can pay ya."

"I said—"

The drunk shouted, "Now!"

Both side windows of the taxi imploded. The two occupants didn't even manage to turn as two six-foot lengths of scaffolding pole shattered the side windows. One scaffolding pole glanced off the driver's shoulder and smashed through his jaw, driving broken bone and torn flesh into his brain. The rear passenger's left eye socket splintered under the second pole and he was dead before his head smacked into the door to his left. The man reaching into his jacket by the security light, folded at the knees and then dropped forward onto his face; the rear of his skull had popped like a balloon and the scaffolding pole had punched through his brain like an apple corer.

Tymo was in agony. The lucky hit from the dying man outside the Turkish tearoom had caught him just below the rib cage on his left side. He didn't know if that was his liver area, or whether it had punctured a lung, or what. He wasn't a medical man; and on top of that, he couldn't think straight.

Luckily, Nix was a thinking man, and he'd told the taxi driver – a man they all called Rahool, to come straight here to see the Doc. Nix had called ahead, got one of the guys to raise the Doc and meet them here along with another four men to guard the outside of the medical centre.

There was still the thick end of forty grand inside the taxi, so it would need protecting.

Tymo was a self-made man. Not a gang lord or a gang boss in the traditional sense of the word; he worked with his men on as many jobs as he could, got his hands dirty and bloody, and never asked them to do anything he wouldn't himself. If Tymo had applied himself as well in the outside world as he did in the underworld, he'd be a company CEO by now, no doubt. But he preferred this kind of life; living on the edge, they called it.

The only problem with living on the edge, with getting your hands bloody, was the risk of ending up in places like this.

He couldn't go to hospital because the police would work out pretty quickly what had happened, and where it had happened. Game over. So he had to rely on the medical expertise of a Polish doctor called Pawel Gryzbowski who was known locally as Dr Pawel, or in circles inhabited by people like Tymo, he was known as Doc or just plain Gryz.

Gryz had given him morphine while he tried to stop the bleeding. Tymo was bleeding out quickly and his face was that of a man struggling against the inevitable.

Standing next to Tymo was Shack; a big man with scars across his face, and he stared at Gryz with growing agitation.

Another man, smaller, called Heiny, said, "Come on, Gryz, fix him up, man!" He was never still, fidgeting, walking around the surgery, out into the waiting room, back into the surgery, peering out of the windows between the blinds, fretting, "Come on, Gryz," he said again.

"Shut it," Shack said. "Gryz, can you fix him or not?"

Gryz's hair stuck out at weird angles; underneath the shirt he wore, he had on his pyjamas and on his feet were a pair of slippers that glistened from fresh drops of blood. Gryz worked on Tymo. He slowly shook his head, "I don't think so. He needs a hospital. He's lost too much blood, and he's likely to have a heart attack anytime soon."

"Fuck."

"He's bleeding inside, Shack, and I can't stop it."

"Fuck!"

"Sshhh," Heiny slid the blinds open again, "did you hear that? I heard glass break, did you hear that?"

"Go check it out," Shack growled, and Heiny flitted across the room and out of the door.

Tymo opened his eyes and looked at Shack, "Get me to a hospital, man."

"Call an ambulance," Gryz said, "they can help quicker."

Shack took out his phone.

Heiny made it into the waiting area, the receptionist's desk in front of him and the exit door round to the left. He stopped, swallowed, and took out his gun. He didn't like this. It all seemed too quiet; where was Davis? He should have...

Sitting in the waiting room was a man he recognised from earlier this evening. He had a black plastic bag tied around one of his legs. He also had a look of arrogance on his face, mixed with anger. "Payback time," he said.

And then he remembered where he recognised the guy from.

To his right something moved quickly and before Heiny could raise his gun and turn, he hit the floor and his gun skittered across to the desk. Heiny coughed once and then the scaffolding pole finished him off.

Monty picked up Heiny's gun and together with Slade hobbling, he strode up towards the doctors' surgeries, Jagger limping behind. In the lead, Tyler and one other man, Eton, stopped at the door. Inside they could hear the clattering of stainless steel tools on stainless steel trays – it could have been a dining room.

And then they heard, "Heiny?"

Slade shoved past his men, ignored Monty's hand trying to pull him back and marched straight into the room.

"Shack," he said. "Good to see you again."

Shack had a phone to his ear but when he saw Slade Crosby and several others filling the room, he simply put the phone away and looked straight at him. "He's dying," he said. "I need to get him to a hospital."

"Why burden the NHS? Don't you think they're overworked as it is?"

Tyler slid past Slade and walked calmly towards Shack, his hand out.

Shack opened his jacket pocket and slid the gun from a small holster attached to his belt, picked it up between finger and thumb and just handed it over.

Gryz took a step back, pulling off a pair of latex gloves. "Please," he said, "take your fight outside, this is—"

"Doc, good to see you too. Now go fix my man up while Tymo and me work out our problems." He raised his eyebrows at the doctor's impending protests, "There's a good man, eh?"

Jagger sat in a plastic chair and began untying the shredded bin bag. Gryz reached for more gloves, looking ever more harrowed.

Monty turned to Eton, "Keep an eye out," he said, handing over Heiny's gun.

Slade approached the table, looked down at Tymo and saw the mess in his side. "Ooh," he hissed, "looks nasty does that." He came close to Tymo's sweating face and whispered, "does it hurt?"

Tymo's eyes flickered open.

"Who told you?" Slade asked. "Who told you we had a little job planned?"

Tymo smiled, slid his eyes closed again.

"Tell me, and I'll let Shack ring for an ambulance."

"I..."

Slade watched Tymo's lips move slightly, leaned even closer.

"A copper," he whispered, "name of..."

"Go on, lad. What's he called?" Slade waited, and then asked, "Was it Phil Gibson? Or Dom Thompson? Maybe Jimmy Akhtar? Eh? Well who the fuck was it!"

Tymo's body tensed slightly for a moment, then relaxed utterly, as he finally breathed out. Unfortunately, sometimes living on the edge called for dying on the edge too.

Slade looked at his face. Looked at Shack. Then back at Tymo. "Lad?" he said. "Don't you fucking die on me now!" He slapped Tymo's face and there was no reaction. "I said answer me, you bastard."

"He's dead," Shack said.

Slade pointed a finger, and spat, "Don't you fucking interrupt me." And he punched Tymo in the stomach, a barrelling blow that had no effect other than to expel more blood from the wound. "Bastard!"

"Let's go, chief."

Slade turned around quickly and pointed a gun right at Shack's forehead.

"Chief?"

"Shut up, Monty." Slade smiled at Shack, "Do you know who told him about our job?"

Shack said nothing. He merely looked past the gun into Slade's narrowed eyes.

"Last chance."

"He never mentioned them to me."

"What about those names? Recognise any of them?"

Shack considered for a moment, and then shook his head. "No, Mr Crosby."

"They're coppers, Shack. They worm their way into our groups, and they taint them; they gather information about them. Only these bastards are going one step further." He jerked the gun, and Shack's eyes widened for just a moment. "These bastards are trying to take us all out. That's a different ball game entirely. And we all need to work together on this to stop them." Slade paused. "Am I getting through your fucking thick skull?"

"Yes, Mr Crosby."

"Yes Mr Crosby," he mocked. "Is that all you can fucking say?"

"If I hear of anything, I'll let you know."

"Remember today as the day I let you live. I saved your life, Shack, and you owe me."

They had to wait another fifteen minutes for the trench in Jagger's calf to be cleaned and dressed. There was no skin left surrounding the wound to stitch to, Gryz had said, so he'd just have to keep it clean and apply new dressings frequently.

When Jagger hobbled out of the surgery, he saw Shack dragging the bodies of his men out of the glow from the security light, ready he guessed, for a pickup truck to come and get them for disposal later. His own team, already in a pickup truck with a black holdall full of cash, waited for him to climb into Slade's car before following them away.

Chapter Thirty

The Moonlight and a Window Seat

IT WAS LATE AND his body was crying out to rest. His mind however, had other plans. He lay the in the darkness, watching the faint slice of blue-white moonlight creeping around the gap between the curtains and the window frame. Ros was on his mind and for the hundredth time in the two hours he'd lain there, he told himself to forget it, at least for tonight. Nothing he could do about it now, was there? May as well sleep and think on it tomorrow.

Oh okay.

No chance.

He punched the pillow and sat up, turned on the lamp and lit a cigarette. And then it hit him. It was almost something physical. Why she wanted him to come and work with her at MCU. All that talk she gave him about being sorry for not contacting him over the last two years was utter bollocks. Wait; that wasn't entirely correct. She was sorry, he felt sure of it now, but ever since he had started working there, there was something wrong, some slight misalignment of the old Ros that betrayed her weak attempts at normality.

And that's what gave the game away.

Eddie climbed out of bed, slid a pair of boxers on and went into the kitchen. Cigarette dangling from his mouth, he put the kettle on and searched for a teaspoon.

She wanted him with her at MCU for protection. Not protection against anyone there per se; but she just wanted him close. She was under threat and now he'd worked out who that threat was. This was the worst possible situation as far as Eddie was concerned. If the threat was someone at work, sorting it out wouldn't be too difficult, because if Eddie couldn't smooth things over with words, he was quite handy with fists, and either method would do so long as it got the desired result.

But her problem was nowhere near work. Her problem was the bastard she slept with. That was why she was so desperately upset that day in McDonald's when he knew, he knew, there was something she wasn't telling him. She had been so upset because the timing was awful. She married this Brian fella because she was afraid of being a spinster, she didn't want to be alone – understandable, it wasn't always the jar of honey it was made out to be. But she only married him because he was pleasant and he was available and, no doubt, he was like a wasp around the Ros honey pot.

The kettle clicked off and Eddie made coffee, stirred it with a knife, and threw the cigarette end in the sink before lighting another.

Then he ambled into the lounge and sat in the window seat, the moonlight slipping past the curtains in here too to give his blank eyes something to play with as his mind toiled on with the problem.

If she'd known that Eddie's marriage had died roughly the same time she bailed out of CSI... well, wasn't being big-headed when he suggested to himself that she would have said yes to him in the blink of an eye. Not at all; Ros had made it quite clear they had a good, deep, friendship, and both of them had known it would have grown into something much more.

Ros had thought that if she went back to her old life, then she could expect just that, her old life, where she shared

Eddie, and always came off second best, always got the crumbs.

Frustration. So, he guessed, that was part of her problem; it was a mental thing, a feeling she'd been cheated out of something because fate and luck – The Laws of Fuck – had thought it a splendid trick to play on her. The other part of the problem was Brian.

Eddie was convinced of it.

It explained so much. It explained partly why she was always so shitty with Eddie. It explained why she didn't like being touched.

Question was, what was he going to do about it; how was he going to help her? And knowing how very proud she was, would she even accept help, would she even admit to there being a problem?

Chapter Thirty-one

The Flowers, The Tablets, and The Briefing

— One —

TODAY WAS A GOOD suit day. Normally, Tyler wore jeans and a leather jacket, or a cheap suit if he was on collections – he liked to look the part but wouldn't risk ruining a good suit with blood should things turn nasty.

But today he'd worn a good suit, one he kept for special occasions. Today was a special occasion. Today, he was going to nail Blake's killer.

"Paying by card or cash, love?" She looked up at him and pushed her half-moon spectacles back up the bridge of her nose for the fifth time since he'd been in the shop.

"Cash."

"She must be a special lady," she smiled at him from across the counter as she curled some pink ribbon and interlaced it with the roses.

"How much?"

The smile drifted away. Embarrassed, she cleared her throat, "Forty-five, please, love."

He slid fifty across to her and made a grab for the flowers before she could waste any more of his time with frilly bits that he didn't ask for or want.

"How about a card, dear, for your sentiments?"

He sighed, "Okay."

She slipped a small card into an envelope and tucked it inside the paper. Then took the cash. When she looked up the door was closing behind him.

According to Google and Thompson, there were seven bookkeepers in the Castleford postal area. Hitting the sweet spot at the first attempt had a slim fourteen per cent chance of success. But there was no other way to go about it, except trying them.

Castleford had once been a mining town with a flour mill at its centre next to the River Aire. Of course, like everything else these days, the flour mill had gone and Castleford was turned from a place of hard-working colliers and millers into one big shopping centre with a dozen pubs and a handful of nightclubs.

Tyler parked at the kerb outside the first address that the satnav brought him to. It looked just like a council house. It was an end-terraced building with a regular front door and regular lounge window. "Fuck," he said. But reason suggested he check it out along with all the rest, because if he wasn't thorough, he'd never find her.

As he was about to step out of the BMW, a thought suddenly struck him. What if, after being raped, this Angela woman, this Angel666, had called one of her friends from work and told them all about it? He would be setting himself up for a fall then. And while this thought rumbled along the stony path inside his mind, a second followed it: she hasn't called the police, so why would she call a friend?

"That's bollocks," he said. People were strange and there was no telling what they'd do after being traumatised. Anyway, even if she had been raped, she might not call the police because as well as being a victim, she was now a murderer. There were no answers to these suggestions, and the thoughts became dust and left him as he climbed out and locked the car.

Over the door was a small hand-painted sign proclaiming, AAB Bookkeeping Services. He wasn't sure if he should knock, but he went straight in, forcing himself to look hopeful and happy, instead of hopeful and vengeful. It was a tough act.

A middle-aged woman stared at him from behind a wide old teak-effect desk.

"Help you?"

"Oh, my name's Blake and I wondered if Charlie was about." He made no effort to conceal the flowers.

She looked at him sideways on. "Charlie?"

"She does work here, doesn't she?"

"No one by the name Charlie works here."

"Angela, her name's Angela." He smiled but it was painful.

"Then why did you call her Charlie?"

Tyler let the smile go; it was just too much work. "Does anyone called Angela or Charlie work here? Female."

"No."

By the fifth attempt, he was about ready to go home. Only Slade's face kept him in the game; that, and the fact that the odds had now increased to thirty-three per cent.

He parked outside a rather more upmarket establishment than those before it. This had a full-length plate glass window with Williams and Collins Accountancy and Bookkeeping emblazoned across it in a fine gold font.

— Two —

"Kill me." Deep inside it was all black. There was no pain any more but the blackness was cold, not comforting. The sparkle had withered and fizzled, and then it had died. It would never come back. The man had raped her and he'd taken away the sparkle too. She had been a shy but bubbly kind of person two days ago, even a little dizzy at times, she would have admitted; but now she was a husk of blackness with no thoughts and no plans and no concept of life outside of the blackness.

Nothing really mattered any more.

"I did nothing wrong."

She had waited down by the stream until darkness had swept across the land, and then she had waited some more. Not for anything in particular, she was just afraid to leave her nest of bracken and the soft lullaby of the nearby stream.

She had watched his motionless figure as it had slowly become invisible against the darkening hillside on which it lay; the light had faded and the body was still there though she couldn't see it. And she grew cold. And she became hungry and thirsty. And she was in pain. But she waited. Scared to move. She had walked back through Garforth and all the way to The Spinney Nook to her car at nearly two in the morning.

And now she was home again, but it didn't feel like home. It didn't feel like anything. She had lain in bed for almost a day and a half, although she wasn't keeping count. Her head peered over the quilt, saw the daylight fighting through the curtains, and wondered again if she'd locked and bolted the front door. Somewhere near her feet, Panda kneaded the quilt and purred incessantly.

Charlie kicked out and the cat fled.

Charlie cried again, and her stinging eye, the one she couldn't see through properly, flared up with a raging heat again as the tears rolled. Her nose was bust, and flaking blood had set in the creases of her skin, and more of it lay in her bed; a reminder of the not so happy times with her one and only date in sixteen years.

This was all Michelle's fault. If she hadn't told her to try a dating site, none of this would have happened; if she'd kept her damned mouth shut and her nose out of other people's business, this pain she swam in wouldn't exist. She would be planning what to do with the rest of her holiday from work instead of wondering if twelve paracetamol was enough to kill herself with.

She didn't think it was. And the tears came again. There was no cure for this.

"I even drove to a pub. I wouldn't let him know my address."

It wasn't fair.

How long would it take to die?

— Three —

Ros had looked so gaunt this morning that it was scary. "You're a bit early for Halloween," Eddie said. Truth be told though, he didn't exactly feel like a million bucks himself this morning either.

"Up yours," Ros said.

Eddie slid his chair across to Ros's desk. She sighed and shoved aside the briefing notes for today's fun and frivolity. "What?"

"What do you mean, 'what'?"

"What do you want, Eddie?"

"I wondered if you were okay."

"I'm okay. I'm fucking wonderful. Now leave me alone."

"Wait, wait, hold on a minute." Eddie came even closer, bowing his head, elbows on the desk. "I thought we sorted out our troubles yesterday. What's bothering you today?"

Ros took a breath and turned to him.

Her eyes were puffy; a thin film of water seemed to shimmer across them. He'd taken the piss before with the Halloween comment, but actually, she did look horrific. "I'm sorry, I just didn't sleep too well last night."

"Oh," he said. "Anything I can do—"

"Okay, listen everybody, please." Everyone looked around to see Jeffery standing in the middle of the floor. "New assignments for some of you today."

Eddie groaned, Ros sat still and stared through her monitor, elsewhere it seemed. Across the far side of the desk, James Whitely and the old geezer, Duffy, stared at him; James with his marine's haircut that was, frankly, so unnaturally perfect that it must have been moulded that way and glued on, and Duffy resting his chin on a fist, eyes hovering somewhere near where Jeffery stood, but with no interest in them at all. Each blink, Eddie noticed, was longer than the previous one, until it seemed as though he was taking really short naps.

"Gang shooting in Harehills. Indoor and outdoor scenes. And one vehicle scene. It seems to have centred around a cash machine robbery within a Turkish tearoom. When the gang exited, another gang was waiting for them, and they opened fire.

"Outside the back of the premises, local CSI have found a vehicle in which there is a body. They also found a second dead male near the van, just outside the back entrance to the teashop, but I managed to convince them to tent it and walk away.

"Around the front of the premises is a further scene. No body though because ambulance found a pulse and took him to St James' where he was pronounced dead on arrival.

"I couldn't keep hold of the tearoom scene: that's down as a burglary and so falls within divisional CSI remit. However, under Operation Domino, we have the van and the two bodies. Needless to say, if OSU finds anything of value as they search the surrounding area, I want us to be their first port of call for evidence, okay?"

James nodded enthusiastically. "I'm on-call tonight, Jeffery, but count me in."

Jeffery smiled. "Ros, I want you to process the body in the van, then have the van recovered; James and Duffy will take the second body. When you're done there, get round the front, I want shots of that scene.

"Lisa Westmoreland will keep us posted of any developments, and I expect you to do the same. I have my phone if you need me for anything. DI Taylor and his designates will be exhibits officers. And I want full Niche compliance when you get back – we have to link in with division on this one." Then he looked directly at Eddie, "You'll be on the other scene we spoke of yesterday, okay?"

Eddie nodded.

"You okay with that, Ros?"

She just smiled at Jeffery, and that was all the response she gave.

Then Jeffery stepped up to Eddie, leaned in closer. "There's intelligence to suggest that the Crosbys killed Tony and his wife. The two brothers did it personally." He stared into Eddie as though making sure the penny had dropped.

"Leave it to me, Jeffery."

— Four —

Considering this was MCU, Eddie was shocked at how blasé they were about security. It wasn't this slack even out at division. He walked along corridors and down the stairs into the foyer, looked at Miss Moneypenny for a second, and then turned left towards the stock room and stores. He passed half a dozen people along the way and no one asked who he was or where he was going. His ID card was jammed in his back pocket; he hated wearing it around his neck on a lanyard; damned thing kept banging into him, generally being in the way and annoying the shit out of him.

Eddie took a right, slurped coffee from a flask and found the door marked Store. Next to it was a serving hatch, and a small bell. Eddie peeked inside. All the lights were on, but there was no one at home. "Hello?"

He waited, pushed the bell. "Hello?" Nothing.

He tried the door but found it locked.

"Fucking great."

Eddie checked his watch. Almost ten, and he wanted to crack on with the scene, not stand here all frigging day looking at the carpet. He looked up and down the corridor, then he placed his coffee down on the counter and scrambled through the hatch like a burglar through a transom.

In under three minutes, Eddie had found the aisle he needed, found the plastic storage box he needed, and found the property he needed. All courtesy of a property number and a decent filing system. There was still no sign of a storeman when he got back to the hatch. So he climbed back through the hole, grabbed his coffee and returned to the office to collect his stuff.

Eddie had been given a blue Vivaro van. It wasn't his own, but he was the only one who was ever going to choose it. And he chose it because it looked like a beaten-up piece of old shit that had escaped from a scrapyard. The aircon worked, and one of the electric windows did too, so it suited him fine. There was no police radio fitted, the tax disc was a real one, and the number plates were real too, not like the usual undercover police vehicles that still had the tell-tale signs. In the logbook, kept hidden in a tray under the driver's seat, Eddie could see no one had driven this old girl in more than two months. And that more or less settled it for Eddie. This was his van. He liked it because no one else seemed to; a kindred spirit.

It was kitted out in the back as an obs van; seats, blacked-out windows, and a small desk. In between it and the meshed off cab area was his kit storage space, accessed by a sliding door. It had his forensic kit, camera, laptop, foul weather gear, and most importantly of all, coffee making facilities.

Eddie climbed aboard and opened the window. He slid his shades on and lit a cigarette.

Eddie hit the road, heading for Alwoodley on the north eastern tip of Leeds, in the heart of his old CSI division.

— Five —

Tyler made sure his tie was straight, and walked into the office. It was the size of his dad's living room, with three desks pushed against the wall and a mirror over the far side that reminded him of the old westerns where the town saloon always had a mirror over the bar. Except this one didn't proclaim Jack Daniels as the new medicine, this one was a replica of the plate glass window. Next to it were twenty or so awards and certificates from some guild or another, telling potential clients what safe hands their accounts would be in.

Still, he thought, it was a league above the last couple of dumps he'd been in.

"Hello, sir. Can I help you?"

Her name badge proclaimed the ginger-haired woman who sat behind a new-fangled desk with two flat-screen monitors obscuring the best bits, as Michelle.

"Well," he smiled his best smile, a cross between I-know-what-I'm-doing and I'm-very-shy-and-humble. It said, I am safe! "I wonder if I might ask if Angela works here? Angela... goes by the name of Charlie." He looked hopefully at her. Made sure she could see the flowers.

Her eyes lit up. "Charlie, oh yes, Charlie works here." She trailed off, eyes full of pink ribbons and yellow flowers and green bits, "Are you..." she looked around and then leaned a little closer, smile on her face, "Are you the new boyfriend?"

He smiled in return, "Well," he blushed, "I am, yes. This is quite embarrassing really—"

"No, not at all—"

"I lost my phone," he whispered, as though disclosing something horrific. "It has Charlie's details in it, so I couldn't ring her."

Michelle smiled at him, almost falling in love with him herself.

"I knew she worked as a bookkeeper... So, well I thought I might leave these here for her."

"Or you could just take them round to her." Michelle leaned forward to get a closer look at the bouquet.

"No, he couldn't." In the archway that led to a small staircase beyond the back of the shop, presumably to an upstairs series of offices where Scrooge and Marley worked, stood a short, dumpy woman who looked like she'd been stung by a whole nest of wasps.

Tyler's mood swung low as she stepped forward. Michelle shrank back into her seat.

"You may leave them here, and we shall contact her." She stared at Tyler, and then gave a quick reproachful glance at Michelle. It was like a slap; Michelle turned quickly away.

"Ah, that's very kind of you. If you're sure it's not too much trouble."

"Nonsense, hand them over."

"Did you enjoy your date?" Michelle dared to speak.

"Oh it was wonderful, thank you yes. She's a fantastic lady."

"She is! I knew you'd like her," Michelle stood again, broad grin taking up her whole face, hands clasped together as though in prayer. "And her hair, did you like her hair?"

Fuck, thought Tyler. Whatever you do, don't ask me what colour it was. "Absolutely."

"And the colour, what did you think of the colour? I chose it for her."

"Well, what can I say. It was beautiful, but I confess," he smoothed his hair, "I was admiring her face."

"Oh yeah, anything else?" Michelle was almost, but not quite, cheeky.

The fat prude cleared her throat, and Michelle recoiled again. "May we do anything else for you, Mr..?"

"No, you've done enough, thank you very much."

"I trust she has your details?"

"Oh yes, yes she does." His cheeks were aching, and then he looked at the flowers, a frown closing in, giving his smiling cheeks a break, "How long do you suppose they'll last, I mean before they begin to look second hand?"

"Difficult to say. I'm a vegetable woman myself." She stared at him. He felt decidedly uncomfortable.

"Right," he said, backing towards the door. "Well, you've been most kind. Thank you very much."

Tyler turned and headed out of the shop, closed his eyes and took a deep breath once the door had closed behind him.

Chapter Thirty-two

Back at the Murder House

— One —

Ros ARRIVED AT THE scene by herself. James had tagged along with Duffy and that was just fine by her. Today, all she wanted was to be left alone.

She'd had precisely no sleep at all last night. It was difficult, she found, with the threat of a knife in your throat. And she wondered how the hell she would ever sleep again. It made no sense; all the stuff Brian ranted on about last night, beginning with the almighty punch in her stomach, and ending with him kneeling over her, pressing a blade into her windpipe. It wasn't like him; he was placid. He was... well, whatever he was, he wasn't a lunatic.

Until now.

Now he was very much a lunatic. And living with a lunatic equalled no sleep last night, and none tonight. None ever again. She shook her head as she pulled up to the cordon, but didn't get out. Her desire for work today, she had to admit, was less than normal.

She had to think of something before the shift was out. She had to go somewhere, find somewhere to stay without seeming needy. Nobody liked a needy person; it made them wonder what was going to befall them too. A hotel maybe?

No, no hotel. Brian will simply come to the office the next day asking awkward questions. And how's it going to look when you're having a domestic in reception?

Almost in a daydream, Ros climbed from the van and, unusually, the first thing she did was get a scene suit out and put it on together with the hood and face mask. The place was heaving with press and TV cameras, and the last thing she wanted was to be someone's entertainment for the morning. Anonymity restored, she crossed the cordon and signed in, then walked across to the rusty blue van.

All around her, shutters clicked and frontmen talked into cameras, holding fluffy microphones before them. This was going to be very awkward due to the press being so intrusive. Across from the van, CSI had erected a scene tent over the exposed body of a dead male, and even that was attracting a fair bit of attention. James and Duffy nodded at her.

The police had closed Harehills Lane at the front of the Turkish tearoom to carry out a fingertip search by suited members of the OSU, looking for shell casings and such. More press stood at either end of the cordon.

And the traffic from the closed road was rolling slowly right past her scene. Ros closed her eyes; this was going to be a nightmare.

She had, on occasion, sought the cooperation of the media by offering them a photo shoot of her performing some mundane, meaningless task that didn't throw focus on the main job or bring attention to a body or a bloodbath. She scanned the faces; there were just too many of them, and she would get no consensus from them.

There was a body lying across the seats of the van, and across the far window was a curtain of blood and spattering of brain, and she didn't want the press photographing that. Yet she had to get to it, had to work through it.

Then Ros had an idea. She smiled and went to see the OSU sergeant.

— Two —

"And it's got a tracker fitted to it, so no fucking about." Slade stared at him. "Do you understand me; are we clear?"

Jagger nodded. "I know asking you to trust me won't get you to trust me, but... you can trust me, you know."

"We'll see, lad," Slade said. "Takes years to earn my trust."

Monty reached in and handed Jagger a fat envelope. "Harbour master is Geoff Willoughby. Speak to no one else, okay?"

Jagger nodded. "Geoff Willoughby, right."

"And when you've collected it, you ring me, let me know it all went smooth, and then get your arse straight back here. No speeding," Slade warned, "I do not want that boot searching, you get me?"

"I got you."

Slade slammed the door and jerked a thumb. Jagger selected drive and the Mercedes glided away.

— Three —

Eddie had a cigarette dangling from his mouth as he flicked through James Whitely's report on the murder scene. His van idled on the driveway in front of a door that now had a West Yorkshire Police security sheet across it. As further protection, there was a WYP alarm installed too, the entry code stamped on a tag attached to the house keys.

James had been thorough, spending two whole days there; occupied mainly with photography, views of each room, views of the dead woman, and views of the landing including Tony Lambert himself.

And it seemed Eddie's advice to him hadn't been lost. He'd taken footwear impressions from the bannister rail, and had managed to get the slip marks off the landing floor with some degree of success. At least they all now knew it was a double murder. He shook his head at how close it came to being a murder-suicide, and he wondered what the consequences of that would have been.

Apart from the murderer walking around free, laughing his bollocks off, there was a man and a woman in that house who would have been stigmatised. And who knew what effect a death certificate labelled as suicide instead of one labelled as homicide would have had on the wills and probate and insurance and all that other nonsense that leaves the grieving relatives worse off. And of course, what of the relatives? They at least knew their son wasn't a weak-willed suicide "victim" who chose to take his poor wife with him; he was now a hero, and his portrait would hang in his local nick, and his grave would be tended.

Amazing what a difference a "homi-" could make in place of a "sui-".

Eddie opened the window and flicked the cigarette end away. And in the rear-view mirror, he saw a neighbour walking up the driveway towards him. He closed his eyes, cursed himself for not just getting out of the van when he arrived and getting inside the house.

"Hello again."

Eddie opened his eyes and looked at her. She was familiar, but he couldn't quite place her.

"You're a detective, right?"

"I couldn't detect water in a swimming pool," he said, still confused.

"You don't remember me, do you?"

"Thanks for that."

"What?"

"I hate that song. Hot Chocolate."

Now she looked confused. "You got me there."

"I thought you were quoting lyrics at me." He stared at the folder still open on his lap, and slowly closed it. "It's going to stay in my head all day now. Shit."

"Shall we start again?"

"Are you a neighbour?"

"Don't think so," she said, "why, where do you live?"

Eddie blinked. "This is surreal." He stopped the engine, climbed out with the folder and slid open the side door.

"Are you here about the murders?"

That stopped him dead. "No," he said calmly, "I'm a decorator."

She laughed, even patted his shoulder and then stood back to let him get his kit out of the van. "No you're not. I saw you here that day, when it all kicked off."

Ah. That's who she was. The reporter. The one who was sorry for his loss. "I, er, I didn't recognise you," he said, clicking his fingers. "Suit, and outside broadcast truck." He turned and really saw her properly for the first time. She was in a loose – but not too loose, he noted – T-shirt and jeans, a pair of scabby trainers too. Her hair was tied back but a good swath of it had broken loose and curled around her neck. "Moron?" he pointed at her.

"Close. Moran, Sarah Moran."

"Ah, sorry 'bout that."

"I get it all the time."

Eddie raised an eyebrow.

"Call me Sarah," she smiled. "You are here about the murders though?"

"Excuse me?"

"I'm sorry, I didn't mean to pry."

"Of course you did; you're a reporter. I've worked with reporters before. You can't help it; it's your job."

"Hey, I'm human too."

"Only under the scales, dear."

"Ouch."

"Okay, look. I'm sorry. I am here about the deaths. And I don't mean to be rude, but I have a lot to do."

"I thought it would have been sewn up by now."

"No you didn't." Eddie locked the van door.

"What makes you say that?"

He took out the evidence bag, shook out a set of keys and unlocked the steel shutter over the front door and swung it aside. "Because you're here."

"Ah. My turn to blush."

"Blush? I haven't blushed."

"You blushed when you called me a moron."

He unlocked the front door and then said, "Excuse me." As he pushed open the door a loud beeping came from inside. He stepped into the hall, and then stopped dead. "Fuck."

"You don't know the code, do you?"

"Now I'm blushing."

"That thing is going to be loud, isn't it?"

He nodded, took the keys out of the lock. "Ah!" And then he ran into the lounge. The beeping stopped and moments later he was back outside, collecting his things.

"Okay, can I ask you something?"

"If it's to do with this," nodded over his shoulder, "then you're wasting your time."

"Why did they tell everyone it was a suicide when it was a double murder?"

He stared at her. How the bloody hell did she know that?

"There was too much police activity and for too long for it to be a straightforward suicide."

"And this week's lottery numbers are?"

She laughed and Eddie slid the van door closed.

"I'm going to have to be careful what I think around you, aren't I?"

"So, can you tell me?"

"I just do as I'm asked, Ms Moran."

"Sarah, please."

"Ms Moran, I can't tell you anything. Sorry."

"How come you're not in uniform today?"

Eddie hauled his kit to the front door. "I work for a different department now."

Chapter Thirty-three

Flowers and Blood

— One —

I<small>T WAS TWELVE THIRTY</small> and the wait had been horrible.

But eventually, Michelle had exited Williams and Collins Accountancy and Bookkeeping and closed the door behind her. She worked part-time. Tyler liked to think he knew she was part-time because she was happier than the others who worked under The Vegetable Lady. It made the whole going to work experience a lot more tolerable, easier to dust off the day's crap.

Of course, he could have been wrong, but it didn't matter; he would have waited until five or five-thirty, whatever time they closed. They had the flowers which meant Charlie worked there, and Michelle wouldn't see those flowers go to waste. Besides, Michelle would want to know all about the date with Blake; every detail. And Tyler knew that Charlie hadn't been in touch because there were no tears, and there were no daggers pointing at his chest, and because no one had called the police.

Everything was tickety-boo.

Michelle walked to a small car perhaps a hundred yards away and climbed aboard. Tyler started the BMW and prepared to follow her.

———

Twenty minutes later, Tyler had followed her to a small and picturesque village in North Leeds called Barwick-in-Elmet. It was a maze of tiny roads, and most of them seemed to terminate in the village square where a tall maypole took centre stage and cast a short shadow in the midday heat. Tyler wasn't paying much attention to the maypole or to the surroundings though; he was intent on staying within sight of Michelle without seeming to follow her. It was difficult to do in the small lanes where very often there was room for only one car to pass.

Eventually, Michelle turned down a two-lane road and promptly stopped at a row of old farm labourers' cottages. Tyler carried along the road for twenty yards past the junction, parked, and stepped out of the car.

———

Michelle grabbed the flowers off the passenger seat and smelled them one last time. They were wonderful, and Charlie was a lucky girl. If only Ben were so romantic. She was lucky to get a Creme Egg and a fart out of him these days. But Blake seemed like a wonderful man; tall and muscular, well-dressed and a rock-star face. Wow.

Daydreaming over with, Michelle got out of the car, locked it and headed up the path to Charlie's front door. There were still milk bottles on the doorstep, and mail hanging out of the letterbox. These things didn't attract Michelle's attention; not yet anyway. First, she rang the bell, and waited patiently. There was no reply, but she thought she could hear movement inside.

She rang the bell again and this time raised her hand to the glass and peered through the lounge window. Then she looked up at the first-floor windows.

Now she was beginning to get a little worried, and it was then she noticed the milk and the mail. And then she looked towards the road, and saw Charlie's car. "Strange," she said. Then she walked around the back of the cottage and peered into the kitchen. Nearby was a playground with kids shouting and screaming; everything seemed normal, yet something was wrong. It took a long time for Michelle to acknowledge that, but now that it was here, she shivered. She banged on the door this time, and could hear Panda squeaking in the kitchen, and then he appeared on the windowsill rubbing against the glass. "Where's your mummy, Panda?" she said, stroking the glass. "Eh? Where's mummy?"

Mummy was lying in bed with her hands over her ears, her mouth wide open in a silent scream, and tears tracing weird tracks down her screwed up face. Someone was at the front door and Charlie thought she was going to explode with fear. She felt sick. She was breathing quickly, shallowly, and she was sweating yet felt cold. She was screaming in her head so loudly she thought she was going mad, and when finally she took her hands away from her ears, there were strands of hair caught under the bloodied nails. The hair was the colour of ginger biscuits, and it was the colour chosen by Michelle.

Michelle had started all this.

And then the knocking and the banging at the front door stopped, and Charlie's arms flopped by her sides and her breathing slowed a little. Her nose was still blocked and her eye, where he'd punched her, wasn't working properly; she could only see slight blurs out of it. And she was sore and she daren't go to the bathroom and she shivered and she wanted the blackness to come back; the cold yet homely blackness where nothing could touch her, and before she could think of anything else there was a knock at the back door.

Charlie froze. And then the nerves bit deeply again and she screwed her face into a mask of fear and curled up into a ball, wishing the whole world would just leave her alone. She wanted to die.

There was no reply at the back door either.

Michelle swallowed and suddenly became quite nervous. Something was definitely wrong. No way would Charlie go out and leave Panda all alone for very long. And the curtains round the front were still drawn and the mail and milk were uncollected. The phone was switched off – she'd tried before leaving work. And her car was still there, so she hadn't gone out for a drive. "What the hell's going on?"

Michelle didn't know what to do. She bit her lip and wandered back around to the front of the house, looked up at the curtains across the windows again. Perhaps she's ill? No, Charlie is never ill. Perhaps she's in the bath with her earphones in.

It was possible, but she'd never leave all the curtains closed, never leave the mail in the door.

Reluctantly, Michelle went back to her car and sat in silence wondering what to do. And then she felt guilty, because if Charlie was ill and was trying to rest in bed, she might have disturbed her. Michelle returned the bouquet to the passenger seat and started the car. She drove away. Had she looked in her rear-view mirror, she would have seen a good-looking man in a smart suit walking up the road to Charlie's house.

— Two —

The OSU sergeant reversed the large police van right across the only view the press had of the blue van with the corpse inside. There were mutterings as the sergeant disappeared back to his men, but it allowed Ros to work largely unobserved. The last thing she wanted was to have gruesome pictures all over the tabloids.

She began with photography of the van's exterior, all four corners, before concentrating on the front driver's side, its smashed window glass, and the shell casing that had rolled a few feet under the van. Once it was packaged, she could move on to opening the van door and making an assessment of how easy it might be to remove the body – and from which side.

Her mind though, wandered often, and more than once she found herself with her hands on her hips looking at nothing in particular, mind slowly trundling back from thoughts of Brian and his knife.

And there was always another thought that hurried back after its big brother, always late back into its box. It was of Eddie. And it was the reason she had gone to such extremes to make sure he came and worked for MCU after all her efforts to keep him out of her life.

She opened the driver's door gently, but despite the care, more glass fell inwards. He had wet himself and the van stank after a few hours of warm sunshine. Already the flies had begun congregating on the man's head and several were crawling along his fingers, disappearing under the cuff of his sleeve. Ros shuddered.

She pushed the door to and then took her camera around the other side, scene suit crinkling as she went. This door was locked, and she closed her eyes at the thought of leaning across him to unlock the damned thing. And then she wondered if the sliding door was unlocked, tried it and it slid back, allowing her to reach in and pop the button on the passenger door. Her glove came away reddened.

Eddie was her defence if things got too hot at home.

She hated herself for thinking that, really she did. Eddie was, in fact, a bloody good friend, and to use him like that – to label him as her defence – was a horrid thing to do. He was her... she shook her head. What was he? He was her best friend. He was almost her lover, very past tense. But he cared for her as she did for him.

The Brian situation. If only she could bring herself to tell Eddie about it. Of course she couldn't, who was she trying to kid? She'd shat on Eddie from a massive height, and now she wanted him to put on his armour and come to her rescue. "Silly bitch!" she said.

The flies were having a ball in the hole in the side of the man's head. His brains had congealed in the blood on the glass, had caused streaks down it, bits of hair stuck to the glass, and bits of glass stuck in his hair and in his face. His right eye had vanished, no idea where it was, just a gaping hole that moved in the midday sun as flies hopped about inside it, looking to deposit their eggs.

It seemed this was the better side to pull him out of. And there was no way she was going to tape him and generally mess about with him while he was still slumped across the seats like that. It was much better, much neater to get him out, get him inside a tent so no one could see, and take all the necessary samples in the cool shade.

And then she drifted back to what she'd said about Eddie being her protection. How presumptuous was that? Poor Eddie might not want to get involved with you, she thought. He might, and quite rightly, think you were using him as a shield against Brian. And whoa, what do you mean "if things get too hot at home"? What was last night exactly, a little warm? What is hot then? Is hot having a twelve-inch blade poking out of your back? Is that hot enough?

No, I think having a knife held to your throat is quite hot enough.

Yet there was something about Brian too; the way he seemed capable of manipulating her when she was at her weakest. Of course, he made her weak with his threats and his violence, but then he'd try to speak to her like a rational man having a debate about politics. He was mesmerising sometimes, and she felt compelled to take him at his word, compelled to blame herself. But wait a minute, she reasoned; didn't you throw a bucket of cold water over him while he was asleep?

I did, she conceded. But does that give him the justification to hold a fucking knife at my throat and speak to me as though he's a psycho? Does it? I don't think it does.

Yet last night, she'd have said that it did give him the right, the justification – that he'd been goaded into it, and he was acting rationally. Something about him, the soft way he spoke to her, the words he used, he was like a hypnotist. Jesus.

So, what do we do then?

Move out? I don't think so, it's my house–

But it's not safe there.

It's safe! Just the man who also lives there is not safe.

Better think of something, kiddo.

"Need a hand?"

Ros screamed, and almost put her gloved hands to her face – but was glad she didn't as her fingers were covered in blood.

"Sorry," James said.

Ros closed her eyes and took a moment to compose herself. "Yes, please. Tent."

— Three —

Eddie sat in the lounge taking a closer look at James's photographs of the crime scene. From a photographic point of view, they were quite good; nice use of bounce flash, a little over exposed in places, but good enough for court. From a scene examiner's point of view, they were in the average bracket. There were standard quarter shots of each room, but there was no detail, no real close-up shots of, for example, the drag marks on the landing floor, the footwear mark on the bannister rail.

Eddie lit a cigarette and threw the pictures to one side. If there was still anything left to be found, then he was going to have to begin from scratch. He didn't wear a scene suit; he didn't see the point because eighty-five per cent of him believed there was nothing more to be gained from this scene, it had given up all its secrets already, and the other fifteen per cent was just along for the ride. Okay, he reasoned, dropping ash on the floor and heeling it into the pile, there was still a slim chance that James had missed something in the original part of the exam – he was not perfect, after all.

Actually, he lied. The fifteen per cent along for the ride was only ten per cent. The remaining five per cent knew there was something else.

Westmoreland wanted that something else – no, no, wait; it was Jeffery who wanted that something else and the request had come from Cooper who worked for Crime Division. And that was understandable because Tony Lambert was Cooper's man on the inside. He was the guy who collected evidence against the gangs. Eddie shook his head; he couldn't imagine a more dangerous profession. He'd seen the gang's handiwork and it wasn't pretty.

He exhaled, and looked at the burnt down cigarette. "Where am I gonna put you?" He went through the kitchen and found the ground floor toilet, and dropped the butt into the water. Then he took the Maglite from his belt loop and looked at the toilet flush lever. He could clearly see glove marks on the shiny chrome but couldn't tell if they were leather or nitrile. So either the murderer used the toilet, or more likely James did, choosing the downstairs one because it was farthest away from the action. He shone the torch at the bare floor and could see no Adidas Wince, just lots of smudged "scene examiner" marks. "Tut tut, James," he said, and flushed the butt away.

Eddie stopped in the kitchen, looked around; saw how many cups and glasses were out, checked the dishwasher, the sink, looking for things that just didn't add up. The scenario he had in mind was of the two murderers knocking or ringing the bell, and Tony admitting them. And why would he let them in? He'd let them in because he knew them, and even if he thought his cover was blown because they'd shown up at his private home address, he wouldn't risk it by refusing them entry.

"Then what?"

This was a tougher question. "How do you get from letting two men in, to them killing your wife and hanging you from the fucking ceiling?"

They knew something. They had to, because they'd had the balls to even show up here. So they knew he was a copper. "Who told them?"

If they knew who he was, why risk killing him here where his wife might have overheard and tried to ring the police? Why not wait until he went out where it would be safer for them?

"They had to kill him quick. He had information about them."

He strode through the dining room and back into the lounge. It was swish; deep pile carpet, marble hearth, fake real-flame fire, huge flat-screen TV, plush sofas. "Very nice," he whispered. "And since he was a copper, and he'd managed to worm his way into their little gang, they wondered if there were any other coppers they should know about."

If that were true, why would they kill his missus? "Because he refused to tell them." Not for fucking long though, I bet, he thought. Once they started being serious, he'd have talked until his throat fell out. Which it very nearly did, he recalled.

Nothing in the lounge.

The stairs were carpeted, the bannister rail covered in aluminium powder. Nothing here either.

So far, it looked as though the eighty-five per cent part was spot on. But Eddie wouldn't leave just yet. He walked straight past the landing where he had found the good Mr Lambert suspended by the neck, and into the bedroom. It was a murder scene, but it still felt like someone's home. It was full of private stuff, get-well cards across the dressing table, scattered around silver photo frames of Tony and her, and of a dog they used to have, and of parents too. There were make-up bins, a special tray that held a pair of hair-straighteners. A stainless steel bin on the floor, a pair of furry slippers under the comfy chair over in the corner. This was a happy room. Once.

"He's spilled the beans, he's screaming for them to leave, but for some reason they don't. Because he's a copper. They're still here and they're serious about ending Mr and Mrs Lambert. Who gets it first?

"Has to be her," he said to the empty room. "Even if she's a heavy sleeper, she's going to wake up when they slip the noose over his head and he starts thrashing about. Unless he was unconscious. No, not unconscious. He'd be too heavy to move then."

He reasoned, it was the wife who got to the finishing line first. And maybe they used her death as a punishment or a carrot for more info.

"In which case, he'd be here watching."

Eddie shook his head; he couldn't think of anything worse than watching some bastard throttle your wife. It must have been awful.

"And how much would you struggle?" He'd be a handful for any one man to hold him steady. And how would you hold him steady, how would you control all that bucking and thrashing?

That took some thinking about. He placed himself in different locations in the room, trying to work out where to watch the grizzly strangulation from, where would give the least obstructed of views. Given that the killer would be at the far side of the bed where she was found, anywhere over this side would be good, he concluded. Except the doorway, because of the bedside table lamps. No, he'd be further into the room, and he'd be cuffed at the back.

"If it was me," he whispered, "I'd have him on his knees, and I'd control him by lifting his arms out behind him." And then he shook his head. No, that wouldn't work; there's nothing to stop him from standing, or from just falling forward so he wouldn't have to look. And once he was on the floor, how are you going to get him to stand so you can walk him out there and hang him?

"Bear hug. Even though he'll still thrash..."

Eddie stopped talking to himself. He was standing in the centre of the room, maybe five feet from the bed, a perfect place from which to watch your wife being strangled to death. Eddie put himself in Tony's position, hands behind his back, a horror show of incalculable terror playing out before his eyes, unable to prevent it. But he tries to prevent it.

On the carpet directly between Eddie's feet was something that shouldn't have been there. Tiny. Something easily missed.

Chapter Thirty-four

Hide, Charlie, Hide

— One —

TYLER WATCHED HER DRIVE away, and as he walked, his cold eyes fell on the end-terraced house he now knew belonged to Charlie. He walked quickly, pulling on his leather gloves, and aiming initially for the front door. But it was too exposed, even with all the shrubs in the front garden to protect him from view. He changed course and made his way around the side of the house, convinced the stupid bitch was home despite not answering the door to Michelle.

She would be scared, no doubt, hiding in the cellar or in a cupboard somewhere, afraid to even venture outside the safety of her house. She'd be too scared to even answer the door. At that moment, Tyler hated Blake and was glad the dumb bastard was dead, but he couldn't be seen to leave his murder unavenged; family honour and all that.

He reached the back corner of the house and peered around quickly to make sure there were no neighbours watching, and then walked to the kitchen window, peered in, and saw no movement, nothing of interest.

She was in, he was sure.

And there was another reason why she wouldn't answer the door to Michelle, even if she'd known it was Michelle out here and not the brother of the man she killed. She wouldn't answer for the same reason she hadn't rung the police and for the same reason she hadn't rung work. Embarrassment. Rape could do that to some people. It made them feel worthless; as though it was all their own fault, as though they'd subliminally invited the attack.

Rape fucked people in more than one way.

There was no way Michelle could relax now. How could she sit down and watch TV all evening, pigging out on Ferrero Rocher and a bottle of Sainsbury's red, knowing that Charlie was... Was what?

Michelle brought her car to a halt and turned it around. At the very least she ought to ring the police, get them to come and check it out. Something was not right! And then, after pulling over at the kerb near Charlie's house, she thought about it again. Could you get into trouble for asking the police for help, and then finding out Charlie stayed at a friend's house last night and wasn't even home?

Get real. Charlie doesn't have any friends.

As she turned off the ignition, Michelle looked around and saw what looked very much like the man who'd given her these flowers, disappearing around the back of Charlie's house, pulling on some black gloves.

Tyler shook his head, disgusted at his brother. But now he was angry because he was having to clean up his fucking mess. He was going to drag a young woman out of her house so his father could kill her later, probably for a bit of sport as well as some kind of revenge – and he was a man not particularly well known for his good manners and sensitivity.

Tyler looked at the back door. It was made of wood and it was painted bright red. He aimed a foot at the cross beam and kicked.

The door held, and he had to kick it another three times before it burst inwards. A black and white cat appeared in the doorway, saw him, hissed, and ran out of the door. He stepped into the kitchen and ran through into the lounge, looked behind the settee, noticed a bunch of keys on the mantelpiece; house keys and car keys, they looked like. She was home then, for sure. And then he made for the stairs. He took them two at a time and was panting when he reached the first floor. And then he stood in her room, and he stared at the bed. "Fuck," he said. Within a stride or two he was at the wardrobes, pulling the doors open, shoving hanging garments aside.

In the bathroom, he yanked the shower curtain down, tapped the side panel on the bath with a foot and then began to grow really angry. On the floor was recently discarded underwear, red with blood, and a torn white thing, could have been a skirt. Tyler shook his head.

"Where the fuck..." and then he found the tight, curving staircase into the attic rooms. He checked them out, and in under a minute he was back in Charlie's bedroom, shaking his head, wondering where the hell she could be. She had to be in the house. Her keys were in the lounge, doors locked from the inside, front door even had a chain on. So where was she?

There was only one place left to look.

Tyler descended the stairs rather more quietly and walked into the kitchen. He looked around for the cellar door – all these old cottages had cellars, it's where they kept the coal in the old days – and then he saw her, standing by the sink, an open drawer nearby.

"If you come near me," she snarled, "I'll stab you, I swear to God."

Tyler smiled. "Hey, Michelle, no need for all this; I was just looking for her—"

"By kicking her door in and scaring her cat!"

"I just—"

"The police are on their way. They had a unit nearby, they said." She stared at him.

He could see the determination in her eyes, unblinking.

Did he believe her?

She didn't look away from his stare. She was focused.

Tyler licked his dry lips; he believed her. He had no choice but to try again later for the girl. He stepped out of the open door and disappeared around the side of the house.

— Two —

Eddie took out the magnifying glass from his kit box and knelt down over the mark. It certainly looked interesting, like a droplet of blood, but black.

"Only one way to find out." First job was photography, as always. Then he broke the seal on a sterile swab, moistened its tip with sterile water and swabbed out as much as he could. Then he checked it was blood by using the Kastle-Meyer presumptive test, rubbing the swab against a piece of filter paper, and then applying two drops of reagent followed by two drops of hydrogen peroxide. The filter paper immediately turned pink, so he was right on the money. To be doubly certain, he took out another kit, a Hexagon OBTI kit, to make sure the sample was human blood. This kit looked like a pregnancy test kit, and gave a positive reaction when two blue lines appeared in a small viewing screen. "Bingo," he smiled. "Human blood."

Eddie opened the front door and peered out. There was no one around. He breathed again and stepped outside the door, and unlocked the van. He'd loaded in the camera and most of his kit, and then she reappeared from somewhere round the back of the van.

"So who told them?"

Eddie jumped, put his hand over his chest. "Jesus!"

Sarah smiled. "Sorry."

"Sorry! I nearly shit my pants then."

She laughed and walked closer, trying to peer inside the house. "Well, who told them he was a copper?"

"Look, Miss Moran, I have no idea what you're talking about, and if—"

"He was killed by bad men, Mr Collins. His wife too—"

"How come you know so much?"

"So I'm right?" She smiled again. "I don't mean to put you on the back foot; I just watch a lot, I talk to people. Two bodies came out of there. And no one, except the person who put out the press release, thinks it's a murder-suicide. So the bad men got to him."

Eddie said nothing.

"Besides, my sister used to work with him. It was a long time ago, ten or more years, she says. She used to be a copper; they joined at the same time."

"Ah. So you've got a vested interest then?"

"She's just recently arrived back in Yorkshire. Tony Lambert was a very good friend of hers. So she made a few enquiries with her old colleagues." Now she wound her eyes wide open, made sure he was looking directly at her, as she said, "He was working undercover. Crime Division."

Eddie looked away quickly.

"I just wondered who'd told them."

Eddie looked at her blank-faced. "Tell me, and we'll both know," he said. Then he looked confused; why would he say something like that? It's what school kids say. It's what flustered school kids say! Was he flustered?

"Here." She handed him a business card.

"Thanks," he said, "but I'm trying to cut down. I don't have a wallet large enough for any more shit."

"It has my personal number on the back."

Eddie looked at the card. "You asking me out?"

She smiled again. "I'd like that very much, thanks."

"What?"

"It's a kind offer. I accept."

"Wait a minute... Look, you don't want to get mixed up with me. I have more baggage than Heathrow lost property."

"I like you."

"I'm not going to tell you anything."

"Shall we say seven?"

"Seven. Feel better?"

"Seriously, Mr Collins; I'd really like to have a drink with you."

"How did you know my name?"

She nodded at the stupid ID badge floating over his stomach.

"Look, I have to go—"

"I'll be at The Rhubarb Triangle at seven o'clock. I hope you'll join me. Really," she said, "I'd enjoy the company."

Eddie watched as she strolled away. There was a lot to watch, and he peered around the van to make sure he took it all in. Then he shook his head, and set the house alarm. He closed and locked the front door and the metal sheet door, and climbed into his van as quickly as he could. "Hope you like eating alone, dear," he said and got out his CID6 and a pen. When he finished, Eddie breathed a sigh of relief, and that's when his phone rang.

— Three —

Both officers had searched the house, every room from the attic rooms to all the small storage rooms in the basement, and Angela Charles was not in the house.

When they'd arrived, they found the back door almost hanging off its hinges; inside was a young woman called Michelle standing in the kitchen holding a bread knife. She was shaking, and she was crying, and it took almost five minutes of placating before she'd put the knife down. At the foot of the back wall was a dead cat.

And then she came out with a story that both fascinated and shocked them.

Almost half an hour later, they had calmed her down sufficiently to get her into the beat car where one officer climbed aboard and took her to Killingbeck Police Station for a statement.

The remaining officer, Steve Worthington, called in to division for a workman to come and board the door, after what he termed an aggravated burglary.

He then thought some more about the clothing he'd found in the bathroom; the bloodied pants and the ripped skirt. And he believed Michelle's story; it had credibility. She thought the new boyfriend was a nutter and he'd wanted to find out where Angela lived so he could finish off what he'd obviously tried to do on their date.

This made the bigger picture something much more than an aggravated burglary. And it also put him in a bit of a spot too, because he should have rung his sergeant or, at a push, his inspector, and told them what he'd found and what his beliefs were. And they'd immediately ask what Angela was saying. And that's where the brick wall was. They would then say pending a complaint from the alleged victim, there was nothing more that could be done.

But Steve thought there was more that could be done. And to save facing that brick wall, to help Angela wherever she might be, he'd made a call to Topaz, the dedicated rape detectives. Advice, they always said, was free.

Topaz had thanked him for his call and promised to ring him back shortly.

"Shortly" had been nearly forty-five minutes, by which time the battery on his phone was almost dead just as he was about to reach his highest score on Angry Birds. When they finally did call back, all they told him was to hang fire, stay on as scene guard and if the boarder got there before MCU, to ask them to standby.

When Steve had asked why MCU were getting involved, he was told nothing, other than he'd made a good call, and he would get a Per39 – a pat on the back – for his efforts.

— Four —

The phone call had been a quick one from Jeffery. He'd asked if he'd finished, and when Eddie replied, yes, he'd finished, all Jeffery then said was, "Get back here quickly."

And this upset Eddie a little. For one thing, Jeffery didn't even think to ask if he'd found anything; and he had, he'd found something at the absolute centre of the murder. He'd found something that would finally bring Tony's murderer out into the open, and that deserved a little pat on the back at the very least.

But the other upsetting thing about Jeffery's curt call was that it was just like being back as a divisional CSI, where there was no time for appraisal, no time to reflect on a job well done or pick out the parts of an examination that could have been done better. It was all about getting to the next job. And on top of all that, Eddie had a feeling that if he'd said he hadn't finished, Jeffery would have pulled him back anyway.

"I mean, how fucking important could a double murder be?" Eddie thumped the wheel and pulled up sharply outside MCU. He opened the window and swiped his card. The gate took a fortnight to open and then Eddie was through, knocking his wing mirror in the process.

He proudly carried his paperwork and the bagged swab into the office and Jeffery was aiming for him already like an Exocet missile.

"Eddie. I need you to go back out. Get yourself up to Barwick-in-Elmet, here's the address..." Jeffery handed over a piece of paper, but Eddie stood there, CID6 book in one hand, swab in the other, motionless, staring at Jeffery as though he'd had a shot of morphine. "Eddie, no time to piss about."

"Good. Then you won't mind if I finish my very important work."

"Eddie, not now—"

"Yes now!" He shook the swab in Jeffery's face, didn't even see Lisa Westmoreland standing in her doorway watching, "This is going to tell us who killed Tony and his wife. And if ever a job was worth doing right, it's this fucker." He stared wide-eyed and angry at Jeffery. "So don't tell me about pissing about."

Jeffery stared at him, lips tight and bloodless. "Five minutes," he said.

"Ten," Eddie took his seat, turned his computer on, and there was the faithful old egg timer. "And if you want us to work faster, get us some computers that run on electricity instead of fucking steam!"

Jeffery marched away from Eddie's desk and almost screamed when he got the line about the steam-powered computers. The man was almost impossible to reason with when he had his stubborn head on. And not since being here, two years ago, had Jeffery wished he was at home with a large, a very large, glass of port.

And then, as he was about to slam his office door, he saw Lisa Westmoreland staring at him. She didn't look happy either. And then she beckoned him with one hooked finger. Jeffery changed course, stared at the carpet running backwards under his feet, and then he was with her. "Inside," she said and closed her office door after her. "What's he talking about?"

"He's been to—"

Lisa hadn't said anything to stop him talking, but she was holding out her hand in a way that said stop. "Calm down, Jeffery."

Jeffery breathed, shoulders slumped a little, and then he began again. "He's found something at Tony Lambert's scene that—"

"What?"

"I said he's—"

"Who sent Eddie Collins to Tony Lambert's scene?"

Jeffery smiled, confused. "I did. Why?"

"Why would you? I thought we'd bottomed that scene."

"James gave it a good go, but I thought... Cooper from Crime Division asked if there was any chance anything could have been missed. And, frankly, I couldn't give him a straight 'no'."

"So we've been running a multiple gang murder scene all day short-handed, and you decide it would be a good idea—"

"Yes. I did. I apportioned the jobs this morning, no one was stretched." Jeffery stood, "And I believe I'm still in charge of my scene examiners, and how they're deployed."

Lisa sat at her desk, head down. After a moment, she looked up, a halfway smile back on her face, an attempt to smooth over the rough edges of the conversation. "I'm sorry," she said, "you're right, Jeffery, of course. I didn't mean to interfere."

Jeffery relaxed, jutted his chin out, and mumbled, "S'okay."

"I was very keen that's all, to have him at this Angela Charles scene as soon as."

"Me too. But you've seen how obstructive he can be."

"Are you saying you can't handle—"

"You were the one who wanted to appoint him!"

Silence fell on the office for almost a full minute. Jeffery had curled his hands into fists and Lisa clenched her teeth so hard that her jaws ached. But eventually, she mellowed again, blinked as though freed from a trance, and stood. She strode around her desk and extended a hand, "I owe you an apology, Jeffery. Again," she smiled wider. "I think the stress of today is getting to me a little."

Jeffery graciously accepted, mumbled "S'okay," again and turned to leave.

"Jeffery?"

"Yes?"

"Just get him there as soon as you can, eh?"

Jeffery closed the door gently behind him and walked straight to Eddie's desk. Eddie looked up. "I've finished. Okay? Wasn't so bad, was it?"

"Cut the smart-arsed stuff will you, I'm not in the mood."

"Aw, did you lose at solitaire again?"

"This address I need you to go to at Barwick-in-Elmet. We think it's the home of Blake Crosby's murderer."

"Ah, not Blake Crosby's rape victim?"

"The one and the same."

"He got what he deserved, the fucking pervert."

"That's as may be, but we have to follow this thing through; this is all part of Domino, and where there's Leeds gangs involved, we have to be one step ahead."

"You mean instead of being a marathon behind?"

Jeffery stared.

"Tell me what you've got."

"A female friend of the... of the rape victim found the address empty, but attending officers have found what they believe to be blood-stained pants, and a torn white skirt. It was the only outstanding stranger rape in Leeds according to Topaz, and they knew it was part of Domino so referred it to us."

"And where's the poor victim?"

Jeffery shrugged, "No idea. She's not at the house, the officers have searched it."

"And the gang? Won't they be interested in her?"

"They've already been up there apparently; the girl who phoned it in gave a description of Tyler Crosby. He's been in and left empty-handed."

"Not likely to come back?"

"Wouldn't have thought so. He's seen Angela isn't there."

"So you want the blood-soaked stuff."

Jeffery nodded, "And anything else with control DNA you can find: toothbrush, hairbrush, whatever you think. We just need to match her to him and the scene."

"The blood at marker four, eh?"

"And the penile swabs."

"Why do I shudder every time someone says that?"

"Okay, crack on."

"Right, I'll see if I can find any sign of Tyler Crosby while I'm there."

"Okay, good."

"I have to put this in the freezer first," he held up the evidence bag containing a single swab. "And I want you to authorise my submission of it to the lab. On an urgent turnaround."

Jeffery nodded, took it from him, "I'll put it in the freezer, and I'll authorise the submission. Just get up there urgently, please."

"Okay, you're the boss." Eddie collected his CID6, then he walked out of the office.

"I sometimes wonder." Jeffery read the handwritten label on the bag, 'Swab of blood, bedroom carpet: tested +ive blood/human.' Impressive, Eddie.

"What's impressive?" Lisa walked by carrying her briefcase.

"Home or a meeting?"

"Meeting, then home," she said. "It's been a long day." She nodded at the bag, "What's that?"

"Eddie found blood on the bedroom carpet at Tony's scene. Sounds promising, doesn't it?"

"Super! If it comes back IDd, that'll be worth a bottle of something to him."

"Oh, not a good idea."

"Ah," she remembered, "maybe not," and laughed. "Want me to lodge it in the freezer on my way past?"

"If you're sure?"

"Give it here."

There was a sparkle in Lisa's eye, and Jeffery was glad to see her back to her usual self but he still couldn't understand why she'd been so upset in the first place. Strange, he thought.

Chapter Thirty-five

Dented Shining Armour

— One —

IT WAS WAY PAST five o'clock when Eddie's van pulled up outside the end-terraced house in Barwick-in-Elmet. Just as he made a note of his arrival time, a small car drove away from the kerb behind him, and a police officer was at his door before he could even get out of the van.

"Eddie Collins?"

"Fuck," Eddie said, recognising the officer, "is nowhere safe these days?"

"I thought you'd bailed?"

"New pastures, that's all."

"Good to see you again, mate. You want me to run through what we've got before we leave you to it?"

Together they walked to the front of the house, and in through the front door to the foot of the stairs. "What do you mean, leave me to it? You want me to examine a house and keep an eye over my shoulder at the same time?"

"Mate, really, we've got to roll. The damaged back door is boarded and you can lock the front."

Eddie shook his head. "Definitely no one in here, right?"

"You frightened she's gonna shoot you?"

"Well, she's already killed one fella, another won't make any difference. Anyway, how the hell did you know about a shooting?"

"Division, mate. No secrets." Steve tapped his nose.

"So there's no one here, right? Thoroughly searched?"

"No one here." He nodded after the car that just drove away, "That was Michelle Hudson; she's just got back from giving us a statement. Her description sounds like Tyler Crosby; she threatened him with a knife and he buggered off. He won't be back; he already searched the place for this Angela Charles woman."

"Right."

"You know about the clothing upstairs?"

"Yep."

"And the flowers?"

"What flowers?"

"Ah. Crosby dropped some flowers into Michelle's office this morning pretending they were for Angela. Then he tailed her up here to find out where Angela lived."

"Clever."

"We've left them in the kitchen; don't know if you can do anything with them."

Eddie heard a toilet flush and then heavy feet on the stairs.

"Ready, Steve. I was fucking bursting, man." Another officer, pulling at his zipper, joined them. He nodded at Eddie, then asked, "You ready?"

Eddie began with the back door. It had obviously been kicked several times. Its bottom hinge had snapped altogether and the top one wasn't looking particularly healthy. The boarder had sheeted right over the frame, so the door was hanging inside like a huge red tongue. He began with photography and then skipped powdering for the footwear marks themselves, going straight to a black gelatine lifter which brought the dust off the door and with it the shoe pattern. Then he taped a clump of tight-knit fibres caught in the sharp splintered wood.

Next, he photographed the flowers, and wondered what the hell he could do with them. As he carefully removed the cellophane and opened it out on the table, a card inside a small white envelope fell out. Eddie smiled.

He lifted three marks from the uncrushed parts of the cellophane wrapper. The part used to carry the bouquet, around the stems of the flowers, was no good, too crinkled, too crushed, but the envelope... Ah the envelope was an excellent candidate for magneto-flake powder. A good thumb on one side and reasonable index came up on the reverse side cheered him, as did finding more on the shiny surface of the card itself, developed using aluminium powder. More photography, more lifting.

Eddie photographed the lounge, then made his way upstairs into the bathroom where the soiled and torn clothing was. More photography and then, using fresh sterile gloves and covering his mouth with a mask, he opened out the skirt and the pants onto a sheet of brown paper. After further photography he carefully wrapped them and slid them into brown paper sacks.

There was just one more simple job to do, then Eddie could get back to the office, deposit his exhibits and the keys to this place in the freezer and store, and then go home. He brought upstairs two knife tubes and two exhibit bags; one tube for Angela's toothbrush, and one for her hairbrush. He slid the toothbrush into the tube and screwed the lid on; wrote out the exhibit bag, slid the tube inside and sealed it.

Then he went into her room, sat heavily on the bed and repeated the procedure for the hairbrush that he'd seen on the bedside table. Then he stood and walked out the door, turned to nudge off the light switch and stopped dead.

— Two —

It had been a hard day for Ros. She hadn't stopped, not for a break, not for lunch, not even for the toilet, and she was exhausted. Not only because of the physical activity all day, but because of the lack of sleep from last night. Her eyes felt heavy and abraded by coarse sandpaper, but she worked on.

She had the dead guy in the tent and had taken every possible sample she could think of from him; the rest they'd have to do at the mortuary. She stood, arched her back and looked at her handiwork. She had swabbed and taped him, wrapped his head, hands and feet in separate plastic bags to preserve any trace evidence, then she'd placed him into a body sheet, and finally a body bag.

Only when she emerged from the tent into the brightness of the daylight did she see a second shell casing twinkling in the sun just ahead of the van's front tyre. More work to do. She sighed and reached for the camera. Thankfully, most of the shells were just outside the back entrance to the tearoom, so James and Duffy would collect them.

After she had photographed and packaged it, she made a call to DI Taylor, to have the vehicle and the body recovered. The press were still there, snapping away at anything they thought might add mystery to their front pages tomorrow.

James and Duffy had finished with their body, and had gone off to swab some blood from the far end of the triangle, and then gone to photograph around the front of the teashop and recover more blood from there too. Sweat glistened on Ros's forehead, and blood had dripped from her fingertips. One of those days.

The last thing was to hand her exhibits over to Taylor's nominated exhibits man, and get the hell out of here.

— Three —

He'd only ever seen one of them before. He'd been at a burglary at an Asian house. They'd taken to hiding their jewellery there. It was a good place to hide things; no one would think to look there.

But he was certain. And now he was more than a little afraid.

Eddie squatted down facing the end of the Ottoman double bed. He clicked on his torch and shone it at the hole between the mattress and the base; it was a hole plenty wide enough to slide a hand into, which you'd need to do if you were going to lift the mattress for access to the storage space beneath.

He cleared his throat, and then he remembered Blake Crosby's body – the one with the bullet hole in the back. The one caused by a gun. The gun they had not yet recovered.

For all he knew that very same gun was pointing at him right now.

Eddie whispered, "If I promise that you are completely safe, will you come out?"

No reply.

Eddie licked his lips. "Please," he said. "I won't harm you. I'll make sure you're safe. Angela?"

Nothing.

Eddie stood, and faced a decision. Ring for back-up, or take a shot – ooh, he thought, wrong choice of word – and lift the mattress, and see what was inside. If she was in there, she would be scared shitless, and how would the poor woman react to seeing a load of coppers prancing around her bedroom? And if she wasn't in there, how would he react to a roomful of coppers taking the piss out of him? He decided to be stupid, and stepped up to the mattress. He grimaced, and then reached down and lifted it up.

He stood back, and what he saw almost broke his heart.

She was a naked ball of grief. She peered at him through eyes that squinted in the brightness, through eyes that rippled with tears, one almost swollen closed. She had drawn her knees up, her fists curled beneath her chin seemed to clasp something silver. It wasn't a gun though; it looked like a brooch to Eddie. Her chin trembled and her mouth moved but he couldn't hear any words.

He knelt at the foot of the bed and tried hard to keep his own eyes dry. It was difficult. "Angela," he whispered, "my name's Eddie. I'm going to help you, okay?"

Inside his mind, he struggled on several planes: keep stable. The last thing a distraught person needs is another distraught person. But remember, she's a killer too, she's scared, easily panicked, and easily provoked; and she may be injured more seriously than you can see from here. And whatever you think, think this: she's been to a hell you could never imagine; she is the victim here, not some bastard Crosby.

He opened her wardrobe, brought out jeans and a top. Then he went to her chest of drawers and found a bra and pants. He hated this; it felt to him as though he was adding to her grief, not only by going through her private things, but just by being here – a male in her very feminine world, a world hung out to dry by males. He hated himself and wondered if Ros would be better. Well of course she would, he thought. But if you invite someone else in here now, the girl would blow her stack.

And then he went into the bathroom and brought out a bath towel, trying to think of some way she could keep her dignity.

Eddie returned to the bed. She hadn't moved. "Angela," he tried again, holding out his hand, "I'm not going to hurt you. I'm here to help you. Come out, please, let me help you."

"He raped me." Her voice was a ragged flower trampled underfoot.

Eddie closed his eyes, fought the tears. "I know, sweet," he said, and he heard the wobble in his own voice, cleared his throat. "I'm going to get you some help."

She shook her head. "You're going to lock me away."

"No. I'm going to get you some help."

"You think I shot him," her voice grew in strength, almost vehement as she stared at him unblinking, tears rolling down her face.

"I think you had every right to..." And then he stopped himself. "Come on, we can sort all that out later, let's get you some help first." He held out his hand again.

She stared at him for a long time and then she began to move, slowly, stiffly, first her legs and then her arms. Eddie spread the towel over her as she came nearer, and found he was crying.

He daren't leave her in the room to dress by herself in case she jumped out of the window. All these things came to him, including one important question: Now what? Hospital? Police Station?

Got to be hospital; who knows what that bastard did to her.

So he stayed in the room, facing her, but looking at the floor as she dressed, slowly, with sobs, in the clothes he'd gathered for her.

"Okay," she said at last.

Eddie looked up, cleared his throat again.

He wondered if it was the sadness in his eyes, maybe it was the pity she saw there, that caused her to burst into fresh waves of sobbing and Eddie couldn't stop himself from closing in on her and holding her in his arms as she wept into his shoulder. She was utterly rigid with fear at his touch, and it took a long time before she yielded and softened, and almost relaxed, and Eddie was grateful that she had. He felt honoured that she seemed to trust him after what she'd been through.

"I didn't kill him," she said.

"It's okay, Angela—"

"I didn't kill him!"

He pulled away and looked down into her reddened face.

"I said it wasn't me."

And those were the words that changed Eddie's life.

All the evidence he found at the scene, all the theories, everything – everything – pointed to her. Yet he believed her implicitly. How could he not? She was at her most vulnerable, the most vulnerable a person could ever be, and he could see she wasn't lying.

"Come with me," he said.

"Where?"

"You can't stay here, Angela."

"Charlie," she whispered. "Call me Charlie."

He smiled briefly at her, "Charlie, then."

"Are you arresting me?"

He shook his head, "No. No one's arresting you."

"But you're taking me to a police station, right?"

"No, I think—"

She was shaking her head. "No hospital, either." Her eyes shone. "I couldn't go to those places. I mean it... I would have to..." She held her arms across her chest, thumbs digging in.

"So what, then? Everyone thinks—"

"I'll explain it to them; I'll sort it out." And he wondered just how the hell he was going to do that. The evidence said she was 100 per cent guilty, no chance of error, no chance of parole.

"You can't, can you?"

"I'll find a way." And then he looked at her, close up, in her face. "Do you trust me?"

"Yes," she whispered.

"You can't stay here, Charlie. I'm taking you somewhere safe."

There really was only one place he could take her.

If he took her to the hospital, they would both be questioned, and before they'd finished treating her and examining her, the police would arrive and she'd be taken into custody as a murder suspect. It was the right and proper thing to do, of course. It would ensure she was fit, had no lasting physical injuries and it would ensure she had the chance to put across her version of events and prove her innocence.

All well and good. But it did nothing for her mental well-being.

And as for the proof thing, Eddie knew she didn't kill Crosby. He just knew it. All he had to do was prove it, because he was damned sure Charlie couldn't prove it by herself. They would eventually pulverise her into admitting it; forcing her to look at the evidence they presented to her – and really, the evidence said she did it.

It was growing dark as he loaded all the exhibits into his van, and meanwhile Charlie sat on the steps wrapped in her dressing gown to keep warm, and cried for Panda, not seen all afternoon. Over the next few hours, Angela Charles would do a lot of crying.

Eddie closed and locked the house and then helped her down to the van, got her seated and started the engine. "There's one proviso," he said.

She looked across at him.

"You have to promise me you won't do anything stupid."

She stared.

"I mean you won't try to commit suicide. You have to promise me that. I know you're upset, and you have every right to be; but if I'm going to help you, I want your word."

She seemed to give it some thought, but eventually nodded, "Okay," she said. "I promise. But if I end up with the police," she said, "I will kill myself, I couldn't go through..."

The journey was half an hour old before anyone spoke. She said, "You haven't asked me."

"Haven't asked you what?"

"You told the men that I'd killed someone. I heard you. He used the toilet, and he went down stairs and you told them I'd killed someone. But you haven't asked me how he died."

"I trust you. That's why I didn't ask you. I also didn't ask you if you had a gun hidden somewhere, because I trust you."

"I didn't kill him," she said. "But I'm glad he's dead."

"So am I."

Twenty minutes later, it was almost fully dark, and Eddie pulled the van up alongside a single-storey cottage. "We're here."

"Where's here?"

"My house." He looked across at her, "You'll be safe here, I promise."

And then she began to cry again.

Eddie unlocked the front door, flicked on the lights and went back to help her out of the van.

"I thought you were going to take me to the police station."

"I told you to trust me, Charlie. I said I believed you, and I do."

He settled her down in the lounge, all the blinds closed. He showed her the small bedroom where she'd be sleeping; he showed her the kitchen and watched her as she looked at the sharp knives on a magnetic block on the wall. He apologised for the mess because he was ashamed – even though he defended his right to live like a slob, it couldn't have been very pleasant for her to see a week's worth of washing up, and his dirty underwear thrown across the floor. "Oh," he added, "I have a teaspoon thief. Sorry."

She looked around hastily, "You share this place with someone?"

"No, no," he smiled, "I mean I can never find a bloody teaspoon. There's no one else here. Okay?"

He showed her the bathroom, got out clean towels and a spare toothbrush for her but said, "I don't want you to bathe yet, and please don't take a shower yet either."

"Why?"

He hesitated. "I'm going out for an hour. Two at the most."

"Where are you going—"

"I have to go back to work and drop off the exhibits I got from your house."

She looked petrified.

"Hey," he soothed, "I've stuck by my word. I wouldn't bring you here to my home and then turn you in, would I?"

She looked at the floor.

"Just, don't shower yet till I've figured out what to do, okay?"

"Okay."

"You know where the coffee and the tea is. I don't recommend the milk though. But help yourself to any food you want. Check it's in date first though," he smiled. But she didn't. She still looked petrified, all twitches and nerves, as though the slightest sound would either give her a heart attack or would see her embedded in the ceiling.

"Do you like my hair," timidly, she said, "the colour, I mean?"

He shrugged, "Yeah, looks good to me." He stood and headed for the door.

"I wanted it pink."

"Cool. Back soon."

Eddie rushed into the office with an armful of exhibits. He threw them on the desk and fired up the computer, aiming to get through it fast and then get some serious thinking done. What he had done was stupid. It could get him fired; not that he was especially bothered about the job. Like he'd said to Westmoreland, he was quite happy just being a bum. What he wouldn't be quite so keen on was a prison cell. Perverting the course of justice carried with it a healthy penalty, as did aiding and abetting a criminal – as yet unproven, well at least conclusively. She was still technically only a suspect. A very good one at that, he granted, but still just a suspect. Innocent until proven guilty and all that bollocks, he thought. She was guilty as hell in their eyes. No question. Crosby raped her, she killed him. Manslaughter at least. Ten years. Murder at most. Fifteen years.

And that's what made him do what he did. She was innocent, and he couldn't let justice take its course because sometimes the course of justice was so long-winded, so easily derailed, so easily corrupted; and her mental state was fragile enough without putting her through a mill and then spitting her into a cell.

All he had to do was prove her innocence and then miraculously "find" her. Easy!

Jeffery closed his office door.

Eddie looked around. "Where's Ros?" he asked.

"Came back to the office, filed her stuff and left. You know you're on overtime, don't you?"

"No shit. You sent me to do a quick job and you knew I'd be ages."

Jeffery smiled. "Well, thanks for doing it anyway, appreciate it."

"Yeah, yeah."

Jeffery walked over to Eddie's desk, "Get much?"

"Yes, I got much. I got Crosby's fingerprints. Well, I think they're his fingerprints."

"Great! Where?"

"He lured a girl from Angela's work with a bunch of flowers he'd bought for Angela, and she drove them up to her house. He followed."

"Sneaky. So where's Angela now?"

Eddie shrugged, "No idea," he said. "Hey, did all the exhibits from Blake Crosby's scene go to the lab?"

"No, not all of them. No need."

"Which ones didn't go?"

"Well, the tox and histology from the PM went, but stuff like plucked hair didn't. The soil samples didn't... Why do you ask?"

"My theory," he said, "I've just been mulling things over, you know."

Jeffery sat on the desk, clasped his hands. "And?"

"What if someone else killed Crosby?"

"Don't see how that's possible."

"Did you send off the blood sample from the tree?"

"Why would I? It's another 300 quid for no good reason."

Eddie closed his eyes. He breathed deeply through his nostrils and tried to keep his warming temper under control. "I just... I just think maybe there's an outside chance that the victim may have fled, and there might have been someone else up in the tree."

Jeffery laughed, and clapped him on the shoulder. "Nice one. Get finished and go home and sleep."

"Jeffery. Please, just put it through."

"Why? It's a done deal."

"It's nowhere near fucking done." He sighed, "Sorry. But please, just put it through."

"You think the same person who propped the white skirt against the tree using the blood-stained branch is the same person who was raped?"

"I don't know, that's—"

"I wondered if your theory would hold water. So I submitted the swabs from the branch along with the swabs from marker four."

"And?"

He shrugged, "They're a match. Whoever was raped propped that skirt there as bait."

Eddie looked confused. That couldn't be right. If the killer used Charlie's skirt as bait, then he must have propped it there. Not Charlie.

"Goodnight," Jeffery got up and walked.

"Hold on, hold on a mo," Eddie was out of his seat and standing at Jeffery's side in a second. "I know it doesn't make much sense right now; but please, I'm convinced I've fucked up somehow. Please, Jeffery, send off the blood from the tree."

"Listen, Eddie. Much as I think you're an arsehole, you do have a good nose for this sort of thing. I had a forensic strategy meeting with Westmoreland yesterday and yours was the only reasonable conclusion we came to, and the results bear it out. You did well. You should be happy."

Now Eddie was getting angry. "First," he said, "if I have a nose for this kind of thing, why the fuck won't you listen to my nose now?"

Jeffery took a small step backward. The humour had vanished from his eyes, the joviality melted with Eddie's change in demeanour.

"And second, I found the tatters of the white skirt at Angela's house. It means she was the last person to handle that stick – and her hands would have been bloody, that's why there was a match between the blood on that stick and the blood at marker four."

Jeffery looked at the carpet.

"But the blood up the tree could belong to someone else. And while ever there's a 'could' in the equation, you can't call the rape victim a murderer. You can't say for sure that Angela killed the bastard!"

"But—"

"It's called reasonable doubt."

"But—"

"I'll pay the 300 myself!"

"Shut up! The skirt you found at Angela Charles's house, might not be the same one you sampled fibres from at the scene."

"I'm going to hit you in a minute."

"But it's true!"

"So send the skirt away for comparison with the fibres then."

Jeffery's mouth moved as though he were chewing something, as though he was mulling it over. He turned away from Eddie, "I'll think about it," he said.

"No! Send them off, Christ's sake!"

"What the hell has got into you?"

He stepped closer, and Eddie could see him sucking air in through his nose. "Don't even ask it, Jeffery."

"So why are you so twitchy over this?"

"I don't want this girl to be locked up for something she didn't do. I can cope with most things, but I couldn't cope with that."

Jeffery paused. "I'll authorise it first thing tomorrow."

Eddie sighed loudly, even returned the clap on the back to Jeffery and smiled, "Thank you," he said. "Now you can go home and finish your knitting."

———

The coffee he'd made went untouched; it grew cold as he worked and a skin had formed on its surface by the time he turned off the computer after dumping his exhibits into the stores and the freezer. He'd been here an hour – bloody quick work, but he daren't leave Charlie much longer.

Except he had one last call to make before he returned to her and made sure she was okay. Eddie grabbed his jacket off the chair and left.

Chapter Thirty-six

Can't do Right for Doing Wrong

EDDIE KNOCKED HARD AND fast, almost breaking the damned door with his fist until, after a minute or two, it opened an inch.

Ros peered out, "Eddie?"

"I need you," he said, massaging his hand.

"I er, I'm not good company tonight."

"I don't want your company; I need your advice."

"Why," she said, "what have you done?"

He licked his lips, looked up and down the street. "Look, I don't want to talk about this on your doorstep."

"You can't come in."

"I don't want to come in. I want you to come out; I have something—"

"Not tonight, Eddie."

"You have to, Ros. I need—"

"No!"

She closed the door and Eddie stood there looking like a prick. This was not happening to him; he needed help. Ros's help. That was all there was to it. End of. He banged again, furious that she'd slammed the door, angry that she... wait a minute. What was wrong with her?

He replayed the slice of face he'd seen, and within the slice was an eye and in the eye were tears. And did the cheek he'd seen appear red? He thought it did. And her voice too, it was croaky, as though she had a sore throat.

This was no summer cold though.

Eddie closed his eyes, resigned to fucking up another friendship; resigned to being blind to anything that wasn't a crime scene.

He looked around, saw her car, but no other. You'd have thought Brian would have had a car too.

He banged again on the door. A new determination made him crack the wood and at last he heard the bolt sliding back, and the door opened again, but stopped on the chain. "What's happened?" he said.

"Nothing."

"That's what people say when everything's happened."

"I'm okay."

"And I've just graduated from the school of tact and diplomacy. Now what the fuck's happened?"

"Eddie, go away—"

"I'll bust the door in, Ros. You know I will."

"Eddie..."

"You stubborn cow. Open up, Ros."

The door closed and Eddie was ready to kick the damned thing in; no way was he losing her again. He knew she was married and he suspected things weren't exactly rosy for her right now, but no way on God's earth would he let her suffer if he could help it.

And then she surprised him by taking off the chain and opening the door.

"Oh God," he said.

Her face was red across one cheek, and the skin beneath her eyes was puffy, eyelashes stuck together in tear-soaked clumps. She bit down on her bottom lip in embarrassment, as though declaring herself ready for inspection, as though she was going to say, "Happy now?"

"Ros," he whispered, and that was enough to get her crying. "What's he done, sweet?"

"It's my fault, Eddie."

He stepped forward and he embraced her, and a small part of him that he felt revolted by enjoyed holding her close again; it was like old times refreshed, a new memory to add to those of yesteryear. But a bigger part of him wondered how anyone could leave her, Ros, in such a state. She was... she was a bundle of goodness, through and through, top to bottom, left to right, and front to fucking back; how could anyone make her cry?

And then, as though his mind had shut with a clang, he wondered how many times he'd made her cry. And then he felt guilty, and cold; he felt like he shouldn't be holding her so closely, so tightly.

He slackened his grip. But she didn't.

"This is really shitty timing, Ros—"

"What's happened?"

"I can't tell you. I have to show you."

"Eddie," she sniffled, "I'm really not up to it tonight."

"I know," he nuzzled into her hair. "But I know this too. I can't leave you here with him. I just can't. I know you're not supposed to get between a man and his wife, I know that... but," he was shaking his head, "I just can't see you in pain like this. It's killing me."

"If he comes back now, he'll save you a job."

"Come with me please, Ros."

"If I go with you, he'll kill me too."

He pulled away from her, and through gritted teeth, said, "Why didn't you tell me?"

She smiled. "What could you have done?"

He looked away, knowing she had a point, but you could only help a person if they wanted to be helped. And at least until now, he knew she didn't want help; Ros, the famous battler, wouldn't stoop so low. Ros was the helper, not the helpee. "Grab your coat, you're coming with me."

"Oh no I'm not." She pulled away from him and tried to take cover behind the door.

"I mean it. There's not many times in my life I make bold decisions," except the one he made only a couple of hours ago, he conceded, "but I'm making one tonight."

"That's kidnap."

And then he smiled at her, thinking of all the things he could be locked up for right now, "Kidnap is so low down on my offences list, you have no idea," and the silly smile turned into a grin. "Grab your coat, and I promise in less than half an hour, you'll forget all about Brian." He shouldn't have said that. It was belittling her problems, and not only that, when he'd used her for advice and guidance, she was going to have to come back to Big Bad Brian and face the music, and where would Mr Bold Decision be then? Well, that was something he'd address when the time came. For now, he had priorities: sort Charlie out, and then deal with Ros.

It sounded awful, but that's just how it was.

Ros took a deep breath. "Wait there," she said.

"What's the deal between you two?"

"Thanks for taking me out for a drive, Eddie, but I don't want to talk about that."

"You really are a stubborn—"

"Cow?"

"Yes, dammit. I want to help you, and you're too fucking proud to let me."

"You don't need to help me."

"How often did you prop me up, eh? How often did you bail me out of the shit with the stuff in my head, or with Kelly? A thousand times, that's how often. And was I too proud?"

"You were too stupid to have pride."

Eddie stared forward. He wasn't known for his high IQ, but... well, it was below the belt. And it hurt.

"I'm sorry, I shouldn't—"

"It's okay. You don't need to apologise. You're right. But even so, let me help you for a change."

"I don't need help."

"Your glowing red cheek suggests otherwise."

"It was just a silly misunderstanding."

"Okay." He drove on.

They covered another three miles before she spoke again. "What is it you're so desperate to show me?"

"If I tell you," he said, "I wouldn't need to show you."

"Tell me!"

He blew out a sigh, as though psyching himself up. "I know you'll hate me for this," he ventured.

"This sounds very bad. Have you blown up MCU?"

He didn't answer, just drove.

"Eddie?"

He snatched a glance around at her. "Okay," he said, "you know my theory of how Blake Crosby died was utterly waterproof, utterly bulletproof?"

"You went to Angela Charles's house tonight, didn't you?"

"Jeffery tell you?"

"Spit it out."

"She didn't kill him," he said again.

"I'm a little afraid to ask how you know that."

"I'm a little afraid to tell you, if I'm honest."

Ros turned in her seat; didn't say anything to him, just watched him.

He felt nervous now, tapped the wheel, swallowed and then whispered, "She told me she didn't kill him."

Ros blinked, and a noise like a cross between a sigh and a half-hearted laugh fell out into the car. "You found her?"

"She's petrified, Ros. Poor kid's been hiding in her house for two days."

"Eddie—"

"The gang is after her. They traced her home, they broke in. They want her dead."

Ros's mouth fell open. She stared forward, and then confusion blossomed on her face.

"She didn't kill him."

"And you believed her?"

"Yes. I believed her. If you'd seen her. She was shaking with fear; Ros, she's been raped."

"Why are we going to your house, Eddie?"

Eddie didn't answer.

"Eddie, tell me you just called it in and got the police to pick her up."

Eddie didn't answer.

"You did the good Samaritan bit and took her to the hospital. Where you called it in."

Eddie turned on to his road.

Ros closed her eyes. "Eddie, you idiot."

"If I call it in, she ends up in a cell until we can prove she's innocent."

"That's because she's guilty!"

"She isn't. She saw who killed him. And if the gang don't get to her then she'll go nuts inside a cell. Ros, we have to help her."

"We?"

He brought the car to a halt. "Well..." he looked at her. Was she serious? He thought, out of all the people he could choose, that Ros would be the one. It's always been Ros; she would help anyone. He stared at her, a real fear on his face now. "She's injured. If I took her to hospital, they'd call it in. She needs your help."

"My help? Jesus, Eddie, I'm not a gynaecologist; what am I supposed to do?"

"I can't do anything. At least you... You could, I don't know!"

"You are so fucking dumb sometimes."

"Thanks."

"And what, you're going to keep her here until she's proven innocent?"

"Yes."

"What if we can't do that?"

"We can. I've sorted it."

"If you get caught with her, you're heading to prison. You know that, don't you?"

"She needs help." He thumped the steering wheel, "Why is this so fucking hard?"

Ros breathed hard. "Okay," she said, "let's go and see her."

"She's afraid, Ros, I've never seen anyone so scared."

"Okay, I hear you."

Eddie turned onto his drive and he looked at Ros, "Thanks," he said. "I am very grateful."

But she wasn't looking at him. Ros was looking right past him, right through the side window. Eddie turned. "Oh fuck, no!"

Chapter Thirty-seven

And Then the Police Came

— One —

EDDIE WAS OUT OF the car and at his front door in seconds. And he stood there, rigid with anger. Ros walked up to him.

The door was open, kicked open. On the floor were shiny bits of metal from the ruptured locks, and Charlie's safety had poured out into the night like Metaxa brandy down the toilet. Slowly he stepped into the house, the lounge and bedrooms to the right, the kitchen straight ahead, and the bathroom to his left. It was dark. It was silent.

His greatest fear while he was away for two straight hours was that she would get scared and decide her best chance of freedom was out there. He was afraid she'd just open a window and step outside. He never once thought...

Eddie walked into the lounge, turned on the light. There were cushions on the floor. He'd left her sitting by the window, in his favourite window seat, padded out with cushions, with a small table an arm's length away where his ashtray was, where the coaster was.

Lying on the floor among the cushions was a smashed mug, tea splashed all over the floor and up the sofa front. Eddie walked through the lounge, "Charlie," he said barely above a whisper. There was a quiver in his voice as he reached the lounge doorway that gave onto a short hall. Off the hall were three other doorways; one for each bedroom, and one at the end, a second entry to the bathroom.

He swallowed and walked the hallway. "Charlie, it's me," he said, "Eddie."

He nudged open the first door, the one to his bedroom. Nothing out of place. So he walked on; one flat footfall after the next until he was standing in the doorway of Charlie's room. He didn't need to turn on the light. He could guess what had happened.

"Go on," said Ros from behind him.

He stepped forward and turned on the light.

Charlie was huddled in the furthest corner of the room, squeezed into the corner, sucked there by fear. She had been shot in the head. In her hand was a small silver brooch; looked like a cameo.

Eddie fell to his knees and sobbed. Ros stood over him, rubbing his shoulders. "Why?" he said. "Just a couple of days, that's all I needed." He stood and was about to walk over to her, but Ros gently held him back.

"No," she said. "Stay back now, Eddie."

"I made her a promise, Ros. I was only trying to help her."

"I know you were."

"I told her she'd be safe here." And then Eddie turned to face her; both their eyes wet with tears, and Eddie drew her to him and he whispered. "She trusted me, Ros. I told her she could trust me. I made her trust me."

Ros didn't try to speak. She just looked at Eddie with eyes full of pity.

"I'm going after them, Ros."

— Two —

The car rocked as Ros climbed back in. "Well?"

"He was great about it." Her voice gave away the surprise she felt.

"He wasn't pissed off with you?"

"No," she said. "Not at all."

"That's good," said Eddie. But his face was just plain worried.

Ros made no reply, and even though he didn't look at her, he knew she was scared. When you expected a bad reaction from someone, and you got a good reaction instead, it usually meant it was a bad reaction dressed up to look disarming.

***

It was a little late to start following protocol.

Eddie sat in the car with the door open, feet scratching in the dirt on his driveway, and he flicked ash. He'd called three-nines. He was going to call Jeffery at home, but wondered what the point of that would be. Even if he came out here, Jeffery would tell him to call it in the same way anyone else would call it in if they found a woman's body in their house. They had procedures to follow; he understood that. But it didn't make the wait any easier.

He stared at his hands. The overhead lamp in the car and his solitary streetlamp told him they were trembling. And he wasn't surprised. He was nervous of the police, despite working for them for God knew how many years. He had seen justice doled out inconsistently in the past; and he knew all it would take would be one pissed-off copper for him to land his sorry arse in a cell at least for the night as a murder suspect.

Other emotions swamped his mind right now that elevated the nerves a little. One of them was sorrow. Abject sorrow. If he'd taken her to a hospital or a police station she would be alive right now; and although she'd be under arrest until he could prove her innocence, he didn't think she'd have killed herself, as she'd threatened to. Surely, if she were going to kill herself, she would have done it before now. And he was sure that, shit as the justice system could be at times, it would treat her with sympathy and courtesy.

My, thinking fucking straight now, eh? Pity you didn't think this straight a couple of hours ago.

But it had been different a couple of hours ago. Standing before him a couple of hours ago had been a scared and defenceless young woman who'd been through the most horrific trauma; it was easy to be blinded by her fears, it was easy to offer her comfort and see that she made it through the dark times. All he'd wanted to do was help her on a basic human level – nothing more; he didn't want recognition, he didn't even want thanks, he just... he wanted to make sure she was okay.

No, no; he'd wanted to put right what someone else had done to her.

His eyes opened wide. That was it; that was his base feeling.

He could never do it, though. How could you put right something like that? It was like asking someone to unlearn something. Couldn't be done.

And then he finished off the thought: if I'd just turned out her bedroom light and walked away, she'd still be alive. If I'd taken her to the station or the hospital, she'd still be alive. I rescued her, and now she's dead. I led them to her. "I killed her."

He sighed, shoulders rounded. He felt like shit. It was because of the one single overarching emotion he felt right now.

And then Ros leaned over and rubbed those shoulders. For a second he stiffened just as Charlie had back in her bedroom. And then he seemed to remember where he was and who had touched him, and he sighed, flicked away the cigarette. "I'm sorry I got you into all this," he said.

"So am I."

"I didn't mean to—"

"Eddie, stop talking while you still can. I know you did your best to help her, but you messed up. Again. And this time you messed up really big."

"You don't say?"

"I'm not saying you killed her though."

"I did though; sure as if I pulled the fucking trigger."

"Start feeling sorry for yourself, and I'm leaving."

"Long walk home."

"I'll get them to drop me off."

Eddie looked up and suddenly his little roadway and his little cottage were awash with headlights. The single streetlamp seemed utterly insignificant now, its feeble light bleached into orange shadows by three vehicles – a van, a police car and a plain car. Eddie closed his eyes for a moment, checking his tripping heart, and then stood to approach them.

"Don't forget," he said, "she gave me no name."

––––––––––

"Have you noticed?"

"What?"

"Everyone around you turns into a corpse." Benson growled, "You're a shit-magnet."

Eddie said nothing. He wasn't in the mood for small talk.

"You really are one dumb fuck, Collins."

He peered out of the windscreen, watching the officers, and said, "I asked you to make sure they didn't touch the front door. And make them stay off the kitchen floor."

"This is your house," Benson said, "it is not your crime scene."

"It is a crime scene! And they're fucking ruining it!"

"Never mind them." Benson tapped him on the shoulder, and Eddie looked round, "you should be concentrating on me; you should be impressing me with the honesty of your answers; you should be making sure your arse stays out of the clink; you should be making sure I don't suspend you from fucking duty."

Eddie turned away again and watched Ros answering questions in the ARV. It was a little late to try and keep the witnesses apart, but they were following procedure. He wished he could swap places so he could get his hands on the M16 they kept in a box between the front seats. He could put it to some very good use.

"Tell me where you picked her up."

"Garforth," he said without looking around.

"Why did you pick her up?"

"I was on my way back from a job in Barwick-in-Elmet. She was standing at the roadside waving at me."

"And?"

Eddie sighed, turned to face Benson. "She looked distraught, worried. She looked unkempt. I wanted to make sure she was okay."

"So you picked her up?"

"Yes. No, I mean I wound the window down—"

"Did she have any baggage with her?"

"What? No, she—"

"Did she offer you money?"

"Why would she offer me money?"

"I wondered if she thought you were a taxi."

"In a fucking van?"

Benson stared hard at Eddie.

"She said she needed to get away," Eddie said, "that she had nowhere to go."

"Ah, Eddie Collins, the good Samaritan."

"Don't take the piss."

"I don't believe you."

Eddie smiled. "I don't care."

"You should. I'm the one who's stopping them driving you to the Bridewell."

"On what charge?"

"I refer to my earlier comment: you really are a dumb fuck. Why do you think?"

"I didn't kill her, Benson."

"What's her name?"

"Charlie is what she said."

"Charlie?"

Eddie nodded.

"No surname?"

He shrugged.

"And what did you plan on doing with 'Charlie' when you got her home?"

"I didn't plan at all. I wanted to help her," and that bit was still true, no lying involved there. "I said I had a spare room she could use."

Benson raised his eyebrows.

"Not everyone thinks like you do."

"A judge would."

Eddie looked forward again through the screen, could just make out Ros nodding to the officer in the ARV. The officer nodded back, looked down as though writing something. Then another officer tapped on Benson's window and beckoned him outside.

"Stay in here," he said, and then stepped out.

Eddie lit a cigarette, wound the window down. He couldn't hear what Benson was listening to, but he could guess.

Within a minute, Benson was back. "I forgot to tell you I found out her name."

"Yeah, Charlie."

"Angela Charles."

Eddie looked at Benson quickly. "Angela Charles? She's the—"

"Killer. I know." Benson stared at Eddie, not speaking for a long time.

Eddie drew on the cigarette then flicked it away, wound the window up.

"You knew that. I think you found her at her house—"

"How? That bastard Crosby didn't. The two bobbies who searched her house didn't. So how the hell did I?"

"I think you found her. What I can't figure out is why you didn't turn her in. You knew she was a killer—"

"She didn't..." Eddie turned away quickly.

Benson's eyes searched his face. "You were saying?"

Eddie wiped his eyes, didn't look at Benson.

"I think you found her and thought you'd help her, hide her somewhere."

"Rubbish."

Benson smiled at Eddie, raised his chin as though he'd had a sudden flash of intelligence and he knew what had happened. "Stay here," he said again, and left the car. He knocked on the ARV's window, and the officer wound it down. Benson leaned in.

Eddie closed his eyes. This was either the part where he'd be driven to the Bridewell to be booked in for the night, at least, or it was the part where Benson would have to believe him. Eddie swallowed, fingers curled into knots, foot tapping the carpet.

Benson finished with the officer, and he sat back next to Eddie again. Eddie looked on, expectant, hopeful, fearful. "Where were we? Oh yes; for some reason you didn't want to turn her in, or you didn't dare take her to the hospital – which is what any sane person would have done, or any person who had that woman's health and well-being in mind." He took a breath but his eyes never left Eddie's. "Instead, you decided to keep her out of the loop, and try to hide her from the Crosbys who," he said, getting more wound up, "also seem to think she killed Blake Crosby!"

"Since when—"

"Shut up!"

Eddie clamped his mouth shut, jaws grinding.

"I think you're pretending not to know her fucking name so I won't bang you up for perverting the course of justice."

"I never—"

"I said shut the fuck up!"

Eddie swallowed.

"I could bang you up on kidnapping and false imprisonment charges."

Eddie's mouth was open, ready to spit another line of innocence out, but Benson stared, daring him. Eddie remained quiet.

Benson turned in his seat and faced Eddie. "I think you knew exactly who she was, Eddie." His voice was calm, almost a whisper. "I think you actually did try to protect her. And I think, well I hope, that it tears you up inside to learn that you indirectly killed that woman."

There was nothing he could say to that. He'd spent the last hour thinking the very same thing. His head fell. Benson was spot on.

"I wonder," Benson went on, "just how close you came to being dead. They followed you, found out where you took the girl. Lucky for you that you went out again. Unlucky for everyone else."

Eddie swallowed.

"If I ever learn that you took her from her home, that you didn't just pick her up in Garforth, I will charge you. If I find out that you knew who she was, I will charge you. Do I make myself clear?"

Eddie nodded, still looking at the floor.

"Now get out."

"You're not locking me up?" Eddie asked the question before he could tell his mouth to shut up. He simply couldn't believe it: how did Benson know he didn't kill the girl himself; it was just another part of the protocol – lock up the people at the scene and then go about ascertaining their innocence.

"She dialled three-nines," he said, "at twenty-three minutes past eight. You were sitting at your desk at the time."

"And Jeffery was with me."

"Yes he was."

"Can't believe you checked on me."

"I'm a fucking detective, Collins. And this is you we're talking about, you slimy little shit. If I thought for a second you had anything to do directly with her death, you'd be bleeding on the floor of the shittiest cell I could find."

Eddie looked at him, whispered, "Thanks."

"Now get out of my car."

"What about them, the Crosbys?"

"Don't you worry about them, we'll get round to 'em." Benson paused, and then repeated, "Now get out of my car."

Eddie did. And it wasn't until he stood shakily outside in the cooling breeze that he realised how much he was sweating. His face was wet, his pits were saturated.

The place was alive with police. Another car had joined the outing, it seemed, and a CSI's van too. Officers were busy stretching tape everywhere; huddles of people talking, pointing, gesticulating, laughing. Just another major scene under way.

The window slid down, and Eddie turned to see Benson leaning across the seats, looking out at him. "One more thing," Benson said.

Chapter Thirty-eight

Trembling All Over

— One —

"Ready?"

Ros nodded at him and he opened the door for her, "Let's get you home." And just those words caused her pallor to change. He noticed it like he'd notice a chameleon changing from green to blue. Just the thought made her tense.

I mean, he thought, being at a murder scene was fine, but the thought of going home to dear old Brian – when he was in a "good" mood, seems to scare the shit out of her.

"All set?"

"How come he was here and not regular CID?"

"She rang in," he said. "Must've given her name and it flagged MCU up straight away." He said nothing for a while as he imagined Charlie inside the cottage with people trying to break in through the door. He could imagine how scared she must have been – petrified, knowing who it was, knowing it was the same maniac who'd searched her house and from whom she'd successfully hidden and survived, only for it to end badly a few hours later anyway. She had the good sense to at least call the police.

Eddie took a breath, blinked to clear his eyes and then looked at Ros, "You okay?"

She just nodded again and got in the car.

Tonight was a night for sighing and Eddie did his best one so far as he crossed the front of the car and got behind the wheel. It wasn't a sigh for the mess those bastards would make in his house – he probably wouldn't notice anyway. Nor was it a sigh for Charlie. He'd sighed plenty for her, and he would shed more tears for her too, later. But the prize-winning sigh of tonight was for Ros. She sat there staring straight ahead with her stubborn chin held high.

She was like a proud prisoner facing the firing squad: resolute, stiff upper lip and all that.

He wished she would trust him again.

Again? Did she ever trust you? And then he checked himself; yes, she had trusted him. He might be the world's most despicable idiot, he thought, but he was good where it mattered. And she knew it too. He knew she knew it. She had trusted him in McDonald's.

And as they drove, he decided he ought to cut her some slack. She was going in to a house where a man who slapped her during arguments lived. She was preparing herself for a confrontation, maybe; she was preparing herself to resume the argument, or to put it on pause until Eddie had gone, or until the morning. And Eddie cursed himself for getting her into all this trouble tonight, not just with the dead girl, but with her husband as well. And then he cursed himself some more for being too flippant about other people's lives and their problems.

Just because he lived alone, he decided, didn't mean he had no effect on other people's lives.

But he was there for her. For what good it would do. They would part at the door and Eddie would drive away oblivious to the raised voices and ill-feeling he would leave behind.

The journey was silent, only punctuated by a squeal of brakes as the car halted behind a big Dodge pickup truck. He saw her take a breath just as she opened the car door and just as Brian opened the front door. Eddie rushed to get out.

The car shook and vibrated as it rolled along. And that was good because it meant she couldn't feel her hands shaking. She said nothing, and she heard nothing. Eddie could have been talking Martian for all she knew.

But maybe he wasn't.

Finding that dead woman had shaken him up quite badly. It must have been like rescuing a puppy from a cruel owner only for it get hit by a car on its first day of freedom. Except it wasn't. She didn't suppose it had really hit him yet, but it would. Maybe tomorrow he'd wake up and realise he had blood on his hands – indirectly of course, but there was no doubt that he had caused her death. And Eddie would take that very hard. He was as tough as granite on the outside, but Ros knew his heart was easily injured.

Perhaps troubling him too was how easy he'd made it for the gang. They had followed him; he'd been almost gullible. And now he was vulnerable. They knew where he lived, and... don't be silly, she thought, the days of gangs killing coppers and police staff were–

She was about to say "long gone". But look at Tony Lambert and his wife. Was nothing safe anymore? Time was as a copper, the badge you wore protected everything about you; it almost granted you immunity from gangs – they didn't want the trouble. But now, now the rules were skewed and everyone was a target.

She sneaked a quick look at him, and his eyes were focused well ahead of anything in his field of vision; unsurprisingly he was lost in thought. Lucky he wasn't locked up for this evening, she thought. And she wondered if Benson had granted him freedom because of the past they had shared. It might have been full of animosity – yes, they hated each other's guts – but there was obviously some kind of professional respect there. And that's what Benson must have seen in Eddie's eyes. Anyone else, anyone at all, would have been in a cell.

And that thought brought her round to Brian. And then she began shaking again.

He'd been great on the phone when she'd rung him from Eddie's place. She had expected him to go wild. But he hadn't. And somehow that was even more worrying. She didn't want to upset him again. He could be nasty when she upset him. She'd learned her lesson, and they got along fine now that she had learned it; but it was better not to take chances.

She swallowed, and wiped her hands down her legs as Eddie brought the car to a halt behind Brian's truck.

Brian was half way down the short driveway and Ros stood there waiting as Eddie came to her side. She looked nervously between the two men.

"You must be Eddie." Brian held out his hand, big smile on his face.

Eddie shook, and returned the smile.

Ros looked into his face but couldn't read anything.

"I'm sorry I took Ros from you—"

"Hey, I know how important work can be. It's fine." He turned to Ros, "You okay, babe? Glass of wine waiting for you."

"Thank you," she whispered. She could, however, read Brian's face.

"You'll stop for a glass too, Eddie?"

Ros pitied Eddie. She could see that the poor man didn't know whether to stay and protect her from Brian, or leave so they could work things out in peace. There were things to work out – no doubt about it. That was part of the expression she could read on Brian's face. We have issues, it said. We need to re-establish the pecking order.

And then Ros looked back at Eddie. And she almost burst into tears; she could see herself leaping back into the car, wanting to drive away from here as fast as she could. With Eddie at her side. And that was about the biggest lump of regret she could feel bubbling up inside her throat, so large and so hot that it could choke her to death. Her chin wobbled and she took a huge breath. "See ya," she whispered to Eddie, and walked up the path without looking back.

— Two —

"And?" He stood in the lounge with his arms folded, and he stared at her.

Ros looked up at him and wondered what the hell she ever saw in him. Surely being a spinster would have been the better option. Of course it would have been, but she didn't know all this shit back then, back when she said I do. "I'm sorry, Brian."

"I nipped out for an hour or two and when I came home..." he shrugged. "No wife." He smiled broadly, took a step closer.

Ros's heart sank. "I called you," she said.

"From his house."

"There was a dead woman in there!"

He said nothing and the magic smile disappeared.

"Brian," she whispered. "Please, I won't do it again."

Chapter Thirty-nine

A Cold Bath and a Hot Whisky

— One —

IN THE DARKNESS THE tap dripped.

She watched the moonlight reflect off the rippling water onto the wall tiles to her left, and then stiffened as he whispered, "Watching you."

All she could think of was Eddie. The look on the poor man's face when he found that girl dead. It was enough to make her cry too. Eddie was a dancer with two left feet; he tried to be serious and sensible and everyone thought he was a clown. But he wasn't serious or sensible. Ros could still see right through the tarnished veneer and saw a vulnerable man who cared about things, and cared about people; and he was always getting his fingers singed, was always stepping on his dance partner's toes.

He tried. And that's why she lov–

Ros's eyes sprang wide at the realisation.

— Two —

There was a chair in the corner of the room; something like a Shackleton's high seat chair. It was one of those crusty old things you'd find in an old folks' home. The smell of piss didn't bother him. He sat in it quietly, feet up on the creaking old bed, looking at the patterns on the frayed curtains, and the slim orange stripe of street light from outside that showed the fleur-de-lys wallpaper. Between his fingers, a cigarette curled smoke into the room, and on the bedside table next to him, a cup of something they called coffee was cold and untouched.

Next to it was a half-bottle of cheap whisky. The seal unbroken.

Eddie flicked ash and took a drag, rubbed his aching eyes and considered the words Benson had spoken: Everyone around you turns into a corpse.

Down the hall, outside his room, a door banged and he could hear people shuffling about in the next room, mumbled voices.

What was the point of life if you did no good with it? What was the point of life if you just died and left nothing of yourself behind? Because once he was dead, he thought, and those around him died too... who would remember Eddie Collins? No one. He would leave no legacy, nothing on this shitty earth would be any better for him having been on it for thirty odd years. Certainly no body, no person, would have been better off for him having been here. And that was the point, surely; to make someone's life better.

But he'd tried.

He'd tried to help Charlie, and look what happened. He'd made it worse, he'd gotten her killed. She was worse off for knowing Eddie Collins. He was in negative equity.

"Don't you worry about them," Benson had said, "we'll get round to 'em."

"Bollocks," Eddie whispered to the empty room. MCU had been dealing with gangs and organised crime for years. And there were still gangs and organised crime around. Most of the crimes he'd dealt with as a divisional CSI were propagated by organised crime and street gangs.

Noises from the room next door grew louder until Eddie's thoughts dispersed like mist in sunlight, and all he could hear was groaning; getting louder, more intense. He banged on the wall. "Hurry up and come, will you!"

There was a muffled laugh, and then a muffled retort, "Piss off!"

Eddie sighed. His thoughts might have dispersed, but his anger hadn't. He reached for the bottle of whisky and his car keys.

— Three —

In the darkness the tap dripped.

Her teeth chattered. She tried to sit up.

"Watching you."

Eddie would never do something like this to her. Eddie cared about her. And she wanted him to care about her, she wanted him to protect her, and that's why she'd invited him to MCU in the first place. He would never do anything like this to her.

Of course it was all her fault. She had come to realise that over the last half an hour. Brian was right after all. And she was genuinely sorry; yet Brian's punishment did not fit the crime. But he was in control now, he steered their ship and she went wherever he sent her, and he doled out the punishment for her misdemeanours as he saw fit. She couldn't complain. And she wouldn't complain.

— Four —

He had very little idea of what he wished to achieve. All he knew was he was pissed off and the chances of the law actually getting off their fat arses and doing anything about it were pretty slim. Eddie decided to do something about the Crosby bastards by himself.

Had he stopped and thought more about it instead of cracking the seal on the whisky bottle, he might have saved himself a lot of trouble. Eddie was one of life's deep thinkers. But tonight, he wasn't. Tonight, Eddie was angry. Tonight,

Eddie had given someone his word, and these bastards had broken it for him. And that was more than he could tolerate.

He drove the Discovery straight through the automatic gates and they folded sideways as though they were made from toilet rolls and crepe paper, and Eddie brought it to a halt outside the front doors just as the lounge light came on and the curtains were pulled back. And then he was out of the car and kicking the door until it crashed inwards.

Across the courtyard, the front door of the staff house opened and a lad wearing dirty white trainers stood there for a moment before disappearing back inside. He returned with his handgun and walked across to the main house.

Inside the house, Eddie began shouting, "Tyler Crosby!" He staggered down the hallway and was met at a door to his left by a big black man. Eddie stopped, swayed, and said, "Where's Tyler Crosby?"

From behind the black man, a voice said, "Bring him through, Monty."

Eddie looked up at the man called Monty, and tried to point a finger, "Is he in there?"

Monty grabbed Eddie by the arms and dragged him through into the lounge. Eddie looked around at the curved leather suite, the huge wall-mounted TV, the projector hanging from the ceiling, the ornate and far too grand fire place with real plastic logs glowing in the grate. In the centre of the room, a circular glass coffee table.

Spittle hung from Eddie's mouth as he surveyed the two men sitting there. One was old, fat, and bearded: Slade Crosby, dressed in a shirt and slacks, and the other was Eddie's age, jeans and T-shirt, blood across his face, nursing a drink: Tyler Crosby. A man walked into the room and closed the door. He stood in front of the silent TV, handgun sticking out of his black leather belt.

In the kitchen beyond, and out of sight, there were other people, muffled voices, moving around. Considering it is gone three in morning, thought Eddie, this place was fucking alive.

"Which one of you bastards is Tyler?"

"Who the fuck are you?" Slade looked at him; he didn't seem particularly perturbed by Eddie's presence, or the fact he'd ruined the posh gates and bust the lock on his front door. Slade looked preoccupied. Slade's knuckles were smeared with blood.

"Fuck me, it's Grizzly Adams!" Eddie shook his arm free, smiled at the bearded old man and staggered around the coffee table towards Tyler. "I'm guessing you're the twat that kills innocent women?"

Tyler glanced at his father.

Slade sneered then nodded at Monty. Monty took a step forward and said, "Gillon," nodding at the kid with the white trainers. Gillon strode over to Eddie, stuck the gun in the back of his neck. Eddie froze, eyes wide. The spittle fell from his lips and he swallowed.

"Boss?" Gillon said.

Slade shook his head. "Not here."

"Why did you kill her, you dumb fuck? She didn't kill your stinking piece of shit rapist bastard brother!"

"I'll ask again," Slade said. "Who are you?"

Eddie swayed as he turned to Slade, almost fell over and caught himself against the mantelpiece. "I'm the fella who rescued a young lass called Charlie. Charlie was hiding in her house, scared shitless because of him," he nodded to Tyler. "I found her. I told her she'd be safe at my house—"

"You!" Tyler spoke at last, an involuntary gasp of recognition.

"Yeah, me, you prick. You broke into my house and killed her!"

"She deserved—"

Eddie half fell and half ran at Tyler, and as Tyler scrambled to his feet, Slade stepped sideways and threw a punch into Eddie's stomach strong enough to throw him off balance and leave him writhing on the floor.

Tyler seemed to gain confidence then, to become brave. He stepped forward and kicked Eddie in the ribs, before Slade slapped him. "Leave him," Slade said. "He stinks like a fucking brewery, and you don't get to do anything until I say so." Slade nodded at Monty, "Drink, please."

Slade retook his seat, pointed at Tyler, "This!" he screamed, "this is what happens when you don't do as I say!"

"She was—"

"Shut up!"

Eddie coughed, and sat up, propping himself up with one hand while the other massaged his ribs, feeling inside his jacket for the pocket. He still swayed and tried to see past Tyler's chair and out into the kitchen; he could see movement still, even caught sight of someone through the crack in the open door, but they were gone in an instant. Strange, but they looked familiar somehow.

"What are you doing here?"

Eddie was shocked at the question. In the motel with his feet on the bed, even while smashing his way through the front door here, he'd never thought they'd ask him outright; it just never occurred to him. What am I doing here? he thought. "I yam here to plant a bug on behalf of Wesh Yorshier Police Force." He smiled, deadpan.

Slade eventually chuckled. "Don't piss me about, son; I'm not in the mood."

"I wanted to see the man who thought he was God." He stared at Tyler. "You roll through life taking whatever you want, whenever you want. You never give any thought to the lives you ruin or take along the way, do you? You're above all that. You're above the law." Eddie almost fell forward, but controlled it enough to stay upright.

Tyler smiled at that.

Monty handed the drink over then looked at Gillon, "Put it away."

"Don't you care?" Eddie asked.

Tyler shrugged, rubbed his lip.

Eddie looked at Slade. "And you, don't you care? Your son rapes her, and then this prick kills her. And she was innocent."

Slade smiled. "Casualty of war. I'll send a wreath."

Eddie smiled in return, and that made Slade's face straighten up pretty quickly.

"So who did kill him, if it wasn't this girl?"

Eddie took a long slow blink, "I haven't worked that bit out yet."

"I think we got it pretty much spot on," Tyler said.

"Shut up, boy!"

"But I'd be happy to share it with you," Eddie said, "if you'll forget my little intrusion."

"I don't need nothing from you, whoever you are."

Tyler laughed.

Eddie looked at him, "And as for you, prick, I'm having you; I'll make you into a casualty of war. I'll make you shake like a shitting dog. I'll make you terrified just like you made her terrified—"

Monty leaned over, grabbed Eddie by the throat and lifted him into the standing position. Eddie clawed at the giant's arms, eyes wide and frightened, bubbles of air grazing down his constricted throat, snot running out of his nose, face a bloated red. And just as he was about to black out, Monty took the pressure off and Eddie sank to his knees coughing and clutching his neck, a raspy noise coming from his throat as he breathed out, a squeaky noise as he breathed in. Tears blurred his vision, and he had a pressure inside his head that felt like his ears were going to pop.

"After tonight, you'll be in no position to make threats against my boy in my house. Now, I like to know the names of the people I kill. So what's your name, you pisshead?"

Eddie swooned, and the oxygen racing into his brain almost made him black out again, but the big guy had done him a favour, and he was now in the perfect position to see through into the kitchen. A face stared back at him. And when he recognised it, it disappeared again as though it knew it had been spotted. "I see you," Eddie pointed and giggled.

The kitchen door opened, and a blurred shape stood in the doorway. Eddie looked, and despite wiping his eyes, he couldn't make out any distinguishing features. Until she spoke.

"His name's Eddie Collins. One of my forensic geeks. And until now, a reformed alcoholic."

Eddie furiously rubbed his eyes, and squinted at her. "Lisa?"

"That's why I don't need nothing from you. See?"

She shook her head at Eddie, as though he'd disappointed her. Slade lit a cigarette and tapped his shoe on the floor, as though the nerves were getting him.

"What the hell are you doing here?" Eddie tried to rationalise her presence; was she part of a sting, was she here under a warrant, searching the place? Each option came pre-stamped in big red letters: N O. "I don't get it."

"I'm making corrections to your work," she waved an evidence bag in front of him. He couldn't see what it was, not from here, and so he tried to stand but just then, the kid with the gun stepped on his hand hard enough to make him hiss.

"What? What do you mean 'making corrections'?"

Lisa Westmoreland turned around and walked back into the kitchen.

"Hey, what do you mean?"

Slade called, "Does he have friends?"

From the kitchen, Lisa laughed. "He's a loner. And a loser."

"Boss?"

Slade looked at the kid who was standing on Eddie's hand, and though Eddie couldn't see the kid's reaction to Slade's shake of the head, he heard the gun being replaced for the second time. And then the penny dropped, and he understood why Lisa was here. No, that wasn't quite right; he didn't understand why she was here or what "corrections" she was making, but he did understand that she wasn't too bothered about Eddie seeing her fraternising with the enemy. And that scared him.

"So how come you went to such lengths to employ me then?"

"You don't need a character reference where you're going, lad," Slade said. "Monty, get this piece of shit out of my sight."

Eddie snarled, "Shut up, you old prick."

And then Eddie found himself face down on the floor again with a foot in his back and pain in his ribs, and his arms so far outstretched that one hand rested under Tyler's armchair. But evidently they did have time for a character reference, because now Lisa Westmoreland stood again in the doorway, her arms folded, a resolute look on her face.

"Because you shot your mouth off at Tony Lambert's scene?"

Eddie grunted.

"If you'd left it as a straightforward murder-suicide, you could have been blissfully unemployed now. And still alive tomorrow."

"Aw, bless ya; you saying I was too good for your fucking clowns?"

"Something like that." She glared at Tyler. "I had to keep you close, where I could keep an eye on you."

"It's a little late for flattery." Eddie tried to laugh, but his ribs put a sharp stop to it.

"And then you had to go back, didn't you—"

Slade yawned. "Look, this is all very Agatha Christie, and really, I'm enjoying the exposé, but it's time you stopped breathing, Mr Collins."

He smiled up at Slade, and tried to stand, "I'll be going now, mate, thanks for the hostipatily."

The kid with the gun stepped forward and raised his eyebrows in a question to Slade. Slade nodded, "Cable tie his wrists. Get Jagger to follow you. And make sure his body is well hidden. Okay?"

"Yes, boss."

"But Dad—"

"Shut it, you."

Suddenly Eddie didn't feel quite so jovial anymore. As the ties nipped the skin on his wrists, and he looked at the people who stared at him, it all became very real. And he wondered if this was his final hour.

"Don't take no chances, Gillon. I'm trusting you." And then he turned to Eddie. "Now you know why I'm above the law, son. And he's not God, I am."

———

They used wide cable ties to make sure Eddie remained compliant, and then a third one looped through the first two and tied into the rear seat belt ring of Eddie's Discovery to make sure he didn't try anything foolish on the journey.

Eddie first saw Gillon in the courtyard as they dragged him from the house. He caught Tyler a good kick in the balls on the way but all it did was earn him a punch in the abdomen that saw him paralysed, unable to breathe at all for what seemed like an hour, until he thought he was going to pass out or die prematurely. But eventually he had hauled in hicks of breath and then a long one and the cold night air and the flicks of rain had brought him back around again. It would have been cruel, he thought, to have denied Gillon his first kill.

Gillon was whooping with delight, dancing around like an idiot and slapping Eddie on the back of the head. Monty caught hold of the kid as Tyler and Jagger installed Eddie on the rear seat. "Stop fucking about," he'd said to the lad. Eddie saw him become serious almost immediately, but he also saw the sly glance at his new prisoner, and understood what was crawling through his shallow mind even as he nodded and apologised to Monty for his foolishness.

"It's not too late, Tyler," Eddie whispered. "Just untie me and we'll call it quits."

Tyler just smiled and yanked on the tie harder.

"I mean it, let me walk. You'll never be free—"

Tyler slapped him. "I wish it were me putting that gun to your head." And then he was gone. The door slammed shut and the interior light blinked out. Eddie was alone. He could hear voices outside, and the voices became shouts and he caught a part of the shout that he wished he hadn't. "Gillon gets to do it!" Eddie closed his eyes; they were arguing over who got the thrill of killing him like a pair of kids arguing over who got to open the last date on the advent calendar, or who got to ride the bike and who got pillion. Bile rose in Eddie's throat, and the heat stung as Gillon climbed aboard and closed the door.

The reflection in the mirror told Eddie he was pleased. He turned in his seat, staring at him, and then laughing. "You look scared fucking shitless!"

"You don't say."

"I'm gonna fucking love this!"

"I'm happy for you."

"I've always wanted to do this."

"I want you to know," Eddie said, "that I will come back and haunt the fuck out of you. Each time you're on the shitter, I'll be there, each time—"

"In fact, I'm gonna stick one right up your arse first. I wanna see if that'll kill you." He disappeared into a brief moment of thought. "Hope not," he said, "I just can't wait to put one in your brain."

"I have the advantage there then."

Jagger drove a blue pickup truck past them and out through the broken driveway gates. Gillon engaged gear and set off after it.

After ten minutes, Gillon turned on the wipers as big fat lazy raindrops splattered onto the screen, to be replaced minutes later by a steady, lighter rain. He goaded Eddie all the way. After a further fifteen minutes, the streetlamps ran out and they were heading away from town and up into the countryside somewhere approaching Otley, he guessed.

All Eddie could see was one red tail light from the pickup and the fan of the Discovery's headlamps in the hedges to his left, rushing by at a thousand miles an hour.

"On a serious note," Gillon cleared his throat, and then lit a cigarette, "I always wondered about kneecapping. You'd hear all this shit on the news about the Irish doing it, and they say it's really painful."

Eddie shook his head.

"I might give that a try first."

"Put some Pink Floyd on, would ya."

"Making you nervous?" Gillon stared at Eddie through the rear-view mirror and Eddie could see his eyes squint up as he laughed.

"Making me bored, you prick."

Gillon switched the cigarette to his left hand and pulled out a gun with his right, then he swung it backwards over the seat. "Still bored?"

"Now I'm delighted. I'm sitting over the petrol tank, you wanker. I'd love you to join me in death." He saw the kid think about it, and then he laughed meekly and pulled the weapon back into his lap.

They passed a sign for Bramham, and Eddie heard the kid curse, "The fuck are we going?"

It didn't stop the goading or the questions but things calmed down a lot for Eddie over the next twenty minutes.

The constant hum of the rain on the roof, the wheels turning through water, and the noisy wipers creaking their way across the screen, successfully combined to drown out Gillon's incessant bullshit. But even those sounds began to recede in layers as though Eddie were slowly unpacking the pass-the-parcel goodie. A numbing silence crushed him, and all that existed was the rocking of the Discovery.

Eddie grew peaceful; sad, but peaceful. This was a horrible way to go, he thought, but at least it would be all over. No more fretting about work, no more worrying about money, or paying the bills, or getting the roof repaired; no more searching for teaspoons, convinced someone was just trying to piss him off all the time, with speed bumps and traffic cameras, and people like Benson who glared and stared and laughed at you behind your back. No more not punching Jeffery for being an arsehole, no more… And then he looked into Ros's face before she disappeared up the path with Brian, and he saw fear in her eyes.

Suddenly all the noises from the road, and the rain and the wipers and the arsehole at the wheel thundered home and Eddie shook awake, eyes wide and scared. The calmness had gone, and now he was panicking, now he was looking at the cable ties, pulling at them, trying to get his teeth hooked into them until he saw blood appear on his wrists. And still Gillon yabbered about kneecapping and all Eddie wanted to do was scream.

But then the pickup truck's red lights grew bright and an amber turn signal flashed on and off. Gillon stopped talking and Eddie swallowed hard. They were near.

A road sign briefly proclaimed Dalton Lane before the vehicle lights washed across it. Eddie saw nothing but black fields to his left, black woodland to his right, and then burning red lights to the front as the pickup stopped.

"Guess we're here," Gillon laughed and jumped out of the Discovery, headed over to Jagger.

The rain pounded on the roof, heavier now they'd stopped, it seemed, and in the headlamps he could see Gillon and Jagger, collars up, shoulders hunched against the downpour conferring, nodding some agreement, and then Gillon headed back this way. Eddie's heart sank, and he knew the end was coming. There would be no rescue, no cavalry suddenly appearing over the horizon. He trembled slightly.

Gillon reached in, a pair of cutters in one hand, a gun in the other, and grinning a stupid idiot's grin as widely as ever. He reached in and snipped the tie holding him to the seat belt anchor. Eddie's arms fell into his lap and the blood rushed along them, pins and needles tingled in his fingertips. "Ready?"

Eddie considered kicking out at him.

"Don't even think it."

Eddie slid along the seat and climbed out onto shaking legs. Rain drenched his hair; mud splashed up his jeans and as soon as he began walking, pushed along from the back by Gillon, his legs felt wet and cold. Soon, his teeth were chattering. He walked slowly towards Jagger. Jagger didn't smile.

Beyond the pickup truck, its lights speared through the rain and shone into a niche in the trees where scrubby underbrush ran rampant in a deserted corner of woodland. There was no footpath, and Jagger led the way twenty yards through the clinging grass, limping through the sucking mud, pulling against the thorns that tugged at his jeans, rain dancing on his head.

"Okay, lads," Eddie found himself saying. "Enough is enough. I'm suitably frightened and I promise to pay for the gates."

It earned him a poke in the back and a grunt. But they walked into the niche where the falling rain seemed ever stronger, as though this was the focus of the storm. The truck's lights showed Gillon's shadow bouncing around at the side of Eddie's own, lit up Jagger's shiny jacket, shone through the drops of water falling from his gun.

"Here," Jagger shouted.

Gillon nudged Eddie to where Jagger pointed.

"Shit," Jagger staggered past them, "spade," he said, and then, "not till I get back, Gillon."

The laughter seemed to have died in Gillon now, his giddiness at the prospect of joining the killing club had subsided because it had all become very real for him too. He still wore the sickly grin, Eddie noticed, but it was just a mask stuck in place for the benefit of street cred later. Gillon nodded, "Kneel down."

"Don't I get a last request?"

"No."

"Gimme a cigarette."

"Ha, in this?" Gillon came up close, "Maybe next time, mate," he winked. "Now kneel down."

"Fuck off. You do it the hard way."

"Turn around and kneel down or I'll—"

"You're going to see my face when I die."

Gillon punched him in the stomach and Eddie went down on his knees into the mud, panting hard. Then Gillon stepped behind him, and brought the gun up to the back of his head.

Chapter Forty

The Fat Lady Takes a Deep Breath

— One —

"YOU TRUST HIM?"

"Gillon? Course I do."

"If he doesn't die—"

"Of course he'll die. Do you think they've gone out for a fucking McDonald's?"

"If he lives I'm ruined. If I'm ruined," she said, "you're ruined too."

"That a threat?"

"Don't make me lose my temper, Slade." Lisa walked up and down the lounge wringing her hands together. Then she stopped, looked at him. "Well?"

"I trust him. And I trust Jagger." Slade sighed, looked at Monty who merely shrugged and ate another digestive. "Gone are the days when we bring their heads back in a bag. What the hell do you want?"

"I don't know. And don't mock me." She resumed her stroll around the coffee table. "Tell him to send you a picture."

"What?"

"A picture, by phone. I want a picture of him dead."

"You are crazy, you know that?"

She stopped in front of Slade. "Please?"

Jagger slid his gun into his jacket pocket and pulled back the tarp, poking his hand into the darkness searching for the spade. His hand brushed it and dragged it free as he cursed the weather, and suddenly he felt a vibration against his leg and closed his eyes. He knew it was coming and it came just at the right time. He limped back towards Gillon and Collins, pulling his phone out of wet jeans. The display flashed a number, but no name.

He stepped to one side so the headlamps from the truck shone directly on Eddie who was on the ground, head bowed forward, rain pouring off his hair, and he could also see Gillon, twitching, shifting his weight from one foot to the other like a golfer practising his swing, getting ready. Jagger's eyes grew wide. He pressed OK and shouted, "What?" he dropped the spade and took the gun out of his belt, hobbled through the mud as he saw Gillon stiffen, locking his arm, feet planted firmly. He didn't listen to the phone, couldn't have heard it properly over the pelting rain anyway; he aimed as he ran and saw in the minutest detail the tendons in Gillon's arm grow tight, saw the trigger move and then Jagger screamed, "No!"

"Jagger?" Slade stared into nothing. "Jagger?" and then he heard someone shout "no" and Slade looked around the room as though someone here could tell him what the hell was going on.

Lisa stopped pacing, Monty stopped eating, and even Tyler, dabbing his bust lip, stopped, and stared at his father.

Everyone heard a single sharp shot quickly followed by a second. Slade had a worried look on his face. "Jagger? Jagger! What happened?"

And then Jagger came on the phone, and Slade's eyes refocused. "He fucking shot him. Gillon."

"What? Gillon shot him, right?"

"No!"

"What do you mean, 'no'? You're not making any—"

"He took Gillon's gun and shot him!"

"How the fuck—"

"Because I wasn't covering him."

"Why weren't you—"

"Because I was answering the fucking phone!"

Lisa's voice was high, reedy, "Is he dead?"

The line died and Slade looked at her.

"I don't know."

Jagger stepped closer to them. Gillon was lying on his back, feet towards the truck's lights, head in the shade, but it was easy to see the blood, it was a black sheet draped clumsily over the side of his face and neck; yet the rain pattering into it, bouncing up into the headlamp beam was scarlet. Gillon wasn't moving.

He looked across at Collins as his phone rang again. "What?" No scream this time, just a resigned whisper barely audible. "Yes, Collins is dead. But so is Gillon." He listened. "Yes, I shot him. He's dead!" And then he listened closely, and he almost laughed, "What? Why do you want—" he stared between the phone and Eddie Collins. "Okay," he said, and hung up.

Collins had landed face first into the brambles and the rocks. The brambles had torn him up pretty badly, one thorn was embedded in his top lip drawing it back over his teeth in a macabre sneer, blood stained his teeth and part of his lower lip. Another thorn had pierced his eyelid, dragging it towards his eyebrow, showing the pale pink underside against the stark white of his eye. The eye did not move, and there was no blood flowing from the wound. His face was contorted further by a rock part-protruding from under his lower jaw and part pushing his cheek outwards. A slug edged its way over the rock.

Jagger pressed buttons on his phone and then got down on his knees, pointed it at Collins's face until a flash fired. He checked the picture, and then sent it to Slade.

———

Slade opened the image and smiled. He didn't look at the screen long before handing it over to Lisa. She took the phone eagerly, studied the bloody underside of Collins's face, the shiny matted black hair on top, the twisted lip and the dead, staring eye. It looked evil; it looked like something a horror movie would have been proud of. The dead pupil, the red-eye, the barb sticking through the lid.

"Happy?"

Lisa nodded.

"No way he could not be dead, is there?"

She shrugged, thinking, "No, suppose not."

"So, are you happy?"

"Yes, I said yes, didn't I?"

"Good. Then you can take that back to your stores now?"

Lisa took a deep breath, picked up the exhibit bag from the coffee table and headed for the door, Monty following her with her jacket.

———

Jagger knelt by Collins and the phone rang again.

"Bury them both. Shift his car a mile or so away, then go home. Come and see me tomorrow at noon."

— Two —

"Hey baby."

Ros held her breath, but she couldn't stop shivering. Her shoes tapped the side of the bath making the water ripple as though there was an earth tremor, as though the big quake had already happened and this was the aftershock. She closed her eyes as the door squeaked open. She could pretend to be asleep but the shivering would give it away. No way could you sleep while you were shivering.

"I brought you some breakfast," he said, a kind of excitement in his voice as though it were her birthday and he was treating her to breakfast in bed with a red rose draped across the tray and a kiss-filled card propped up next to the teapot. He placed the tray on the shelf at the foot of the bath and then sat down on the toilet. She could hear him rubbing his hands together. "I want you to know something." He cleared his throat, "I want you to know that I forgive you, Ros."

She lay there motionless, trying to relax so she wouldn't shiver; but failing because the shiver was long past being one caused by the cold. Now it was fear that made her shake.

"Open your eyes, sweetheart."

She didn't. She lay still, holding her breath, tiny fingers of wet hair shaking against her neck.

"Open your fucking eyes!"

Ros sucked in a huge breath, frightened by the echoing scream, and stared at him, trying to keep the shaking under control, but succeeding only in giving herself neck ache. She couldn't feel her legs properly. She looked up at him as he wiped the spittle away from his lips.

The lips smiled at her. Warm, pleasant, reassuring and gentle. "I love you," he whispered. And suddenly he was at her side, on his knees, elbows on the edge of the tub, hands together, chin resting on them, smile balancing on the chin. She looked up at him, could see the crumbs of toast from his own breakfast stuck in the stubble at the sides of his smile, a smear of butter on the round of his chin. And his eyes, eating her alive. "I loved you from the first moment I saw you." His eyes drifted away to a past only he seemed to enjoy. "Did I ever tell you that? I did," he whispered, "I loved you then and I love you even more now."

"Brian—"

"And I want you to know," his arms levelled out across the top of the bath, lowering his face until it too was on the top of the enamel, until it was closer to her, "that I've been thinking over what happened last night. And I've been thinking that some of it might have been my fault. I mean, if I hadn't gone out, then..." The smile re-emerged, and she could see grease on his lips too. "Well, no need to dwell on it."

And then he looked at her and saw she was shivering.

"Cold?"

No, she thought, I'm cleaning the bottom of the fucking bath! "A bit."

He reached over and pulled the plug, hung it over one of the taps and resumed his earlier position. The water, only about three inches deep, but plenty enough to keep her cold all night, more than plenty to make her limbs ache as it leached all warmth from them, squealed down the plughole, sounding like a cat caught in some machinery. He waited until the final gurgle passed, before saying, "I know this seemed like a lenient kind of punishment; I wouldn't make a very good Nazi would I, but you made me do it again," he laughed. "You brought this on yourself—"

"I didn't do anything to deserve—"

He flicked an arm in the air and Ros recoiled, bringing her hands up to her face, pulling her stiff legs up and screamed at the pain in them, as he only reached for the plug.

"You want some more?"

She was shaking her head, "No, please, Brian. I'm sorry, please, don't do it again."

"Are you sorry? Really sorry?"

She nodded vehemently, as though demonstrating that the harder she nodded, the more sorry she was. Her lips were numb, her nose was running, and the shivering had turned into waves of shaking. Perversely, the water, though cold, had kept some of the heat in, in the same way that swimming in the sea felt freezing, but as soon as you climbed out onto the beach, that's when it got really cold.

"Okay, then. Enough of this nonsense, Ros. You start behaving like a decent woman for a change. You start being a good wife for your hard-working husband, and there'll be no more of these silly punishments." He took the weight on his hands and stood. "Fuck knows why I put up with all this shit from you." He reached for a towel, "Come on get up, get out of those wet clothes, and eat the breakfast I made for you."

Ros tried to move and couldn't. She reached over the sides of the bath and pulled, but nothing happened. And then she cried, "I can't move, Brian." She covered her face with her hands, and sobbed.

He stood there with hands on his hips and eventually the hard face softened and reached down to her. "Here," he said, "take my hand. Come on, take it. Take it!"

Eventually she reached up to him, and he smiled as though helping the cat out of the machinery with a here I am, rescuing you again, but you know I can't resist helping a loser look on his face.

"See," he raised his eyebrows, "how silly you've been now?"

She nodded as very slowly she stood, water draining from her clothes. And still she cried for the aches in her body, her locked limbs, her wrinkled skin, and the pain that drummed everywhere, and she breathed tiny breaths through blue trembling lips that clamped around a shivering jaw. Then he went and stood by the door. "I've helped you enough, Ros." He threw the towel at her, "Wise up or suffer."

Chapter Forty-one

Sophie Grew a
Spine

— One —

WHEN SOMETHING IN YOUR life grows with each hour until it obliterates your horizon, until you can think of nothing else simply because you can neither see nor feel anything else, it becomes the sole point of your life until it's dealt with; the entire focus of your waking hours. Like it or not. Life stays on hold until you grow a spine and sort things out.

Twenty-four days ago, Sophie grew a spine.

Sophie had licked her lips. They were dry, her whole mouth was dry, yet she could feel the sweat oozing out, beading on her forehead, running down her back. She stared on, the nerves making her twitchy.

She'd waited nine years for this moment, and now that it was here, she didn't know whether to rejoice, running up and down between the tables screaming her happiness, or just to turn around and walk back to Sarah's place with her tail between her legs. After all, she'd thought, a dream was only a dream while it was inside your head. Soon as you tried to make it real, that's when things tended to go wrong, that's when it all fell apart and landed in a crumpled heap at your feet.

So maybe it would be better to let sleeping dogs lie. Of course, that was utter rubbish. Even if the dream was crushed until nothing good was left, and all the memories that propelled it were suffocated, it was better than living with a hollow hope; a shadow of uncertainty. At least she'd know, and surely that was better than forever wondering.

And, look on the bright side – a small smile had grown on her lips – if the dream came true, think how fucking happy you'd be! At last.

Sophie had taken the drink with her; it was good to have something to hold when you were this nervous, like a comforter. She'd walked across the room, towards the window seat where Lisa Westmoreland sat.

She looked great. She was a good-looking kid who'd grown into a great looking woman; elegant, refined. Distinguished. Sexy.

Sophie walked in a daze, feeling tremendously uncomfortable, as though all eyes were on her. Sophie's eyes had never left Lisa's handsome face, waiting for the moment when she looked up from the table and saw her.

And before she could wonder what her reaction would be, Lisa looked up.

It was an effort, but Sophie had smiled at her; the worry she felt twisted it slightly, making her appear unsure, uncertain... It must have shone through.

The clattering of cutlery, the soft hum of chatter died away and Sophie heard only the soft creak of her black leather jacket and her heart booming in anticipation. Or was it fear? Dread?

Lisa had recognised her immediately. Her eyes widened instantly, and for the briefest of moments, she smiled. Then the smile turned black and died. She looked shocked. Embarrassed.

"Hey," Sophie said.

Lisa squirmed, suddenly much less elegant.

"How are you?" Sophie watched her, saw her swallow, saw her looking around as though searching for an exit, or maybe hoping for back-up. But the reply was worse than that when it finally came.

"Do I know you?"

Sophie's world had ended then. The hopeful smile she wore, all welcoming, all forgiving, turned sour and limped away. Tears filled her eyes. But she tried again, "It's me, Sophie."

"I think you've made a mistake."

But she hadn't made a mistake. It was her, no doubt at all; it was Lisa. It was her Lisa.

And then Lisa's back-up did arrive. He was tall, wore a businessman's suit, pink tie, shiny shoes, and he had a salesman's smile.

That's when Lisa's eyes had lit up, and that was when she became elegant again, relaxed even. Exactly the opposite of what they did when Sophie had approached the table.

"Hello, dear," he said.

Lisa was embarrassed now. She licked her lips and felt awkward. Sophie could tell, didn't need a fucking shrink to tell you that.

"Who's your friend?" he asked, taking off his jacket.

The fingers of the hand holding the glass turned white, and Sophie held her expectant breath.

"I've no idea; I think she made a mistake. Didn't you? I think you made a mistake."

Sophie had looked between Lisa and the salesman. They stared at her. Her world shrank into something the size of a fist. Her eyes clouded over and her chest boiled. In tears, she turned and walked away. And she could have been wrong, but she thought she heard them laughing. When she reached the door, Sophie was full on crying.

The dream had been crushed and the memories propelling it turned to dust and simply blew away.

— Two —

The weeks that had passed felt like a year, but to someone who'd waited a decade, time was easily manipulated. If you played it right, you could fool your mind, you could make time pass quickly. It was a prison thing: sleep often, keep busy, don't dwell.

Since her first encounter with Lisa, she had hardened considerably. The hope had gone of course, she wouldn't allow herself any more hope; it was a false feeling, a self-destructive feeling. In its stead stepped loathing. Not quite hatred, but not far off.

She had thought of the restaurant every day since and played it back using different permutations; had altered her role, changed the way she'd approached the table, changed the first words, even made a scene. But it all came down to one thing: rejection. Oh, make that two things: rejection, and denial.

Today would make up for it, for the denial at least. The rejection she could handle, but Sophie would not let Lisa deny her for a second time.

Sophie pressed the doorbell.

This time her mouth wasn't dry, and she didn't sweat. This time, she held no comforter. This time, she had anger on her side. This time, she wouldn't fail.

Lisa opened the door and Sophie walked right inside, pushing her aside. "In the lounge," she said.

Lisa stared at her, and then slowly closed the door.

"How dare you not acknowledge me? How fucking dare you pretend you didn't know me—"

"I beg your—"

"Shut up. Sit down."

Lisa looked at her, saw the grimace and the throbbing cheeks. And then she sat.

So too did Sophie. "Ten years has been good to you."

"I'm sorry—"

"Why?"

"What?"

"Why are you sorry?"

Lisa paused. "You want a drink?"

"No, I want some answers."

"How did you find me?"

"I used to be a copper, remember? It wasn't so hard." And then Sophie stared her straight in the eye, "I used to be your lover too."

"Things have changed."

"Why did you stop writing to me? Why did you stop visiting me? Have you any idea, any fucking idea at all, how much I looked forward to the letters and to seeing you once a fortnight? They were the only things keeping me sane."

Lisa looked at the floor.

"Well?"

"I met someone, Sophie."

"Good for you," she smiled sarcastically. "I had my own cell!"

"Look, I've said thanks, I really was grateful, I really am grateful."

"But not quite grateful enough to introduce me to your..." She paused, thinking, "Of course, I should've known," she whispered, "I'm an embarrassment to you."

"No, Sophie—"

"Ah, no I've got it. Your past is an embarrassment to you."

Lisa was silent.

"The last ten years have been hell, Lisa. Hell!" And then she laughed, "But you know what, I'm not embarrassed about my past or about what I did to protect you. You killed Chloe. I took the blame for you, because I loved you. No sense in us both doing time. I had the girl's blood all over me, all over my clothes. You had the chance to get out and get away. I gave you that chance, and you took it—"

"I was a kid,"

"Me too."

"Sophie—"

"But you know what, I'm not afraid of my past anymore. All my dirty secrets are out in the open; I've paid for my mistakes – or rather for your mistakes, and I have nothing to fear." Sophie leaned forward. "You're still scared shitless of your past."

"I need a drink." She made to stand up, and Sophie barked at her.

"Sit down. I haven't finished with you yet."

Lisa shrank back into the chair, seeming to prepare herself against a barrage of harsh words.

"You spent your ten years well. Made it right up to DCI, I hear. Got yourself a good-looking boyfriend, nice house, nice car..."

"What do you want?"

"Took your time getting to that." Sophie rubbed her hands together and grinned. "I lost my job, my life. I sometimes think I also lost my self-respect. But actually I didn't; it was just dormant. You however, you have no self-respect."

"I have—"

"Sssshhh, Lisa." She got off the chair and sat on the sofa, sinking into the soft leather next to Lisa, invading her space, getting very personal. "You look at me and you see what you'd have become. You look at me and you're scared."

Lisa pulled her gown tighter.

"I'll be honest," Sophie smiled, "I didn't want anything from you in that fancy restaurant. I wanted to say hi, and I suppose I wanted you to ask how I was. It would have been good to learn why you stopped writing and visiting. But I'm not stupid, I never expected you to wait for me, not really; I knew you'd move on with your life.

"But you didn't ask how I was. You pretended I was some deranged fool who'd made a mistake. I made the ultimate sacrifice for your freedom, Lisa, and you stabbed me in the fucking back."

"I'm sorry, I—"

"Not yet you're not." Sophie stood and looked down on her. "I want recompense. You've turned this from personal to business. So I want fifty grand."

"What?"

"I think that's more than reasonable. It's only five grand a year. And you must be on, what, forty-five, fifty grand per year?"

"Where the hell am I supposed to get hold of fifty grand, Christ's sake!"

Her eyes narrowed. "See what I mean? You didn't even argue that you owed me; just how much you owed me. You're a piece of shit, Lisa. I hope your fucking castle crumbles around your ears."

"Look, I didn't ask for this—"

"Neither did I!" Sophie was panting, the veins stood proud on her neck, and she felt like she was only seconds away from strangling the sad bitch. How the hell did she fall for her in the first damned place all those wasted years ago? She was nothing special; she had no loyalty, no respect.

But she didn't strangle her. Instead, she got up, yanked her jacket straight, and said. "You got to come to terms with your past, girl."

"I can't get fifty grand, Sophie!"

Sophie smiled. "I was kidding. I don't want your money." And then she headed for the door, "But I will make you face your past."

Chapter Forty-two

Missing

LISA WESTMORELAND SAT QUITE still at her desk. She hadn't even turned on the computer yet and she'd been here twenty minutes already. Her mouth felt perpetually dry. Every time someone came into the large office where the detectives and the CSIs and the admin worked, every time a shadow passed the large window that looked out onto that office, her head snapped up, her eyes searching.

At this rate, she wouldn't last the day without having a heart attack or at the very least, coming down with a migraine. She stared at the desk, hands trembling ever so slightly. And then she tried to reassure herself that the picture Slade's man had taken of Eddie out in the woods last night, was proof he was dead. And it worked, slowly. She still felt twitchy – murder was a hell of a thing to live with; it was harder to pretend everything was normal, much harder, than she'd thought.

She swallowed again. Squeezed the bridge of her nose.

Last night, when Eddie walked into the Crosbys' lounge like the drunken idiot she'd been warned about, she had nearly fallen through the floor. Of all the chances... How often had she been to Slade's house? Three, four times? And then he had to show up, and then on top of that, Slade had invited her to show herself. He'd wanted her to select a flagpole and nail her colours to it. It also said to Eddie that he would never see the inside of MCU again; he'd never see anything again. It reassured her; but not much.

Why had he shown up? She still couldn't figure it out.

And that was on top of the other problem: Sophie. Why on earth couldn't she have stayed away? Why did she have to come back and try to resurrect an old relationship? When you said to people on holiday, "You must keep in touch", you didn't mean it! You were being polite, you were saying you enjoyed their company for the week and now you'd like to part on good terms and never see each other again. But some people misconstrued that; some people had to follow you around like a damned shadow.

And yes, of course Sophie had done a wonderful thing for her, and she was very grateful to her. And she claimed she didn't want the money, she only wanted to make her remember her past. How abstract was that? Either she wanted money or she didn't. Why even ask for it if she didn't want it?

But what was clear was that Sophie Moran wasn't going to let this go; she'd become holier than thou, all self fucking righteous. And then it dawned on her: Sophie was going to tell the police about Chloe in the nightclub.

For a moment, as the thought crossed her mind, she smiled. But it was short lived. She smiled because there was no way anyone could prove Lisa had killed the girl. No way! It would be Sophie's word against hers. Simple. And look who'd win – especially since Sophie had admitted to the murder in the first damned place.

The smile, though, had died for one simple reason. Proof didn't matter in this career, on this side of the line. Suspicion was enough to cast doubt; doubt would get you suspended while they carried out an investigation; doubt would get you off the security clearance register; doubt would see you in disciplinary meetings. Doubt could even see you demoted, if not out of a job.

That's why the smile died. Sophie's veiled threat to expose her was no veiled threat at all. It was very real. It was a potential career-killer. Couldn't turn back time and try a different move the second time around, buddy! It was done; you accepted the dive, and you "...set me free!"

"Everything alright?"

Lisa jumped and looked up to see Cooper standing there, arms folded, leaning against the doorframe. Lisa began to feel sick. The dry mouth was still there, her fingers tingled, and her palms grew damp. She smiled up at him, "I'm not feeling well."

"You got a minute?"

She swallowed. "What's up?"

Jeffery looked at the clock. 0810. Still no sign of Collins. He signed the paperwork granting authorisation for the DNA samples that sat inside a red cooler bag on the admin desk. Two swabs, that's all they were, individually wrapped in tamper-evident clear bags with all the details correctly filled out on the accompanying panel on each bag, all signed correctly, all dated, complete with exhibit numbers and crime identification details.

One was a swab from the bedroom carpet in Tony Lambert's house, and one was a swab from the tree branch at Blake Crosby's scene. He ticked the box for 24-hour turnaround, and signed again at the Premium Charge Acknowledgement box.

"Thanks," Melanie said. "I'll get them over to the lab."

Lisa Westmoreland watched them from her office.

Jeffery asked, "Heard from Eddie this morning?"

Melanie looked blank, "Sorry no. I thought maybe he'd got the day off or something."

Jeffery smiled at her, and then made straight for Ros. Her coat was over the back of the chair, still wet from the rain, and she sat at her desk staring at the log-on screen, as though she'd forgotten what to do. "You okay?"

Ros blinked, and then looked at him, a far-away gaze in her eyes.

"Ros?" He squatted next to her.

"I'm fine."

He could see she wasn't. Her eyes looked shiny, her hair was tangled, a mess he'd never seen before, and her skin was pallid. "You don't look so good; you coming down with something?"

She shook her head, got her fingers busy on the keyboard, and Jeffery stood up ready to leave her alone. "Heard anything from Eddie?"

Her head snapped around, she checked the clock, "No," she said, eyes suddenly alive.

"Don't worry; he's always a bit late. We'll give him till half past before we start to fret, okay?" He smiled warily at her because this wasn't Ros. She looked fragile somehow, as though one wrong word would shatter her. "Okay?"

She nodded and then checked her watch just for confirmation.

"Jeff?"

Jeffery turned, saw Cooper nod at him, and left Ros alone. He walked across the office, mumbling that his name was Jeffery, not Jeff! It said Jeffery on his birth certificate, and he liked it, it was—

"Come on, haven't got all day!"

Cooper guided Jeffery into Lisa's office and closed the door, then leaned back against it. Lisa was seated behind her desk, eyes wide with a distrust that seemed to calm slightly as Jeffery entered, hands tied together in a knot of writhing fingers. Tom Benson sat in a chair by the window, slightly reclined and with his legs crossed, casually. Jeffery took a seat next to him and Cooper began talking.

"I wanted to get you all together to bring you up-to-date with a job that happened last night, and one that might have repercussions for Operation Domino. Eddie Collins examined a scene yesterday where the suspect for Blake Crosby's death lived. Her name is Angela Charles.

"We believe that Tyler Crosby also went there looking for her, but didn't find her."

"Have you heard from Eddie," asked Jeffery, "because..."

"I'm coming to that."

"Sorry."

"CID called Tom last night to pass on details of a three-nines from an Angela Charles. She'd told the call-taker that a man was trying to kill her. It's on tape that there was a lot of background disturbance, doors being kicked in, items being knocked over. She was very distressed. Then a shot was fired."

Cooper took a moment to study their faces; especially Lisa's whose fingers had at last stopped their private wrestling match and rested star-shaped on her desk. She was aghast. Benson stared at his shoes; Jeffery was paying attention like Jeffery always did.

"She made that call from Eddie Collins's house."

"What!"

Cooper raised his hands to Jeffery, "Bear with me. Eddie was here at the time of the call, as you know, Jeff, working late."

"Why would he take a murder suspect home?" This from Lisa.

Cooper shrugged, was about to speak, when Tom Benson cut in. "He says he didn't know who she was. He picked her up from Garforth on his way back here. She looked needy, he said."

"Doesn't sound right to me," she said.

"I agree," Benson added, "but I can't prove that he knew her. He says she was called Charlie, and is adamant that he didn't find her in that house in Barwick-in-Elmet."

"So what happened?"

"James is working that scene," Jeffery said. "I thought I recognised the road name – but he never mentioned it was Eddie's house when I spoke to him a few hours ago."

"Is he anywhere near done?"

"Should be back any time."

Cooper resumed, "What happened, I'm guessing, is that whoever tried and failed to find Angela at her house in Barwick-in-Elmet was watching Eddie, saw him pick the girl up and followed him home. Luckily for him, Eddie left and came back here to finish off some work, and that's when she was killed."

"And Eddie?" Jeffery asked. "Where's Eddie?"

Cooper braced himself. "We don't know."

"Why don't you know?" Lisa asked. "He was a suspect at a murder scene, and you didn't arrest him?" She stared right at Benson.

"He checked out!"

Jeffery looked disappointed, "Lisa, he's your employee."

"He's still a suspect!"

"Everyone calm down," Cooper said. "There's probably a very good explanation for his absence this morning." He looked again at Lisa, but her face was passive except for a smear of anger directed at Benson. "I think he got spooked and ran." Still he watched Lisa.

She turned away from Benson, eyes scooting the floor, and then whispered, "Which reinforces the theory that he's guilty of something."

"Maybe he got drunk. This is Eddie Collins, after all." Jeffery hated saying it, his face gave it away, but it needed saying, everyone was thinking the same thing.

"I thought he didn't drink anymore."

Jeffery shrugged, "Who knows though. It must have been a great shock to find someone shot dead in your house."

"He was shocked," Benson agreed. "I'm no fan of his, but he was horrified at what had happened."

"He indirectly caused her death," Cooper said. "If he'd taken her to the hospital or to a police station, then she—"

"You can't blame him for that. If it's true, that he didn't know she was Angela Charles, why would he even consider taking her to the hospital or the nick?"

"I just can't believe you let him bloody go!"

Benson stared at her. "I already told you. He checked out, there was no reason to hold him."

"Well it might have prevented him going missing!"

Benson avoided her eyes, looked instead at Cooper, itching to respond.

"Protocol suggests he should have been arrested, yes; but—"

"Protocol is written for when we know nothing at a scene; it's a safety net," said Benson. "I knew he had nothing to do—"

"It's also written to protect people," Lisa said, eyes boring into Benson.

"Whoa, hold it there," Jeffery said, standing, "Are you saying they might have come back for him? The Crosbys? You saying they might have snatched him?"

Lisa said nothing.

"Why would they?" Benson said. "They have nothing to gain from him. They killed the woman who killed—"

"Angela Charles didn't kill Blake Crosby," Jeffery was adamant. "Eddie believes it, and I believe him." Jeffery pulled open the door, shoving Cooper aside.

"Where are you going?"

"To ring him, see if we can sort this out." And he turned to Lisa. "I hope to Christ I never need your support."

Lisa shouted, "What do you mean Angela Charles didn't..." But Jeffery had gone.

"To ring him," Benson laughed. "Why didn't I think of that?"

And when Jeffery had gone, Lisa faced Cooper. "I can't believe you didn't bollock him," she nodded at Benson, "for not arresting Collins."

"I'm still here, you know," Benson shouted.

"We've had words," Cooper said.

"Super! Is that it, words?"

"You think I should poke him in the eye or something?"

"You think this is funny?"

"Shut up, Lisa." Cooper took a pace towards her. "Right now you don't want to know what I think is funny."

Benson stood.

She squinted. "What's that supposed to mean?"

"Alright you two—"

"Shut it, Benson! I said what's—"

"I think your mind's not on the job."

Benson stared wide-eyed at Cooper. "Boss," he warned.

"What did you say?" Lisa stood and glared at him.

Eventually he smiled and then left the room. Benson sauntered after him.

Lisa was dumbfounded, and then sank into her chair.

———

Ros stood outside the office. It was like a kindergarten in there, everyone shouting over each other, pointing fingers, making threatening remarks. Through the glass and the small gap in the door, the odd word, the odd sentence even, made it clear to her what had happened. And then, when Jeffery barged out of the office and ragged snipes ricocheted around the walls at full volume, it left her in no doubt.

Like a dumb robot, Ros turned and followed Jeffery into his office. He had his back to her, hunched over his desk, and then suddenly she heard an electronic rendition of a recognisable voice.

"Congratulations! You've found me. Don't leave a message 'cos I won't reply anyway."

"Eddie, it's Jeffery from work. Nothing to worry about, but could you ring me as soon as you get this message please? Thanks."

"They took him, didn't they?"

Jeffery spun around, "Ros. I... No, I'm sure he overslept or..." He walked towards her and gently took her by the arms, guided to her to the seat by the wall and sat her in it, crouched before her. "No one knows, Ros. But I'm sure it's something simple."

"Are you? After what they said?"

"Speculation. And bluster. They haven't a clue."

"But what if they're right?"

He smiled at her, a fatherly smile, concerned, yet not entirely comfortable. He looked as though he were about to break some bad news. "Why don't you go home? I'll let you know soon as we get in touch with him. Promise."

She shook her head, looked away. "I'll stick around."

"I could run you home; you'd be there in twenty minutes—"

"I said no. Thank you. I'd rather stay here."

"What's the matter, Ros?" The fatherly smile had gone now. "You look awful."

She tried to stand but he put his hand on her shoulder. "Nothing," she said. "Maybe a cold coming on or something."

"Ros, have you heard from him? Is there something you're not telling me?"

Now she looked confused. "No," she said. "I haven't heard from him at all, that's why I asked you!"

And then James rolled into the office with eyes that came straight out of a vampire movie; bloodshot, tired, and droopy. He didn't make small talk; he sat at his desk and began work straight away, thinking of nothing but getting the hell out of here and crashing into bed where he'd stay for the next fourteen hours.

The next time he looked up, a crowd had gathered around him.

"Well?" Jeffery asked.

James dropped his pen, instantly looked worried. "Have I done something wrong?"

"What did you get from Eddie's house?"

"Probably some rather nasty disease, actually. It's filthy!"

Lisa stepped forward, "Has Eddie been back to his house?"

James added confusion to the worried look. "Erm, no," he said. His eyes shifted one person to the next, "What's going on, why is everyone staring at me?"

An hour later, James's chair was empty. His exhibits, an LCN swab from a 9 mm shell he found in the bedroom, a poor-quality footwear mark from the outer surface of Eddie's front door, and a set of photographs, were going through the mill of exhibit processing, and James was already at home, several fathoms below the surface when Cooper called another meeting with Benson, yawning, and Lisa, spiky.

"I'm worried that Eddie has been snatched by them," he said immediately.

Lisa stared at him, Benson stared at her.

"I've got the financial boys working on tracing any credit card movement; I've got a nationwide PNC report circulated for his car, including ANPR awareness. Any other suggestions?"

"Division," Lisa whispered. "Have you passed it to them?"

"Yes."

"Well that's all you can do then."

"Not quite all," Cooper said. "What do you think of us contacting Slade Crosby directly?"

"What? Are you out of your mind?"

"I used to like you when we first met," Benson said. "Now you're downright rude."

"You're calling me rude?"

"Why not contact him?" Cooper asked again.

"Because he'll laugh at you, he'll accuse you of carelessness, losing one of our CSIs. It'll give him a psychological advantage over you."

"He's got that advantage anyway, I'd say," Benson said. "He killed Angela Charles when no one else could even find her."

"And you really expect him to tell you?"

Cooper shrugged.

"What about your men? You must have someone inside Crosby's empire."

Cooper shook his head. "I did have, Tony Lambert. Now I have no one in there."

"Shame," Lisa looked away.

"I think you're safe." Lisa checked in the rear-view mirror, keeping a watchful eye out.

"I knew I was."

"I mean he's just told me he has no one inside your organisation."

"Ah, righto, that's good to have it confirmed. But I always knew we'd winkled out the last of 'em when Pearson, or Lambert, or whatever his name was, went down."

"Thought you'd like the confirmation."

"I appreciate that," Slade said. "Now what have you really called me for?"

Lisa sighed. "I need the job bringing forward to this week."

"Impossible."

"Please. You have to try otherwise it's all been for nothing. I lose everything."

After a long pause, Slade said, "Tell you what we'll do; you get me that name we spoke of last night, and I'll work on bringing the plans forward. I ain't saying it'll happen, but I'll give it my best shot."

Lisa tapped her fingers on the steering wheel, wore a grimace as he spoke to her and stared hatred towards the Bluetooth mic hanging down from the overhead console. "I've done more than enough for you over the last few weeks—"

"Let me remind you of your last sentence... 'I lose everything', I think it was."

"I can't just—"

"Get me his killer's name!"

The mic clicked as Slade put down the phone, and Lisa slapped the steering wheel.

She took a full half an hour to compose herself before she could pluck up the courage to go back inside. For all she knew, her cover might already have been blown out of the water, and Benson could be there waiting with the cuffs.

Inside the main MCU office, Jeffery was hunched over a desk on the phone to someone, and his hand was covering his eyes, pinching the bridge of his nose. Ros watched him closely. She couldn't hear what he was saying, indeed, he'd looked across at her twice, and turned away deliberately so she couldn't hear.

Eventually, he replaced the receiver gently and then walked calmly over to Lisa's office and closed the door.

Ros couldn't stand it any longer. She had stayed at her desk all morning, grumbling at the pain in her back, shoulders and knees, but consistently refused to go home. And now she knew Eddie was missing, she wouldn't even entertain the notion of leaving – she needed to be here when he phoned in all apologetic. Drunk probably, she had to admit. But even that was better than...

It was obvious Jeffery had heard something and she wasn't prepared to wait for the grapevine to swing into action. Ros got to her feet and ambled over to Westmoreland's door, knocked and entered. They both stared at her, and that made her feel worse, "Well?"

Jeffery licked his lips, "They found a receipt in a B&B he stayed in last night. He'd bought whisky."

Ros smiled instantly, and exhaled the breath she'd been holding. "Thank God." He's pissed as a fart somewhere, but that's good, he'll show up soon enough—

"There's something else too."

Now Ros looked up at him, down to Lisa who sat behind her desk looking pensive. "What else?"

"We found his car abandoned up in North Yorkshire."

"Oh my God, no."

Lisa coughed. "There is a cut cable tie in the back seat."

Ros looked confused for a moment, and then dismayed.

"Look," Jeffery whispered, "we have no idea what's happened, Ros. No need to jump—"

"I'm not stupid, Jeffery. I can work out for myself the implications of that."

"Want me to drive you home, Ros?" Lisa asked.

"For the last time, I am not going fucking home!" Her chin was trembling, and Jeffery opened the door.

"Come on," he said, "out. Let's grab a coffee."

"I don't want—"

"I said out."

As they dragged Eddie's Discovery onto the back of a recovery lorry, a police dog van slewed its way through the mud towards some dense woodland up a track that was mostly overgrown but had obviously been used recently.

Of course, with the heavy rain overnight and that which persisted even now, the tracks were of no forensic value even if they'd led anywhere important. The lane was dead-ended by thistles and nettles and thorn bushes, a small outcrop of rocks, and then an expanse of mud before the trees abruptly began. They'd already told him where to look, so it wasn't going to take him long, which was fine by him in this pissing weather, but being told the location kind of took the challenge out of it. It would have been nice for them to have given him some coordinates and left the detailed bit to him. He liked a challenge and so too did Deefer.

Deefer whined in the back, and eventually, with the van wheels spinning, he elected to stop and they'd walk from here. Deefer leapt from the van and was off. He smiled and walked at a more relaxed pace.

In less than twenty minutes, they'd found two freshly dug mounds of earth. There was blood too, trapped in creases of earth, in wrinkles in the sides of rocks where the rain couldn't wash it away.

Chapter Forty-three

Speculation and Bluster

— One —

ROS WOKE WITH A customary headache and he was staring at her.

"Hello, sleepy-head," he smiled.

Ros ignored him and tried to turn over, but he'd placed a hand either side of her body, almost pinning her to the bed by the quilt and he seemed reluctant to release her. She opened her eyes fully then, and tried not to make a fuss, even though she suddenly felt claustrophobic, hot and trapped, with his god-awful face less than a foot from hers. She was breathing the same air he'd exhaled, and it smelled rotten.

"How you feeling?"

"Achy still."

"You need a doctor?"

She shook her head. No, what she needed right now was for him to piss off to work, to get out of her life and leave her the hell alone. Unlikely though. "What time is it?"

"Half six. You up to making breakfast?"

"I have to go into work."

"I rang them already." He smiled even wider now, and she noticed his teeth, the blackness between them, the cracked lips. He was slowly turning into a horror movie all by himself. She heard him shriek, Here's Johnny! and closed her eyes.

"Got you the day off."

"You what?"

His smile faltered. "I can't work," he said, "been rained off again. So I thought, since you were under the weather, we could..."

"What? We could what?" Now the quilt wasn't tight enough around her, she pulled it up to her chin.

He merely nodded at the bed, sickly suggestive smile on his face, slimy, slug like.

She shuddered. "I have to go into work, I'm working on something," she tried to pull the quilt aside, but he held firm.

"They said you could take the—"

"I'm not taking the day off, I have some important—"

"Not so long ago, you'd have jumped for joy at not going in." He paused, then said, "I might begin to think you didn't want to spend the time with me."

She closed her eyes, wishing she had the strength to just tell him the truth, wondering why it wasn't obvious to him by now! "Of course I do," she lied, "but I'm really involved with this case—"

"What case?"

"I can't tell you that, Brian. You know—"

"How convenient: you're really involved with something, but can't tell me what."

"You knew all that when we first met—"

"Nothing to do with Eddie Collins then?"

Her heart stopped, and all of yesterday's fears tumbled back into place one by one until she felt as scared for him now, as she had yesterday. "What do you mean?"

He leaned close, nuzzled her ear and her neck, and she shivered, felt nauseous as he grunted like a pig. Just as she could feel bile rising in her throat, he pulled away and stood up. "You mentioned him in your sleep last night." He folded his arms.

She swung the covers aside and climbed out of bed, and hurried to get inside yesterday's clothes that she'd thrown over the back of the chair. She had no time for showers and tarting up her hair this morning, not even time to get out some fresh clothes – she just wanted to be out of this house. "Nonsense, Brian," getting as far away from this creep as quickly as possible was the only priority right now, "I'm just worried about this job I'm on. It's going wrong, I can feel it," and how the thought of never coming back thrilled her, but how the thought of being stopped by him scared the life out of her, "and if I don't act soon, then..."

"Then what?"

She was dressed now, mouth felt claggy still, eyes full of sleep still, but she had to leave, had to get away from him. It had become progressively harder to stay in the same room as him, but if he suspected her feelings for him, her true feelings – how could he not, she thought – then he would cage her up and chain her to the sodding wall and torture her until she died.

She shrugged, "Don't really want to think of that," she smiled. And then she surprised herself, as she wrapped her arms around him, sank her face into the side of his neck and kissed him. There was a part of her brain that had shut down, the tender part; it had closed for business so that the survival part of her brain could score points with Brian, so it could earn her safe passage away from him, at least temporarily. And had she not done that, showed some counterfeit affection, she may not even have made it out of the front door.

As it was, he returned the hug, even pulled away slightly so he could look at her, searching the feigned affection in her actor's eyes, and then he kissed her.

The survival part of her brain went into emergency mode, and she was able to return the kiss, blotting out the night spent in cold water in the bathtub, blotting out him fucking his bit on the side. Blotting out the fact she was scared of him, that she hated him, that she detested him.

She pulled away then, and smiled up at him, and she could tell he was convinced by it all. Her only concern now was that he'd force her to undress again and climb back into bed. She turned away before he had the chance, but he caught her by the arm, and she felt like screaming. Her heart pummelled, the needle on the Emergency Department gauge wavered around the red segment of the dial, and she was ready to collapse and just give in.

"You just be careful out there," he said. And he appeared to say it with sincerity.

Bollocks, she thought.

"Be home on time, eh?"

She nodded. "Do my best."

"I mean it. You don't want another night in the bath, Rosaline, do you?"

And then she was gone, down the stairs, out of the front door, car keys rattling in her shaking hand, and she shuffled saliva around her mouth, cleaning away the taste of him, before spitting it all out on the grass.

— Two —

He's going to kill me. That was her overriding thought as she swiped her card and let herself into the main office at a little before seven-thirty. There were lights on in Westmoreland's office and in Jeffery's too. Even farther along the office, she could see a glow through the blinds in Cooper's office as well. But it all meant roughly nothing to her as she took her seat and turned on the computer, staring out of the window into the car park below.

Rain hit the window, and trailed yesterday's dirt down it so that the muddy smear on the sill outside shimmered.

There was a feeling of hopelessness in Ros's mind now; it had persisted throughout yesterday, and had coalesced overnight, and now it was almost solid, like the pool of mud on the sill. And it dragged her down into a darkness, a blackness where nothing else really mattered. Her fear was for Eddie – entirely. Of course, the troubles at home were real too, they ring-fenced her fear for Eddie with a thousand shiny spears, but the blackness was more powerful and infinitely more severe.

"Ros?"

Her head snapped around and she saw Jeffery approaching. He looked like he hadn't slept much either. At least he had fresh clothes on this morning, a new tie, dark blue – conservative, like his demeanour, and his shoes, as always shone, but his eyes did not. He looked solemn.

"News?"

He sat next to her, no smile, no How are you? just an appraising stare. "I hate to say it, but you look like shit."

"Any news?"

"Go take a shower downstairs. Get yourself cleaned up. I'm sending out for breakfast."

"Jeffery. Answer the fucking question." She growled at him through clenched teeth.

He closed in, no hint of compliance in his eyes. "Go. Shower. Now." And then he stood up and walked away.

— Three —

Lisa Westmoreland was in a state of near paralysis. Like the others in the office, she had snatched minutes of sleep in what turned out to be a very long night for her. She had a fitful slumber that consisted of a fairground ride where each segment of its journey passed through one nightmare after another, rotating slowly so she got the full experience each time. She got her money's worth.

In one segment, Eddie would pop up and ask her if she was enjoying the ride, big smile on his face and a thorn pinning his top lip into his right nostril – looked like a permanent sneer, looked like an exaggerated impression of Elvis, and of course, he could blink in one eye only because the other was pinned open. Tears streamed down his face, and they'd mingled with blood to produce a water-smear like running red mascara after a crying fit. His eyes glared at her with a redness in their centres, a glow reserved for some kind of robot from those sci-fi films, like a Terminator. He was grotesque and she couldn't shake the image no matter how hard she tried. Eddie would put his drunken arm around her and ask her why she'd fucked about with his evidence like that.

He'd stood next to her in Crosby's kitchen, and watched one of his men use the liquid nitrogen from a van they'd pulled around the back. They took a tamper-proof evidence bag – the one bearing Eddie's signature, the one with a swab inside it from Tony Lambert's bedroom carpet – and they'd wafted it in and out of a metal container with liquid nitrogen pouring over the sides like an eerie spectral vision of the Niagara Falls.

Eventually, the bag had cracked open at the seal, the adhesive – super strong under normal temperatures, and of course, tamper-proof – had parted and the swab inside fell out onto the worktop. The bag now was super fragile, it would snap if touched too hard, had become brittle enough to shatter if subjected to extremes of temperature variation, and would remain so until it slowly came back up to room temperature again. So one guy had kept it hovering inside the container without actually immersing it, while another guy had slowly slid inside it another swab, pre-prepared by Lisa.

She could see Eddie in Slade's lounge now; he was on the floor and had been kicked in the side, and he was slurring his words as though pissed. Then the door had opened further and Eddie saw her, and his eyes opened wide in recognition, and that's when her heart had stepped up a notch. But by then it had been too late to step back out of the way – the damage was done. Eddie had just signed his own life away. And that's when Slade invited her into the lounge.

But then, Eddie was right beside her again; he had nudged her, thumbs up, "Feckin good job," he'd said. He spoke and a dribble of saliva splashed onto the floor because he couldn't close his mouth properly. "You've really thought thith through," he slurred.

And she had. But it was all Eddie's fault. If he'd stayed away from Tony's scene, none of this, none of it, need ever have happened.

And that's when the carousel spun majestically around a little further and the nightmare had continued on to another scene. This one featured bright sunlight bouncing off the white walls of a pub called The Magic Carousel; bright enough for her to be squinting, shielding her eyes from the brightness with a hand like she was giving a permanent salute to the man she stood alone with. His name was Slade Crosby, and he was a fat bearded man like a Hell's Angel, but he didn't wear oil-stained denim and a scratched leather jacket with spikes all over it. He wore jeans, and boots, but with a shirt and cotton jacket. He wore aviator shades so she couldn't read his eyes.

And she was speaking to him as though she trusted him. And she knew she couldn't. He was a gangster, and you could never trust a gangster. Gangsters worked towards their own ends, and once those had been satisfied, there was little chance your own piece of the deal would be concluded correctly. But she'd had little choice.

A young woman had approached her several weeks prior to this meeting. The young woman though had grown wide, not fat yet, but wide. She'd become incredibly less beautiful than she'd remembered; now she was clad in black leather, black-painted nails, black lipstick and black eye-liner. A dozen years ago, about two years before the young woman went to jail, she'd been lithe, sensual and beautiful in every department. She could have been a model, she was fit, as the saying went, but she wasn't a model, she was a copper, like Lisa. They'd gone through probation together and became lovers the night before they had graduated.

Of course, they didn't graduate by themselves. Back then there'd been a healthy intake of new police officers. Fifty people in all, four waves of probationer officers. And during the twenty-six weeks they'd spent together, a good few of them had become close friends. Lisa and this one young lady called Sophie, in particular. But fringing them, good enough friends to be invited on nights out and parties at each other's houses, were several others. In particular, there was a guy called Tony Lambert, distinctive because of the gap between his front teeth that was wide enough to park a bike in. He'd disappeared off the radar not long after graduation. He'd gone to work out of Stainbeck police station in Leeds, and then he disappeared, rumoured to have been picked up by Special Branch – and Christ knew what happened to people when they went into the secret squirrel world of plain-clothes.

But in the case of Tony Lambert, Lisa knew exactly what had become of him because over Slade's shoulder she could see him right now. He was squinting against the sunlight too, drawing his lips back as he screwed up his eyes, showing the gap between his front teeth.

At first, she hadn't really noticed him; she was involved in some rather fragile negotiations with Slade. But then she'd seen him, really seen, really paid him some attention, and she was utterly convinced it was him. She had problems bringing his name to mind at first. She got the Tony part immediately, but the surname evaded her.

"She's into me for fifty grand," she whispered to Slade. Of course, that wasn't necessarily the truth – Sophie had said she was kidding. But the point of it all was the threat, at least that's how Lisa perceived it: a threat. And that was good enough reason to be here right now, cutting a deal with a bastard. Didn't matter what currency.

Slade's eyebrows had risen at that. A handsome figure.

"I've no chance of raising it."

"You shouldn't anyway," he said. "What's to stop her coming back for more? You'd never be free of her."

"That's where you come in."

"Why would I want a piece of that?"

"Because I'm going to get Blake off a charge of rape for you."

Slade slid his aviators up his head, looked at her through deep brown eyes, shadowed crow-feet to the sides. "I'm listening."

And she'd gone on to state how she'd risk her career to lose some evidence, namely semen, recovered from the scene. When it went to court and CPS couldn't produce, they'd have to cancel the hearing or risk it being thrown out anyway.

Slade had warmed to the idea of course, and he'd agreed to take care of Sophie for her. But then, he'd surprised her by asking how he could trust her. A fair question when you actually stopped and thought about it.

"You want to know if you can trust me?" she'd asked. He nodded. "Okay," she said, "Don't look around, but the man who drove you here today. Do you know him?"

"Course I do. He's one of my men. Why?"

"Last I heard he worked for Special Branch. Probably into Crime Division by now."

"Bollocks."

"Name's Tony..." and there she paused for a moment, because it still wouldn't come; it was still just out of reach, and then, like a penny dancing down the board, striking pins left and right at the fairground, it landed in her hand, and she said, "Lambert. Been on the force for twelve years. Same as me."

"You sure?"

"Joined the same time as I did. He doesn't know I've seen him, but I know he recognises me. You should ask him."

Slade was quiet. Thinking. "Lambert?"

"It's what I know him as, yes."

Slade pulled the aviators back down over his eyes again.

"So you trust me now? We have a deal?"

It turned out they did indeed have a deal. And Tony had died as a result of it. Turns out his wife had too. And Lisa was sorry about that. No, really she was; she didn't want this thing with Slade to get bigger than one simple job in return for one simple favour. But, as predicted – if she'd stopped and given it some serious thought – it had spiralled into favour after favour, and still Sophie waved the threat over her and still Sophie laughed at her, with her high morals and low self-esteem.

It was a laugh. But it wasn't in the slightest bit funny, as The Magic Carousel revolved a bit further, still spinning even though she'd been awake and in her office for the last hour or so. There was so much happening inside her mind that Lisa shrieked when her phone rang.

— Four —

It was a large office and there were phones ringing all the damned time. Over at the admin desk in particular where Melanie worked, but also there were phones and conversations happening all around her, and yet Ros managed to pick up on just one out of the cacophony.

Jeffery was summoned into Lisa Westmoreland's office and the door closed. This was becoming like a ritual. It was getting to the point of obsession on Ros's part, and she climbed from her chair, about to walk across the carpet and let herself into the office. Through the window, Jeffery obviously saw her, and he put his hand up as though stopping traffic. She stopped, and then he waved her back, telling her to get back to her desk. There was pain in his eyes.

Chapter Forty-four

Respect at the Graveside

Northern England. A graveyard and a wind howling among the stones like a ghoul in a vampire movie. And of course the rain, incessant, pounding; umbrellas being ripped inside out, the vicar's garments floating up around him like some weird occult version of a Marilyn Monroe scene. He finished his chat at the graveside, bowed his head in respect for the people standing there in the rain, and left them to it.

Among the dozen or so police officers who had arrived wearing pristine dress uniforms, and who now looked like a bedraggled fancy-dress party, were Cooper and Benson, heads down, praying silently for, or just contemplating, a man doing his duty, an officer of the law trying to bring order from chaos. Much missed. Sadly defeated by an evil that roamed freely among them like the vampire movie ghoul.

"So where did it all go wrong?"

Benson squinted through the rain at Cooper. "It went wrong," he shouted over the wind, "with that stupid bitch, Westmoreland."

Cooper nodded.

"And I have to say, boss, it went wrong when you didn't take a firmer stand against them."

"Slade Crosby?"

Benson shrugged. "All of them; all the crews in Leeds. You've got enough to bang them up, certainly the leaders. I don't know why—"

"I was waiting," he said. "I knew there was something big coming along—"

"There's always something fucking big!"

Cooper looked at him.

"And look what happens when you wait," he nodded at the mounds of mud before them. "I need a drink," he said, and walked away, leaving Cooper feeling empty, betrayed, and worthless. But he wasn't alone. Standing at the far side of the new grave was a young woman dressed in a black leather jacket. She wore black lipstick and black eye-make-up; looked like a fucking Goth, Cooper thought. For a moment he wondered who she was and why she was there. Then it didn't matter anymore, and he walked away too, chasing a drink with Benson.

It was time to bring Domino to a close.

Chapter Forty-five

Heartbreak

— One —

LISA'S NIGHTMARE VANISHED LIKE smoke in a force nine. For the first time in days, she felt invincible again, like her plans were working, like they'd been positioned in the path of success by gods favourable to her. Eddie was dead, sunk into a muddy grave up north, and so surely it wouldn't be too long before her final problem was out of the way. Slade would deal with Sophie soon, as soon as she'd given him the news that the swab from Tony Lambert's bedroom carpet came back as horse blood. He would have to act then; it was her payment, her final payment to him to get on with the damned job of erasing Sophie and her malignant threat.

The nightmare carousel would be still tonight, she hoped.

The call she'd taken was from division, saying they had discovered two shallow graves up north not far from where they'd found Collins's car. It seemed a little strange that division had called her, but Collins was her employee, after all. Anyway, the feeling of elation completely obliterated any reservations she'd had. The silly bastard was not going to come walking back through the office door. She could relax, breathe deeply and concentrate once more.

Out in the office though, things were not so smooth. Lisa peered through the glass at Ros, and couldn't help feeling a little sorry for her.

— Two —

Since Kojak and Columbo were out of the office, it fell to Jeffery to pass on the news to Ros. He stepped out of Lisa's office and felt like running away. He saw Ros's eyes staring him down, and he was sure she could tell just how nervous he was. He looked not at her, but past her, out of the window just so he wouldn't have to see the pain of expectation in her eyes, and then he looked at the carpet, unable to deal with it any longer.

"Jeffery?" Melanie beckoned him.

Jeffery stopped, pirouetted left, like some kind of ballet-dancing puppet, and said, "Please tell me it's not more bad news," he approached her desk, "I cannot take any more bad news today, my bad news bank is overflowing and if I have any more then—"

"Just look," she said, cutting him dead. She slid a piece of paper across the desk.

He picked it up and read it. It was from the forensic science service – lab results for exhibit EC15, which was the swab from Tony Lambert's bedroom carpet, and from EC8, which was the blood swab from the tree branch at Blake Crosby's scene in Garforth. He perched on the edge of Melanie's desk, absorbed by the news.

"This can't be right," he said.

"What?"

"This!" He flicked the page, and in a high voice said, "Get me Eddie's scene report from the revisit at Tony Lambert's house."

"But—"

"Now!"

Melanie beat the keyboard up and then turned the screen so Jeffery could see the scanned report of Eddie's second attendance at the scene.

Then Ros was by his side. "What is it?"

"It's the lab results from Eddie's exhibits."

"Not that," she said; "what were you coming to tell me?"

"Nothing," Jeffery was distracted, scrolling through the report.

"Tell me."

"It'll wait, Ros, I'm just—"

"It won't fucking wait! Tell me!"

Jeffery closed his eyes, sighed and turned to her. He took a moment, and then quietly said, "They found two shallow graves not far from Eddie's car."

Like a machine shutting down, spiralling downwards towards a complete halt, Ros's eyes closed, and her breathing slowed, her tense posture relaxed and then she hit the floor going straight down like a building being demolished. Melanie shrieked and raced around the desk; Jeffery dropped the report and tried to catch her but got twisted up in his own feet and fell to the ground just beside her.

Lisa's door banged against its stop as she rushed from her office, "Get her some water!"

— Three —

Benson and Cooper left the pub and climbed into the car.

"Well, we should go see him," Benson said.

"Okay, let's do it."

In twenty minutes they left the main road, circled around onto a quiet lane, and pulled up outside an old-fashioned cottage with a single streetlamp outside, and a tuft of crime scene tape tied at its base fluttering in the wind.

In the rain they stood by the new front door and knocked loudly.

Eventually it creaked open and he stood there with a blurry expression, swollen lip and badly bruised eye. Across his forehead was a gash an inch and a half long with glue and tape holding the two sides of the flap together.

"Fuck me, it's Dempsey and Makepeace." Eddie strolled back inside and headed for the kitchen.

They closed the door behind him and he sighed as he realised his peace and quiet had just gone straight to ratshit hell. He sprinkled some coffee into a swilled-out mug and looked up at them, "Want one?"

They looked at the mug and both shook their heads.

"Suit yourselves." The kettle boiled and he poured the water. "You get anything useful from the bug?" And then he picked up a knife.

"What bug?" asked Cooper.

"Why are you stirring your coffee with the handle of a knife?"

Eddie looked at Benson as though he was stupid, "Because if you use the blade it sloshes everywhere."

"What bug?" Cooper asked again.

"I meant to tell you about that, boss."

"But you forgot, eh?"

"Gentlemen," Eddie said, "no shouting, I have a headache, okay?"

"How are you feeling, Eddie?" Benson hovered around him as Cooper took a seat in the lounge.

"Concussion. A lip that stings, an eyelid that hurts like fuck and throbbing in my head like there's a guy with a sledgehammer practising percussion for Motörhead. And the drugs they've given me... I can shit through the knee of an idol."

"What. Fucking. Bug?"

"So you didn't actually get shot at all?"

Eddie shook his head. "Nope. That prick Gillon was about to but Jagger got him first. He fired as he hit the floor fortunately."

"How come you got all the injuries?"

He shrugged. "I dunno. I kind of fell forward when I heard the shot, like a reaction. Dinked myself on some rocks and thorn bush things. Just plain old lucky, I guess."

Benson laughed, "Prick."

"I also shit my pants. But I'd like that to stay between us."

"Is anyone going to tell me about this bastard bug?"

Benson sat next to Cooper. "I knew there was someone inside working with Crosby, and I wanted to find—"

"You didn't think running it by me would be useful? Or courteous?"

"Girls, please."

"I tried to plant one myself," Benson continued, "but I failed and he was the perfect candidate—"

"Oh, the perfect candidate. Forgot that I was brave there for a second."

"You weren't brave, you arsehole, you were angry! And that's how I knew you'd get inside."

"I got inside 'cos I drove my car through the fucking gates!"

Cooper put his head in his hands. "Do you two have any idea how far over the line you both went? We have strict rules on covert surveillance."

"Like Jagger said to me yesterday morning, you have to play very dirty with these bastards. Play by the rules and you might as well walk away, for all the use it does. You don't start making headway with these pricks unless you take chances."

"Chances—"

"And I made some serious headway, Cooper, and don't you forget it. Who told you Westmoreland was your mole, eh? Who saw her tampering with evidence?"

"What evidence?"

"You're asking me," said Eddie, "when I've been out of it for—"

"We don't know what she's messed with yet," Benson said, "But it confirms what you said about the semen sample going missing from the stores at Blake's first rape, don't you think? Remember her outside the court that day, when she went and spoke with him on the steps?"

"Where's the proof?"

"Getting inside the stores is a piece of piss," Eddie sipped his coffee and winced at the pain in his lips.

They stared at him.

"It's almost never manned; I guess he goes off for a lie down somewhere, or he's playing with Miss Moneypenny under the receptionist's desk." He smiled but they just stared at him. He sighed, "When I went to Tony's house, I needed the keys from the stores. I knocked and buzzed and there was no one around, so I climbed over the counter and helped myself. She'll have done the same with whatever it is you're talking about."

Cooper and Benson looked at each other. "Is there CCTV in there?"

"Yup," said Eddie. "I waved at it on my way out." And then he looked at Benson, "Hold on, you said you knew there was someone on the inside?"

Benson nodded.

"So you'll have kept my death close to your chest then?"

"Damned right. If we'd blabbed you were alive, it'd put Jagger in danger from Crosby, and our mole would've done a runner pretty fucking swift; and then—"

"No one knows I'm alive?"

"Are you deaf?"

"You haven't even told Ros?"

Lisa Westmoreland topped up Ros's glass with fresh water and carried it to her. She looked very pale, shockingly so, and she was crying constantly, saying things like, "I'm being punished for doing this to him."

No one could get any sense out of her. Eventually Lisa looked across to Melanie and asked her to take her home.

"I'm staying here!" she screamed.

"Whoa," Lisa said, squatting down beside her, "you're in shock, Ros. You need to be home in bed."

"I'm not going home." She looked at her, "Please, don't send me home."

Lisa thought about it. "Ten minutes," she said. "If you're no better in ten minutes, then I will send you home; I have your health and safety to consider."

Ros looked down at the carpet, and cried quietly to herself.

Lisa pulled Jeffery to one side and asked, "Do you think we should call an ambulance?"

He shook his head. "That was fine, I think. We'll see how she is in ten minutes. If she's no better, Melanie can run her home." Lisa was about to turn and head off when Jeffery added, "I think you should look at the lab results."

"What lab results?"

He walked with her to Melanie's desk, picked up the sheet and handed it to her. "Eddie went to Tony's scene and found a red stain on the bedroom carpet. Well out of the ordinary for such a clean house."

She scanned the report, "It says no human nuclear DNA present."

"I know. It wasn't human blood."

"Stupid man—"

"No, no, he's not. Take a look at his report," he pointed to the screen on Melanie's desk. "See, he tested it at the scene using a KM kit, so it's definitely blood; then he tested it again with Hexagon OBTI, so it was definitely human blood."

She looked at him, confused.

"The lab have cocked up," he concluded. "It's the only thing I can think of."

"So that's that, then. Unless we can trace their error, that blood is lost?"

"Yes, that's right."

"And we can't revisit the scene?"

"No point; we always swab all the stain."

Inside, Lisa was jubilant. It had worked wonderfully, and it kept Tyler out of jail. And with Tyler kept out of jail, Slade would be happy, and if Slade was happy, then Sophie would be out of the way in the morning, she was sure of it. Her mood had lifted considerably, and she could think of nothing more enjoyable than contacting Slade right now and giving him the good news.

"But we do have some good news," Jeffery said, bringing the lab report back into view.

Just then Ros threw up all over the carpet, and all over Melanie.

And this time there was no discussion and no protesting from Ros. She looked very sad but also resigned. When Melanie came back from cleaning herself up, Ros surrendered and walked out of the office, still in tears.

Lisa was marching towards her office when she stopped dead at the side of James's desk. On it were colour photographs of some woman. Dead. But that wasn't the reason she stopped and stared at them, leafing through them as though they were shots from a glossy magazine. "Jeffery?"

Jeffery came over, the lab report still in his hand.

"See these?"

"Angela Charles's photos for the coroner. What about them?"

"The flash. See the eyes?"

"What am I looking at?"

"The flash, see. Why isn't there red-eye? Every time—"

"Ah no. You don't get red-eye from a corpse."

"What? What's that supposed to mean? Explain it!"

Jeffery took a pace backwards, surprised obviously by the fire in her voice. "It means that when you die, the retina isn't so blood-rich anymore, not so fresh or full of oxygen. When light hits a living eye, there are massive amounts of blood vessels all full of rich pumping blood and that reflects the flash back."

"But not in a dead person?"

"No."

"Ever?"

"It's never happened to me before. The eyes need a heavy supply of blood, and when the heart stops..."

"How long after death before the retina loses the ability to reflect flash light?"

"I've no idea really," he said. "But not long, less than a minute I should think."

She took a long breath, and the pictures in her hand began to shake. "Where are Cooper and Benson, do you know?"

"Erm, at Tony Lambert's funeral I think."

She dropped the photos and headed for her office.

"What about the lab report?"

Within seconds, Lisa Westmoreland had collected her keys and her coat and was on her way to the exit, eyes focused entirely on the doors, jowls bouncing with each hurried step.

"Lisa, it's good news on here!"

She stopped at the doorway, and slowly turned around. She stared at Jeffery.

Jeffery licked his dry lips, suddenly nervous.

And then she walked back to him. She snatched the report and read with ever-widening eyes the result from the blood stain on the tree branch: exhibit EC8. She looked at Jeffery in shock, and then in ever deepening thought. "Copy this for me."

———

"So what happened to Jagger?" Eddie asked.

"Nothing happened to him. He took a picture of you after you hit your head, and sent it to Crosby as proof you'd been killed."

"But what about Gillon, how did he explain his death?"

"Says you wrestled his gun from him and killed him first and then he killed you."

Eddie raised his eyebrows, "Smart kid."

"Lucky for you he's on the ball. And he got you to Harrogate hospital quick enough."

"So where is he now?"

"Back in the loving bosom of Slade Crosby."

"I don't know how they do it, undercover cops I mean."

"Special breed," Benson said.

"Changed your tune, you said—"

"I know what I said; but they have to play by the rules these days. Jagger did well considering the constraints we supposedly put on him; I respect him. But he agrees with me; you have to grab these bastards by the balls and pull as hard as fuck. They should be taken down using whatever means we can find."

"No, using whatever means is fair by law," Cooper said.

"Fair?"

And then Cooper's phone rang. He took it out and looked at the display; it said 'Office'. "Hello?"

"It's Jeffery, can you speak?"

"Yes, go ahead." He pressed some buttons and then said, "You're on speaker."

"Got the lab results back from Eddie's swab at Tony's scene."

"Go on, spit it out, Jeff."

"There must have been a mix up because it's coming back as no human DNA in the sample."

"What!" Eddie almost fell off his chair.

"In English."

"Erm, it's not blood."

"How can it not be blood?"

"Either the lab messed up or Eddie messed up. But his report is thorough; his sample tested positive for human blood."

"That was definitely blood!" Eddie screamed. "That's what evidence Lisa Westmoreland was fixing at Slade Crosby's house!"

From the phone, Jeffery said, "Who's that? Cooper, who's there with you?"

"Benson and Eddie Collins."

"What? What do you mean Eddie's with you?"

"I'll explain later." Cooper ran a hand down his whiskered face and said, "So we still don't know who killed Tony Lambert?"

"Sorry, no."

"I have the feeling that's not all. You have some more news?"

"I sent off a swab Eddie collected from the tree branch overlooking Blake Crosby's body."

Eddie ranted in the background, "She's not getting away with this."

"Why would you do that? You said it would belong to Angela Charles, right?" Cooper looked up to see Eddie shrugging a jacket on.

"No, it doesn't belong to Angela Charles."

"Just a minute, Jeffery," Cooper looked at Eddie. "Where the hell are you going?"

"Run me into work."

"Wait, wait, no one's running—"

"I said run me into fucking work." And then he reached the front door, "Forget it, I'll drive myself. Lock the door when you leave."

"Christ's sake!" Cooper looked at Benson, "Stop him, man!" And then into the phone, "I'll call you back." He hung up and chased Benson to the front door.

Chapter Forty-six

Behind The Magic Carousel

LISA WESTMORELAND WAS SO eager to break free of the MCU building that she took the passenger wing mirror off her car against the gatepost. She was screaming at the fucking thing to open quicker. Once outside, she got a mile away before pulling over and dialling Slade Crosby. Her hands were shaking, her stomach ached and her head was spinning.

"It's me," she said. She added a shaking voice to her list of troubles this afternoon.

"What's up?"

"We have to meet urgently: they're on to me and I have to get away quickly and I have to tell you—"

"Whoa, whoa, slow down!"

Lisa breathed deeply, tried to make her heart slow down. She stared at the traffic flying past, feeling its wake rock the car gently. "I need your help," was how she chose to begin. "I need cash, twenty grand should be enough."

"Twenty grand? Where the fuck do you—"

"Please, Slade! You don't have to help, I know, but... please. They're on to me." Silence from her phone. "And, I have some very important news for you too."

"News? Like what?"

Her mouth was dry, she swallowed but all she got was a clack. "Will you help me?"

"Is this about that Sophie woman? Because I've said we'll deal with her tomorr—"

"No, no, forget her; this is much more urgent."

"How do you know they're on to you?"

"Meet me. Please."

"Okay. Behind The Magic Carousel. Twenty minutes."

"Thanks—"

"This had better not be a trap, woman. And make sure you're not followed."

Slade hung up and then looked at the phone as though it were going to do some tricks. Across the room, Tyler shook out the newspaper and stared at his dad.

"What was all that about?"

"Fucked if I know. Where's Monty?"

"Dunno. He left about an hour ago. Bookie's I expect."

Slade made it to his feet, grabbed his stick and said, "Go get twenty grand from the safe."

Slade was in the car park of The Magic Carousel in fifteen minutes. He'd already completed two circuits of the surrounding lanes, and he made sure Tyler parked facing the exit, and when Lisa's car pulled up alongside, he made Tyler get out and check her boot, her back seat and then go stand at the roadside, thirty yards away. He was cautious under all circumstances, was Slade, but this kind of thing was verging on extreme. And though he would have liked another six men taking care of security right now, he had no one. They were out collecting, or out pissing it up, or like Monty, at the bookies.

He looked at Lisa through the side windows of both their cars, and when Tyler nodded, he beckoned her to sit next to him.

"What's so urgent?"

"Did you bring the money?"

He studied her face, and could see real anxiety on it. Her eyes flicked around like she was on speed, never still, never trusting. Whatever was bothering her, it was real, not a trick. Slade pressed the glove box button and took out an Asda bag. "Twenty grand," he said, handing it over.

"Thank you." She had tears in her eyes.

"Okay, what the fuck is going on?"

"They're on to me—"

"You said that already. How do you know they're onto you?"

"The red-eye. The photo your man took of Eddie Collins?"

"What about it?"

"Apparently dead people don't have red-eye." She looked at him, square on.

Slade studied her for a moment before reaching inside his jacket for his gun.

Lisa immediately raised her hands and began crying. "I'm not lying," she sobbed, "it's true; that's how I found out they knew about me. They kept it from me, they said he was dead, that they'd found his car and two graves. But he's alive!"

Slade was quiet for a moment, and then he put the gun away. "That means Jagger's in on it. That means he's a fucking copper."

She nodded.

"And you didn't know?"

"No! No one knows who they are, except Crime Division. I swear, Slade. When I checked him out for you, he was kosher."

"Bastard!" He smashed a fist into the dashboard, and glared at her. "If you're fucking me about, I swear I'll mutilate you."

The tear fell, and she mumbled, "I'm not. Honest."

"So that's why you're not bothered about the Sophie woman?"

"I'll be long gone before she calls for her money."

Slade sat still in thought for a moment, cheeks throbbing as he ground his teeth, eyes like slits as he planned Jagger's execution. "Go. Leave me alone."

She opened the door wide, and then hesitantly took a folded sheet of paper from her jacket.

"What's that?"

"This is the news I have for you." She looked worried. "I have nothing to gain from this, so it's up to you if you believe it or not."

He snatched the paper, then turned to her. "What is it?"

"It's a lab report from a blood stain."

Slade shook his head, "I have no idea what you're—"

"This is the name I promised you; the one responsible for Blake's death. He was killed by a rock thrown from a tree."

"What?" And then he half-laughed, like a snort. "That's like a kid's way of killing. I always thought he woulda been shot."

"We found blood on the branch where the murderer sat."

Slade unfolded the piece of paper and squinted, trying to make sense of all the numbers, and the names, and the processes it mentioned.

Tentatively, Lisa reached over, and pointed to the line that said, "No nuclear DNA detected. That's the results from the swab of Tyler's blood on Lambert's bedroom carpet. Remember, I said I'd fix it?"

"Yeah, so you fixed it. So what else am I looking at?"

"I just wanted you to know that you can trust me; that I did my bit."

"Yeah, yeah, I see that!"

"Below it is Exhibit EC8, the blood Collins swabbed from the tree branch..."

Slade's eyes followed the row that began with Exhibit EC8, followed by the date, the time, the place. Then came the lab process used to extract DNA. Then came the result as a number. That number was converted to a Nominal index number. The Nominal index number equated to 'CROSBY, Tyler Michael'. He read it through again, and then he read it through one last time before looking at Lisa with a mixture of confusion and disbelief.

She nodded, "It's true."

Slade bit down hard on his lower lip. "You saying he killed his own brother?"

She looked at him, not daring to speak.

"Why would he kill his own brother?" Slade's eyes left her and they stared out of the windscreen into nothing at first, just drifted as though searching for an answer. And then they settled on Tyler standing by the entrance smoking a cigarette, keeping an eye on the traffic. "This is true?"

"Yes."

"No way it could be falsified, like you did with the bedroom carpet blood?"

"It hasn't been tampered with. And I've nothing to gain by lying to you."

Slade closed his dampened eyes, and eventually he said, "Go." The car rocked slightly as she got out and there was a muffled thud as she gently closed the door. Then he heard her drive away. When he opened his eyes again, the tears fell.

But the sorrow didn't last long. The anger came pretty quickly.

Sophie used her elbow to smash one of the small panes in the rear door. Most of the glass fell onto a bristle mat just inside the door, and the back garden was secluded, shielded from view by a six-foot fence, sounds well muffled by the shrubs and the trees that grew nearby. She waited for a minute or two just to make sure no one had overheard.

No one had, it seemed, so she pulled the cuff of her woollen sweater from beneath the leather jacket, and down over her fingers, then reached inside and unlatched the Yale lock.

Five minutes after Slade left the house, Jagger opened the gates and the police rolled in. They came in vans. Nine of them. Forty police officers, sniffer dogs, OSU search teams, CSIs and divisional detectives all commandeered by Crime Division to conduct a thorough and detailed search of The Grange, the staff quarters and the surrounding outbuildings, and any vehicles found on site. Armed officers gave initial protection to method-of-entry officers and when the house was cleared, they took up position at the gates.

X99 floated overhead, and spotters circulated the neighbourhood, keeping an eye out for erratic behaviour and signs of impending trouble.

Jagger didn't anticipate Slade being back any time soon. And that was good, because war would break out if he did. All this had begun with a hurried phone call to the Divisional Commander this morning at 0430 hours from Cooper – shortly after Eddie Collins woke up in a Harrogate hospital and began talking to Jagger. And then there was a face-to-face meeting at 0700 at Killingbeck Police Station.

It had been hurriedly concocted, hastily brought together, and all those gathered under the operational name Domino had been on standby two miles away for the last three hours.

Units had been placed at the ends of the road which ran past Slade's house, and at all junctions in between. Each unit had pictures of all nominals connected with the Crosbys, and all the units were allotted an operational channel to communicate with each other directly, or exclusively with a control room staffed by three, and watched over by a Silver Commander.

From a shaded balcony across the street, a young woman took pictures of all the activity and made audio notes into a recorder. Her name was Sarah Moran, and a man called Eddie Collins had rung her earlier with an address that, he said, might be of very great interest to her, providing she could secure a decent vantage point.

Other units were also deployed to a café called Fat Sam's, known to be owned by Crosby, and fourteen tenement flats in some of the newer apartment blocks in the city centre. Over the course of the day, eleven disused properties were raided; six of them turned out to be fully-fledged cannabis farms, two were crack houses producing methamphetamines, and a further two were inhabited by women and girls of all nationalities in makeshift brothels. Another address in south Leeds yielded Slade's fraudulent passport business, complete with the 150 superbly forged passports that Jagger had collected from Scarborough.

Further, smaller scale raids occurred simultaneously at sixteen addresses through Leeds and Bradford, but this was the biggy, this was the kingpin. When Slade Crosby fell – they would all fall.

They hadn't found them yet, but over the course of the next two days, search teams would find detailed records of his protection rackets, contacts at various ports around the UK; names and interests of junior and senior politicians, even references to police officers.

"Can't you drive any fucking faster?"

Benson scowled at him. "I could, but what's the point in rushing?"

"What's the point? The point is, dipshit, Lisa Westmoreland ruined evidence against the son of a Leeds gang lord. Until you have that evidence, you can't charge him with killing one of your men! Oh, and his wife. But if you're—"

"I know that, but the lab'll be closing soon, and he ain't going anywhere is he?"

"—not interested then just drop me at the nearest bingo hall."

"Very fucking funny."

"I put my neck on the line for you lot; I was inches away from being dead, and you're worried about a speeding ticket. And would you rather he was charged just for killing his brother, or for killing a police officer?"

"Okay, okay."

"Pity we can't hang him twice really."

Eddie said, "And there's something more important, too."

"What?"

"You buried the poor bastard with everyone still thinking he killed his wife and topped himself. You need to put that right urgently. Think of his family."

The car went quiet for a few minutes following that little revelation. Of course it was something that each of them knew, but it was good to have it refreshed, and said out loud.

From the back seat, Cooper said, "He's right, Tom, get your foot down. If Eddie can get anything from Tony's scene, I want it dealt with now, the lab techs and scientists can work overnight if needs be. Domino is running and the last thing I want is loose ends flapping in the breeze. I should be in the control room now, not fucking about with you."

"Boss," sighed Benson.

"And when we get to MCU, I want you to find Westmoreland."

"I thought you lot always swabbed everything anyway. You said there was only one spot of blood."

Eddie ignored him, took out his phone and searched for Ros's number, then pressed 'dial'. All he got was five rings and then a recorded message. He searched for her house number and tried that. All he got was constant ringing, not even an answerphone.

"Who you ringing?"

"Trying to get hold of Ros. She still thinks I'm dead, remember?"

"I'll let her know," Benson said. "She'll be in the office."

They arrived at MCU and the gate rolled slowly, achingly slowly, back. Eddie noticed a wing mirror near the gatepost and chuckled to himself. No sooner had Benson stopped the car, than Eddie climbed out, wincing at the pain in his ribs from the kicking Crosby's crew had given him.

He limped to his van, and was back at the gate before it had time to begin closing. Cooper followed in his car.

Chapter Forty-seven

Nearly There

— One —

"WHERE TO?"

Slade stared across at Tyler as the car moved along. He said nothing for a long time, he just stared. He was thinking about his son as a boy. Not so long ago really. And what tugged at his mind in the way an often used memory will, was a time when Slade and Maureen, Tyler and Blake were in Cornwall on one of the very few family holidays they'd ever had – Rachel had elected to stay at a friend's house.

Part of the reason it stuck in his mind was because it was the first time Tyler had ever sworn at him. He'd be about twelve or thirteen years old. Maureen wouldn't permit the kids to swear, not until they were sixteen, she said – and even then, never in front of her. It was a stupid rule, because he and Maureen frequently swore. They can know the words, she'd said, but while ever they're under my roof or under my care, or in my company, they will not use them.

But Tyler had. And this was his first time.

Slade had bought Blake and Tyler a mobile phone each. Funny how when you go on holiday you have to browse the same shops as you would back home. And even funnier is the mentality that you can spend more while on holiday. Anyway, he'd bought them a phone each. Nokias, he thought they were. Except Tyler's didn't work. Blake's was fine, but Tyler's wouldn't even switch on.

They had a fight and Slade had got between them and given them both a good clout around the ear. Blake had cried, as he always did – and really, he hadn't deserved it – but Tyler had flown into a rage and screamed at Blake and his dad, called him a bastard and one or two other choice words. So Slade thumped him on the chin, nothing too hard, just a reminder of who was boss. That had made Tyler cry. And it made him furious too, shouting and screaming that he always got worse treatment than Blake, that Blake was the favourite, that he could do no wrong, while Tyler always had the shit kicked out of him. Soon after that, Tyler called his brother Blake-the-Snake. And that name stuck for months.

"What you grinning at?"

Slade looked at his son. And he found that he was indeed smiling. Memories did that to you too. "Head out to Garforth."

"Garforth? What's in Garforth?"

"I was remembering Blake-the-Snake," he said. "You remember that?"

Tyler nodded, saw the beam on his dad's face and smiled too. "Yeah, he was though," and he laughed.

"And then—" Slade's phone rang, spoiling the moment, and it brought him back to now. Not a pleasant place to be, especially after the memories he'd allowed himself to see. First time in a long time. He took out the phone, "Where the fuck have you been?"

"Chief, it's me."

Slade sighed. "I know it's you, Monty. Where are you?"

"I'm with Shack, chief. Remember the names we got off that copper fella, Pearson; the undercover coppers? They're here! We found 'em, chief!"

"What, all three of them?"

"Nah. Two of 'em, though."

Slade thought about this. They have two of them; I can make that a flush. "Where are you now?"

"Woodhead's scrapyard. Off Pontefract Lane in Hunslet."

"Right. Gimme an hour." Slade pressed end and put the phone away. And then he said to Tyler, "Take a left here, here now!"

"Okay!" Tyler swung the car off the road, and it bounced onto a rutted track, still slick from the earlier rain. The track appeared to go nowhere, disappeared around a bend. "What we doing here?"

"Just drive. Slowly!" And then he was back in Cornwall, being called a bastard by Tyler. Good days. But they got worse. Tyler had swapped phones with Blake and World War Three had broken out. Slade took his belt off and gave Tyler's bare legs three of the finest wallops he'd ever handed out. They'd left marks so vivid you'd have thought he'd sat on a freshly painted bench. The boy had screamed for hours, and then the screaming died down a bit and the ranting began, the pleading of innocence, the blame, the finger pointing at Blake, and then the tears. 'Why won't you believe me?' It went on for hours. "Here," Slade said, "Pull up here."

Tyler rolled the car to a gentle stop. They were half a mile away, maybe more, from the road. The place was immersed in silence; only an occasional bubble of birdsong interrupted it. Perhaps it didn't interrupt it, merely added to it, an enhancement, Maureen would have said.

"Dad, what the hell are we doing here?"

"Turn the engine off and get out. I want to show you something."

Once outside the car, Slade said, "You ever been told you never had time to stop and smell the roses?"

"I've heard it before. But I'm not interested in flowers."

Slade looked at him for a moment, and then it dawned on him; Tyler hadn't a fucking clue what he was talking about. "We're having five minutes," he said. "Five minutes of father-son time; five minutes out of the rat race just to ... chill out."

"Cool."

"Come on, wanna show you the stream."

It took them almost ten minutes to walk the 200 yards away from the car. They stood at the top of the banking, Slade favouring his bad leg, and breathing heavily. The stream ran, heavy with recent rainfall, twenty-five yards away. Its sound was hypnotic enough to induce a trance-like state, and Slade allowed himself a moment of clear meditation. That's what he called it anyway. He closed his eyes and the rippling water reminded him of Cornwall again. Absently, he wondered why he couldn't get Cornwall out of his damned mind. And that brought his trance to an abrupt end.

To the right, another thirty or forty yards away, was a great old oak tree. "Recognise this place?"

Tyler shrugged. "Nope."

"Not even that tree?"

"Should I?"

"I thought you would, yes. This is where Blake brings his... used to bring his 'girlfriends'."

"Where he raped women, you mean."

"Precisely. To my knowledge he brought two of them here. The first he managed to walk away from; we even got him off the charge when she got the police involved."

"Yeah, the copper woman."

"That's right. The copper woman." Slade shifted his stick to his other hand and reached inside his jacket for a folded sheet of paper. "The second one though, he didn't walk away from."

Tyler stared blankly at his father.

"That's where he died," he nodded to a spot below the oak tree, "just down there."

"This place gives me the creeps."

"Still don't recognise it?"

"I already said."

"Alright, alright." He held out the paper. "Read this then."

Tyler reached out and took the paper, but his eyes stayed on his father, a confused look in them. "What's this?"

"Read the fucker and find out."

Tyler unfolded it, turned it the right way up and began reading. The bewilderment grew on his face.

"Check out the line that begins with 'Exhibit EC8'."

Slade watched Tyler's face change from incomprehension, to understanding, stopping off at fear and disbelief on the way.

"What is this shit?"

"That shit is proof that you killed your brother."

"Are you serious?"

Slade didn't answer.

"Come on, Dad. It's a fucking lie. It's a piece of paper, means shit."

"You look me in the eye and tell me you didn't drop a rock on your brother's head from that fucking tree over there."

"I didn't... what's it mean, 'swab of red stain'?"

"Red stain. Red stain – that's blood, you prick! Your blood! They found it on a branch up that bastard tree!" Spittle flew from Slade's screaming mouth.

"I didn't! Dad, you have to believe me, I never killed Blake! I can't believe you think I killed my own brother!"

"You wanted my empire. You hated him rapin' women; you always thought he was a danger to your future."

"Bollocks!"

Slade calmly took the gun from his inside jacket pocket.

"Dad. Wait, wait, Dad. Don't do anything stupid."

Slade looked up at that.

"Wait, I didn't mean... I can't believe you'd take their fucking word over mine!" The veins on the side of his neck stood out, and his face glowed red; desperation now hunched him over in a submissive posture towards his father, hands out, pleading. "Dad you have to believe me I wouldn't kill Blake I loved him Dad don't do this!"

Slade aimed and pulled the trigger.

The echo took but a fraction of a second to disperse. Tyler still stood even after it had. But not for long, and then, momentum slowly won the battle and it toppled him backwards onto the banking. He collided with a tree root and landed with half of his face in a bunch of nettles. And the peacefulness came back. No birdsong however, just trickling water from the stream and a clear silence.

Slade bent and retrieved the paper, took Tyler's wallet and the car keys. He slid the gun inside his jacket pocket, took hold of his stick and began walking back to the car.

Ten minutes later, he rested against the still warm bonnet of Tyler's BMW and smoked a cigarette. "Now who gets your empire, Slade?" he whispered.

After he smoked the cigarette, he flicked it away and lit another, and then he took out his phone and called Jagger. "Come pick me up," then gave directions and hung up.

It was almost over now. Just one crooked piece of the jigsaw remained, and its name was Jagger. Soon, the puzzle would be complete. Slade smiled to himself as again his mind wandered back to Cornwall, and how, as it turned out, Blake had swapped the phones over just so Tyler would get the belt. All Tyler's pleading and crying had been genuine after all. Slade suddenly stopped smiling.

— Two —

Eddie wasn't sure, but he thought Tyler had done a pretty decent job up till now of evading the 'thou shalt not' parts of English Law. He'd done a pretty thorough job of getting others to do the risky things for him, the things that would see them caught. He also seemed to have done a reasonable job of leaving no fingerprints or DNA at any of the robberies or beatings Eddie had heard about. Except Charlie's of course. But what was that? Burglary. Whoopee.

He pulled into the cul-de-sac up in Alwoodley fourteen-and-a-half minutes after setting off from MCU, closely followed by Cooper, thankful not to have been stopped for speeding. Cooper met him at the side of the van. "Did you bring the house keys?"

"Still in the van from last time," he winked, "I forgot to put them back."

"We still need to follow protocol, Eddie. No point if—"

"Stop whining and grab the camera."

Eddie turned off the CPS alarm and turned on the lights. It was cold in here; had a weird atmosphere that he refused to put down to anything other than the house now being empty; no one opening windows, letting in fresh air. That's all it was.

He peered up the stairs and was not surprised to see no body hanging from a length of blue nylon rope from the attic hatch. Of course not.

"Shouldn't we be putting scene suits on?"

Eddie jumped, and growled. "Just a mask and gloves will do; we haven't time to fanny around." He swallowed and climbed the stairs. He switched on the light in Tony Lambert's old bedroom. All curtains were drawn, and the daylight that managed to seep through was weak, pasty, diluted by cloud and incessant rain. It was summer time, after all.

Cooper pulled the mask over his face and drew the nitrile gloves on. "Well, where is it then?"

"You think I swabbed it and left a marker just in case some bitch decided to screw with my evidence and I had to come back?"

"Okay, okay, stop being so snappy!"

"Snappy?"

"Get on with it, Collins!"

Gingerly, Eddie pulled the mask on, wincing at his stinging lip and swollen eyelid. Armed with his Maglite, Eddie crossed the patterned carpet to an area that offered the same kind of vantage point of the far side of the bed, as the last time he was here. It wasn't as though the original blood spot stood out – if it had, James would have seen it; if it had, Eddie would have spotted it far more easily. But no, it had hidden in the pattern of green and red swirls, the golden flecks confused the eye and Eddie ended up on his knees searching the carpet inch by inch.

"I wish I'd brought my scene photos," he said. "I could've narrowed it down a bit."

And then Cooper's phone rang. He took it out and spoke through the mask, "Hello."

"She's gone. Jeffery said she left not long after the lab results came in. In a hurry too, he said."

"Bollocks. Get to her house, Tom. And get some back-up there too."

"There won't be any back-up; there's no one left. Domino sapped it all."

"So be careful then!"

Eddie shouted, "Did you tell Ros?"

Cooper listened to Benson's reply. Shook his head at Eddie, "She's gone home, sick." Cooper hung up, and said to Eddie,

"Find me some blood, and quick; this thing is beginning to sink – if that bitch gets away, I'll... I'll..."

"Kill her?"

"Not fucking funny!"

More valuable minutes escaped as Eddie searched with the Maglite, using a folding magnifying glass on the pieces of carpet that he thought looked most familiar. "Gotcha!" He could see it, a tiny smear of red against one of the green swirls. He pinpointed it with the torch, never took his eyes off it as he said to Cooper, "Get me four adhesive arrows out of the camera kit."

"Good lad!"

Eddie stuck all the arrows so they pointed at a section of carpet no more than 5 mm across. Then he stood back and photographed it, closing in with each new shot until in the final frame, he could see individual strands in the carpet fibre, and the smear of redness clinging to a slender bunch of them.

Once swabbed, Cooper snatched it from him and was making his way down the stairs when Eddie called, "You okay with the paperwork?"

"Fuck the paperwork." And then he was gone out of the front door, and moments later he was wheel-spinning his way out of the cul-de-sac.

Eddie left the arrows in situ for some reason he couldn't quite fathom, then he hurriedly assembled all his gear and marched down the stairs for the last time. He had somewhere very important to go next.

— Three —

Lisa parked on the drive, wrenched the handbrake on and stepped out of the car, fumbling with her house keys so much that she dropped them and privately screamed. Once inside, she closed and locked the door, left the bag of cash on the hall table and sprinted up the stairs.

When she came back down again, in clothes more comfortable for travelling, with a soft leather briefcase, and her passport clutched in her hand, the money had gone.

She stood and stared at the table. Her heart thundered and her hands sweated again. She'd left it there, she knew she had. She didn't need to go check in the car, and she didn't need to go and check upstairs – she left the fucking thing right there!

Lisa swallowed and walked slowly into the lounge.

"What's this?"

Lisa's bottom lip trembled slightly. No point asking how Sophie managed to get in; besides feeling the draught from the back door, it didn't really matter. "I assumed you were going to contact me with a date and a place."

"The money thing... it was a joke. You pathetic cow. I don't want your fucking money. I said back then that I didn't." Sophie looked at her through the corner of her eye, and lifted the bag. "This isn't for me anyway, is it?"

What could she say?

Sophie looked up from the bag, dropped it between her feet, and smiled. "You look like you need a glass of wine. Stressful day?"

"Just a bit."

"Planning a weekend away?" Sophie nodded at the passport. "Or a lifetime maybe?"

"Sophie, please—"

"You remembered my name! And you're being polite to me."

"I have to go. Right now."

"Bad misters after you?" Sophie grinned, "But you work for the police! Detective Chief Inspector, no less!" And then she laughed. "Why would you of all people be running from the bad misters?"

"It's a long story."

Sophie reclined in the chair, her leather coat creaking, and crossed her legs. "I have time, Lisa. Looks like you don't though, huh?"

And then, as if someone had thrown a switch inside her head, Lisa blinked; Sophie was a threat to her. Ever since their last encounter, whenever she had thought of Sophie, which was often, she'd thought of the word threat.

But the switch flipped again, and the threat vanished. It didn't matter if Sophie reported her as being responsible for killing Chloe all those years ago now did it? The police were after her now anyway.

Lisa blinked again. And she smiled.

Clearly this unsettled Sophie; she was the one in charge, she had the upper hand, she was the one who smiled as though belittling a minion. The minion obviously should not smile back; the minion was under the thumb. Something had happened to change it all around. Sophie licked her lips, "How come you didn't go to Tony Lambert's funeral?"

Lisa sat down on the sofa opposite her, crossed her legs and leaned back. "It would have been a little two-faced considering I had him killed." She stared as Sophie's mouth fell open. Smiled again.

"You what?"

"Because of you as it turned out."

"Me?" She barked a laugh, "What the hell did I have to do with it?"

"It was all because of you. You showed up and I damaged your ego by not leaping on you and sticking my tongue down your neck after you'd been away for ten years. And because you felt sorry for yourself, you decided to blackmail me—"

"I wanted—"

"You wanted me to suffer!"

"Like I suffered!"

"And now everyone has suffered because poor little Sophie is back on the scene. I couldn't afford fifty grand and I couldn't afford the risk of you waltzing into some fucking police station and opening old wounds."

"They're not old to me!"

"So you left me no choice."

"What the hell did you do, Lisa?"

"I turned to someone for help."

"You were gonna have me executed, weren't you?"

"Moved along, I think they term it."

"You went to a gang then, eh? And..." the realisation dawned on Sophie's face. "Tony was there, wasn't he, working undercover? And he saw you."

Lisa looked at the floor. She whispered, "See what you did now, Sophie? See what you started?"

Sophie didn't move or speak. She let it sink in, and then suddenly she looked up. "This is quite surreal," she whispered. "I didn't want anything from you. Especially not money. But you know what I did want? I wanted you to acknowledge me, and maybe even just shake hands, to thank me for sparing you ten years inside. I think I deserved that. Don't you?" Lisa made no reply. "I went shopping."

"Look, I really have to—"

"One minute. That's all this will take. Promise." She stood up and walked around the sofa to the stereo. Sophie opened the CD player. "I still can't believe you had one of your old colleagues killed. I mean that's, that's incredible; it's the kind of shit you see in films. It doesn't happen in reality." She wiped the CD against her black leggings, dropped it on the tray. She pressed buttons and the CD tray closed. "You must be some weird kind of bitch to do that to someone you worked with."

"What are you doing?"

"Ssshhh, just one sec."

And then the music started playing.

"Oh please!"

"Listen."

Sophie turned around and knelt down behind the sofa that Lisa sat on. And the bass erupted across the room, all four speakers singing the Sugababes' A Freak Like Me, and memories of that night a decade ago thrashed back to life, of them dancing, of them embracing, kissing, fondling.

Killing.

Sophie reached an arm up and around Lisa's neck and pulled. Lisa's throat was in the crook of her arm and Sophie tightened the grip and pulled backwards against the sofa.

Sophie maintained a determined and persistent grip. Through clenched teeth, she said, "I hate you for making me do this, you murdering bitch. But you're not running away from what you've done again, Lisa. Gonna make sure of it. Remember," she grunted, "I said I wanted you to face up to your past? Well, that's exactly what you're going to do. And you can tell them I blackmailed you if you want, but do you think they'll believe you? I already confessed to 'killing' Chloe. And now you're going to have to confess to killing poor Tony."

Lisa's arms flailed, whacking the sofa, pulling at Sophie's arm, scratching the leather of the jacket she wore, nails like claws reaching back for her face, trying to gouge her eyes. Tears squeezed from bulging eyes that were wide with terror, and her feet thrashed about wildly, her chest heaving.

"Nearly there," Sophie whispered into her ear. "Tony's gonna get the decent burial he deserves, and all this shit between you and some gang is coming out in the press. I promise you. Everything."

It went on forever.

The thrashing had stopped now. Sophie watched the back of her pretty head. Noticed her hair, could see individual hairs, saw the tops of her ears, the fine downy hairs on her cheeks. And as she released the pressure on Lisa's throat, she could see the side of her face, the closed eye, the curl of her eyelashes, and the beautiful curve of her nose. And she could see her throat, a good strong pulse in the side of her neck. "Perfect," she said.

Still the music played but Sophie didn't hear it any more. Her thoughts were so immersed in her actions, her eyes so occupied with feeding on Lisa that there was no room for audio. But now it thundered rudely back into her spectrum, and it wasn't music anymore, it was just noise, too loud, too much. She hit stop, and knelt on the floor breathing hard and sobbing.

Slowly she got to her feet, and looked down at her handiwork. Lisa's white hands rested on the sofa, her head cocked to the side, dry lips pulled slightly back over her teeth. If it wasn't for the shallow rise and fall of her chest, you could easily mistake her for dead. But did this make her happy? Did it make up for Tony's death? Was it a punishment for, as Lisa had put it, not sticking her tongue down her throat and carrying on where they'd left off? Was it payback for not writing or visiting anymore?

Was it justified?

"No," she whispered.

Sophie heard a car pull up very quickly out front and then she snapped awake, and stared the bag of cash. Then she left through the back door and hopped over the fence at the foot of the garden.

Benson hauled the handbrake on and was out of the car before it had stopped, engine still running as he sprinted up the drive alongside Lisa's car with the broken off wing mirror and tried the front door. It was locked and he ran around the back. When he saw the broken glass, he stopped.

"No, no, no, this isn't good," he panted.

He nudged the door inwards and stepped over the glass and into the kitchen, listening all the time. But it was silent. He wondered if she was upstairs, but the broken glass kept telling him something was badly wrong. He peered around the door into the lounge; saw her slouching lopsided on the sofa. "Lisa?" He entered the lounge. "Lisa?"

A wheezing breath came from Lisa's mouth, and her throat was cherry red.

"Just fucking super," he said.

Chapter Forty-eight

A Present for Jagger

SLADE HAD GOT THROUGH another five cigarettes before he heard the sound of tyres approaching on gravel. It was Jagger in the silver Mercedes. Slade turned and hobbled to the passenger side, and climbed in, throwing his stick into the back.

"What's happened?"

"Nothing."

He nodded at the BMW. "You just leaving that there?"

"No, I thought you could drive them both at once. Prick. Course I'm leaving it there; we'll have a couple of the lads come by and pick it up later." He looked across at Jagger, and despite having just ended his last son's life, he felt like smiling at the slimy bastard. He knew now that Jagger was a copper and he knew Jagger was pretending; everything he'd done over the few months he'd worked for Slade was a fucking lie. But he was good; yep, he blended in nicely, did his work without any grumbles and worked the hours too. He was fucking good.

But not good enough.

And that's why Slade turned to the front. "Drive," he said. "Hunslet." Because he was going to smile and that would give it away. Didn't want that to happen. Not yet anyway.

"What's happening in Hunslet?"

"Just drive!"

There were a lot of things spinning around in Slade's mind as the journey progressed. How he'd lost his wife to a stupid drunken road accident more years ago than he cared to think about; how he'd lost his daughter when she grew old enough to realise how Slade paid for the fancy cars, and the house extensions, and the jewellery. But worse, she'd seen how Slade behaved with people who weren't on his team. How he'd come home with bleeding knuckles and always seemed to smell of cordite, vomit or shit, or cheap perfume.

And then he'd lost Blake who couldn't control himself around women who didn't work for the firm. He had big problems fitting into a society that didn't revolve around the Crosbys – he was spoilt, thought Slade bitterly; couldn't handle the word no. Ever. And one day it bit him in the arse.

And the arse biter, so to speak, was his other son, Tyler. Tyler fitted in very well with society – to the extent that he hated the way Blake treated the world as his personal playground, that he smudged consideration and consequence until neither meant anything to him. Of course, out of the two boys, Slade had always thought Blake was the insecure one, the one that needed most guidance. But he'd been wrong there, big fucking time. Turned out Tyler was the insecure one; couldn't handle his brother's blasé attitude and the possibility that he'd inherit the family firm. Or maybe Tyler just couldn't abide a rapist, even if it was his own brother.

Suddenly Slade felt like crying. Indeed, if he'd been an employee, he would have resigned. Today would have been the day Slade Crosby walked away from it all. He'd had enough. And for this lifestyle, he'd given enough – in fact, he'd given far too much.

And as the gates to Woodhead's Scrapyard approached, he thought only of this one last task of killing Jagger and the other coppers, and then... who knew. Maybe he'd hand the keys over to Shack or even Shylock. And then just leave town. Leave England maybe.

Jagger drove the car into the yard. The gates closed behind them.

"What are we doing here, boss?" he said.

Slade detected a bit of nervousness in the man's voice, and he liked it. "Got a surprise for you."

From a breeze-block cabin, Monty walked out into the grey light of another shitty day. He didn't smile though, which Slade found surprising; he was sure he'd be happy at bagging all three of the slimy bastards. Jagger opened the door and stepped out while Slade grabbed his stick and went to meet Monty.

Behind Monty strode the new leader of Tymo's mob: Shack. Slade recognised several of Shack's men, but there was a new guy. They all stopped, facing each other in a rough circle.

"Slade," Shack nodded.

"Who's that?" Slade looked at the new man.

"I'm Phil."

"Phil who?"

"Mind your own fucking business."

Slade stared at him. "Cocky bastard, eh?"

"I took over in Harehills when Shylock passed away." Phil made the sign of the cross, and smiled widely.

"Shylock's dead?"

"He tripped," Phil said. "Fell on a gun."

Slade looked at Phil, didn't much like him. To Monty, he said, "You have a present for me?"

And as though it was some kind of password worked out in advance, Shack and his crew, and this new guy, Phil, drew weapons and pointed them at Jagger.

"Whoa," Jagger raised his hands and stepped back, "what's going on?"

Slade laughed and walked over to him. Jagger eyed him, looked at the weapons pointing at him, took another timid step back. Slade slapped his face. "You fucker. I sussed you out, you twat. And we sussed out your two buddies as well. Didn't we, Monty?"

Monty stayed silent.

"I'm so going to enjoy ripping you into tiny pieces. I always wondered how much pain one man could take before his heart packed in. I always meant to find that out but never really had the time. I'm going to spend some time on you, boy."

"You're gonna have more time on your hands than you'll know what to do with." Shack laughed hard and Slade looked his way as the weapons swivelled to point directly at Slade. "The fuck's going on?" Slade shouted.

Jagger slapped him back, and Slade almost fell, catching himself on the bonnet of the Mercedes. Monty took a step forward, and Shack shook his head at him, "Don't forget where your loyalties lie, Monty. There's a good lad."

"Monty? What's he talking about? What the hell's going on?"

"Slade, Slade, Slade," Jagger smiled widely. "You've no idea have you?" He took out a pair of blue nitrile gloves from his jeans pocket, put them on and delved into Slade's jacket pocket. With his fingertips, he brought out Slade's gun and passed it to a man also wearing gloves who then disappeared inside the breeze-block hut.

Slade stared from one to the other, lingered on Monty, and settled finally on Jagger.

Jagger said, "Him there," he nodded at Shack, "he's taken over the Middleton operations. The Middleton crew have been permanently disbanded. His real name's Dom. And Phil over there is head honcho in Harehills. He has a crew of three. All of them work for Crime Division, and all of them are winding down operations in that area, collecting data, sifting contacts. I am the new head of the Chapeltown gang. I am a detective sergeant – hopefully inspector this time next year. And my real name's Jimmy. Jimmy Akhtar, at your service."

"You—"

"Shut up. No need for melodrama, Slade. I have a team right now of 167 police officers and staff. They are dismantling everything you've worked for. They are uncovering everything you've ever fucking touched. Welcome to Operation Domino, Slade Crosby."

"Bastard!"

"Monty is being of great value to us. Aren't you, Monty?"

Monty's head bowed, and he whispered, "Sorry, chief. I knew that—"

"Shut the fuck up you piece of shit! I'll fucking have you, man. If it's the last thing I do, I'll fucking have your head on a spike!" Slade spat at Monty. His lower lip trembled with fury; the big veins in his neck stood proud and throbbed, and his eyes were dampened with a red rage. And then he looked back at Jagger, "You ain't got nothing on me anyhow. And when my lawyer—"

"Well," Jagger pointed a stern finger, "I think we got that one covered too." He nodded at Shack. Shack went to the breeze-block hut. "We needed a start, see. Something that gave us authority to blitz the fuck out of you," he grinned. "Came up with this."

From the breeze-block hut, Shack gently escorted a young lady. The left side of her face was Post Office red; she wore a gauze across her left eye, and a bandage over a shaved part of her head. Shack whispered something to her.

She squinted, then she nodded. Then she screamed, "That heem, that heem!" Her hand went to her mouth and Shack had to hold her up as she broke in fits of tears.

Slade looked on shocked. "The Polish whore," he whispered.

"We got her underwear," Jagger said. "So we got you for rape. And we had the Pooh Bear mug, the one you broke over this girl's fucking head, fingerprinted. So we got you on a Section 18 assault. And then, not an hour ago, we got you for murder."

"What?" Slade was getting hyper, chugging shallow breaths, feeling pins and needles in his fingertips, and watching as his field of vision seemed to shrink.

Jagger was in no hurry. "I'm going to tell you something now, Slade. But you have to promise me you won't have a fucking coronary and croak." He clapped his hands together in glee, "I've just got to see you on the stand! I have to!"

"Fuck you."

"Remember when Blake and Tyler came back from killing Tony Lambert and his wife, Shelly?"

"I ain't saying nothing."

"Don't have to. Anyway, remember how Tony gave Tyler a bust nose? Blood everywhere. Turns out that Tony did us all a favour; he actually killed the guy who murdered him and his wife."

Slade stared hatred.

"Tyler mopped all the blood from his nose with tissues. Like a scruffy bastard, he just left them on the back seat."

Jagger pointed through the screen of the Mercedes, "You can probably still see one or two there now. Anyway, I took a few of them, kept them. And when Monty told me that Blake had lined up a new woman, it didn't take Einstein to work out where he'd take her. Trouble was, I was a bit late getting there.

"He'd already raped the poor woman; she was nowhere to be found when I arrived. And anyway, someone else seemed to know him pretty well too, because when I got there, they'd already dropped the rock on your boy's swede and put a round into his back. When I got near the tree, I saw someone running away."

"You're full of shit, boy—"

"Listen, Slade, you'll like this bit. This is where I win my inspector pips." And then he looked around at his colleagues, "nobody except these fine gentlemen knows about it," and he laughed at Slade's perplexed face. "I worked out the rock thing, that it'd been dropped from the tree, and so I took the tissues with Tyler's blood on them, I dampened them in the stream, and I smeared his blood all over that fucking tree branch."

"You lying piece of—"

"Shut up!" Jagger screamed. "I'm just getting to the really good part," he smiled. "So you shot poor, poor Tyler for doing nothing wrong except having a nose bleed."

Slade's eyes filled with water.

"Want to know who actually killed Blake?"

Slade blubbed, the spittle from his lower lip let go and splashed onto his shoes.

"If I remember rightly, she had pink hair. I saw her running into the woods." Jagger blinked, watched Slade's expression turn to despair. "Pretty sure your daughter, Rachel, has pink hair." He tapped his lower lip, looked to the clouds, "I wonder if they're one and the same person. What do you think, Slade?"

Slade collapsed to the muddy concrete and sobbed like a wronged child.

Jagger squatted by his side and whispered, "So tell me; how much pain can one man take before his heart packs in?"

Chapter Forty-nine

The Long Soak

HE WANDERED THROUGH THE back door and the kitchen and into the lounge.

"You should whack her."

"No, no. I couldn't hit a woman unless it was in self-defence. What kind of man do you think I am?"

"Well I don't bleedin' know, do I? I can barely remember you!"

"Okay, look I'm coming over tonight—"

"Bring some Stella."

He laughed meekly, "Right. Stella, yes."

"And don't be long."

"I won't... Kirsty? Kirsty, you there?" He listened but she'd hung up already. Brian dropped the phone back into its charger and paced the floor again, nibbling on his thumb nail. And through the lounge window he saw a car draw up outside. He peered, squinting into the late afternoon brightness that almost passed for sunlight, pulled back the net curtains and saw the sad bitch climbing gingerly out of the passenger seat of some old car as though she were a ninety-year-old woman.

Brian cracked his knuckles and smiled to himself as he went and opened the front door. He watched as she staggered closer, wondering what the bloody hell was wrong with her now. "Stupid cow," he whispered and went outside.

Then he saw someone else getting out of the car, and he broke into a trot, "Rosaline, what's happened, honey?"

He supported her by the elbow and wrapped his arms around her, cooing until the driver appeared at their side.

"I think she'll be alright," said the young woman.

"What on earth's happened to her?" Brian asked in his best voice of concern.

"She's upset; a colleague of ours passed away today."

"Oh you poor thing," he said to Ros, and to the young woman, "I've got her, thank you very much for bringing her home. It was very kind of you."

"No problem. You alright now, Ros?"

Ros whimpered, closed her eyes and allowed Brian to escort her inside.

As soon as the hallway gloom hit them, he kicked the door shut. "Who died?"

She shook herself free of his uncaring embrace and walked through into the lounge where she continued to sob quietly into a tissue.

"Don't ignore me, Rosaline. You know I don't like to be ignored."

"Eddie," she croaked.

"Collins? The man you went out with?"

She nodded, peered at him over her trembling hand.

"Christmas and birthday all in one." The smile he wore eventually drifted away as he considered this. She was crying full on now, and by the looks of her puffy eyes, the eyelashes stuck together and the disgusting trail of snot hanging from her nose, she'd been crying all fucking day! And that thought prompted another, one that made his chest glow hot with anger. "I wonder," he whispered, "if you'd cry like that for me."

"Please, Brian; not now."

"Not now? Not now? Not now what?"

"I don't want to get into a battle with you. I just want to go—"

"Ha! A battle? Why would we get into a battle? It was a simple question. I just wondered if you'd be this upset for me if I passed away. That's all. A simple question."

"Of course I would."

But she was lying. He could see it! Plain as day. Hollow. Words that meant nothing. Words so he'd be happy and leave the selfish bitch alone to go to bed and weep tears for a man she barely knew.

Barely knew?

His eyes squinted in thought. How did he know she barely knew him? She could've been... of course, she was. It made sense now! Ever since he started work in her office she'd been like a lovelorn teenager. And how often had she spoken of him? All the time! Never stopped! Eddie this and Eddie that.

Yes, of course, that's where she went last night with him. Out with him.

"Come upstairs."

"Oh Brian—"

"I said upstairs! Now!" He left the room and mounted the stairs with a determination in his face; a gruesome determination. Brian was nobody's fool. He wouldn't tolerate his wife sleeping around like some common whore, laughing behind his back, making a fool of him. He could imagine the young woman who'd dropped her off, laughing her tits off on the way back to the office or home or wherever she was going. Laughing her tits off because she knows Rosaline is shagging someone behind my back – and like a dumb idiot, I knew nothing about it; I welcome her home, help her inside, treat her well, trust her, and she makes a mockery of me. A mockery!

———

Ros looked at the front door through stinging eyes. He'd locked it, taken the key out. And so she took the phone from the handset, sneaked back into the lounge and dialled 999. She listened to the handset, and all she could hear was nothing.

Ros turned slowly around. Brian stood in the doorway with the lead in his hand.

"Who were you ringing?"

"No one."

"I've had about all I can take from you."

"Brian, I—"

"Get up those fucking stairs now!"

Before she could move he was in front of her and had her by the hair, pulling her out of the lounge and up the stairs as she screamed a futile protest.

There was a certain foundation to all of this emotion. Of course it had begun a couple of days ago with her night-long immersion in three inches of cold water, fully clothed. That was the start; it had brought her down to earth with a spine-jarring thud. She hadn't recovered from it, the aches and the shivers that had spread through to her bones had persisted since then. But then, the news that underpinned that foundation, that Eddie had been shot and was in some shallow grave up in North Yorkshire, had warped her mind so out of true that she couldn't think straight anymore.

At first she thought it was a crazy, morbid prank that Eddie had played to get back at her. And of course she'd deserved it – she'd done exactly the same thing to him for almost two whole years. She could see why he'd want a little retribution: taste your own medicine, Ros, and see how the hell you like it! This is what you put me through. But if it was a joke, a lesson, it was extremely elaborate – and it involved the whole office. There was no way Jeffery would allow that to happen. It was way off the morbid scale.

And so it was real. Had to be. And that's when things became a little blurred for her, fuzzy round the edges like an old photo, sepia toned and scratched and beaten. Just when she'd become used to having him back in her life, just when she'd stopped chastising herself for leaving him out in the cold for so long, and most painfully of all, just as she'd come to terms with hooking up with last-chance-Brian when she really ought to have checked on Eddie's marital status before jumping to conclusions, he'd been cruelly and stupidly taken from her.

What a waste.

Why go to the Crosbys in the first place? Did Eddie really think he would leave there with his legs intact, let alone his life?

And that set her off into fresh wails again.

Brian was filling the bath.

"No, Brian, not that—"

"Take your clothes off, Rosaline."

He said it in such a blasé way, as though he'd offered a cup of tea and a digestive. Take your clothes off, Rosaline, and would you like a McVitie's with it?

"No, Brian, please—"

"Why d'ya always test me? Huh? That's what teenagers do to see how much power they got; they test their parents by being obstinate, by asking questions and refusing to obey commands. Why do you do it?"

She stared at him.

"Take your clothes off." He whispered the command, but here was real menace in his voice.

Slowly, she began to undress.

"Come on, come on, I haven't got all night!"

She undressed quicker, throwing the T-shirt in the corner, pulling off her jeans and socks. She stood there, swallowing her grief and feeling ashamed. But she didn't know what for. Why was she feeling ashamed? Why was she allowing herself—

"Bra and pants too, come on, chop-chop."

"No."

Brian stopped still. Slowly he turned to face her. "Excuse me?"

She said nothing.

He turned off the tap. It dripped. "Take them off. If I have to ask again, I'll whack you."

Ros stood motionless for a moment or two. Then she burst into tears again and reached around and unclasped the bra, slid her pants off.

Brian smiled.

"Kneel down."

"Why?"

He made to slap her and she recoiled, gasped and hid her face. Then she knelt down.

"In front of the bath, stupid! You really are tryin' my patience. I have places to be this evening, and here I am wasting my time with you. D'ya think I want to do this? D'ya think I enjoy it? Hurry up, dammit!"

Ros knelt before the bath, head down submissively, her lips moved slightly.

And then he grabbed her by the hair and pushed her head under the water.

Ros panicked, arms thrashing in the bath, elbows banging against the hard enamel, trying to pull his hands off her, kicking out with her bare feet and making absolutely no impression at all.

"Eddie Collins is dead."

She screamed and a hurried torrent of air bubbles broke the surface, and then she really did panic, and for a moment she managed to break the surface, gasped in some air, but got a mouthful of water too, and she tried to cough, but he already had her back under the water.

"I love you, Rosaline."

And Ros was drowning.

Inside her head, there was tumult. It was filled with her own internal screams, and it was filled with the sounds of thrashing in the water, and sounds of air leaking out, and the heat of cold water burning in her lungs, and she felt the strangest most irrelevant things like her toenails digging into the carpet, like the faint scum-line of soap around the upper edge of the bath. And she could see the bottom of the tub. She could feel the coldness of the water against her eardrums. Her elbows hurt and she didn't know why.

And she could hear her own heart above all this tumult, slowing down, and she blinked less often, and she could feel the last few air bubbles running up the side of her face, almost tickling.

Brian hauled her out of the water. She coughed water, belched it and vomited it. She sucked in lungfuls of air and coughed it all back out again. Ros screamed.

"You do love me, don't you Rosaline?"

"Fuck you," she gasped. "I love Eddie."

His grip on her hair tightened, and this time he rammed her head beneath the water. And this time the air flowed in larger bubbles up her face, she pushed it out. And she stared at the bottom of the tub feeling nothing. Her toenails sent her no strange messages; she didn't even feel for the scum-line this time.

She let her hands settle on the bottom, closed her eyes...and breathed in.

There was a brief moment or two when it was all so serene. Of course, she knew it was death coming along, and really, it didn't matter. Death came to everyone eventually. And drowning wasn't as bad as people made it out to be. Everyone always wanted to die in their sleep, naturally she supposed, because it was like not being there while something horrid happened. But drowning was not totally unpleasant. There was the initial shock where your lungs don't get air, they get water. And that was the worst part, she thought. But after that, when the convulsing was over with, it was so enormously peaceful. It was the transition from life to death, and it was utterly wonderful. Extremely relaxing.

Death was simply a change of state, that's all. And people were frightened of it, not necessarily because they'd miss whatever they left behind, but because they'd never done it before – and people were always scared of new things.

But then that tumult she'd experienced a little earlier came back.

Daylight fell out of the air like cinders at a bonfire. In its place, a mellow, cool yet insipid darkness washed over the land as quickly as an artist's watercolour brush; the contrast dispersed and with it came a silence that was almost eerie.

Eddie ambled up the driveway, almost afraid to knock on the front door, now he'd rushed all the way here. What the hell was he going to say if Brian answered? Hi, just thought I'd pop by and tell Ros I'm not dead. It didn't have the strength he was looking for, and more importantly, it was like a boast, it assumed she'd give a shit that he was alive anyway.

And if Ros herself answered, what was he going to say? Fooled ya! And again, he could imagine her expression: Yeah, so what? See you at work tomorrow. And the door would close in his face.

Maybe this was a bad idea. It all made him appear conceited. Eddie raised his hand to knock, and then bit his lower lip. As he turned and took his first stride back to the van, he heard it, as plain as twilight. A scream. He stood there with his eyes wide, as though it would make the situation clearer to him, as though opening his eyes wide would open his ears wide too.

And then he tried the front door, found it locked and wondered for a second whether to shoulder it. He would, he decided, if he couldn't get through the back door. He leapt over the side gate, down the path and found the back door slightly ajar. Eddie checked himself before entering; it felt uncomfortable somehow, and technically it was burglary—

There was a shout, and a muffled scream; the sounds of splashing water confused him. But it didn't matter what was happening; his legs took care of the distance while his mind wondered what it would find when it reached the source of the noises.

He thudded up the stairs two at a time, the splashing clearer yet more subdued, lazy.

Eddie reached the doorway and was utterly mesmerised by what he saw. Mesmerised, and horrified. Ros was naked, her head held under water by Brian who crouched above her, a twisted sneer on his face. His arms shook with tension as he held them dead straight, keeping his wife's head submersed as little bubbles popped on the still water. She was limp though; he could see her feet were just there, there was no movement, no reflex, no jerking. Her arms were lazily hanging in the water, hands grazing the bottom of the bath as though her life was over.

Suddenly, Brian saw Eddie, and the sneer changed to a weird mixture of anger and embarrassment; being caught, being disturbed while doing this most private of activities – killing your wife – was almost comical. But Eddie didn't laugh.

"Get out of my house!"

Eddie blinked. Did he just say that? *Am I supposed to apologise for interrupting and close the fucking door behind me?* Eddie stepped into the bathroom and swung a mighty left-handed blow to the side of Brian's exposed head. Brian's face crumpled and he arched backwards, then his legs folded and he bounced into the sink and landed awkwardly on the floor. He was groaning as Eddie reached down and pulled Ros out of the bath.

She didn't splutter. She didn't make any sound. Water cascaded from her hair, and Eddie dragged her onto the landing, directly beneath the shining ceiling light.

There was an undercurrent of panic trying to get to the surface inside Eddie's mind, trying to take control and leave him totally frozen, rigid, and useless. He wouldn't let it; he had to act almost on instinct because to stop now and think of what the hell to do in situations like these was just asking for trouble.

But he couldn't stop a snapshot of a memory from a distant first aid course flitting across his mind; how he'd slouched there with his arms folded, stifling yawns and struggling to keep his eyes open as the instructor rambled on, a monotone rumble like the sound of a fucking air conditioning unit at the front of the class.

He listened at her mouth, knew she wasn't breathing and went straight into tilting back her head to expose and straighten her throat. And then the panicky little voice advised him to empty her lungs of water first. Its voice was high-pitched and annoying, but Eddie heard it and wondered how to do that – he was sure the air conditioning unit never mentioned that in the course.

Eddie turned her onto her side, and lay behind her, then curled his arm around her abdomen and pulled. Water shot from her mouth and poured through the spindles and down the stairs wall. He did it again, listened as it flowed less and less. And then he began to tingle all over, because he was sure he'd wasted too much time, and had inadvertently killed her. He pulled her onto her back, tilted her head, opened her mouth and pinched her nose. He took a breath and forced it into Ros's mouth. He felt his lip split open again from the thorn wound, and when he sat up, she had blood all over her mouth and a trickle of it running down her cheek – it looked like lipstick applied by a three-year-old.

And then the panicky voice shouted again – chest compressions!

He looked at Ros's chest, said, "Excuse me," and crossed his hands over her sternum and pressed, and pressed and pressed. And then he didn't need the panicky voice anymore, because he was panicking by himself right now. He breathed into her again, watched her chest rise and fall, and he pressed her chest again, and he breathed, and he pressed, and nothing happened.

"Fuck!" he screamed.

"This is where you open her eyes and say you love her."

Eddie looked up. Brian stood in the bathroom doorway, fists pumping by his sides, blood from a bust lip hanging like a pendulum from his chin. "And maybe you drop a tear onto her face too, that sometimes works."

"Brian. Stay the fuck away from me, or I swear to God, I'll—"

Brian laughed, a snorting kind of laugh that just enraged Eddie. But he didn't matter; what mattered was Ros, and he wouldn't give in until exhaustion claimed him.

He reached over and he breathed into her, a long breath that filled her lungs so much that she arched her back from the floor. Still nothing. And then he clasped his hands and beat on her chest, got progressively wilder, a little more violent than he thought was safe; and then he got faster, heavier, and more frenzied than he knew was safe. And then he cried as he worked on her. Unashamedly cried.

And then, as Brian stepped closer and took a hold of Eddie by the neck of his jacket, she spluttered. It sounded like an old car cranking into life. The splutter happened again, and then she took a breath by herself, and then she breathed deeply, and then her eyes opened, and then she threw up on the landing, as Eddie's fingertips brushed her skin. And Brian had him. Ros cried in between hitches of breath and began to take notice of her surroundings, began to be aware of where she was and what was happening around her and what had been happening before she went under – wherever under actually was, and what she saw made her scream again.

Eddie's fingertips, the ones with essence of Ros on them, curled into a fist again and as Brian lifted him clear of the floor, the momentum gathered produced a magically wild punch directly beneath his chin.

Eddie heard Brian's jaw snap, heard the teeth clamp together, and saw splinters of them shoot out between clenched lips. His head jerked back and smacked into the corner of the bathroom doorframe. And for the second time, Brian hit the floor. But he didn't groan this time, and really Eddie couldn't give a sideways shit. No sooner was Brian's hand free of his jacket, than Eddie turned his attention back to Ros.

And he still cried, but not with sorrow, he cried because he couldn't believe that she was alive – still woozy, disorientated obviously, but she was coming back now, eyes lighting up again like someone was turning up the power.

She looked up at Eddie, and her face began to smile, and she simply said, "You're alive."

Of course it was a shame. The ambulance took Brian away. They said he'd make a full recovery once the jaw had healed. Eddie had expressed his dismay by asking the paramedics if there was any way they could think of to kill him without anyone finding out. They smiled and drove away; a police car followed the ambulance.

Ros had refused an ambulance ride of her own despite being warned that she should have ECGs and a thorough examination. Eddie promised to give her a thorough examination when she felt better, and that had perked her up no end, and for the first time in two days, she cracked a smile and even laughed a little. She didn't laugh when he said, "I promise I never looked at your tits."

Chapter Fifty

Epilogue

BRIAN GOT TO KEEP his clothes and his toothbrush. He didn't get to keep the Dodge Ram, nor did he set foot inside Ros's little house ever again. He made his way to Kirsty's place on the bus from the hospital, thankful that Ros didn't press charges for attempted murder. Kirsty was pissed off because he forgot the Stella. No one knows what happened to him afterwards.

Lisa Westmoreland made a full recovery and had some awkward questions to answer prior to taking up residence in the segregated unit of HM Prison New Hall. To her credit, she never mentioned Sophie by name – even though Slade had; claiming her attacker was someone not known to her. Sophie left West Yorkshire, content that she'd finally made Lisa face up to her past. A few years later, she returned, and lived with her sister, a reporter called Sarah, for a while.

Ros moved into Eddie's cottage. She had the phone line repaired and redecorated the spare room where poor Charlie had died. Eddie bought new teaspoons and smoked a lot. They carefully selected a landscape gardener to get rid of the nettles out the back, had some decking constructed high enough so they had an undisturbed view across the fields towards Temple Newsam House and the surrounding woodland.

They sat on the decking, shiny with suntan lotion; Ros just soaking up rays on the lounger while Eddie studied a crossword, a cool glass of beer on the table by his side, a cigarette stuck in his lips.

"I thought you'd fallen off the wagon," Ros said.

"Hmph? I've never been on the wagon."

"They found a receipt for a bottle of whisky in your motel room."

He looked up. "You cannot call that place a fucking motel. Sorry, you might get by calling it a midden, but motel, no."

"But the receipt?"

"Oh yes, that was real enough. When Benson asked me to go into the Crosbys' gaff, I thought I'd better go prepared."

"So you got drunk?"

"What? No. I poured some into my hands and rubbed it into my face."

"Seriously?"

"People have some wonderful misconceptions about me – being a drunken bastard is one of them. I have no idea why I've got that reputation because I'm, no more a drunken bastard than you are."

Ros bit her lip and looked away.

"But anyway, people don't take you seriously, they think you're incapable of fighting, and they expect you to fall down a lot." He flicked ash and took a sip of beer. "I wanted to fall down so I could plant the bug without it looking too obvious."

"Oh, I see. Very clever."

"And I'd rather hoped they'd just kick my arse out of there. Was a bit of shock when they decided to kill me. Kinda ruined my day a bit, did that."

"You surprise me."

"Besides, it worked in my favour when Lisa Westmoreland poked her head round the door. She knew my history and like you, she assumed I'd fallen off the truck again too. Or wagon, skateboard, whatever."

An hour later, after Eddie finished a crossword, and a glass of apple juice, he began chuckling. Ros opened her eyes and looked at him. "I'm listening," she said.

"It just came to me."

"What did?"

"Black by Rose. You remember it was written on the scrap of paper?"

"What about it?"
"It's an anagram of Blake Crosby."

Acknowledgments

There's a long list of people to thank for helping to pull this book, and all of my books, into something that reads like it was written by someone who knew what they were doing. Among them is my amazing wife, Sarah, who makes sure I get the time to write in the first place.

To <u>Kath Middleton</u>, Alison Birch from <u>re:Written,</u> a huge thank you for making sure the first draft wasn't the final draft – you will always be the first people to read my books, and consequently always the first to point and laugh at my errors. It's because of you that this book has turned out so well, and it's because of me that you had so much work to do to get it there.

Thanks also to my Facebook friends in the UK Crime Book Club, my Andrew Barrett Page, and my Book Group for their constant encouragement – who knew readers could be so assertive, demanding... and kind.

Black by Rose

is dedicated to Kath Middleton

About the Author

Andrew Barrett has enjoyed variety in his professional life, from engine-builder to farmer, from Oilfield Service Technician in Kuwait, to his current role of Senior CSI in Yorkshire. He's been a CSI since 1996, and has worked on all scene types from terrorism to murder, suicide to rape, drugs manufacture to bomb scenes. One way or another, Andrew's life revolves around crime.

In 1997 he finished his first crime thriller, A Long Time Dead, and it's still a readers' favourite today, some 200,000 copies later, topping the Amazon charts several times. Two more books featuring SOCO Roger Conniston completed the trilogy.

Today, Andrew is still producing high-quality, authentic crime thrillers with a forensic flavour that attract attention from readers worldwide. He's also attracted attention from the Yorkshire media, having been featured in the Yorkshire Post, and twice interviewed on BBC Radio Leeds.

He's best known for his lead character, CSI Eddie Collins, and the acerbic way in which he roots out criminals and administers justice. Eddie's series is six books and four novellas in length, and there's still more to come.

Andrew is a proud Yorkshireman and sets all of his novels there, using his home city of Leeds as another major, and complementary, character in each of the stories.

You can find out more about him and his writing at www.andrewbarrett.co.uk, where you can sign up for Andrew's Reader's Club, and claim your free starter library.

He'd be delighted to hear your comments on Facebook (and so would Eddie Collins) and Twitter. Email him and say hello at <u>andrew@andrewbarrett.co.uk</u>

Also By Andrew Barrett

<u>The CSI Eddie Collins series:</u>
The Pain of Strangers
Black by Rose
Sword of Damocles
Ledston Luck
The Death of Jessica Ripley
This Side of Death

Did you enjoy Black by Rose? I hope you did. You'll need the next in the CSI Eddie Collins series; it's Sword of Damocles.

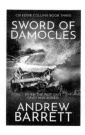

The novellas are available from Amazon in paperback format, as is each individual book in the SOCO Roger Conniston trilogy.

Try a CSI Eddie Collins short story or a novella. Read them from behind the couch!

Have you tried the SOCO Roger Conniston trilogy?